BY TERRY BROOKS

A PRINCESS OF
LANDOVER

A PRINCESS OF
LANDOVER

TERRY
BROOKS

BALLANTINE BOOKS · DEL REY · NEW YORK

Published in the United States by Del Rey, an imprint of
The Random House Publishing Group,
a division of Random House, Inc., New York.

DEL REY is a registered trademark and the Del Rey colophon
is a trademark of Random House, Inc.

Map by Russ Charpentier

Library of Congress Cataloging-in-Publication Data

Brooks, Terry.
A princess of Landover / Terry Brooks.
p.   cm.
ISBN 978-0-345-45852-0 (hardcover : alk. paper)
1. Magic Kingdom of Landover (Imaginary place)—Fiction.   I. Title.
PS3552.R6596P75   2009
813'.54—dc22   2009021288

Printed in the United States of America on acid-free paper

www.delreybooks.com

2 4 6 8 9 7 5 3 1

First Edition

Book design by Liz Cosgrove

To Shawn Speakman,

*for Web Druid services expertly rendered
and valued friendship freely given*

So she was considering in her own mind (as well as she could, for the hot day had made her feel very sleepy and stupid), whether the pleasure of making a daisy-chain would be worth the trouble of getting up and picking daisies, when suddenly a White Rabbit with pink eyes ran close by her.

There was nothing so *very* remarkable in that; nor did Alice think it so *very* much out of the way to hear the Rabbit say to itself, "Oh dear! Oh dear! I shall be too late!" (when she thought about it afterwards, it occurred to her that she ought to have wondered at this, but at the time it all seemed quite natural); but when the rabbit actually *took a watch out of its waistcoat-pocket,* and looked at it, and then hurried on, Alice started to her feet, for it flashed across her mind that she had never before seen a rabbit with either a waistcoat-pocket, or a watch to take out of it, and burning with curiosity, she ran across the field after it, and was just in time to see it pop down a large rabbit-hole under the hedge.

In another moment down went Alice after it, never once considering how in the world she was to get out again.

—Lewis Carroll, *Alice in Wonderland*

CONTENTS

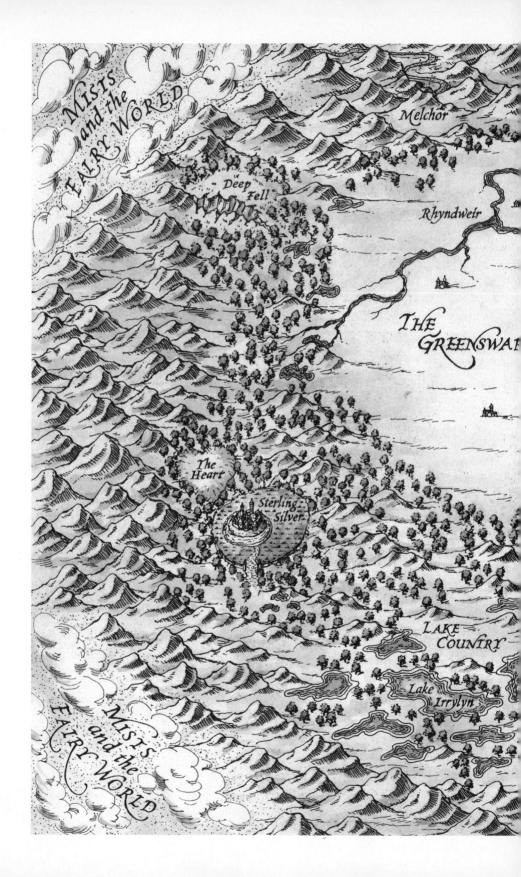

MISTS
and the
FAIRY WORLD

Fire
Springs

EASTERN
WASTELANDS

The
MAGIC KINGDOM
of
LANDOVER

Libiris

MISTS
and the
FAIRY WORLD

K. CHARPENTIER '69

A PRINCESS OF
LANDOVER

IT'S ALL HAPPENING
AT THE ZOO

The crow with the red eyes sat on the highest branch of the far-thest tree at the very back of the aviary, dreaming its dark and terrible dreams. Had there been substance to those dreams, they would have scalded the earth and melted the iron bars and steel-mesh netting that held it prisoner. Had there been substance, they would have burned a hole in the very air and opened a passage to that other world, the world to which the crow belonged and des-perately needed to return. But the dreams were ethereal and served only to pass the time and grow ever darker as the days wore on and the crow remained trapped.

The crow was Nightshade, Witch of the Deep Fell, and she had been absent from Landover, trapped in her current form, for more than five years.

She thought about it every day of her captivity. She sat on this branch, aloof and apart from the other birds, the ones that lacked the capacity for critical thinking, the ones that found some measure of happiness and contentment in their pitiful condition. There was nothing of either happiness or contentment for her, only the bitter memories of what had been and what might never be again. Her lost world. Her stolen life. Her true identity. Everything that had been hers before she sought to use the girl child of the King and Queen for her own purposes.

Mistaya Holiday, Princess of Landover, was the child of three worlds—and of parents who knew nothing of what she needed or what she could become, who knew only to keep her from a destiny that would have made her the witch's own.

Even the sound of her name in the silent roil of the witch's thoughts was like the burn of acid, and her rage and hatred fed on it anew. It never lessened, never cooled, and she was quite certain that until the child was dead or hers once more, it never would. She might be kept a prisoner in this cage for a thousand years and might never regain her true form, and still there would be no peace for her.

In her tortured mind, the witch replayed the last moments of her old life, the way it had all been, had all ended, and had suddenly become the nightmare she now endured. The child had been hers: subverted and won over, committed to her new teacher of dark magic. Then everything had gone wrong. Set against the girl by circumstances and events beyond her control, she had tried to make the child understand and had failed. Confronted by the child's parents and allies, she had fought back with magic that had somehow been turned against her. Instead of the child being sentenced for insubordination and disobedience to banishment in a foreign world, *she* had been dispatched instead, made over into the form of her familiar.

She had tried endlessly to reason out what had happened to make things go so wrong, but even after all these years she could not be certain.

The other birds avoided the crow with the red eyes. They sensed that it was not like them, that it was a very different species, that it was dangerous and to be feared. They kept far away from it and left it alone. Now and then, one of them erred and came too close. That one served as an object lesson to the others of what might happen if they failed to be careful. It was never pretty. It was seldom even quick. The other birds tried not to make mistakes around the crow with the red eyes.

Which was the best that Nightshade, Witch of the Deep Fell, could expect if she failed to escape.

Vince stood at the edge of the enclosure and studied the odd bird just as he had been studying her for the better part of the five years following her abrupt and mysterious appearance. Every day, right after he got off work—unless there was a pressing reason to get home to his family—he stopped for a look. He couldn't have explained why, even if pressed to do so. Woodland Park Zoo was filled with strange and exotic creatures, some of them species so rare that they had never been seen in the wild. The crow with the red eyes was one of these. Whether she was truly a species apart or simply an aberration was something ornithologists and experts in related areas had been trying to determine from the beginning, all without success. It didn't matter much to Vince. He just found the crow intriguing and liked watching it.

What he didn't much care for was the way the crow seemed to like watching him, those red eyes so intent and filled with some unreadable emotion. He wished he knew its story, but he never would, of course. Crows couldn't talk or even think much. They just reacted to the instincts they were born with. They just knew how to survive.

"How did you get here?" Vince asked softly, speaking only to himself, watching the bird watching him.

It had popped up at the local animal shelter, not there one day and there the next, come out of nowhere. He still wondered how that could be possible. The shelter was a closed compound, and birds didn't just fly in or out. But this one had. Somehow.

The experts had tried to trap it repeatedly after it had been transported to the zoo, hoping to get close enough to study it more carefully. But they should have thought of that before they released it into the aviary. All their efforts had failed. The bird seemed to know their intentions ahead of time and avoided all their clumsy attempts to get their hands on it. They had to content themselves with studying it from afar, which they did until more pressing and fruitful pursuits had turned their heads another way. If the bird had not been a bird, but one of the big cats or lumbering giants of the African veldt, it would have gotten more attention, Vince thought. There would have been more money for research, more public interest, something to drive the effort to learn its origins. Vince knew how things worked at the zoo. The squeaky wheel got the grease.

Vince watched the bird some more, perched way up there in the branches, a Queen over her subjects. So regal. So contemptuous, almost. As if it knew how much better it was than the others.

He shook his head. Birds didn't think like that. It was stupid to think they did.

He glanced at his watch. Time to be getting home. The wife and kids would be waiting dinner. There was a game on TV tonight that he wanted to see. He stretched, yawned. Tomorrow was another workday.

He was walking away, headed for the parking lot and his car, when something made him glance back. The crow with the red eyes was watching him still, following his movements. Vince shook his head, uneasy. He didn't like that sort of intense scrutiny, especially not from a bird. There was something creepy about it. Like it was stalking him or something. Like it would hunt him down and kill him if it were set free.

He quit looking at it and walked on, chiding himself for such foolish thinking. It was just a bird, after all. It was only a bird.

UNEXPECTED CONSEQUENCES

Headmistress Harriet Appleton sat straight-backed at her desk, a huge wooden monstrosity that Mistaya could only assume had been chosen for the purpose of making students entering this odious sanctum sanctorum feel uncomfortably small. The desk gleamed gem-like beneath repeated polishings, perhaps administered by girls who had misbehaved or otherwise fallen afoul of the powers that be. Surely there were many such in an institution of this sort, where *fair play* and *justice* were primitive, possibly even passé, words.

"Come in, Misty," Miss Appleton invited her. "Take a seat."

Said the spider to the fly, Mistaya thought.

Wanting nothing so much as to tell this woman exactly what she could do with her suggestion, she nevertheless closed the door behind her and crossed to the two chairs placed in front of the desk. She took a moment to decide which one she wanted, and then she sat.

Through the window of the headmistress's office, she could see the campus, the trees bare-leafed with the arrival of December, the ground coated with an early-morning frost and the stone and brick buildings hard-edged and fortress-like as they hunkered down under temperatures well below freezing. New England was not a pleasant place for warm-blooded creatures at this time of year, and the buildings didn't look any too happy about it, either. Hard to tell with buildings, though.

"Misty," the headmistress said, drawing her attention anew. She had her hands folded comfortably on the desktop and her gaze leveled firmly on the young girl. "I think we need to have a talk, you and I. A different talk than the ones we've had previously."

She reached for a folder, virtually the only item on the desk aside from the telephone, a stone image of an owl, and a school cup filled with an assortment of pens and pencils. There was a framed picture, as well, facing away from Mistaya. Although she was interested in who might be in the picture, she could not see without standing up and walking around to the other side of the desk, something she would under no circumstances do.

The headmistress opened the file and made a point of shuffling through the pages it contained, even though Mistaya was quite certain she had already read it enough times to have memorized the contents. Miss Appleton was irritating, but no fool.

"This is your third visit to my office in less than three months," Harriet Appleton pointed out quietly, voice deliberately lowered in what Mistaya could only assume was an effort to convey the seriousness of the situation. "None of these visits was a pleasant one, the sort I like having with my students. Even more distressing, none of them was necessary."

She waited, but Mistaya kept quiet, eyes locked on the other's sharp-featured face—a face that reminded her a little of Cruella De Vil in that dog movie. Were there no beautiful headmistresses in the schools of America?

"The first time you were sent to me," the headmistress of the moment continued, "it was for fomenting trouble with the grounds crew. You told them they had no right to remove a tree, even though the board of directors had specifically authorized it. In fact, you organized a school protest that brought out hundreds of students and shut down classes for three days."

Mistaya nodded. "Trees are sentient beings. This one had been alive for over two hundred years and was particularly well attuned to our world, an old and proud representative of her species. There was no one to speak for her, so I decided I would."

The headmistress smiled. "Yes, so you said at the time. But you will remember I suggested that taking it up with either the dean of students or myself before fomenting unrest among your classmates might have avoided the disciplinary action that followed."

"It was worth it," Mistaya declared, and sat up even straighter, chin lifting in defiance.

Harriet Appleton sighed. "I'm glad you think so. But you don't seem to have learned anything from it. The next time you were in this office, it was the same story. You didn't come to me first, as I had asked. Once again you took matters into your own hands. This time it was something about ritualistic scarring, as I remember. You formed a club—again, without authorization or even consultation with the school teaching staff—to engage in a bonding-with-nature program. Instead of awarding patches or other forms of insignia, you decided on scarring. An African-influenced art form, you explained at the time, though I never understood what that had to do with us. Some two dozen scars were inflicted before word got back to the dean of students and then to me."

Mistaya said nothing. What was there to say? Miss Applebutt had it exactly right, even if she didn't fully understand what was at stake. If you didn't take time to form links to the living things around you—things besides other students—you risked causing irreparable harm to the environment. She had learned that lesson back in Landover, something the people of this country—well, this *world,* more correctly—had not. It was exceedingly annoying to discover that the students of Carrington Women's Preparatory were virtually ignorant on this point. Mistaya had provided their much-needed education in the form of a game. Join a club; make a difference in the world. The scarring was intended to convey the depth of commitment of the participating members and to serve as a reminder of the pain and suffering human ignorance fostered. Moreover, it was accomplished using the sharp ends of branches shed by the trees that were part of the living world they were committed to protecting. It made perfect sense to her.

Besides, the scarring was done in places that weren't normally exposed to the light of day.

"I didn't see the need to bother anyone about it," she offered, a futile attempt at an explanation. "Everyone who participated did so voluntarily."

"Well, their parents thought quite differently, once they found out about it. I don't know what your parents allow you to do in your own home, but when you are at Carrington, you have to follow the rules. And the rules say you need permission to form clubs or groups actively engaged on campus. The students are underaged girls, Misty. *You* are an underaged girl. You are only fifteen!"

Well, technically, perhaps. If you measured it by how she looked. Her real age was a matter of debate even in her own home. There was the age you were physically and there was the age you were mentally. There was the number of years you had lived and the extent to which your mind had developed. When you were born from a seedling nourished in the soil of a land where magic was real and a part of you, the commonly accepted rules about growth did not necessarily apply. No point in getting into that, however. Miss Harriet Half-Wit would never understand it, not even if Mistaya spent from now until the end of next year trying to explain.

"Which brings us to the present and the point of this third visit," the headmistress continued, shaking her head to emphasize the point. "Even I didn't think you would ignore my second warning about not acting on your own when it had been made clear to you that it would not be tolerated under any circumstances. What were you thinking?"

"Is this about Rhonda Masterson?" she asked incredulously.

"Yes, it is about Rhonda. It is exactly about Rhonda. She's hysterical! She had to be sedated by the nurse. Her parents will have to be informed. I can't imagine what I am going to tell them. That you traumatized their daughter by threatening her? That you scared her so badly that the entire school is talking about it? I am appalled, Misty. And I am angry."

Mistaya could tell that much. But she still didn't see the problem. "She called me a name. She did it in front of everybody. She did it to make me angry, and it worked. She got what she deserved."

"For calling you a name? What name?"

Mistaya tightened her lips. "I can't repeat it. I won't."

"But what did you do to her to frighten her like that?"

Well, that was hard to explain, and Mistaya knew she better not even try if she wanted to keep the truth about herself a private matter. Princess of Landover, born of a human come from this world and a sylph who occasionally turned into a tree—how could she explain that? Telling them the truth about her father was out of the question. Telling them about her mother might give some credence to her commitment to saving trees, but it wouldn't do much for her overall credibility. Telling them about her real life, which was not in Landover, Maryland, as they all thought, but in the Kingdom of Landover, which was another world entirely, would only lead to them locking her up for evaluation. There just wasn't much she could say.

Still, she had to say something.

She sighed. "I just told Rhonda that if she kept this up, I was going to get her, that's all."

But Harriet Appleton was already shaking her head in a sign of dissatisfaction with the answer. "It had to be something more than that to frighten her the way you did. You whispered something to her, and then—this is what some of the other students told me— you . . . you did something else to her."

Other students. Rhonda's sycophantic followers, all of them blue-blooded East Coast snots from lots of money and little brains. They had been on her case since she arrived at Carrington, making fun of her, teasing her, pulling mean tricks on her, doing anything they could to make her life unpleasant. This time they had pushed her too far. Though forbidden to do so under any circumstances, she had used her magic. Just a little of it, but enough to make them sit up and take notice. A quick conjure of an image of someone she knew from Landover, someone they should hope they never encountered in real life.

She had shown them Strabo. Up close and personal. Especially Rhonda, who had been made to smell the dragon's breath.

"What is it that I am supposed to have done?" she asked, deciding to turn this around.

"The girls said you made a dragon appear right in front of Rhonda."

Mistaya feigned disbelief. "I *made* a dragon appear? How am I supposed to have done that? Magic or something?"

Miss Appleton frowned. "I don't know, Misty. But I think maybe you did what they said. You are an unusual young lady. You have demonstrated a capacity for commitment that exceeds that of the other students. You are a natural leader and a determined, if all-too-frequently reckless, advocate of the causes you believe in. Once you have set your mind to a task, it seems nothing deters you. You are a brilliant student. Your grades are excellent. If anyone could make Rhonda think she saw a dragon, you could."

She leaned forward. "The point is, you did something that terrified this girl. This isn't the first time you've broken the rules, and I am quite certain that if things continue on as they are, it won't be the last. I cannot have this sort of disruption. This is an institution of learning. In order for that learning process to function as it was meant to, the students must adhere to the rules for proper behavior and apply themselves accordingly. I don't like using this term, but students must find a way to *fit in*. You don't seem to feel that this is necessary."

"You're right, I don't," Mistaya agreed. "I think we are here to discover ourselves so that we can do something important with our lives. I don't think we're meant to fit in; I think we're meant to stand out. I don't think we are meant to be like everyone else."

The headmistress nodded and sighed. "Well, that's true for when you are older, but not for when you are in a college-preparatory boarding school like this one. Carrington trains you for growing up; it isn't a chemistry class for the actual process. Not the way you see it, anyway."

She reached into the folder, produced an envelope, and handed it to Mistaya. "You are suspended from Carrington effective immediately, Misty. The details of the reasons for this are contained in this letter. Read it over. A copy has been sent to your parents. I have tried calling them, but cannot reach them at the home number. I suppose they are traveling again. I did reach a Mr. Miles Bennett, your father's attorney, and he promised that he would try to get word to them. But it might be better coming from you. You don't have to leave until the end of next week, when classes are finished and the Christmas break begins."

"My parents . . . ," Mistaya started to say, then forgot the rest and went silent. Suspended? For making Rhonda Masterson see a dragon? This was ridiculous!

"I want you to go home and think about this conversation," Harriet Appleton continued, refolding her hands on top of the file. "If you can persuade yourself to become a student of the sort that Carrington expects you to be and if you can convince me that you can be one of those students, I will consider reinstating you." She paused. "Otherwise, I am afraid you will need to find another school. I'm sorry, Misty. I truly am."

Mistaya stood up, still in shock. "I understand," she said. "But I don't think it's fair."

"I am certain you don't," Miss Appleton agreed. "Go home and think about it. After you've done so, maybe you will be of a different mind. I certainly hope so. I would hate to lose you as a student at this school."

Mistaya turned and walked from the room. All she could think about was how angry her father was going to be.

She stalked out of the building into the midmorning cold, her frustration building incrementally as she replayed the particulars of her meeting with the headmistress and the events leading up to it. She didn't care all that much about the suspension. In truth, though she would never admit it aloud, she wouldn't care if she were expelled altogether. She hated Carrington and she hated the other students and she hated this entire world. It was her father's and not hers, but he had forced her to come to it, anyway. Talk about misguided thinking!

It's time for you to learn about places other than this one, Mistaya. You need to spend time with other girls your own age. You need to have your education broadened by travel and new experiences. Questor and Abernathy have done what they can, but now . . .

Blah, blah, blah. Her father. Sometimes he was just too thick. She didn't need anything other than what she had in Landover, and she certainly didn't need the hassle of living in a world where there was never anything new or interesting happening. She hated the smells, the tastes, and much of the look of it. She hated her classes, which were dull and uninformative. Who chose the subjects they studied there, anyway? Was there a single class on connecting with nature in a meaningful way? Any material on the traits and classification of mythical creatures? Was there any book that smiled on Monarchy as a form of government and suggested there might be more to it than beheadings and adultery?

Still, none of this would be happening, she knew, if she had been able to control herself. It didn't help that Rhonda Masterson had a building on campus named for her family and that she would be a fourth-generation alumna when she graduated. Carrington valued loyalty and wealth, and the Mastersons had both. She, on the other hand, had neither. At least, not in this world. She was a Princess, but only in Landover, a place no one here even knew about. She had no standing of the sort that Rhonda Masterson had. She was just someone to be brushed aside.

She made up her mind in that instant. If they wanted her to leave, fine, she would leave. But she wasn't waiting until the end of next week to leave; she was leaving right now. She was going home where she belonged.

She changed directions abruptly, breaking off her trek across campus to her English literature class, and instead turned toward her dorm. A few other students passed by on their way to class, casting furtive glances, but none of them spoke. She stalked on, tightening her determination even in the face of what she knew would be waiting for her when she got home. She could already hear her father. But what could he do about it? She was suspended and she had been told to go home and that was what she was doing. He would have to live with it.

There was no one in her dorm room when she opened the door. Her roommate, Becky, had gone home for the weekend. A tall, athletic girl with a scholarship in basketball, she was always running home to her family in New York. Which was fine. Mistaya liked Becky. She didn't pretend to be anything she wasn't, and she wasn't afraid to let you know how she felt. Becky had been involved in every mishap Mistaya had organized since her arrival, a full accomplice in all her efforts. But Becky never got in trouble for it. She knew how to be a part of things without standing out. She knew how to blend in—something Mistaya knew she had yet to learn.

She sighed. Miss Appleton had pointed to Becky with pride as an example she would do well to emulate—a clear demonstration that the woman didn't have a clue about Becky's subversive side.

Mistaya began packing her clothes and her books and her personal effects, and then quit right in the middle of her efforts. Everything she cared about was back in Landover, not here. She left it all where it was and called a cab. While she was waiting, she wrote Becky a short note to the effect that this place wasn't for her and she wouldn't be back. Becky could have what she wanted of her stuff and throw out the rest.

Then she marched down the hallway to the front door to wait for her ride. She found herself smiling. She couldn't help it. She was excited about going home. The reason didn't even matter. It was enough that it was happening.

She rode the cab to the airport, caught a long flight to Dulles and then a short one to Waynesboro. Money wasn't an issue when you were a Princess of Landover. She thought about her life as she traveled, measuring the length of the road gone past and estimating the distance of the one yet to be traveled. It wasn't easy to do when you

were half fairy. Her differentness from other girls was hard to over-
state. Nothing about her life had proceeded in recognizable fashion.
She had not grown up at a normal rate, not even by Landover's standards, her progress from infancy to girlhood achieved in quantum
leaps. Talking at two. Walking at three. Swimming at four. *Months,*
not years. Then status quo for almost a year, one of her many dormant periods when nothing seemed to change. She was in one of
those periods just now, her body in a kind of suspended animation.
Physically, she was a fifteen-year-old with a twenty-two-year-old
mind. But emotionally, she was off in the Twilight Zone. She
couldn't describe it exactly, couldn't put a name to what she was
feeling, only that she was feeling *something.* It was like an itch that
kept working at her no matter how hard or often she scratched at it.
She was restless and dissatisfied and hungry for something she
didn't have but couldn't identify.

Maybe going home would help her figure out what it was. She
certainly hadn't been able to do so at Carrington. All of her adventures with trees and nature and Rhonda had just been things to keep
her occupied. Her subjects were boring and easy. She was already
thinking and working at college level, so there wasn't much to be
learned at a preparatory boarding school, despite what her father
might think.

Mostly, she thought, she had learned to be rebellious and troublesome. Mostly, she had learned new and interesting ways to break
the rules and drive the teachers and the administration crazy.

She smiled. If nothing else, it had certainly been a lot of fun.

On landing, she called a private car service and had a town car
take her up into the Blue Ridge Mountains along Skyline Drive. The
day was sunny and clear, but the temperature was way down in the
thirties. The car drove with the heat on, and Mistaya shed her heavy
coat for the duration of the ride, which ended twenty miles later at
a wayside turnaround overlooking the George Washington National
Forest, south of Waynesboro. A small green sign with the number 13
lettered in black, a weather shelter, and a telephone identified the
location. She had the car pull over, slipped her winter coat back on,

and climbed out. The driver gave her a dubious look when she told him he could leave, but she assured him she would be all right, that someone was meeting her, and so he shrugged and drove off.

She waited until he was out of sight, waited some more to be sure, and then walked across the highway to the trailhead and started along a winding path leading upslope into the trees. She breathed the sharp, cold air as she walked, feeling refreshed and alive. She might hate some things about her father's world, but not the mountains. Ahead, an icy stream that had slowed almost to freezing trickled down out of the rocks, the sound faintly musical. She found herself thinking of the weather in Landover, which would be warm and sunny. There were storms, rain and wind and gray clouds, and sometimes there was even snow. But mostly there was sunshine and blue skies, and that was what she was expecting today. She wondered how long it would take her to reach the castle, if she would find anyone to take her there or if she would have to walk.

She wondered, quite suddenly and unexpectedly, if Haltwhistle would be waiting to greet her.

The possibility that he wouldn't show up made her frown. She had been forced to leave him behind when she left for Carrington. Landover's inhabitants, human and otherwise, could not pass through the mists as she could. Her father was the exception, but that was because he had the medallion of the Kings of Landover, and that allowed him to go anywhere.

She, on the other hand, could pass through because of how she was made—an amalgam of elements culled from the soils of three worlds.

Making her different from everyone else.

She grimaced. Maybe her father would take that into consideration when he heard about the suspension.

STRANGE CREATURES LIKE HERSELF

Mistaya continued to climb until the leafless winter trees hid all traces of the highway behind a screen of dark trunks and limbs and a thickening curtain of mist. The little falls had been left behind, and even the trickling sounds of its waters had faded. Ahead, the mist was growing more impenetrable, swirling and twisting like a living thing, climbing into the treetops and filling in the gaps that opened to the sky.

Had she not known what to expect, all this would have frightened her. But she had traveled between worlds before, and so she knew how it worked. The mists marked the entry into Landover, and once she passed through them, she would be on her way home. Others who found their way into these woods and encountered the mists would be turned around without realizing it and sent back the way they had come. Only she would be shown the way through.

Assuming she didn't get careless and stray from the path, she reminded herself. If she did that, things could get complicated. Even for her.

She pulled the collar of her coat tighter, her breath clouding the air as she trudged ahead, still following the path that had taken her up. When at last the path ended, she kept going anyway, knowing instinctively where to go and how she must travel.

A wall of ancient oak trees rose before her, huge monsters casting dark shadows in the failing light. Mist swirled through them, but at their center they parted to form a tunnel, its black interior running back into the forest until the light gave out. Trailers of mist wove their way through the trunks and branches, sinuous tendrils that moved like huge gray snakes. She moved toward them and entered the tunnel. Ahead, there was only blackness and a screen of mist. She kept walking, but for the first time she felt a ripple of uncertainty. It wasn't altogether impossible that she could have made a mistake. There wasn't any real way of knowing.

The consequences of a mistake, however, were enormous. One misstep here, and you were in the land of the fairies.

She pressed on, watching the mist and the darkness recede before her at a pace that matched her own. She hugged herself against the chills that ran up and down her spine. Whispers nudged her from within the trees to either side, the voices of invisible beings. She knew those voices, knew their source and their purpose. Fairies, teasing travelers who passed through their domain. They were insidious, unpredictable creatures, and even she—who was born, in part, of their soil and therefore a part of their world—was not immune to their magic. Partly their child, partly an Earth child, and partly a child of Landover: that was her heritage, and that was what had determined who and what she was.

Her mother, Willow, had kept the secret from her; it was the witch, Nightshade, who had told her the truth. Her mother was a sylph, an elfish creature who transformed periodically into the tree for which she was named to take root and nourish in the earth. She had done so in order to give birth to Mistaya. In preparation, she had collected a mix of soils—from a place in Ben's world called Greenwich and from the old pines in the lake country and from the fairy mists in her world. But when she had gone into labor unexpectedly, she had been forced to take root in a hurried mix of the soils she carried while she was still down in the dark confines of the Deep Fell, the home of the witch Nightshade. The consequences were unimaginable, and while Mistaya had been born without incident she had also been born the only one of her kind.

You couldn't be more different than that.

But being different only got you so far. For one thing, you were never exactly like anyone else and so you never completely fit in. It was so here. Being part fairy was not enough to guarantee safe passage. Staying on the path and keeping your head was what would protect you.

So she did as she knew she must, even though the temptation to step away, to follow those intriguing voices, to try to find even one of the speakers, played on her curious mind. She pushed ahead very deliberately, waiting for the dark and the mist to fade, for the trees to open before her, for the passage between worlds to end.

Which, finally, it did.

Quickly, smoothly, without warning of any sort, the trees thinned and the curtains of mist lifted. She walked out of the darkened forest into a bright, sunlit day filled with sweet scents and warm breezes. She paused despite herself, drinking it in, letting it infuse her with good feelings.

Home.

She had entered at the west end of Landover, and the sweep of the valley spread away before her. Close by, just below, lay the broad, open grasslands of the Greensward; south, the lake country that was her mother's home; north, the Melchor Mountains where the trolls lived; and east, beyond the Greensward, the wastelands and the Fire Springs where Strabo, last of the dragons, made his home. She couldn't see it all; the distance was too great, and when you reached the ring of mountains that encircled the valley, mist cloaked everything.

As she scanned the familiar countryside, enjoying the good feelings that coming home generated, her eyes passed over and then returned to the dark smudge below the Melchor that marked the Deep Fell. Memories she did not care to relive surfaced anew, and she felt a twinge of regret. The Deep Fell was her real birthplace, dark and terrible, and though she would have wished it otherwise, it was a part of her. Nightshade had told her so. Nightshade, who had wanted her for her own child. For a while, she had wanted that, too. Treachery and deception had marked that period in her life, when she was only ten years old. But that was finished now. Nightshade was gone, and she wouldn't be coming back.

She shifted her gaze, fixing it instead on the place where she knew Sterling Silver waited, not too far away now, less than a day's walk if she hurried.

She started ahead at once, moving deliberately down from the foothills into the valley, choosing her path almost without thinking about it. She breathed deeply of the scents of the valley as she descended into it, marking each of them in turn, identifying each one, able to separate them out and match them to their names. She had learned to do that a long time ago while studying under the able tutelage of Questor Thews, the court wizard. Questor, ancient and amusing, held a special place in her heart. It wasn't just because he was so funny, frequently mixing up his spells and causing all sorts of minor catastrophes. It wasn't because he had always treated her like an adult and never a child, better attuned to who and what she was than her father. It wasn't even because he was the dearest friend she had, aside from her parents.

It was because he had saved her life and almost lost his own by doing so. It was because he had done so impetuously and without a thought for the consequences. It was because he had dared to go up against a much stronger sorcerer in Nightshade, the Witch of the Deep Fell.

Mistaya had used her own magic to save him, a combination of newfound talent acquired from studying with the witch and her natural talent. Enraged upon discovering she had been deceived into using both to attack her father, she had lashed out at Nightshade in a red-hot fury. The two had gone toe-to-toe in a battle of sorceries that might have seen both destroyed if not for the timely intervention of Haltwhistle. Her spell turned back upon herself, Nightshade had disappeared in an explosion of green witch fire. Afterward, Mistaya had used her talent and determination to nurse Questor back to health. When he was well again, he had become her teacher and constant companion.

Until her father had sent her away to Carrington where, he insisted, she would learn new and necessary things.

To his credit, Questor hadn't argued. He had agreed with her father who, after all, was King and had the final word on almost everything. He had told her that her father was right, that she needed to see something of another world, and her father's world was the obvious choice. He would be waiting when she returned, and they would pick up right where they left off on studying the flora and fauna, the creatures and their habits, of the world that really mattered to her.

Remembering his promise, she was suddenly anxious for that to happen.

Abruptly, a huge black shadow fell across her, a dark stain that spread wide in all directions as something massive and winged swept overhead in soundless flight. She gasped and dropped into a protective crouch, preparing to defend herself. A beating of great, leathery wings churned the sleepy air into a howling wind that threatened to flatten her, and Strabo hove into view. Body extended, the dragon banked into a glide that brought him about and down into a smooth landing directly in front of her.

She straightened tentatively and faced the dragon as he towered over her. "Good day, dragon!" she greeted bravely.

"Good day, Princess," the dragon replied in a voice that sounded like metal being scraped with a saw's sharp teeth.

She wasn't sure where this was going, but decided it was best to find out sooner rather than later. "You seem as if you have a purpose in coming upon me like this. Are you here to welcome me home?"

"Welcome home," he said.

She waited for more, but the dragon simply sat there, blocking her way. He was a massive beast, his weight something in the area of four or five tons, his body sheathed in leathery skin and armored with bony plating, spine ridged with spikes, triangular head encrusted with horns and legs as big as tree trunks. One yellowish eye fixed on her with determined intent while the other closed with languid disinterest. Neat trick, she thought, and wondered if she could learn how to do it.

"We have a small problem, Princess," Strabo rumbled after a long few minutes. "You have engaged in forbidden behavior. Are you aware of what that behavior might be?"

"I am not," she declared, wondering suddenly if it had something to do with Rhonda Masterson.

"You used your magic to create an image of me to frighten someone," the dragon said, confirming her suspicion. "This is not allowed. This is never allowed. No one is ever, ever, ever allowed to use an image of me, in any form whatsoever, for any purpose whatsoever, without my permission. Perhaps you did not know this?"

She took a deep breath. "I did not. I thought it was a perfectly acceptable usage."

"Think again. More to the point, don't do it again. I don't know what kind of manners they teach you at the castle, or what sort of behavior you have been led to believe is acceptable, but labeling dragons as scary monsters is way out of linc. Consider this fair warning. If you ever create an image of me again without my permission, you shall hear from me much more quickly than this, and you will be made to answer for your foolishness. Am I clear?"

She tightened her lower lip to keep it from trembling as the dragon bent over her like a collapsing rock wall and she got a clear whiff of his incredibly rancid breath. "You are very clear," she managed.

"Good," he declared. When he straightened, he was as tall as a three-story building, and with his wings spread he was twice as wide. "I shan't keep you longer. It is good to see you again, and I wish you well. I have always liked and admired you and your mother; your father, of course, is a different story. Please do yourself a favor and don't take after him. Now farewell. Take care to remember my warning."

Huge wings flapping with enough force to knock her sprawling, Strabo rose into the sky and soared away, flying east until he was lit-

tle more than a dwindling black speck against the horizon. Mistaya
stared after him, aware of how close she had come to finding out a
whole lot more about dragon breath than she cared to.

"Although that was pretty show-offy," she mumbled as she rose
and brushed dirt from her pants.

A sudden movement to one side startled her, and she gave a
small cry of delight as a familiar face poked out through a thatch of
berry bushes and a pair of soulful eyes gazed up at her. "Haltwhistle!" she cried. "You did come!"

She started to rush over to throw her arms around him in greeting before remembering that you couldn't touch a mud puppy, and
so she settled for dropping down on one knee and blowing him a big
kiss.

"I'm so glad to see you!" she said.

The mud puppy gazed back at her with his soulful brown eyes,
and his strange lizard tail wagged gently. Mud puppies were among
the strangest of all creatures in Landover, and that was saying something. His elongated body, colored with patches of brown hair, sat
atop four short legs that ended in splayed, webbed feet. He had a
face that was vaguely suggestive of a rodent, long floppy dog's ears,
and that weird reptilian tail. He looked as if he had been put together with spare parts, but he was so ugly he was actually cute.
Haltwhistle had been a gift from the Earth Mother, her own
mother's spirit protector and self-appointed guardian, who had anticipated that Mistaya would have need of the magic that a mud
puppy possessed.

As it turned out, all of her family and friends had ended up needing the mud puppy to keep them safe.

Haltwhistle sat back on his haunches and regarded her soberly,
his tongue licking out briefly in greeting. "I knew you would be
here," she told him, even though she hadn't really known that at all.
"Good old Haltwhistle."

She patted her thigh to signal for him to follow and set out anew.
The appearance of the mud puppy further buoyed her spirits, and
she was beginning to feel like everything was going to work out.

Her father, while stubborn, was not an unreasonable man. He would listen, weigh, and evaluate arguments carefully. That was what made him such a good King. He didn't just decide and put an end to discussion. He took his time, and he wasn't afraid to admit when he was wrong. If she argued strongly enough, he would come to see that he was wrong here. He would accept that she belonged in Landover and not in some other world and agree to give up the Carrington experiment as a failed cause.

She marched along briskly, anxious to get back to the castle and begin making her case. Haltwhistle, for all that he looked incapable of moving much faster than a turtle, kept up with no trouble. She loved this little animal, and she determined never to leave him again. She would keep him with her always, close by, her constant companion. All she needed to do was speak his name once each day, even if she couldn't see him and didn't know where he was. That was what the Earth Mother had told her when she had given her Haltwhistle, and that was what she knew she must do. She hadn't needed to do so while she was in her father's world, but she had done so anyway just because she missed him so much.

She whistled a bit as she walked, a poor effort since she had never learned properly, and after a bit gave it up for singing. One of Landover's eight moons, the mauve one, hung low in the sky east, pale and ephemeral against the blue, and she sang to it in greeting. The peach moon hadn't risen yet, but when it did she would sing a song to it, too. Swatches of bright color spread across the valley, fields of grasses and flowers that bloomed in every color of the rainbow. Groves of fruit trees dotted the landscape, their smells carrying on the wind. She breathed them in, and suddenly she was very hungry.

Ahead, just visible now, was Sterling Silver, her ramparts rising in bright reflective shapes from the island on which she sat. She gleamed her greeting, so Mistaya sang a song for her, too.

She broke a branch from one of the Bonnie Blues as she passed by a small grove at the edge of the valley floor, stripped off the leaves, and began to munch on them eagerly. The Blues were the staple of sustenance for Landover's human occupants. They were trees formed thousands of years ago of fairy magic, their leaves edible, their stalks the source of a liquid that tasted like milk. They grew everywhere and replenished themselves with dependable regularity. Any resident within walking distance was allowed a reasonable culling. Any traveler was welcome to partake.

"Want some, Haltwhistle?" she asked the mud puppy, even though she knew he didn't. She just wanted him to know she would be willing to share.

She passed on across the grasslands, through a meadow of brilliant firestick, their stalks as red as blood; a field of regal crown, golden flowers on bright green stems; and a long, looping line of pink wisteria that channeled down a border fence for miles. Blue ponds appeared here and there, and silvery streams flowed down out of the higher elevations, a sparkling latticework as they crisscrossed the valley floor. It was all summery and cheerful, a promise of better things.

Though she wished that just once it would snow in Landover. It did snow at the higher elevations, but the snow fell into the fairy mists where it was impossible to get to it. There would be snow aplenty at Carrington once real winter set in. There had been several light snowfalls already.

She brushed the thought from her mind. There was no point in thinking about Carrington. That was over.

She had just reached the small forest that marked the boundaries of the King's land when Haltwhistle nudged her leg. She moved away, thinking she had strayed into his path, but he nudged her again.

This time she stopped where she was. Apparently it was all right for him to touch her, even though she wasn't supposed to touch him. She put her hands on her hips and stared at him in surprise, but he was already walking away, moving off to the left toward a huge old Marse Red that dominated the trees around it by sheer size, its branches spreading wide in all directions.

Something was hanging from one of the branches. She walked

closer and discovered that it was some sort of creature, all trussed up and suspended by a heavy rope from one of the stouter branches. When she got closer still, she realized, despite all the rope looped about its head and body, that it was a G'home Gnome.

Now, everyone who lived in Landover, whether in the deepest reaches of the lake country or the highest of the Melchor or the most desolate of the wastelands, knew about G'home Gnomes. Mostly, they knew to stay away from them. Their name alone—evolved over time by repeated demands that began or ended with "Go home, Gnome!"—said it all. They were a burrow people with little to offer anyone, scavengers preying on small animals and birds—many of them others' treasured pets. They enjoyed the reluctant favor of her father for two simple reasons: because they had been the first to swear allegiance to him when he was named King, and because he believed in equal treatment for all his subjects, no matter how low or how despised they might be. Good thing. There was no one lower or more despised than the G'home Gnomes.

Not by her, of course. She rather liked the little creatures. They made her laugh. But then, she hadn't had a pet eaten by one, either.

She walked up to the bound-and-gagged creature and took a very close look at its muffled face.

"Poggwydd?" she whispered.

She could hardly believe her eyes. It was the G'home Gnome she had stumbled upon when she'd disobeyed Nightshade and gone outside the Deep Fell. She had been tricked into thinking the witch was her friend and was hiding her in the Deep Fell to keep her safe. But eventually, she had given way to an impulse to see something of the world she had left behind. Nightshade had caught them out and tried to kill Poggwydd, but Haltwhistle had intervened and saved him.

All that was some years ago, and she had not seen Poggwydd since.

And now, unexpectedly, here he was.

Quickly she began loosening the little fellow's bonds, choosing to remove the gag that filled his mouth first, which proved to be a big mistake.

"Careful, you clumsy girl! Are you trying to tear the skin off my face? It isn't enough that I am humiliated and mistreated by those rat-faced monkeys, but now I have a cruel child to torment me, as well. Stop, stop, don't yank so hard on those ropes, you're breaking my wrists! Oh, that I should have come to this!"

She kept working, trying to ignore his complaints, a difficult undertaking by any measure. But the knots in the ropes that held him fast were tight, and it was taking everything she had to loosen them.

"Stop!" he screamed. "Didn't you hear what I said? You're breaking my arms! I am in great pain, little girl! Have you no pity for me, trussed and bound as I am? Do I deserve this? Do any G'home Gnomes deserve what happens to them? The world is a cruel place, hard and unforgiving—ouch! And we are its victims every—ouch, I said!—day of our miserable lives! Stop it, stop it!"

She stepped back. "Do you want me to free you or not?"

He stared at her, his lips quivering. "I do. But painlessly, please."

G'home Gnomes looked a great deal like you might expect, hairy heads with ferret faces mounted on stout bodies. They were small creatures, most not quite four feet tall, and due to the circumstances of their burrow life perpetually dirt-covered and grimy. Poggwydd was no exception.

Enough so, in fact, that she wondered suddenly what had possessed her to attempt to free him by touching his filthy body.

She spoke a few quick words, gestured abruptly, and the bonds that constrained him fell away. As did he, tumbling to the ground in a ragged heap, where he lay gasping for breath.

"Was that really necessary?" he panted, looking up at her. Then abruptly, he paused. "Wait! I know you!"

He looked past her to where Haltwhistle sat looking back, and the light came on in his rheumy eyes. "You're the little girl from the Deep Fell, the one that the witch had been keeping hidden! You're the High Lord's daughter . . . What's your name again?"

"Mistaya," she told him.

"No, that's not it." He shook his head and frowned. "It's Aberil-lina or Portia or something like that."

She reached down and pulled him to his feet, where he stood on shaky legs, looking as if he might fall down again. "No, it's Mistaya," she assured him. "What happened to you, anyway?"

He took a moment to think about it, working hard at brushing himself off and straightening his ragged clothing. "I was set upon by thieves," he announced abruptly. "I was traveling to the castle to see you, as a matter of fact. I wanted to be sure you were all right since I hadn't heard from you in quite some time. Rather poor manners on your part, I might point out, not to keep in touch with your friends. Why, if not for me, you might still be a prisoner of the witch!"

She decided not to correct his warped view of old events or to challenge his obvious lie about thieves. She was enjoying herself far too much to spoil the fun. "So the thieves took you prisoner?" she pressed.

"They did indeed," Poggwydd continued dramatically, gesturing wildly with his hands. "I fought them off for as long as I could, but there were too many for me. They stole everything I had, trussed me up, and hung me from that tree. Not a care for what might happen to me, left like that; not one glance spared for me as they left."

"Good thing I came along when I did," she said.

"Well, you could have come sooner," he pointed out.

"Are you all right now?"

"I've been better, but I think I will be all right after I've had something to eat and drink. You haven't any dried meat in your pockets, do you?"

She shook her head. "Why don't you come back to the castle with me and get something to eat there. You can be my guest at dinner tonight."

A look of horror crossed his face, and he shook his head vigorously. "Oh, no, I can't do that!" He swallowed hard, searching for something more to say. "I would like that, you understand. I would be honored to be your guest. But I have . . . I have a meeting of the tribal council to attend, and I must get back. Right away. This incident with the thieves has thrown me well off my schedule, which, by the way, is very demanding."

She nodded. "I suppose so. Well, perhaps another time, then?"

"Yes, another time. That would be wonderful." He nodded and backed away. "Soon, I promise. It was good seeing you again, Mistrya. Or Ministerya. Good to see that you are doing so well. And your strange little dog, too. Does he still go with you everywhere, or does he sometimes wander? He looks like he needs a lot of fresh air and sunshine, so I hope you let him out now and then. Outside the confines of the castle, I mean."

She gave him a look, and he smiled with all his teeth showing. "It was just a thought. Well, thank you for cutting me down from that branch, even if you did almost break every bone in my body." He rubbed himself gingerly to demonstrate the pain he was feeling. "I hope to see you again. I shall, in fact. I have made my home in this part of Landover. A fresh beginning after the encounter with the witch. It took me a long time to get over that, you know. But it was worth it to help you."

Well, she supposed that he did help her, if only indirectly and inadvertently. By engaging her in conversation, he had kept her out of the Deep Fell long enough for her to learn the truth about what everyone thought had happened to her. He had also provided an object lesson in the temperament and disposition of her would-be teacher and mentor. Witnessing Nightshade's efforts to destroy him had given her cause to think, for the first time, that she might be making a mistake by staying.

"Good-bye now," he called over his shoulder to her, moving rapidly away. "Farewell."

She let him go. There was more to this business of being hung up in the tree than he was telling her, but that was usually the case with G'home Gnomes. She watched him disappear over a rise, and then she turned and started walking again toward the castle with Haltwhistle at her side. Time to be getting on.

She was within hailing distance of the front gates, just across the causeway leading over to the island on which Sterling Silver gleamed in brilliant greeting, when she saw Questor Thews appear on the battlements and wave to her with one stick-thin arm.

She thought the wave looked encouraging.

FATHER KNOWS BEST

Ben Holiday sat across the table from his daughter and stared at her in dismay. It was all too much. Here she was, a young girl who had everything she could possibly want. She was beautiful, intelligent, talented, and skilled. She possessed an extremely potent form of magic. She was the daughter of the King and Queen of Landover and had every opportunity to become something special and to accomplish wonderful things.

Yet her wrongheaded stubbornness and poor judgment eclipsed all of her good qualities and extraordinary abilities and reduced her to a source of constant irritation to those who loved her most.

"Suspended," he repeated for what must have been the fifth or sixth time, staring down at the letter.

She nodded.

"For using magic."

She nodded again.

"You used magic?" he repeated in disbelief. "Despite what we agreed? Despite your promise never to do so outside of Landover?"

Mistaya was wise enough to sit there and not even nod this time.

"I don't understand it. Where was your common sense when all this was happening? What about our agreement to give this a try? Did you think that meant you wouldn't have to put any effort into it? That you could just do whatever you felt like doing without any consideration for the consequences?"

She straightened just a bit. "Why don't you just accept that this was a bad idea in the first place? I don't belong over there. I belong here."

His jaw clenched and he felt his face redden. He wanted to tell her that she belonged where he told her she belonged, but he managed to keep from doing so. Barely.

"So what I want for you—what your mother wants for you—that doesn't count at all?"

"Not when it's the wrong thing." She sighed. "If you were in my shoes, what would you do? You wouldn't let someone send you to a place where you didn't fit in, where people made fun of you and called you names, where they didn't even understand the importance of taking care of their trees. Would you?"

Ben didn't know what he would do, and he didn't think that was the issue here. They weren't talking about him; they were talking about her. That wasn't the same thing at all.

He took a deep breath to calm himself and exhaled slowly. King of Landover, ruler of a nation, overseer of a crossroads that linked multiple worlds, and he couldn't even control his own daughter. He didn't know when he had been as angry as he was at this moment. Or when he had been so frustrated. He felt powerless in the face of her emotionless response to what had happened and her clear refusal to allow it to affect her in any meaningful way. She wasn't talking about when she would go back or what she would do to make that happen. She wasn't talking about going back at all. This was his idea, damn it. His idea for her to go to a boarding school in his world and mingle with girls her own age. Not girls with magic at their command. Not creatures strange and exotic, dragons and mud puppies and the like, for which she had such a fondness. Real, live human girls with human quirks and oddities that required that she exercise at least a modicum of diplomacy. But did she do this? Did she even try? Oh, no, not Mistaya. Instead, if this letter was any indication, she had simply run roughshod over students, administration, and rules with no regard for anyone but herself, and the end result was that she had gotten tossed right out the door.

Now she was sitting here as if nothing important had happened, looking not in the least contrite or ashamed, having decided quite clearly that this put an end to his grand experiment as far as she was concerned.

He read the letter from Headmistress Harriet Appleton once more as he tried to think what to say.

"Reading it again won't change anything," his daughter declared quietly. "I broke their stupid rules, and I'm out."

"You're out because you didn't try to fit in!" he snapped. "You keep trying to turn this back on the school and the other students, but it's really about what you failed to do. Life requires that you make concessions; not everything will go your way. That was what I was hoping you might learn by attending Carrington. You have to work at being part of a larger community. How do you think I function as King? I have to take other people's feelings and needs into consideration. I have to remember that they don't always see things the same way I do. I have to treat them with respect and understanding, even when I don't agree with them. I can't just tell them what to do and sit back. It doesn't work like that!"

"Perhaps Mistaya needs a little more time to grow up in Landover before she goes back into your world," Willow offered quietly. She had been sitting off to one side, listening, saying nothing until now.

Ben glanced over at his wife and saw his daughter's features mirrored in her face. But the similarity ended there. Willow was measured and calm in her thinking while Mistaya was emotionally driven, quick to act, and less willing to spend time deliberating. Of course, Willow had been like that, too, when she was younger, before Mistaya was born. Probably she understood their daughter better than he did, but she wasn't saying anything to demonstrate it.

"She's a very mature, smart young lady," Ben pointed out. "Much smarter and more mature than those girls who got the best of her." He shook his head. "She needs to be able to deal with this sort of thing. It's not going to go away just because she's come back here. There will be challenges of the same sort in Landover, whether today or tomorrow or somewhere down the road. That's just the way it is."

He looked back at his daughter. "But we're getting away from the point. You've been suspended from Carrington, and now I get the clear impression that you don't think you're going back."

"It's not an impression," she replied. "It's a fact. I'm not going back."

Ben nodded slowly. "Then what is it that you think you are going to do?"

"Stay here in Landover and study with Questor and Abernathy and learn from whatever they can teach me." She paused. "Is that so unreasonable?"

That's not the issue, Ben thought. *This isn't about being reasonable; it's about doing what's expected of you when there's something to be gained from doing so.* But Mistaya wasn't about to see it that way, and he couldn't think of a way to change that at present. He knew he couldn't let her get away with this, couldn't let her come back and dictate what she was going to do with her life after failing to give the learning experience he had afforded her a decent chance. He just didn't know what to do about it.

"I'll tell you what," he said carefully. "I'll give it some thought. I'll talk it over with Questor and Abernathy and see what they think. They may have some ideas on the matter, too. Fair enough?"

She eyed him suspiciously, but he held her gaze until finally she nodded. "I suppose."

She rose, walked over to her mother, and bent to kiss her cheek. Then, without looking at her father, she left the room.

Ben glared as she closed the door behind her. He waited until he was sure she was safely out of hearing and then said, "I can't let her get away with this."

"This isn't personal, Ben," his wife said quietly. "She's a young girl trying hard to grow up under difficult circumstances."

He stared. "What are you talking about? She's got everything! How much easier could it possibly be for her?"

Willow came over and knelt next to him, one hand on his arm. "It could be easier if she were like everyone else and she didn't have to work so hard at trying to be so. You forget what it was like for you when you first came into Landover. Another world entirely, another life, everything you knew left behind, everything unfamiliar and uncertain."

She was right, of course. He had purchased his right to be King through a Christmas catalog in a scheme that was designed to take his money and leave him sadder but wiser or, in the alternative, dead. He hadn't really believed a place like Landover existed or that he could be King of it, but he had lost his wife and child, his faith in himself, and his sense of place in the world; he was desperate for a chance to start over. He had been given that chance, but it was nothing like what he had expected, and it took everything he had to fulfill its promise.

Willow had been there to help him almost from the start. She had come to him at night in a lake where he had impulsively gone swimming, a vision out of a fairy world, slender and perfect, a sylph daughter of the River Master, her skin a pale green that was almost silvery, her hair a darker, richer green, fine fringes of it growing like thin manes down the backs of her arms and legs. He had never seen anything like her, and he knew he never would again. She was still the most exotic, marvelous woman he had ever known, and every day he spent with her was a treasure he could scarcely believe it was his good fortune to possess.

Willow patted his arm. "It might not seem like it, but she's doing the best she can. Mistaya is a grown woman intellectually, but she is still emotionally very young. She is trying to find a balance between the two, and I don't think she's done that yet."

"What am I supposed to do in the meantime?" he demanded in frustration. "I can't just stand around and do nothing."

"Be patient with her. Give her some time. Keep talking to her, but don't try to force her to do something she so clearly doesn't want to do. I know you think it is important for her to spend time in your world. I know you believe there are things there that would help her to be a better person. But maybe all that can wait a few years."

She stood up, her dark eyes warm and encouraging. "Think about it. I'm going to go talk to her alone and see if I can help."

She left the room and, as always, his heart went with her.

He walked over to the window after she was gone and stared out at the countryside. His reflection was mirrored in the glass, and he looked at himself with critical disdain. His hair was graying at the temples, and the lines on his forehead and around his eyes were deepening. He was aging, although not so quickly as he had before coming over from his old world. Aging in Landover was slower, although he had never been able to take an accurate measure of its general rate of progress because it differed considerably from one species to the next. Some aged much more slowly than others. Some, like Mistaya, followed no recognizable pattern. Fairies, he had been told, did not age at all.

He should be fifty-eight or so by now, by normal Earth standards. But he looked and felt as though he were about fifteen years younger. It was most noticeable when he crossed back through the mists and saw his old friend and partner from the law firm, Miles Bennett. Miles looked years older than Ben did. Miles knew it, but never spoke of it. Miles was like that; he understood that life treated people differently.

Especially if you lived in Landover and you were Ben Holiday.

He remembered anew his own first impressions when he had come into Landover to take possession of the throne some twenty years ago. *Culture shock* did not begin to describe what he had experienced. All of his expectations of what being King would mean were dashed immediately. His castle was a tarnished ruin. His court consisted of a wizard whose magic wouldn't work right, a scribe that had been turned into a dog and couldn't be turned back into a man again, and a cook and runner who looked like evil monkeys but were actually creatures called kobolds.

And those were just the occupants of the castle.

Outside, there were knights, a dragon, a witch, trolls, G'home Gnomes, elves, and various other creatures of all types, shapes, and persuasions. There were demons housed underneath Landover in a hellish place called Abaddon that Ben had been forced to enter several times over the years. There were trees and plants and flowers that were incredibly beautiful and could kill you as quick as you could blink. There were cave wights and bog wumps and crustickers and cringe-inducing vermin you didn't want to get within spitting distance of. Literally.

There was the castle herself, Sterling Silver, a living breathing entity. Formed of hard substances and infused with magic, she was created to be the caregiver for Landover's Kings, seeing to their comfort and their needs, watching over them, linked to them as mother to a child. The life of the King was the life of the castle, and the two were inextricably joined.

Finally, there was the Paladin.

He stopped himself. *Don't go there,* he told himself angrily. *This isn't the time for it.*

But when was it ever the time? When did he ever want to think about the truth of who and what he was?

He shifted his gaze to the land beyond and his thoughts to his daughter's return. He knew he could not just ignore what she had done, but he also knew that Willow was right when she said it would be a mistake for him to force Mistaya into something she had so clearly set herself against. Carrington was still a good idea, but maybe not right now. Given that admission, painful though it was, the problem remained of what to do with her. She would happily return to being tutored by Questor and Abernathy. And why not? Both were besotted with her and would let her do pretty much what she chose.

Which, in part, was why he had sent her off to boarding school in the first place, thinking it might help her to have some rules and some social interactions that didn't involve a hapless wizard and a talking dog.

He returned to his chair. He was still sitting there thinking, mostly to no avail, when there was a knock on the door, and Questor Thews and Abernathy stepped through.

He gave them a critical once-over as they approached. *Now, there's the original odd couple,* he thought.

He loved them to death, would have done anything for either one, and couldn't possibly have succeeded as King of Landover without their help.

Still, you couldn't ignore how odd they were.

Questor Thews was the court wizard, a trained conjurer whose principal duties included acting as adviser to the King and making his life simpler by the use of magical skills. Trouble was, Questor wasn't very good at either, but especially the latter. Ben would give him credit for moments of helpful advice, with a few notable lapses, but the court wizard's use of magic was another matter entirely. It wasn't that he didn't try or didn't have good intentions; it was all in his execution. With the magic of Questor Thews, you never knew what you were going to get. Much of their time together had been spent figuring out ways to correct the many things that Questor's magic had gotten wrong.

Abernathy was the chief case in point, and Questor still hadn't managed to fix that one. To keep him safe from the unpleasant and dangerous son of Landover's last King, Questor had turned the court scribe into a dog. Not fully, of course. He only managed to get him halfway there. Abernathy retained his human hands and his human mind and his human voice. The rest of him became a dog, although he still walked upright. This was not a good thing, because Abernathy still had his memories of his old life and wanted it back. But Questor couldn't give it to him because he couldn't work the spell that would reverse the change. He had tried repeatedly to help his friend—because they *were* friends, despite the fact that they ar-

gued and fought like cats and dogs. He had even gotten it right
once, and for a brief period Abernathy had reverted to his human
form. But mostly Questor had gotten it wrong, and those weren't
incidents anyone cared to talk about.

So here they were: a tall, scarecrow of a man with long white
hair and beard, robes of such atrocious patterns and colors that even
Mistaya winced, and a distracted air that warned of mishaps waiting
just past the next sentence he spoke; and a dog that dressed and
walked upright like a man and sometimes barked.

He could tell right away that they had something to tell him. It
almost certainly had to do with Mistaya.

"High Lord," Questor Thews greeted him, offering a deep bow.

"High Lord," Abernathy echoed, but without much enthusiasm.

Questor cleared his throat. "We need a moment of your time—
that is, if you have a moment to spare just now—to put forth an
idea that we have stumbled upon while attempting to help you
through this crisis with Mistaya, knowing how painful it must be for
you—"

"Fewer words, Questor!" Abernathy growled, almost dog-like.
"Get to the point!"

Ben smiled indulgently and held up both hands to silence them.
"I trust this visit has a constructive purpose and isn't just a misguided effort to advise me where I went wrong with my daughter's
upbringing?"

Questor looked horrified. It was hard to tell with Abernathy; a
dog pretty much always looks like a dog, even if it's a soft-coated
wheaten terrier. "Oh, no, High Lord!" the former exclaimed in dismay. "We have no intention of trying to correct you on your efforts
at raising Mistaya! We wouldn't think of such a thing—"

"We might *indeed* think of such a thing," Abernathy interrupted.
He glared at Questor. "But that isn't why we are here. As you may
eventually find out, I hope."

Questor glared back. "Perhaps you would rather handle this than
I? Would that suit you better?"

Abernathy perked up his ears. "It might. Shall I?"

"Oh, please do."

Ben hoped the vaudeville act was finished, but he held his tongue and waited patiently.

Abernathy faced him. "High Lord, Questor and I are well aware of the fact that Mistaya's return is a disappointment and an irritation. We are also aware of what she thinks is going to happen, which is that things will go back to the way they were before she left. You, on the other hand, would like to find some more productive use of her time, preferably something educational and perhaps a bit challenging?"

He made it a question, even though the force of his words made it clear he was certain of his understanding of the situation. "Go on," Ben urged, nodding.

"We know that she must be disciplined, High Lord," Questor broke in, forgetting that he had ceded this territory to Abernathy only moments earlier. "She is a willful and rebellious child, perhaps because she is smart and beautiful and charming."

"Perhaps because she is your daughter, as well," Abernathy muttered, and gave Ben a knowing look. "But to continue." He turned the full weight of his liquid brown, doggy gaze on Questor to silence him. "What is needed is a lesson that will teach Mistaya at least something of what you had hoped Carrington would provide. Study with Questor and myself, however educational, has its limits, and I think we may have reached them."

Questor bristled. "That is entirely wrong—"

"Questor, please!" Abernathy bared his teeth at the other, then turned to Ben anew. "So we have an idea that might accomplish this," he finished.

Ben was almost afraid to hear what it was, but there was probably no avoiding it. He took a deep breath. "Which is?"

"Libiris," Questor Thews announced proudly.

Ben nodded. "Libiris," he repeated.

"The royal library."

"We have one?"

"We do."

"Libiris," Ben repeated again. "Unless I am mistaken, I have never heard mention of it." He sat back, mildly confused. "Why is that?"

"My fault entirely," Abernathy declared.

"His fault entirely," Questor Thews agreed. He looked pleased with the pronouncement. "He never told you about it, did he?"

"Nor did you," the other pointed out.

"Nor did anyone else." Ben leaned forward again, irritated despite himself. "How is it we have a royal library I know nothing about? As King of Landover, aren't I supposed to know these things? Where in the heck is it?"

"Oh, well, that is a long story, High Lord." Questor looked saddened by the fact, as if the length were an unfortunate accident.

"Perhaps you can shorten it up for me." Ben smiled. "Perhaps you can do that right now, while I'm still smiling in hopes that all this has something to do with my daughter."

Questor cleared his throat anew. "Long, long ago, in a time far, far away, there was a King—"

Abernathy's sudden bark cut him off midsentence. The scribe shook his head. "Now look what you've made me do, wizard! You made me bark, and you know how I hate that." He gestured at the other in annoyance. "Let me tell it or we'll be here all day!"

He faced Ben. "Libiris was founded by the old King, the one who ruled for so long before you, a man more enlightened than his son or the rabble of pretenders who came afterward. He built it to house his books and those of the Lords of the Greensward and others who had libraries of their own. It was his hope that making the books available to the entire population of Landover would foster a greater interest in reading, something that had been sorely lacking. It was a good idea, and it worked for a while. But complications arose, and the King grew old and lost interest, and the entire effort simply bogged down. Eventually, Libiris ceased to function in any meaningful way. It has, in point of fact, fallen into a sad state of neglect. Enough so that it has ceased to function at all."

"But you've never even spoken about it?" Ben pressed.

"There were other, more important concerns for much of the time during our early years together, High Lord. Such as trying to keep you alive. You may recall that part of your life? Since the birth of Mistaya, I simply haven't given the matter any thought. There hasn't been any reason to. Libiris has been closed now for many years."

He shrugged. "I should have said something before, but it just didn't seem important enough to bring up."

Ben found this odd, but given the state of things in Landover, even after almost twenty years of his presence as King, he wasn't entirely surprised. "Well, now that you have brought it up, what does any of it have to do with Mistaya?"

Questor stepped forward, taking command once more. "It was our thought that perhaps you should send Mistaya to Libiris with instructions to reorganize and reopen it. Such an effort fits well with your other programs regarding education through community service, and it seems to us, Abernathy and me, a perfect project for a young lady of Mistaya's capabilities."

Ben thought about it. "You think I should send her there to find out what's needed and then to undertake repairs and rehabilitation of the books and fixtures and buildings? A fifteen-year-old girl?"

Questor and Abernathy exchanged a quick glance. "I wouldn't call her that to her face," Abernathy declared quietly. "And yes, I think she is more than equal to the task. Don't you, High Lord?" He paused. "It would be a mistake to underestimate her capabilities."

"It would provide an educational and challenging task for her," Questor added. "One that would require working with others and finding middle ground for agreement on how to do things. Just the sort of project I think you had in mind when you talked to her earlier."

Well, it wasn't what he'd had in mind at all. He hadn't really had any project in mind, although thinking it through now he had to agree that the general idea was sound. A project of this sort—the reorganization of a library—would keep Mistaya occupied and involved in something meaningful while she grew up a little more and perhaps rethought her decision to leave Carrington. This whole business about having a royal library came as a surprise, but now that he knew about it there was no reason not to do something constructive with it.

"You wouldn't send her there alone, would you?" he asked.

"No, of course not," Questor declared. "I would go with her. Abernathy could go, as well. Later, once she's taken the measure of the place, we'll send for craftsmen and laborers. But it would be her vision, her project, from start to finish."

Ben thought about it some more. "All right. Let me talk to Willow. Then we'll make a decision. But I think you might be on to something."

He regretted the words almost before they had left his mouth, but once spoken there was no taking them back. He would just have to hope that this time was different from some of the others.

Beaming in unison, the wizard and the scribe bowed and left the chamber.

⸺◦❧◦⸺

Once outside, the door closed tightly behind them, Abernathy turned to Questor. "Perhaps we should have told him the rest," he whispered.

The court wizard shook his head, mostly because Abernathy's whiskers were tickling his ear. "Time enough for that later. He doesn't need to know everything right away." He glanced over his shoulder. "Besides, we don't know if *he's* still there. He might have moved on. When was the last time you visited Libiris?"

"I don't remember."

"You see? Anything could have happened. Besides, what if he *is* still in residence? We're more than a match for him, the three of us."

"I don't know," Abernathy said doubtfully. "Craswell Crabbit. He's awfully clever. I never trusted him."

"Then we will have reason to get rid of him first thing. In fact, we will suggest that to the King before leaving, once he has made the decision to send her. Which he will. I could tell by the way he spoke about it that he likes the idea. Anyway, you and I will be with her when she goes. What could happen?"

It was the kind of question Abernathy didn't care to ponder, and so he dismissed it from his mind.

FROGGY WENT A-COURTIN'

That night, when they were alone, Ben discussed with Willow the idea of sending Mistaya to Libiris. She agreed it was a project that deserved Mistaya's time and effort, but she also advised him not to make it a command that Mistaya go. When he talked to her, he should suggest that this was something that might interest her and utilize her strengths, letting her make the final decision.

"But what if she says no?" he demanded.

"Then give her more time to think about it. Don't insist. She's very strong-willed and may react in a way that is intended to test you."

"Test me? Why would she want to test me?"

Willow ignored the question. "Ask her again in another few days. If she still refuses, then let her make a suggestion about what she would like to do. Just tell her that staying at Sterling Silver and studying with Questor and Abernathy is not a choice, that she is too old for that now."

Ben didn't get it. Why all this tiptoeing around something that should be settled right off the bat? He couldn't get past the fact that Mistaya was only fifteen, still a child despite her advanced capabilities, and not yet independent enough to be making decisions of this sort on her own. Plus, she had brought this difficulty on herself by misbehaving sufficiently at Carrington that they had sent her home.

She should be grateful he didn't insist that she go right back and straighten things out. She should be eager to do anything he asked after what had happened.

Willow also suggested that he not do anything at all for perhaps a week and instead allow their daughter time to settle in without any talk about her future. Let her have a short vacation. Let her do what she would like for a few days before discussing what was to happen in the long term.

"I think she needs that right now," his wife said, smiling. She leaned in to kiss him. "Remember whose daughter she is."

Well, he remembered well enough, but what did that have to do with anything? Willow kept saying this, but he didn't see the point. If she was his daughter, she ought to be more like him, not less.

In any case, he let the matter drop. He told Questor and Abernathy that he and Willow thought their suggestion a good one and intended to speak to Mistaya soon, adding that they should keep quiet about things in the meantime. Both seemed willing to do this, although he could not mistake the furtive glance that passed between them when he remarked that, after all, there was no hurry.

The following week passed quickly. Ben was occupied with court business, including a review of a new irrigation program pending in the Greensward that the feudal Lords were refusing to cooperate on implementing despite Ben's orders. He knew this meant making a trip out there at some point—or at least sending a representative—but he was in no hurry to do so. It was their domain, after all, and he had to give them a chance to work it out. He was also facing complaints about the G'home Gnomes, several clutches of which had started to show up in places they were not welcome—which was just about everywhere, but especially where they hadn't been as of yesterday. That, too, meant a visit by someone from the court—probably Questor, certainly not Abernathy—to all those parts of Landover that were being invaded. At times he wished he could simply establish a separate country for the troublesome Gnomes, but they were migratory by nature, so that was unlikely to work. Little did, where they were concerned.

Mistaya did not give him further cause to be irritated with her. She was scarcely in evidence most of the time, working away on projects of her own choosing. Even Questor and Abernathy admitted they had seen almost nothing of her, that she hadn't once asked for their help or requested instruction. No one knew what she was doing, but as long as she was doing it unobtrusively and without obvious consequences, Ben was content to let his daughter be.

Only one strange event occurred. Bunion, the court runner and Ben's self-appointed bodyguard, approached him to apologize the day after Mistaya's return. In his strange, almost indecipherable kobold language, he said he was sorry for hanging the Gnome up in the tree, no matter what it had done, and he promised not to do anything like that again without asking the King's permission first. After showing all his teeth to emphasize the point, he departed. Ben had no idea what he was talking about and decided he was better off not knowing.

Then, seven days later, just as he was preparing to approach Mistaya with the prospect of going to Libiris, Laphroig of Rhyndweir appeared at the gates and requested an audience.

A visit from Laphroig was never good news. His father, Kallendbor, had been Lord of Rhyndweir, the largest of the Greensward baronies, and an adversary of considerable skill and experience who had done much to make Ben's tenure as Landover's King difficult. He had crossed the line five years ago when he had allied himself with Nightshade in a scheme designed both to rid them of Ben and to make Mistaya believe she was the witch's true daughter. The scheme had failed, and Kallendbor had been killed.

If Ben had thought that his adversary's death might mark an end to his problems with the feudal barony of Rhyndweir, he was sadly mistaken. There were at any given time somewhere around twenty families governing the Greensward, and as Lords of the Greensward died off or were killed, members of their own families replaced them unless they died childless, in which case a stronger barony simply absorbed their lands. The number of Lords ebbed and flowed over time, and while they were all beholden to the King, Ben knew enough to leave them alone except in matters directly affecting the entire Kingdom—such as the irrigation project, which was responsible for crops that fed other parts of the land as well as the Greensward.

When Kallendbor died, he left three sons and three daughters. The eldest son—a difficult but manageable young man—became the newest Lord of Rhyndweir in accordance with the rules of how power passed from one member of the family to the next. But he lasted only eighteen months, dying under rather mysterious circumstances. The second son promptly took his place, and several things happened at once. The youngest son vanished not long after, his mother was sequestered in a tower room she was forbidden to leave, and his three sisters were placed in the keeping of other powerful Lords and forbidden by the second son from marrying or having children without his permission. Then Rhyndweir's new Lord promptly took a wife. He discarded her when she failed to bear him an heir, took a second wife, did the same with her, then took a third wife and kept her when she produced a son.

In some quarters, this sort of behavior might have been greeted with dismay. But in the feudal system of the Greensward, it was perfectly acceptable. Ben waited for one of the sisters to come and complain so that he might consider intervening, but none of them ever did.

That would have been due in no small part to the character of the second son, who was Laphroig.

If the first son had been difficult, Laphroig was impossible. He was only twenty-six, but already he had decided that fate had made him Lord of Rhyndweir and the world at large should be grateful because he was born to the role. His father had never liked him and would have turned over in his grave, if that had been possible, on learning that the son he considered ill suited for anything more than menial labor had become his successor.

Laphroig was intelligent, but he was not the sort who played well with others. He was mostly cunning and devious, the kind of man who would never fight you openly with blades but would poi-

son you on the sly in an instant. He was mean-spirited and intoler-
ant of any kind of disagreement or display of independence. He was
controlling to an extent that caused dismay even among his fellow
Lords. None of them trusted him, even the ones to whom he had
dispatched his sisters. At council meetings, he was a constant source
of irritation. He felt he knew best about everything and was quick
to let others know. As a result, he was avoided by all to the extent
that it was possible to do so and deliberately left out of social gath-
erings whenever convenient.

He had proved to be particularly troublesome for Ben.

Not so secretly, Laphroig believed he would be a better King, if
given the chance to prove it. He never said so, but he demonstrated
it at every turn. He constantly challenged Ben, more so than any
other Lord of the Greensward, which necessitated the exercise of a
firm hand and sometimes rather more than that. He did not cross
the line into open rebellion, but he danced around it constantly. He
questioned everything Ben said and did. His attitude was insolent,
and his failure to respond to the King's rule was more deliberate
than obtuse. He appeared when it was convenient and stayed away
if it wasn't. He pretended forgetfulness and complained of pressing
duties. He was full of excuses and, in Ben's opinion, full of a lot
more than that.

To top it all off, both his looks and actions were strange. Although Ben tried not to think about it, he soon found he could not
help himself. It was Abernathy who started it all, announcing after
Laphroig's first visit that he would henceforth refer to him as The
Frog. It was a play on Laphroig's name, but also a reference to his
protruding eyes and his distracting habit of flicking his tongue in
and out of his lips at odd moments. Abernathy, who had no patience
for insolence and lack of courtesy on the part of others when it
came to Ben Holiday, did not like Laphroig. In large part, this was
because the latter had called him a dog to his face on that first visit
and would have gone on doing so if Ben had not put a stop to it. In
smaller part, but only marginally, it was because Laphroig was so
awful to be around that he invited the rude remarks of others.

Ben didn't like Laphroig any better than Abernathy or Questor did—the wizard couldn't tolerate him, either—so he let the nickname stand and soon thought of him in the same terms.

They hadn't had a visit from Rhyndweir's Lord for some months, and for a time they had begun to think he might not be coming back. It had been a happy interlude for all of them, but apparently it was over.

"What does he want?" Ben asked, on being informed.

"He won't say," Abernathy replied. "He says that his words are for your ears alone." He held up one hand. "But he was polite about it."

Ben frowned. "He was?"

"All smiles and goodwill. He kept his tone friendly, he followed all the requisite protocols without complaint, and he never once referred to me using canine terms."

"That doesn't sound like Laphroig."

"No, it doesn't." Abernathy cocked his ears. "I would be careful, if I were you."

Ben nodded. "I'll make a point of it. Show him into the east room. I'll do as he asks and speak with him in private."

When Questor had gone, he departed for the east room, where he held private talks with visiting dignitaries, and prepared himself mentally for what lay ahead. He was not dressed to receive anyone, having not scheduled visits for this day, but he saw no reason to do anything about it since it was only Laphroig. He settled for throwing on a light robe and removing the medallion of office he was wearing from beneath his tunic so that it hung revealed against his breast. The image on its face was of a knight in battle harness mounted on a charger and riding out of a morning sun that rose over a castle on an island.

The castle was Sterling Silver. The knight was the Paladin.

The man who had sold him the Magic Kingdom of Landover, a scheming and manipulative wizard named Meeks, had given him the medallion. Meeks had crossed over into Ben's world and was engaged in the thriving business of selling the Kingdom over and over again to men who thought they could become its King and were doomed to fail. Ben was chosen to be one of them, but surprised both Meeks and himself by finding a way to overcome obstacles that no other had.

He owed his success, in no small part, to the medallion.

He took a moment to study it. Only the Kings of Landover were allowed to wear the medallion, as it was both the insignia of their office and a talisman allowing them to pass freely between this world and others. It could not be removed by force, only voluntarily. Ben never took it off. Removing it would strip him of his identity and consign him to an exile's fate. He had discovered that the hard way when Meeks, after giving it to him, had tricked him into thinking he had taken it off in a failed effort to regain control of the Kingdom. After surviving that, Ben had been careful never to let the medallion out of his possession.

But the medallion had a more important use, one that he had discovered almost by accident and literally meant the difference between life and death. It was his link to the Paladin, the King's champion and protector. While he wore the medallion, he possessed the power to summon the Paladin to defend him against his enemies. This was no small matter in a land where dangers threatened a King at every turn. The Paladin had saved his life countless times since he had assumed the throne. Without the medallion, that would not have happened.

No one but Ben understood the full extent of the medallion's power. No one else knew the whole of its secret save for Willow, and it had taken him a long time to tell her.

The medallion provided a link between King and Paladin because the one was the alter ego of the other.

Ben Holiday *was* the Paladin.

When he summoned his champion, it materialized out of nowhere, a ghost come out of the ether. It rode a battle horse and it was fully armored and armed and ready for combat. It defended Ben, but in doing so it took him inside and made him a part of itself. It did so because the strength of the King determined the strength of the knight.

But there was more. The Paladin carried with it the memories of all the battles it had ever fought for all the Kings of Landover who had ever been. Those memories were harsh and raw and painted with blood and death. They surfaced instantly when it was joined to Ben. They transformed his character in the bargain, infusing him with a bloodlust that was all-consuming. He became the warrior that had survived every struggle it had ever engaged in. Everything else was forgotten; all that mattered was winning the battle, whatever the cost. The battle became everything.

And while he was the Paladin and while he fought, he wanted nothing more than what he had at that moment—a fight to the death.

Afterward, he was always shaken at how completely he had been overwhelmed by the primal emotions of the struggle. While he fought as the Paladin, he loved how those emotions made him feel, how alive he became. But he was left drained and terrified afterward, and he always hoped he would never have to make the change again.

Because, secretly, he was afraid that one day he would not be able to change back again.

Even now, after all these years, he struggled with this dark secret. He could tell no one, although the weight of it was enormous. It was his alone to bear, for all the years of life that remained to him. It repulsed him, but at the same time he remembered how the transformation would feel when it happened again. The mix of the two was troubling, and though he continued to try he had not yet found a way to come to terms with it.

He was in the midst of pondering this when a knock sounded on the chamber door, and before he could respond the heavy portal swung open to admit Laphroig of Rhyndweir.

Ben started to get to his feet and abruptly sat down again, staring in disbelief.

Laphroig always dressed in black. Always. Ben had assumed the affectation had to do with either the impression he was trying to make on others or the one he had of himself. Today, though,

Laphroig wore white so dazzling that on anyone else it might have suggested the angelic. White ribbons and bits of lace decorated his cuffs and shoulders and elbows, a sash wrapped twice around his waist, and a white cloak draped his slender form and hung just inches from the floor.

And a broad-brimmed hat, too. With a feather in it!

Laphroig wasn't a big man to start with. Indeed, he was smallish and slender, his features sharp and his black hair spiky. There was a sly and cunning look to him and a ferret's quickness to his movements. But dressed as he was today, all in white, he reminded Ben of an egret.

What in the heck, Ben asked himself, *is going on?*

The Lord of Rhyndweir approached with something between a mince and a bounce, removed his feathered hat with a flourish, and bowed deeply. "High Lord, I am your humble servant."

That'll be the day, Ben thought.

"Lord Laphroig," he replied, almost saying *Lord Frog,* only just managing to keep from doing so. He gestured to the chair on his right. "Please sit down."

Laphroig swept his cape out behind him and settled himself comfortably. Ben couldn't stop staring. The thought crossed his mind that aliens might have taken Laphroig over and caused him to don the outlandish outfit. But otherwise he looked the same: eyes protruding, tongue flicking out, spiky black hair sticking straight up . . .

Ben blinked. Those inky, depthless eyes: There was a glint of cunning there, a look both cold and calculating. He remembered Abernathy's words of caution and banished his incredulity and bemusement. It was not a good idea to consider Laphroig as harmless. "What brings you to Sterling Silver?" he asked, smiling as if everything were normal.

"A matter of utmost importance, High Lord," Laphroig replied, his face suddenly serious. Then he smiled. "I see you are surprised by my dress. Not the usual black. That is because of what brings me here. Black does not suit the subject of my visit. White is more appropriate, and I decided to honor my purpose by dressing accordingly."

Ben nodded, wondering where this was going.

"I realize I should have sent a messenger requesting an audience, but I couldn't bear the attendant wait, High Lord. Once my mind was made up, there was nothing for it but to come straight here and hope that you would agree to see me. You have not disappointed me; I am most appreciative."

So, Ben thought. *Aliens have taken him over. The Laphroig we know and hate has been replaced by something unrecognizable.* He caught himself. *Well, maybe. Maybe not.*

"What matter is it that brings you to us, Lord of Rhyndweir?" he asked.

Laphroig straightened noticeably, as if bracing himself. "High Lord, I know I have not been the best of neighbors in the past. I know I have been difficult at times, even rude. I attribute this to my youth and my inexperience, and I hope you have found it in your heart to forgive me."

Ben shrugged. "There is nothing to forgive."

"You are entirely too kind, High Lord. But I know differently, and I offer my apologies for all offenses given. I wish to start anew with our relationship, which I expect to be a long and productive one."

Ben smiled and nodded. *What is he up to?*

"I also intend to be a better friend to the members of your court, starting with Questor Thews and Abernathy, to whom I have been less than kind at times. That is all in the past now and will not happen again."

His tongue flicked out as he gathered himself. "High Lord, I have come to ask you for the hand of your daughter, Mistaya, in marriage."

Whatever Ben Holiday might have thought he was ready for, it certainly wasn't this. He was so shocked that for a moment he just stared at the other man. "You want to marry Mistaya?" he said finally.

Laphroig nodded enthusiastically. "I do. It will be a satisfactory match for both of us, I think."

Ben leaned forward. "But she's fifteen."

Laphroig nodded. "Older than I would have liked, but still young enough to teach. We will be a good match: she an eager helper and dutiful wife and I, a strong protector and devoted husband. She is young enough to bear me many children, some of whom, I fully expect, will be sons who will succeed me. She has a pleasing face and temperament to match. She is clever, but not too much so. She is the woman I have always hoped to find."

Ben stared some more. "Am I missing something here? Don't you already have a wife? And a son and heir, for that matter?"

Laphroig looked suddenly sad. "Apparently you haven't heard, High Lord. News doesn't always travel as fast as we might think. My son caught a fever and died not twenty days ago. His mother, in her grief, killed herself. I am left with neither spouse nor heir, and while I would like the period of mourning to go on longer than it has, duty dictates that I act in the best interest of my subjects. That means taking a new wife and producing an heir as quickly as possible." He paused, shaking his head. "Even in my grief, I thought at once of Mistaya."

So that was it. Suddenly Ben wanted to wring his visitor's scrawny neck. He could do it, right here in the reception room, and no one would know. Even if Questor or Abernathy guessed at the truth of things, they would never say a word. The impulse was so overwhelming that he found he was clenching his fists in anticipation. He forced himself to relax and sit back.

"Your dedication to your duties is commendable," he said, trying to decide how to put an end to this.

"Mistaya, I understand, has just returned from her schooling in what was once your old world, High Lord." Laphroig smiled, his tongue flicking out. "I gather she does not intend to go back, but to remain here in Landover. That makes it all the easier for a wedding to be arranged. It is a suitable match, don't you agree?"

Ben knew enough not to tell the other what he really thought. He also understood how marriage protocols worked where the Lords of the Greensward were concerned. Taking wives to produce heirs was standard practice. Young wives were favored to allow for maximum production. Marriages were arranged between the ruling families all the time. Such unions created alliances and strengthened friendships with allies. Nothing that Laphroig had suggested was out of line with common practice.

On the other hand, it was entirely out of the question. Ben and Willow's opinions aside, Mistaya would run screaming into the night if the suggestion were even broached; she hated Laphroig, who was always patting her arm or trying to kiss her cheek. Given the opportunity and the least bit of encouragement, she would have turned him into a real frog. But Ben had cautioned her against doing anything overt, pointing out that he had to live and work with people like Laphroig, and there was nothing to be gained by making it harder than it already was.

He half wished now that he had let her have her way.

"My Lord, this is a matter that will require some thought and discussion," he said finally. "The Queen must be advised of your intentions. Also . . . um, Mistaya must be told."

"Of course, of course," Laphroig agreed at once. "She must be courted, as well. I must win her heart. It was never my intention to ask that she simply be given to me. She must agree to the match, too."

Ben felt a little of the tension drain out of him. If Mistaya must agree, it would be the Twelfth of Never before any marriage happened. "I am pleased you are taking this approach."

Laphroig stood, bowed deeply, his feathered hat sweeping down, and straightened anew. "I shall return home to await your word. But I do want to emphasize that I hope to begin courting the Princess as soon as you have had a chance to consider and accept my proposal.

As I said, I do feel some urgency in this matter, and I do feel I have a duty to my people."

"I understand," Ben advised, rising with him. "You shall hear from me again very shortly."

He watched Laphroig bounce out of the room, wondering how in the world he was going to handle this.

MISUNDERSTANDINGS

Some distance away from the castle, although not so far that she could not see its silver gleam against the green backdrop of the surrounding forests, Mistaya sat talking with Poggwydd about proper behavior. It was a discussion that was taking considerable time and effort, and they had been at it for several hours now. That these two citizens of Landover should be engaged in a discourse on this particular subject was of itself rather strange, and the irony of it would not have been lost on Ben Holiday had he been present to witness it. No doubt he would have had something to say to his daughter about the pot calling the kettle black or how people who live in glass houses shouldn't throw stones.

Willow, on the other hand, would have pointed out that sometimes people worked through their own problems by trying to help others with theirs, and that this could be particularly effective when the nature of those problems was so similar.

"If you want to be accepted by others, you have to be considerate of their feelings," the pot was saying to the kettle.

Poggwydd frowned. "No one is considerate of us. No one wants anything to do with us. G'home Gnomes are friendless outcasts in a friendless world."

"Yes, but there are reasons for this, as I have been saying," Mis-

taya explained patiently. "For instance, taking things that don't belong to you is not a good way to endear yourself."

Poggwydd bristled. "G'home Gnomes are not thieves, Princess.
We are finders of lost items, with which we then barter or trade. It
is a time-honored profession, and one in which our people have
been engaged for centuries. Just because we are not skilled craftsmen or clever artisans does not mean we deserve to be treated
badly."

Mistaya sighed. They were covering familiar ground without
making much progress. "Poggwydd, you do not find 'lost items' in
other people's storerooms and closets. You do not find them in their
sheds and huts. You do not find them in their kitchen cabinets and
pantries, some of which are bolted and locked."

Poggwydd screwed up his monkeyish face and grimaced. "Those
are harsh words. Unpleasant accusations." He thought about it a
moment and suddenly brightened. "Where is your proof?"

"Well, in your case, finding you hung from a tree limb by an
angry kobold who just happens to serve my father would be a prime
example."

"That was a case of mistaken identity. It wasn't me. Probably
wasn't even a G'home Gnome, although there are some among us—
as there are some among you—who do not obey the rules of the
tribe. But if I were pressed for an explanation, I would think it was
probably another kobold—perhaps even the one who accused me."

He nodded with some degree of self-satisfaction, and she
wanted to smack him. "Bunion doesn't lie and he doesn't have any
reason to steal things to which he has free access," she pointed out.
"Besides, Parsnip saw you, too. That suggests you might want to rethink your explanation. The fact is, Poggwydd, you were somewhere you shouldn't have been. You weren't invited into the castle,
let alone into the kitchen and the pantries. This is an example of
being where you aren't supposed to be for a purpose that shows no
consideration for others."

The G'home Gnome pouted. "I would have paid it all back, you
know. Eventually."

"Well, if you hadn't done it in the first place, you wouldn't have had to worry about paying anyone back. And you could have asked for whatever it was you took. Maybe Parsnip would have given you what you needed. Next time, you should just ask for me."

He shook his head. "No, I can't do that. You are a Princess. Why would a Princess even be *told* I was asking for her?"

She brushed back her blond hair. "We're getting off the point. We were talking about proper behavior. Or lack thereof. G'home Gnomes suffer from a failure to recognize what proper behavior is. If they want to be accepted by others, they have to earn their respect."

Poggwydd snorted. "How is that supposed to happen? Everyone's already made up their minds about us."

"And you don't do anything to change those minds. Besides 'finding' things in people's houses, you manage to latch on to their pets, too. Often right out of their pens. And then you eat them."

"That is a lie!" Poggwydd leaped to his feet, flinging his arms about, his wizened face screwed up like a walnut. "We do not eat pets. We eat wild creatures we find wandering about. If they happen to be pets that have strayed, what are we to do about that? How are we to know? People blame us, but they don't want to share that blame! If they took better care of their pets, these things wouldn't happen!"

Mistaya scratched an itch on her nose and smiled. "Why don't you stop eating cats and dogs altogether? There are plenty of other things you could eat. Squirrels or birds or voles. Or even bog wumps, if you could catch one. Eat some of those instead."

"Bog wumps!" Poggwydd was horrified. "Do you eat bog wumps? Does anyone?"

"Well, I don't," she agreed. "But I don't eat cats and dogs, either."

The gnome sat down again. "I don't think you know what you are talking about." He gave her an accusatory stare. "I think you are badly confused about all of this."

She pressed her lips tightly together in frustration and nodded. "Why don't you just think about what I said," she suggested finally.

"In the meantime, stay away from the castle. If you need food, come ask for me. I will tell everyone I am to be told if you do. Is that all right?"

Poggwydd folded his arms across his skinny chest and hunched his shoulders as he looked away from her. "I might just leave. I might just go back to where I came from and forget about trying to make a home here. I don't think this is going to work out."

She got to her feet. Couldn't argue with logic like that, she thought. "I'll come back and see you again tomorrow," she promised. "We can take a walk and not talk about anything, if you like."

He shrugged. "If you can spare the time."

She left him sitting there looking off into space, pretending that nothing she said or did mattered to him, that he was above it all. She had come out to talk with him after hearing from Bunion the whole of what had led to the little fellow being strung up by his heels, wanting to do something to prevent it from happening again. Bunion and Parsnip could promise that it wouldn't, but if they caught Poggwydd again where he wasn't supposed to be she wasn't all that sure the promise would mean anything. Kobolds were not known for their generous natures, and even though these two were her friends, friendship only went so far.

As she strolled back through the grove of Bonnie Blues toward the castle, she tried to decide what else she could say that would make a difference. She needed to do something besides brood on her situation as a former Carrington student, an identity she was trying to put behind her at this point. Her father hadn't said anything more about her suggestion that she go back to being tutored by Questor and Abernathy, but she had a feeling he was considering something else. No one had indicated what that might be, not even her two would-be tutors, who kept hemming and hawing around the subject whenever she brought it up to them.

So now she was thinking that it might be a good plan to come up with an idea of her own, a project that would convince her father that she was doing something useful. Working with the disadvan-

taged had always appealed to her, and there was no one more disad-
vantaged than the G'home Gnomes. If she could demonstrate her
ability to change even one of them for the better, then her chances
of being allowed to try to do so with all of the others would be
greatly improved.

However, Poggwydd wasn't doing much to cooperate, and she
was starting to think this might be tougher than she had thought.

She was still mulling this dilemma over, paying little attention to
anything around her as she meandered out of the forest and onto the
roadway leading to Sterling Silver, when she suddenly found herself
face-to-face with Laphroig of Rhyndweir and his entourage. There
were six or eight of them, all on horseback save for the driver of the
carriage in which Laphroig was riding. She didn't realize who it was
right away, still distracted with thoughts of Poggwydd and G'home
Gnomes, and so she stood where she was as the procession rolled
up to her and stopped. By then, it was too late to consider an escape.

Laphroig flung open the carriage door, leaped down, and hurried over to her. "Princess Mistaya," he greeted warmly, reptilian
tongue flicking out as he executed a deep bow.

"Lord Laphroig," she returned warily, only barely managing not
to call him *Lord Lafrog*. She had heard Abernathy use the nickname
often enough that she had begun doing so, as well.

"So wonderful to see you!" he declared effusively.

He grasped her right hand with both of his and began kissing it
effusively. Rather forcibly, she extracted it from his grip and gave
him a meaningful frown. "It's not *that* good to see me. But thank you
for the compliment."

She had learned something about diplomacy while growing up a
Princess in her father's court. You were always polite, even when
what you most wanted was to be anything but.

"I hadn't dared hope that I would be so fortunate as to encounter
you personally on this visit. But now that I have, I shall consider it
an omen of good fortune."

She nodded, taking in his strange outfit. "What is that you're wearing?" she asked, unable to help herself. "Why aren't you wearing black?"

"Ah, you've come right to the crux of the matter," he replied, giving her a knowing wink. "My clothing is not the usual black because my visit is not the usual visit. It is a different reason entirely that brings me to Sterling Silver. I have been to see your father concerning you."

"Have you?" She felt a sudden chill sweep through her. "About me?"

"I have requested permission to court you with the intention that you should become my new wife and the mother of my children!" he declared, sweeping the hat from his head and bowing deeply once more. "I intend that we should marry, Mistaya."

It took her considerable effort, but she managed to keep her face composed and her emotions concealed. "You do?"

"Your father has already said he would consider the matter. I shall use that time to come calling on you regularly. I shall make you see that we are the perfect match."

In your dreams, she thought instantly. But what was this about her father agreeing to consider the matter? Shouldn't he have dismissed it out of hand? What was he thinking?

"Lord Laphroig." She gave him her most charming smile. "Do you not already have a wife? Are you not already spoken for?"

A cloud of gloom settled over his froggy features. "Unfortunately, no. A terrible tragedy has occurred. My son passed away quite suddenly less than two weeks ago. Dear little Andrutten. A fever took him. My wife, in her grief, chose to follow him into that dark realm of death, and now both are gone and I am left alone and bereft of family."

"I'm sorry, I hadn't heard," she said, embarrassed by her ignorance.

She remembered his wife, a pale, slender woman with white-blond hair and sad eyes. There were stories about that marriage, and none of them was good. She had never seen their child.

He bowed anew. "Your condolences mean everything."

"I should think you would be in mourning for them," she suggested pointedly. "For a suitable time before courting anyone."

He shook his head as if she were clueless. "I will be in mourning for them forever. But duty calls, and I must answer. A Lord of Rhyndweir requires a wife and sons if he is to fulfill his duties. I must not leave the Lordship imperiled, even for as long as thirty days. I must provide an heir to reassure my people."

Whatever this was about, Mistaya was certain that it had nothing to do with duty and obligation. Laphroig was up to something, just as he was always up to something, and somehow his machinations had found their way to her doorstep. She decided to lock and bar the door before it could be forced.

"My Lord, I am hardly a suitable match for you," she declared. "I am young and naïve and not yet well trained in the art of wifely duties." She nearly gagged on this part. "I am best suited for continued study at an institution of higher learning—as I am sure my father has told you."

Laphroig cocked his head. "It was my understanding that you had been dismissed from Carrington."

She stared at him, sudden anger boiling up as she realized that only a spy could have provided such information. "I intend to continue my education elsewhere."

He smiled. "This in no way hinders my plans for you. You can be tutored at Rhyndweir castle for as long and extensively as you like. Tutors can be engaged to educate you on any subject." He paused. "Save those only a husband can teach."

She flushed bright red despite herself. "My Lord, I think you fail to understand the situation—"

He stepped forward suddenly, standing right next to her, his head bent close to her own, his protruding eyes fixing on her as if she were a troublesome child. There was a possessive quality in that stare that repulsed and frightened her.

"I think, perhaps, it is you who fail to understand, Princess," he whispered. "Understand me. I am set upon this match. I am set upon you as my wife, and so you shall be. Do not think for a moment that anything will change this. Not even your father." He paused. "You will come to realize this soon enough. You will come to accept your duty to me. Things will go easier for you when you do."

He stepped back a pace, but his eyes were still dangerous. He took hold of her wrist and held on tightly. "No one defies me, Princess. When they do, there are unpleasant consequences."

Suddenly she thought of his wife and child, both dead, and then of his older brother, dying mysteriously, and his younger, not much older than herself, disappeared and never found. An awful lot of people connected to Laphroig had come to a bad end, and as she stood there facing him she knew with a chilling certainty that this wasn't by chance.

"My father is waiting for me," she managed, barely able to meet his gaze now. "I have to go."

He smiled, releasing her wrist. "Of course, you do. Good day, Princess Mistaya."

He climbed back into the carriage without giving her another glance, and the entire entourage moved away in a rumble of wheels, a thudding of hooves, and a creaking of harness.

Mistaya waited until they were out of sight, and then she set off for the castle in a white-hot heat.

Ben Holiday was at his writing desk, signing work orders for a project that the crown had approved to build a new bridge spanning the Clash Bone Gorge below the Melchor, when Mistaya stormed in, throwing open the door to his study without knocking and then slamming it shut behind her.

"Why did you give The Frog permission to court me?" she demanded, coming to an angry stop in front of his desk, face flushed and hands on hips.

He blinked. "I didn't."

"Well, he says you did. I bumped into him out on the road, and he told me the whole story about his plans for our marriage. He said he asked you if he could court me and you said he could!"

"I said I would think about it."

Her lips tightened into a white line. "Oh, that's all right, then. Obviously. What's wrong with me? Of course, you have to think about it! How can you make an informed decision otherwise?"

"I told him that to buy myself a little time, Mistaya. You know how it works when you're dealing with the men and women in power. Hasty answers—even when you'd like to give them—aren't always the wisest way to go. Besides, his proposal caught me by surprise, too."

His daughter scowled. "I think you made a mistake, Father. A very big mistake. I think you needed to tell him straight out that your daughter isn't going to marry him on the best day of his life and he ought to just forget about it. Putting him off just encouraged him. He thinks you're seriously considering giving him permission. He practically hauled me off to his castle right then and there! He thinks the matter is settled in all but deed!"

She leaned over his desk, her anger a bright fire in her green eyes. "I do not appreciate being dragged into court matters. I am not some piece of furniture to be given away to anyone who comes around asking! I don't care if you are King of Landover! I am not a bargaining chip! If you don't get that, then maybe you'd better do a quick study on the laws of emancipated women in the twenty-first century. Remember how it works in the world you came from, the one you sent me back into to learn more about life? Well, that's a lesson I learned early on. You don't give away young women to rich old men!"

"What are you talking about?" Ben leaped to his feet, anger surfacing in him now, too. "Rich old men? Laphroig? He's not all that much older than you! Anyway, that's not the point! I have no intention of 'giving you away,' as you put it—not to him or to anyone else! But people like Laphroig don't understand how things work in my world, so I can't just drop that on them without exercising some diplomacy—"

Mistaya slammed the flat of her hand on his desk. "You aren't listening to me! He thinks you have already agreed! He implied that it would be smart for me just to go along with his wishes and not to argue the matter. He threatened me out there, Father! He warned me that he was used to getting what he wanted and that I was going to be his latest acquisition whether I liked it or not!"

Ben straightened. "Threatened you?"

"Yes, threatened me!" She straightened, folding her arms across her chest. "He frightens me. I don't like him, and I don't want to have to see him again. I've heard the stories about his brothers. And now his wife and child are dead, too? And he wants me to marry him?" She shook her head. "I want him kept away from me. He's dangerous, Father. Bug eyes and lizard tongue or not, he's scary."

They stared at each other for a moment, and then Ben nodded. "I agree with you. I already sent Bunion to see what he could learn about the death of Laphroig's wife and child. We should know something by tomorrow."

He held up his hands hastily as he saw the anger flood back into her cheeks. "Not that this changes anything where you are concerned," he added quickly. "But I think it better if we find out the whole of the story. It may be that Laphroig has overstepped himself, and we can do something about it."

"So what about me?" she demanded. "Will you tell him he can't court me, and you won't give him permission to marry me?"

Ben took a deep breath and exhaled. "I will. But there's something else we have to talk about, too, and we might as well do it now. Questor, Abernathy, and your mother and I have talked about how you should continue your education. We all understand that you do not want to go back to Carrington. So we won't ask that of you. But we also agree that continuing your studies here at Sterling Silver isn't the best choice, either. So we've come up with an alternative—one that might actually help us all better deal with Laphroig and his marriage proposal."

She eyed him suspiciously. "What is it?"

"We want you to go to Libiris as emissary to the throne, to reorganize the library."

She smiled brightly. "Do you, Father? What a terrible idea. I'm not going."

"Wait a minute." Ben held up one hand to ward off whatever else she might be thinking of saying. He could scarcely believe his ears. "You're not going? Just like that? You haven't even heard my reasoning! Why are you refusing me out of hand?"

"Because, Father."

"Because? What does that mean? Because why?"

"Because," she repeated, putting emphasis on the word. She scowled at him. "Put yourself in my position, if that's possible. How would you like to be sent off to Libiris for an indefinite stay? Libiris is the backside of beyond! Questor told me all about its history during our studies. There's nothing there, and the place is a wreck! So now you want me to go there and put it back together? Me, a fifteen-year-old boarding school dropout? Because I'm so qualified for this, maybe? I don't think so. I think this is just an excuse for getting me out of the way. How do I know what you'll do about The Frog once I'm away?"

Ben was suddenly furious. "Doesn't my word count for something with you, Mistaya? Do you think I would go back on it?"

She glared at him. "Frankly, I don't know what you might do. You haven't exactly distinguished yourself so far where this business of Laphroig is concerned. I don't want to go off hoping you'll do the right thing and come back to a surprise marriage!"

"I'm not going to marry you off to Laphroig!"

"Or anyone else, if you please!" She huffed, pouted, and wheeled away. "Besides, Libiris is beyond help. Even Questor said so."

"Questor is going with you. You can use the travel time to discuss the matter. In any case, it was his idea in the first place."

She wheeled back. "I don't believe you."

"The library was once an important part of the Kingdom," he explained patiently. "It was built because one of my predecessors understood the value of books and reading. His undertaking fell apart after he was gone because no one else made an effort to keep things up. But you could change all that. This is a worthy project, Mistaya. If you can reorganize and repair Libiris, we could use it to better educate the people. What could be more important than that?"

She shook her head. "Have you ever been there?"

He hesitated. "No."

"Do you know what's in those books?"

"No, but I—"

"Or even if the books are still intact? Doesn't paper fall apart over time? What's to say the whole library hasn't been reduced to a giant rats' nest?"

He composed himself with some effort. "If it has, then you can come back home, all right? But if not, you have to agree to stay."

She shrugged. "I'll give it some thought. Maybe after I've heard you tell The Frog he can hop on back to his lily pad, I might go. But not before then and not while I'm feeling like this!"

Ben stood up. Enough was enough. "You are fifteen years old and you don't have the right yet to determine what you will and won't do! Your mother and I still make certain decisions for you, and this is one. Your education begins anew at Libiris. You can have today and tomorrow to pack your things and make ready to travel. Then you are going. Is that clear?"

She gave him a look. "What's clear is that you would do anything to get me out from underfoot. You might even marry me off to someone despicable. That's what's clear to me!" She sneered. *"Father."*

The door opened suddenly, and Willow stepped through. She glanced purposefully from one to the other. "Why are you both shouting?" she asked. "You can be heard all the way to Elderew. Can you please conduct this conversation in a quieter fashion?"

"This conversation is over!" Mistaya snapped.

"Will you please be reasonable—" Ben started to say, but she stomped out of the room without waiting for him to finish and slammed the door behind her. Ben stared after her in dismay, slowly sinking back into his chair.

Well, that didn't go very well, he thought.

Willow crossed the room and sat down on the other side of the writing table, her gaze settling on him like a weight.

"Don't say it," he said at once.

"I think you could have handled that better," she said anyway.

"You weren't here. You didn't hear what she said."

"I did not have to be here, and I did not have to hear what she said. It is enough to know that you both kept talking long after you should have stopped. But you, especially. You are the parent, the elder of the two. You know better. Pushing her to do things— worse, telling her she must—is always a mistake."

"She's fifteen."

"She is fifteen in some ways, but she is much older in others. You cannot think of her in the ways you are used to thinking of fifteen-year-old girls. She is much more complicated than that."

She was right, of course, although he didn't much like admitting it. He had been drawn into an argument that he was destined to lose from the outset. But that didn't change what he knew was right or necessary.

"I know I can do better with her," he conceded. "I know I lose my temper with her when I shouldn't. She knows how to push all the right buttons and I let her do it." He paused. "But that doesn't change things. She is still going to Libiris with Questor the day after tomorrow. I have my mind set on this, Willow."

She nodded. "I know you do, and I know that it would be good for her to go. But I am not certain she sees it that way."

"Well, it doesn't matter how she sees it. She's going whether she wants to or not."

He was bothered by how that pronouncement sounded the moment he was finished making it. In the days ahead, he would have cause to remember so.

FLIGHT

Mistaya marched back through the castle to her sleeping chamber without speaking to anyone—not even to a bewildered Questor Thews, who tried to ask her a question—closed and locked the chamber door, and sat down to contemplate her undeserved misery. The day was bright and clear and sunny outside her window, but in her heart there was only gloom and despair.

How could her father be so unfeeling?

It was bad enough that she had returned home under a dark cloud, suspended from the prestigious boarding school to which he had sent her with such high hopes, her future a big, fat blank slate on which she had no idea what she would write. It was worse still that she was almost immediately confronted with a marriage proposal she didn't need from a man she didn't like, a proposal so outrageous that it should have been rejected out of hand and yet somehow wasn't. But to top it all off, she was now looking at months of exile to a place that no one in their right mind would visit under any circumstances, a gloomy and empty set of buildings that were crumbling and breaking apart, that were filled with dust and debris, and that housed moldering old books no one had opened in decades.

At least, that was the way she envisioned it in her mind as she sat before her mirror and looked at her stricken face and thought to herself that no one should have to endure this.

She grew tired rather quickly of feeling sorry for herself and turned away. She walked over to the window, stared out at the countryside for a moment, then opened the window and breathed in the scents of Bonnie Blues and Rillshing Cedars. She loved her home. She loved everything about it, and what hurt her most about everything that was happening was that she was going to have to leave it. Technically Libiris was also her home, since it was a part of Landover, but not all parts of Landover were created equal. Consider the Fire Springs and the wastelands east, for instance— nothing in that part of the country was particularly charming. But Libiris was worse still.

Or so Questor had led her to believe.

She thought about her friend and mentor for a moment and could not quite make herself believe that it had been his idea to send her there. But her father would not lie about such a thing; it would be too easy to find him out if he did—and besides, he never lied. He did a few other irritating things from time to time, but not that.

She drummed her fingers on the windowsill and thought. There was no point in sitting around feeling sorry for herself. She would have to do something about her situation if she wanted it to improve.

Her first impulse was to talk to her mother. Willow was more sympathetic to her plight, more understanding of her struggles in general. But her mother was unlikely to cross her father in this instance and would probably suggest that Mistaya give Libiris a chance. Questor and Abernathy supported her father already, so there was no point in pleading with them.

She sighed. This was all so *unfair.*

She had a sudden urge to cry, and she almost gave in to it. But crying was for babies and cowards, and she wouldn't do it no matter how much she wanted to. She stiffened against it, reminding herself that teen angst was for those movie magazines and romance novels that she had discovered in her father's world. In Landover, there was no place for it.

All right, her mother was out. Her friends were out. Whatever help she was going to find, she would have to find elsewhere.

Right away, she thought of her grandfather, the River Master. The River Master was the leader of the fairy-born—a collection of creatures that had forsaken the fairy mists that encircled Landover to come live in the world of humans. They made their home in the lake country south of Sterling Silver and more particularly in the city of Elderew. She could go there, and her grandfather would take her in and give her shelter and might not even tell her parents—at least, not right away. Willow was his daughter, but their relationship had never been all that strong. Willow's mother was a wood nymph whom he had never been able to tame or hold, a wild creature that refused to marry or even to settle. Willow was a reminder of her, and her grandfather neither needed nor wanted reminding. He liked Ben even less, an interloper from another world become King through a series of happy coincidences who didn't really deserve the job. Her grandfather tolerated him, but nothing more.

She had learned all this while growing up, some of it from Questor and Abernathy and some from her own observations and experiences. She had never appreciated her grandfather's attitude, but she could see where it might come in handy in this instance. Because even though the River Master was not close to her parents, he loved Mistaya intensely.

Of course, there was always the possibility that he was angry with her for not having come to see him for more than a year. That might require a little repair work on her part—perhaps even a little groveling. She thought about it a moment and then shrugged. Well, she could grovel, if she had to. She would find a way to win him over, whatever it took. Going to Elderew was the best option open to her.

She folded her arms defiantly and nodded. Yes, she would run away to her grandfather. And she would do so immediately. No waiting around for the inevitable; no praying for a miracle. She would leave tonight.

She would pack some clothes and sneak out of the castle while everyone was sleeping. That might not be so easy. The castle was guarded, and her father's retainers were under orders to keep a close watch over her. It helped that Bunion was off checking on The Frog, but there were other eyes. If she tried to leave carrying a suitcase or a backpack, someone would notice and report it and she would be hauled back before she got halfway to Elderew.

Even more troubling was the fact that her father had ways of finding her, even if she didn't tell him where she was going. Once he discovered she was gone, he would use the Landsview or one of his other magical devices to track her down. Then he would simply mount up and come looking for her. She would have to find a way to thwart him.

She frowned with irritation. This couldn't happen in his old world, where you could be found only through technological means and not through magic. But she wasn't about to go back to where she had come from.

Was she?

No, of course not, she chided herself. What was the point of going back to the very place where she had been so miserable? But it did suggest another possibility. She could pass out of Landover into any world; like the fairies in the mists and the dragon Strabo in the Fire Springs, she had that ability. Once she was outside Landover, her father might never find her. It was an interesting thought, and she mulled it over for a long few moments. In the end, however, she discarded it. Leaving Landover wasn't acceptable. She had come home to Landover to stay and stay she would—just not at Libiris.

She flounced back over to the window, breathed in the scents of the countryside, rushed back to her bed and threw herself down, staring at the ceiling as she tried to work out the details of a plan. But planning wasn't her strong point. She reacted to people and events almost solely on instinct—the result of being a child of three worlds, she imagined—so thinking ahead too far was counterproductive.

She was still considering how to make her escape unnoticed

when one of the pages knocked at her door and informed her that she had a visitor—a G'home Gnome, he advised with obvious distaste.

At once she had the answer to her dilemma.

She rushed down to greet Poggwydd, who stood uncertainly at the front entry, gnarled hands clasped as gimlet eyes tried to take in everything at once, his posture suggesting that he had every expectation of being thrown out again momentarily.

"Poggwydd!" she shouted at him with such exuberance that he nearly dropped to his knees in fright. She rushed across the room and embraced him like an old friend. "So you *were* paying attention to me when I told you to come see me!"

He stiffened and gave her a halfhearted bow. "Of course I was paying attention! I took you at your word and then decided to see how good that word was!"

"Well, now you know." She smiled, took his hand in her own, and dragged him forward. "Come see the castle. But don't try to steal anything, all right?"

He mumbled something that she took to be an assent, and for the next hour they wandered the halls of Sterling Silver, looking in all the chambers—(save those her mother and father were occupying)—and talking of how life in the castle worked. She only caught him trying to take something once, and since it was an odd little silver vase, she let him keep it. Gradually, he relaxed and began to act as if he belonged, and they were soon talking with each other like lifelong friends.

As the tour finished and the urgency of her intended mission to escape began to press in upon her, she suddenly had a brilliant idea.

"Poggwydd, can I ask a favor of you?" she said.

He was instantly suspicious. "What sort of favor?"

"Nothing complicated or dangerous," she reassured him. She shrugged disarmingly. "I just want to give you some clothing to keep safe for me until I need it. Can you do that?"

He frowned. "Why would you give your clothing to me? Why would you need to keep it safe?"

She thought quickly, and then leaned in close to him. "All right, I'll tell you why. But you must agree to keep it a secret." She waited for his nod. "I have some clothes my parents gave me that I want to give to someone else who needs them more than I do. But I don't want my parents to see me taking them away because it will make them feel bad."

He struggled with this a moment, his monkey face screwed in thought, and finally he said, "Oh, very well. I can keep them if you want." Then he stopped abruptly. "Wait. How long do I have to keep them? I don't have anywhere to put them where they will be safe, you know."

She nodded. "You just need to keep them safe until tonight. I will come meet you after it's dark and take them back from you. All right?"

She could tell it wasn't, not entirely. Taking things in the course of scrounging or stealing was perfectly all right, but taking them any other way seemed odd. Poggwydd was clearly thinking that this could somehow come back to bite him, taking the personal clothing of Landover's Princess, whether it was her idea or not.

"Poggwydd," she said, taking his hands in her own. "You won't be getting into any trouble, I promise. In fact, this would mean I owe you a favor in return."

He seemed to like the sound of that, and he gave her a crooked smile. "All right, Princess. Where are these clothes?"

She took him to an anteroom off her bedchamber and had him wait while she pulled out travel clothes and packed them in a duffel bag she could sling over her shoulder. Not much, but enough to see her through the few days it would take to reach the lake country and her grandfather. She added a compass, a virtual map ring (really a handy tool for nighttime travel), a small fairy stone (a present for her grandfather), and a book on wizard spells that Questor had given her before she left for Carrington, which she had only just started reading again. This last might offer something useful in the days ahead, and since it was pocket-sized it was easily carried. Then she wrapped the duffel in an old sheet, tied the corners of the sheet in knots to secure everything, and took it out to him.

"I'll meet you at the Bonnie Blues tonight," she promised as she walked him to the front entry. A few curious glances were cast their way, but she ignored them and no one said anything. "Just remember to be there to meet me," she added.

She ushered him back through the gates and went up to her room to wait for nightfall.

It was all very exciting.

---◦⦚∞⦛◦---

She managed to put up a good front through dinner, even pretending that she would think more about going off to Libiris—(*as if!*)— and would take her father at his word that there would be no more encounters with the marriage-minded Laphroig. She had more faith in him on this one. But she was fifteen years old, and no fifteen-year-old ever took the word of a parent at face value and without reservations. It wasn't that parents were deliberately duplicitous— although sometimes they clearly were—but rather that they tended to forget their promises or to find a way to misconstrue their parameters. Whenever that happened, it somehow always ended up the child's fault. Given where things stood in her life, Mistaya was having no part of that.

But she talked and smiled and laughed and pretty much acted the way she knew they wanted her to act and didn't let her anxiety over managing a clean break interfere with their meal. She loved her parents, after all, and she knew they wanted only the best for her. Mostly, they delivered. But in this case they were going to have to start over and find a better route.

When dinner was finished, she excused herself on the pretext of wanting to do some reading and retired to her bedchamber. There she sat down to wait, biding her time until the castle stilled and her parents retired. They always followed the same procedure, looking in on her before going off to bed, so she couldn't try to leave before then. Because she had slipped them a sleep-inducing potion in their ale at dinner, they were likely to check in on her much sooner than usual. So she sat patiently, and before long there was a knock at her door.

"Mistaya?"

"Yes, Mother?"

"Your father and I are going to bed now. But you and I will have a talk in the morning about what's happening. Your father means well, but he is impetuous and sometimes oversteps his parental boundaries. Sleep well."

Mistaya listened to her footsteps recede, and as she did so she felt a pang of regret over what she intended to do. She had committed herself, though, and there was no guarantee that her mother could help her in this business, no matter how well intended she was. Better that she go to her grandfather's and bargain from a position of relative strength.

She gave it another ten minutes, then pulled on her cloak and went out the door.

It was dark and silent in the hallway, and she slipped down its length on cat's paws, little more than a passing shadow faintly outlined by clouded moonlight against the wall. She didn't have far to go, so she took her time, careful not to make a sound or do anything that would alert the watch. Once she was safely down the hallway and had reached the hidden passage, they were unlikely to find her no matter how hard they looked.

She arrived at her destination without incident, triggered the lock in the panel that concealed the door, waited for it to slowly open, and stepped inside. From there, she went through the walls and down the stairs to the cellars, opened another hidden door in the stone-block walls, and followed a second passage to the outer walls and the door hidden there that opened to the outside world. She knew all this because she had made a point of finding out. You never knew when you might need a way to slip out without being seen, and an obliging Questor Thews, not once suspecting her reasons for asking, had revealed it all to her some time back. She supposed this constituted some sort of betrayal of trust, but she didn't have time to worry over it now.

Once outside the walls, she slipped around to where the old rowboat was anchored at the back docks, stepped in, and paddled her way across the moat to the far shore. It took hardly any time at all, and because the moon had slipped behind a bank of clouds, there was no light to betray her to the watch should they happen to look down from their towers.

Smiling with no small measure of self-satisfaction at how easily she had accomplished her goal, she prepared to set out for the stand of Bonnie Blues and Poggwydd. But first she decided to see if Halt-whistle was anywhere around. She called for him in a whisper, and almost immediately he appeared, standing right in front of her, short legs barely enough to keep his mottled brown body off the ground, long floppy ears faring little better, reptilian tail wagging gently.

"Good old Haltwhistle," she greeted, and she kissed at him on the air.

Together they went looking for Poggwydd. They found him waiting in something of a grumpy mood, sitting with Mistaya's sheet-wrapped travel bag clutched between his bony knees, a scowl on his wizened face. "Took your sweet time about getting out here, Princess," he muttered.

"I had to be careful," she pointed out. She reached for her bag, smiling. "Thank you for taking care of my clothes, Poggwydd."

To her surprise, he put both arms around the bag and hugged it possessively. "Not so fast. I have a few questions first."

She fought down a sudden surge of irritation. "What do you mean? What sort of questions?"

"The kind that require explanations. For instance, why do you need a compass, a map ring, a fairy stone, and a book of wizard spells to deliver a bunch of old clothes?"

Her jaw dropped. "Did you look through my things?"

"Answer my question."

She was fuming now. "Precautions against trouble. I have to travel some distance to make the delivery. Will you give them to me please?"

He ignored her. "Traveling is required because whoever you are taking these clothes to cannot come to the castle to get them?"

"That's partly it. Give me the bag, Poggwydd."

If anything, his grip grew tighter. "Hmmm. You know, Princess, it's dangerous traveling alone at night. I think I had better go with you."

"I can do this by myself, thank you. Besides, I have Haltwhistle."

"That's right. You have the assistance of your weird little dog. Clearly, he is a better friend to you than I am."

"What are you talking about?" she snapped.

"Well, you trust him enough to take him along, but not me. He probably knows the truth about what you're doing, doesn't he?"

Her mind was racing. "I don't know what you are talking about."

"Then allow me to enlighten you. Maybe it slipped your mind, but you are running away."

"I am not!" She tried to sound indignant. "If you don't give me my bag right now, I really will stop being your friend!"

"Sneaking out of the castle at night, having me meet you with clothes and travel stuff you could have carried out by yourself, and then telling me you intend to go somewhere mysterious alone? Sounds like someone running away to me."

She regretted ever thinking it a good idea to give her bag to this ferret-faced idiot. But it was too late for regrets. She had thought herself so clever, letting Poggwydd do the hauling. That way, she had reasoned, she wouldn't be burdened with the extra weight and if caught could argue that she was just going for a walk.

"You better tell me the truth about this right now!" he insisted. "If you don't, I'm going to start yelling."

"All right, don't do that!" She sighed, resigned to the inevitable. "My parents and I have had a disagreement. I am going to visit my grandfather for a while, and I don't want them to know where I am. Okay?"

Poggwydd looked horrified. He leaped to his feet, arms waving. "You really are running away?"

"Not exactly. Just . . . taking a vacation."

"Vacation? You're running away! And I'm helping you! And after you're gone, they're going to find out about me, and they're going to say that it is all my fault!"

She held up her hands in an attempt to calm him. "No, they're not. Why would they blame you?"

"Because G'home Gnomes get blamed for everything, that's why! And I'll get blamed for this! Someone will remember that I was the last one to visit you. Someone will remember that I left carrying a bag of clothing. Someone will tell that kobold, and he will come after me and hang me from the tree again!"

"No, he won't. Bunion promised—"

"It doesn't matter what he promised!" Poggwydd snapped, cutting her short. He was beside himself, hopping up and down in agitation and dismay. "This is all your fault! You're leaving me behind to pay for your bad behavior! You used me to help you, and now you are leaving me! Well, I won't stand for it! I shall alert the watch immediately and then they can't blame me!"

He started to turn away, heading for the castle, and she was forced to reach out and grab his arm. "Wait! You can come with me!"

He tried to jerk his arm free and failed. "Why would I do that?" he demanded, stopping where he was. "Why would I come with you?"

"Because we're friends!"

That silenced him for a moment, and he stood there looking at her as if she had just turned into a bog wump.

"Friends don't leave friends behind," she continued. "You were right about my decision to leave without you. I was being selfish. You should come with me."

He seemed suddenly confused. "I *was* right, wasn't I? I knew I was. But . . ." He stopped again, trying to think it through. "You're going to see your grandfather? The River Master? You want me to go with you to the lake country? But they don't like G'home Gnomes there. They like them there even less than they do everywhere else." He paused. "Except maybe in the Deep Fell, where the witch lives."

"We're not going to the Deep Fell," she assured him, although suddenly she was thinking that maybe that wasn't such a bad idea. With Nightshade still not returned from wherever her misguided magic had dispatched her almost five years earlier, the Deep Fell was safe enough. Well, maybe not all that safe, she conceded.

"I think this is a bad idea," he continued. "You shouldn't leave home like this. You should tell someone or they will worry and come hunting for you. If they find you, they'll find me and I'll get all the blame!"

She was massively irritated with his whining, but she recognized that there was a reason for it and that she had brought the whole thing on herself by involving him in the first place.

"What if I write you a note?" she asked him.

"A note? What sort of note?"

"One that says you are not to blame for this. They would know my handwriting. They would know it was genuine."

He thought about it a moment. "I think I will just come with you and take my chances," he said finally.

She almost started arguing against it, then remembered it had been her suggestion in the first place. "Well, that's settled then. Can I have my bag now, please?"

Grudgingly, he released his grip and shoved it toward her. "Here. Take the old thing. Do what you want with it." Surly and grumpy-faced, he lurched to his feet. "Let's get going while we still can."

She started off without speaking, already determined to get rid of him at the first opportunity.

MISERY LOVES COMPANY

Whatever reservations Mistaya might have harbored about her decision to allow Poggwydd to accompany her on her journey to the River Master were quickly proved insufficient.

He started to annoy her almost immediately by talking without taking a breath. He didn't appear to have any idea at all that it was possible to travel in silence. It began to seem after the first hour that his mouth was somehow connected to his feet, and that if one moved, the other must naturally follow suit. He talked about everything—about things he was seeing, about what he was thinking, about his worries and hopes and expectations, about his aches and pains, about his struggles to get by in life, but mostly about the undeserved lot of all G'home Gnomes.

"We have been set upon relentlessly, Princess," he declared, shaking his finger at her as if she were somehow to blame. "We are persecuted from the day we are born until the day we die, and there is never any letup in the effort. All creatures feel it is their bound duty to make our lives miserable. They do so without compunction and without reason. I think it is a game with them—an evil, malicious exercise. They consider it a pastime, an activity in which all must participate and from which great enjoyment is to be gained. They see us as toys—small playthings made for their amusement."

She tried to slow him down. "Perhaps if you—"

"There is no 'perhaps' about any of it," he continued, cutting her short. "Do not try to change the reality, Princess, with encouraging words and empty promises of better days ahead. We Gnomes know better. It is our lot in life to be abused, and however unfair and arbitrary, we have learned to accept it. Teasing and taunting, sticks and stones, beating and flaying, even the burning of our homes"—this one slowed her down a bit, since G'home Gnomes lived in burrows in the ground—"are all part and parcel of our everyday lives. We bear up nobly under our burden. You will not see a G'home Gnome flinch or hear him cry out. You will not witness a moment of despair revealed in our faces."

She could hardly believe what she was hearing, but she decided not to get into an argument about it. "Yet you continue to steal what isn't yours, which just encourages your mistreatment by others?"

"We do what we must to survive, nothing more." He sniffed with obvious indignation. "Most of the accusations of theft are baseless. Most are the product of overactive imaginations and willful resentments. When a G'home Gnome takes something that doesn't belong to him—a rare occurrence, as you know—it is usually because there is no clear ownership discernible of the thing taken or because there is a starving, homeless child to be cared for by a parent trying to do the best he or she can. I, myself, have witnessed this on more than one occasion. But do our persecutors take this into consideration? Do they give one moment's thought to those helpless children so in need of food and shelter? Sadly, no."

"If you kept to your own territories—"

"We are citizens of the world, Princess," Poggwydd interrupted her again. "We are nomadic travelers of all the parts of the land, and we cannot be confined to a single patch of ground. It would destroy us to do so. It would contradict and diminish centuries of Gnomic lives gone before, make mockery of all that we are, belittle our heritage—what little we have—a travesty of unparalleled proportions . . ."

And so on. And so forth.

She endured it stoically, all the while plotting his demise. If she could drop him into a pit, she would. If she could feed him to a hungry tiger flunk, she wouldn't hesitate. She would welcome lockjaw in any form. She kept hoping that something would happen to cause him to turn back. But nothing suggested this was about to happen, as was apparent from his assurances between his endless tales of Gnomic persecution.

"But we are not like them, and so I shall stay at your side, Princess, and do what I can to see you through this trying time." He puffed up a bit at this pronouncement. Apparently, he had forgotten his stand on the matter some hours earlier. "No danger, however dire, shall force me to leave you. We G'home Gnomes are a strong-hearted and determined people, as you shall see for yourself. We do not abandon or mistreat our friends. Unlike some I know. Why, not two weeks ago, there was a farmer with a pitchfork . . ."

And so on. And so forth.

They walked steadily through the moonlit night for several hours, traveling south out of Sterling Silver's boundaries and into the wooded hills that fronted the lake country. All the while, Poggwydd talked and Mistaya gritted her teeth and tried not to listen. Even Haltwhistle, ever faithful, had disappeared from view, obviously not any happier with the irritating Gnome than she was. She tried turning her attention to her surroundings. The sky had been mostly clear at the beginning of their journey, but now it began to fill with clouds. Moon and stars disappeared behind their heavy screen, and the dry, warm air turned damp and cool. By midnight, it had begun to rain—lightly, at first, and then heavily.

Soon the young girl and the G'home Gnome were slogging through a downpour.

"I remember another storm like this, perhaps a couple of years back. Much worse than this one. Much." Poggwydd would not give it up. "We walked for days, my friend Shoopdiesel and I, and the rain just kept falling on us as if it were tracking us for personal reasons. We huddled under old blankets, but it just seemed another instance of how everything works against you if you're a G'home Gnome . . ."

Just shut up, Mistaya thought, but didn't say. She wondered momentarily if magic might silence him, but she had resolved not to use magic of any sort on her journey to her grandfather unless she was absolutely forced to do so. Using magic was like turning on a great white light that everyone who had a connection with magic could see from miles away. She was trying to stay hidden, not broadcast her whereabouts, and there was no surer way of alerting her father.

So she couldn't use it to do anything about Poggwydd or the rain and the cold, either, and she had to content herself with trying to ignore the Gnome and pulling the collar on her cloak a little tighter around her neck and choosing a path that kept her under the tree canopy as much as possible in an effort to deal with the weather.

Poggwydd, for his part, tramped along as if it were a sunny day, ignoring the rain as it streamed off his wizened face and leathery body, his lips moving in time to his feet in a steady, nonstop motion.

Such dedication, Mistaya thought irritably. If only he could apply half of that effort to avoiding all of his bad habits and irritating ways, he might manage to become at least reasonably tolerable.

At some point during the seemingly endless trek, she caught sight of the cat.

She wasn't sure what drew her attention—a small movement or just a sense of something being there—but when she looked, there was this cat, walking along in the rain as if it were the most natural thing in the world. What a cat was doing in the middle of the forest in the midst of a rainstorm escaped her completely. It didn't look feral or lost or even damp. It was slender and sleek, its fur a glistening silver save for black paws and a black face. It was wending its way through the trees, staying parallel to her, but keeping its distance. She waited for it to glance over, but it never did.

She looked away, and a few minutes later when she looked back, it wasn't there.

Maybe she had imagined it, she thought. Maybe it was Haltwhistle she had seen, mistaking the mud puppy for a cat.

Maybe it was a wraith.

When she had walked as far as she could, gotten as wet and cold as she could, and endured the elements and the incessant chatter of her traveling companion for as long as she could, she called a halt. She found shelter under the branches of a closely grouped clump of giant cedar, then took up a position on a dry patch of ground to wait for things to improve. Haltwhistle joined her, curling up a few feet away. Poggwydd chose a dry spot that was some distance off, yet still close enough for him to be heard should he choose to keep talking through the night. Mercifully, he seemed to have run out of steam and was rummaging through his rucksack, searching for food.

Food held no interest for Mistaya. She sat hunched down within her cloak in the rain and the darkness, rethinking what she intended to do. In retrospect, her plans seemed foolish. What made her believe the River Master would welcome her? Grandfather or not, he was a difficult and unpredictable creature, a once-fairy who had no use for her father and little more for her mother. Nor, she had to admit, had he shown much interest in her, at least of late. At best he had exhibited some small pleasure in having her as his granddaughter—much the way one enjoyed having a pet. It hadn't been so when she was younger, but things had changed. Why did she think he would give her any special consideration now, when she was no longer little and cute?

She chided herself for not visiting him more often and certainly sooner than this.

Even more distressing was her growing certainty that she could not avoid being discovered by her father before she was ready. There was no hiding from the Landsview, which could find anyone anywhere in Landover. Unless, of course, they were in the Deep Fell or in Abaddon, home of the demons, and neither was a reasonable alternative to the lake country. She might try using her magic to conceal her presence, but she didn't think she could afford to rely on a spell she had never used. She had to expect that she would be found out and confronted about what she was doing.

She grimaced. A favorable outcome did not seem likely. Whether her grandfather rejected her or her father found her, she would be humiliated and revealed. A physical confrontation with her father was out of the question, so what was left to her? If flight and concealment were not available, then she would almost surely have to settle for a protracted exile to Libiris and a life of drudgery and boredom. Her father would win, she would lose, and it would be business as usual.

She reached into her shoulder duffel and pulled out a quarter loaf of bread, gnawing on it absently. It seemed dry and tasteless amid the cold and damp. But there would be nothing better until she got to her grandfather's, so she might as well get used to it. She should have done a better job of thinking through her escape plan, she told herself. She should have found some reason for going to her grandfather that did not involve running away, and once she was there she could have found a way to make him let her stay. Now she was forced to hope she could persuade him in a matter of hours rather than days. Why was she so stupid?

"Why am I so stupid?" she repeated, whispering it to herself, inwardly seething.

"That is difficult to say," came a reply from the darkness.

She jerked upright and looked around to see who had spoken. But there was no one else present but Poggwydd. She waited expectantly, and then she said, rather tentatively, "Is someone there?"

Poggwydd replied, "Of course I'm here! What does it look like? Did you think I would abandon you?"

"No, I didn't think that, but I—"

"G'home Gnomes do not abandon those who depend on them in times of need, Princess. It is a characteristic of our people that even in the worst of circumstances, we stand firm and true. Forever faithful, that is our motto and our way of life, carried bravely forth . . ."

And off he went with a fresh spurt of verbal energy, chattering away once more. She could have kicked herself for giving him a reason for doing so, but there was no help for it now.

She took a moment to consider her options before pulling out her travel blanket, wrapping herself up tightly, and lying down with

her head on the duffel. She gazed sideways out into the trees, listening to the sound of the rain and smelling the dampness. Things
weren't so bad, really. She shouldn't imagine the worst just because
the future seemed so uncertain. She had faced difficult situations
before and overcome them. She would overcome this one, too. She
would be all right.

The last thing she saw before she fell asleep—and this was just as
her eyes had grown so heavy that her vision was reduced to little
more than a vague blur—was that strange silver-and-black cat.

When she woke, it was morning. But the rain was still falling, the
air was still damp and cold, and trailers of mist were drifting
through the trees like snakes in search of shelter. The only good
thing she could point to was a silent, sleeping Poggwydd.

She looked for Haltwhistle, but he was gone again. She whispered his name, the way she knew she had to if she was to keep him
close, never forgetting that she would lose him otherwise.

Then she saw the other G'home Gnome.

At first, she thought she must be mistaken, that she was seeing
things, a mirage formed by the damp and the mist, perhaps. She
blinked to clear it away, but when she focused on it again, it was still
there. A second G'home Gnome, right there in front of her. Watching her, no less. She couldn't believe that this was happening. The
only thing worse than one G'home Gnome was two.

She lifted herself up on one elbow for a better look. The Gnome
raised one hand and wiggled his fingers at her. He was an unbeliev-
ably odd-looking fellow—there was no disputing that. He seemed
to be younger than Poggwydd, less wrinkled and wizened looking,
less hunched over. His ears were enormous appendages that stuck
out from the sides of his head like bat wings. Thatches of reddish
hair bristled from between them and in a few instances from inside
them. The round blue eyes were in sharp contrast with the red hair,
and the nose was a tiny black button that looked as if it belonged to

someone else. He was short and squat, even for a G'home Gnome, and made up almost entirely of bulges.

He smiled rather bashfully and said nothing as she scrutinized him, seemingly waiting for something.

Then Poggwydd woke up and things really got weird.

"Shoopdiesel!" he screamed excitedly as he caught sight of the other. "You're here!"

He gave a wild howl and leaped to his feet. The second Gnome jumped up, as well, and the two rushed at each other in a flurry of waving arms and wild exclamations. On reaching each other they went into a crouch, hands on knees, and began to chant:

> One, two, three, together we'll always be!
> Three, four, five, as long as we're alive!
> Six, seven, eight, because we're really great!
> Eight, nine, ten, we'll always be good friends!

Then they began clapping hands and thumping chests and exchanging bizarre, complicated handshakes in a practiced ritual that Mistaya was certain held no meaning for anyone but them. She stared at all this, fascinated. Several things occurred to her about what she was witnessing, but none of them required acting on, so she contented herself with just watching the show.

"Princess!" Poggwydd called to her when the show was over and the two G'home Gnomes were embracing warmly. "This is my greatest and most loyal friend in all the world. This, Princess, is Shoopdiesel!"

He said this in a way that suggested it was an important announcement and meant to be taken seriously. She did her best to carry it off. "Very nice to meet you, Shoopdiesel."

The Gnome replied with a deep bow and a grin that consumed the entire lower portion of his lumpy face.

"Might one of you explain what that greeting was about?" she ventured, turning back to Poggwydd.

"That is our ritual secret greeting," he replied, grinning almost as widely as his pal. "No one knows how to perform it except us. That way, no one can ever pretend to be us."

He seemed to think that this was very clever, and she thought it would be heartless to point out that no one would ever *want* to pretend to be them. "How did you find us, Shoopdiesel?" she asked instead.

The newcomer whispered intently in Poggwydd's ear for several long minutes before the other then turned to her and proclaimed, "It was a stroke of good fortune, Princess."

Though she had every reason in the world to doubt this, she nevertheless listened while he explained that Shoopdiesel, having done little but worry about Poggwydd after his abrupt departure several weeks earlier, had come looking for him and found him yesterday sitting on the ground in a stand of Bonnie Blues with an old sheet clutched between his legs. Not certain how to approach him—which had something to do with Poggwydd's leaving in the first place, although it was not made clear exactly what—he sat down to think things over. Then Mistaya had appeared and spoken with Poggwydd for a very long time, and afterward the pair had gone off together, walking south, away from the castle. Having nothing better to do with himself, he had followed them.

"It was difficult for him to keep up with us during the storm without letting us know he was there, but he managed it. He is very unsure of himself, Princess, very shy. It is a fault he is trying to correct, but he couldn't overcome it at Sterling Silver. Then, this morning, he summoned the courage to come into our camp and reveal himself."

He paused. "Besides, he doesn't have any food and he's hungry." He gave Mistaya a toothy smile. "Can he have some of your food, Princess?"

Mistaya sighed, reached into her food pouch, and handed over a quarter loaf of her dry bread. What did it matter if she gave it away at this point? "Do you always travel without food?" she asked.

"He had food, but he ate it," Poggwydd answered for him.

Shoopdiesel did not even glance up from the bread as he gnawed on it, absorbed in his eating. "He got very hungry."

The three sat down together while he ate, Mistaya thinking suddenly that maybe she had found a way out of this mess after all. It might not be a bad thing that Shoopdiesel had appeared. It might have provided her with an excuse for ridding herself of Poggwydd.

"Now that Shoopdiesel has found you," she ventured, as the last of the bread disappeared into the little fellow's mouth, "you probably want to spend some time together catching up on things. So off you go! You don't need to come any farther with me. I know the way from here, and it won't be difficult for me to find—"

"Princess, no!" Poggwydd exclaimed in horror. "Abandon you? Never!"

Shoopdiesel echoed these sentiments with a flurry of waving arms.

"We will travel together, the three of us, until you are safely in the hands of your grandfather," Poggwydd continued. "G'home Gnomes know the importance of loyalty to their friends, and you are entitled to that loyalty for as long as you need it. There shall be no shirking of duty on our part, shall there, Shoop?"

There was another shake of the head from good old Shoop, who apparently left all the talking to his friend. She could have strangled them both on the spot, but she supposed actions of that sort would lead to worse problems than she already had.

"Fine," she said wearily. "Come if you want. But you should remember that this is the country of the fairy-born, and they don't care much for G'home Gnomes."

Poggwydd grinned. "Who does, Princess?"

Both G'home Gnomes exploded in gales of laughter, which she hoped made them feel better than it did her.

GRANDFATHER'S EYES

The morning dragged on. The rain intensified anew, the dawn drizzle turning into a midmorning downpour that soaked everyone and everything. Mistaya was miserable—cold, wet, and vaguely lonely despite Poggwydd's incessant chatter, an intrusion that bordered on intolerable. She kept thinking about what she had given up to avoid being sent to Libiris, and she couldn't help wondering if perhaps she had made a mistake. She didn't like thinking that way; she was not the kind of girl who second-guessed herself or suffered from lingering regret if things didn't work out as she had hoped. She took pride in the fact that she had always been willing to suffer the consequences of her mistakes just for the privilege of being able to make her own choices.

But this morning she was plagued by a nagging uncertainty that worked hard at undermining her usual resolve. Still, she gave no real thought to turning back and comforted herself with the knowledge that this wouldn't last, that things would get better. They were nearing the borders of the lake country now, the forests thickening and filling up with shadows as they pushed deeper into fairy-born territory.

At one point—she wasn't sure exactly when—she noticed the cat was back. A silver-and-black shadow, it walked off to one side among the brush and trees with dainty, mincing steps, picking its way through the damp. The rain was falling heavily by then, but the cat seemed unaffected. She glanced back at the G'home Gnomes to see if they had noticed, but they were oblivious to this as to everything else, consumed by Poggwydd's unending monologue.

When she looked back again, the cat was gone.

Very odd, she thought for the second time, to find a cat way out here in the middle of the forest.

They crossed the boundaries of the lake country. It was nearing midafternoon, and the woods were turning darker still when the wood sprite appeared out of nowhere. A short, wiry creature, lean and nut brown, it had skin like bark and eyes that were black holes in its face. Hair grew in copious amounts from its head down its neck and along the backs of its arms and legs. It wore loose clothing and half boots laced about the ankles.

Its appearance frightened Poggwydd so that he actually gave a high-pitched scream, causing Mistaya renewed doubt about how useful he would be under any circumstances. She hushed him angrily and told him to get out from behind Shoopdiesel, where he was hiding.

"This is our guide to the River Master, you idiot!" she snapped at him, irritated with his foolishness. "He will take us to Elderew. If you stop acting like a child!"

She immediately regretted her outburst, knowing it was an overreaction brought on by her own discomfort and uncertainty, and she apologized. "I know you're not familiar with the ways of the fairy-born," she added. "Just trust me to know what I am doing."

"Of course, Princess," he agreed gloomily. "Of course I trust you."

It didn't sound like he did, but she decided to let matters be. For one thing, his momentary fright had stopped him from talking. The relief she felt from that alone was a blessing.

The wood sprite fell into step beside her without speaking, did not glance at her or make any attempt at an acknowledgment. Within half a dozen paces, he had moved ahead of her and was leading the way. Mistaya followed dutifully, knowing that when you came into the country of the fairy-born, you required a guide to find their city. Without a guide, you would wander the woods indefinitely—or at least until something that was big and hungry found you. Even if you knew the way—or thought you did—you would not be able to reach your destination unaided. There was magic at work in the lake country, a warding of the land and its inhabitants, and you needed help in getting past it.

They walked for another hour, the forest around them darkening steadily with the coming of twilight and a further thickening of the trees. The look of the land changed as they descended into swampy lowlands filled with pools of mist and stretches of murky water. They walked a land bridge that barely kept them clear of this, one that was narrow and twisting and at times almost impossible to discern. Their guide kept them safely on dry ground, but all around them the swamp encroached. Creatures moved through the mist, their features vague and shimmering. Some were unidentifiable; some were almost human. Some emerged from the murk to dance atop the water's surface. Others dove and surfaced like fish. Ephemeral and quicksilver, they had the appearance of visions imagined and lost.

Mistaya could feel the fear radiating off her companions.

"Everything is fine," she reassured them quietly. "Don't worry."

More of the wood sprites appeared, falling into place about them until they were thoroughly hemmed in. Poggwydd and Shoopdiesel were practically hugging each other as they walked, the latter making little hiccuping noises. But the sprites were there to keep them safe, Mistaya knew—there to see that they did not stray from the path and become lost in the tangle of the woods and swamp. Some of the denizens of this land would lead them astray in a heartbeat if the opportunity presented itself. Sprites, naiads, kelpies, pixies, nymphs, elementals, and others for which there were no recognizable names—they were mischievous and sometimes deadly. Humans were less able in this world, more vulnerable to temptation and foolish impulse. Humans were playthings for the fairy-born.

Nor were these the most dangerous of such creatures. The true fairy-born, the ones who had never left the mists that surrounded Landover, were far more capable of indiscriminate acts of harm. In the mists, there were no recognizable markers at all and a thousand ways to come to a bad end. The fairies of the mist would dispose of you with barely a moment's thought. No one could go safely into those mists. Not even she, who was born a part of them. Not even her father, who had done so once and almost died there.

But she felt some comfort in being here, in the lake country, rather than in the fairy mists that ringed the kingdom. Here the River Master's word was law, and no one would dare to harm his granddaughter or her companions. She would be taken to him safely, even through the darkest and murkiest of the woods that warded Elderew. All she needed to do was to follow the path and the guides who had set her on it. All she needed to do was to stay calm.

Even so, she was relieved when they cleared the black pools, gnarled roots, wintry grasses, and mingled couplings of shadows and mist to emerge once more into brightness and open air. The rain had slowed to a drizzle and the skies overhead, visible again through the treetops, had begun to show patches of blue. The fetid smells of the deep forest and the swamp faded as the ground rose and they began to climb out of the lowlands they had been forced to pass through. Ahead were fresh signs of life—figures moving against the backdrop of a forest of huge old oaks and elms that rose hundreds of feet into the air, voices calling out to one another, and banners of bright cloth and garlands of flowers rippling and fluttering on the breeze from where they were interwoven through the tree branches. Water could be heard rushing and gurgling some distance away, and the air was sweet with the scent of pines and hemlocks.

As they reached the end of their climb and passed onto flat ground, they caught their first real glimpse of Elderew. The city of the fairy-born lay sprawled beneath and cradled within the interlocking branches of trees two and three times the size of those they had passed through earlier, giants so massive as to dwarf anything found elsewhere in Landover. Cottages and shops created multiple levels of habitation both upon and above the forest floor, the entrances to the latter connected by intricate tree lanes formed of branches and ramps. The larger part of the city straddled and ran parallel to a network of canals that crisscrossed the entire city beneath the old growth. Water flowed down these canals in steady streams, fed by underground springs and catchments. Screens of mist wafted at the city's borders and through the higher elevations, a soft filtering of sunlight that created rainbows and strange patterns.

To one side, a vast amphitheater had been carved into the earth with seats formed of grasses and logs. Wildflowers grew at the borders of the arena, and trees ringed the entirety with their branches canopied overhead to form a living roof.

Poggwydd gasped and stared, wide-eyed and for once unable to speak.

The people of the city had begun to come out to see who was arriving, and some among them recognized Mistaya and whispered her name to those who didn't. Soon what had begun as scattered murmurings had risen to a buzz that rolled through the city with the force of a storm wind, everyone wanting to know what the King's daughter was doing there.

So much for any chance of keeping things secret, Mistaya thought in dismay.

A crowd quickly began to form about them, a mix of fairy-born united by curiosity and excitement. They spoke in a dozen different languages, only a few of which Mistaya even recognized. The children pushed close and reached out to touch her clothing in quick, furtive gestures, laughing and darting away after doing so. She smiled bravely, trying to ignore her growing sense of claustrophobia.

Then the crowd parted and a clutch of robed figures pushed forward, men and women of various ages. Her grandfather stood foremost, his tall, lean figure dominating the assemblage, his chiseled features impassive as he saw who was causing all the excitement. No smile appeared to soften his stern look, and no greeting came. The gills on either side of his neck fluttered softly and the slits of his eyes tightened marginally, but nothing else gave any indication of his thinking.

"Come with me, Mistaya," he said, taking her arm. He glanced at Poggwydd and Shoopdiesel. "The Gnomes will remain here."

He walked her back through the crowd, away from everyone but the handful of guards who were always close at hand. They passed down several walkways lined with flowers and through a park to a fountain set in the center of a pool. Benches surrounded the pool, and he led her to one and seated her firmly.

There was anger in his eyes now. "Tell me what are you doing with those creatures!" he snapped. "Tell me why you brought them here!"

So this is how it's going to be, she thought. She tightened her resolve. "They insisted on coming, and I did not see the harm. How are you, Grandfather?"

"Irritated with you," he replied, the weight of his gaze bearing down on her. "I hear nothing from you for more than a year, and then you violate our code by bringing into the home city of the fairy-born a pair of creatures who are never allowed in places much less selective about whom they admit. What were you thinking, child?"

She held his gaze. "I was thinking you might be more tolerant than this. I was thinking that at the very least you might hear me out."

"Perhaps you thought wrong—just as I did in believing you would not forget your grandfather and your fairy-born roots." He paused, and some of his anger faded. "Very well, tell me about this business."

"First of all," she said, "it was insulting not to be greeted in a more friendly and personal fashion by my own grandfather. I traveled some distance to see you, and I would have thought you could show some small measure of happiness at seeing me, no matter the time that has elapsed between visits. I would have thought an appropriate display of affection might be called for!"

She paused, but he said nothing. She shook her head. "I have been away at school in my father's world, should it have slipped your mind. Visits back here from another world are not so easily arranged. Yes, I should have come before this, but it wasn't as if I had all that many chances to do so."

He nodded. "I accept that. But there are other avenues of communication, I am told."

She returned the nod. "And I accept *that*. But things have a way of getting away from you."

"So you've come to see me now, something you might have had the courtesy to advise me of. But you sent me no notice of your visit." He gave her a long, hard once-over. "Why would that be?"

"An impulsive act, perhaps? Maybe I suddenly regretted my neglect of you and decided to make up for it?" She made a face at him. "Don't be so stern. It isn't as if I haven't thought about you."

"Nor I of you, Mistaya."

"I decided it was time to make amends. I thought my coming would be a nice surprise."

"A surprise, in any event. Am I to gather that your choice of traveling companions is a part of that surprise?"

"No," she admitted. "I was . . . I was sort of forced to let them accompany me. They worried for me and insisted on seeing me safely here. I asked them not to do so, but they would not hear of it, so I agreed to let them come." She shrugged. "I didn't see the harm. They can be sent away now, if you wish."

Her grandfather studied her once more, his eyes searching her own. "I see," he said finally. He kept looking at her, the long fringes of black hair on the backs of his arms rippling in the cool breeze. She didn't like how his eyes made her feel, but she forced herself to wait on him.

He sighed. "You know, Mistaya," he said finally, "the fairy-born cannot be easily deceived, even by their own kind. Not very often, anyway. Not even by someone as talented as you. We have an instinct for when we are not being told the truth. You have that same instinct, do you not? It is a safeguard against those who might hurt us—intentionally or not." He paused. "Those instincts are telling me something about you, right now."

"Perhaps they are mistaken," she tried.

He shook his head, his chiseled features as hard and fixed as stone. "I don't think so. Something is going on here that you haven't told me. You might want to consider doing so now. Without revising as you go."

She saw that he had seen through her deception, and that lying or telling half-truths was only going to get her deeper in trouble. "All right, I'll tell you the truth. But please listen and don't get angry. I need you to be fair and impartial about what I'm going to say."

Her grandfather nodded. "I will hear you out."

So she told him everything, right from the beginning, right from the part where she had been suspended from Carrington up to her father's insistence on sending her to Libiris to oversee a renovation of the library. It took her awhile, and she faltered more than once, aware of how bad it all made her look, even if it wasn't her fault and entirely unfair. She even admitted that she had used Poggwydd to help her make her escape, and that having done so she found herself obliged to bring him along so as not to alert her parents before she had reached Elderew and the fairy-born.

When she had finished, he shook his head in disbelief.

"Please don't do that!" she snapped at him. "I came to you for help because you are my grandfather and the only one I could think of who would be willing to consider my situation in a balanced way. And you're not afraid of my father!"

He arched one eyebrow. "You don't think so?"

She gritted her teeth. "I am asking for sanctuary," she declared, liking the lofty, important sound of it. "I'm asking for time to find a way to make my parents see the wrongness of what they are proposing. I don't expect you to do anything but let me stay with you until they've had a chance to think things through. I will be no trouble to you. I will do whatever you require of me to earn my room and board."

"Your room and board?" he repeated. "And you say you will be no trouble to me?"

"I do say!" she snapped anew. "And stop repeating everything, Grandfather! It makes you sound condescending!"

He shook his head some more. "So your visit to surprise me has more to do with your falling-out with your parents than a desire to see me?"

He said it mildly, but she could feel the edge to his voice. "Yes, I suppose it does. But that doesn't change the fact that I have missed you very much. I know I should have come sooner to see you, and I might have done so if I hadn't been sent off to Carrington. I might actually visit more often now, if I am not exiled to Libiris. But you have to help me! You understand what this means better than anyone else! The fairy-born would never submit to such treatment—being locked away in some old building with nothing to do but organize books and papers and talk to walls! Their plan is nothing more than a reaction to my dismissal from school!"

"Your intention, then, is to reside with me until something happens to change your parents' minds about Libiris and your future, is that right?"

She hesitated, not liking the way he said it. "Yes, that's right."

He leaned back slightly and looked over at the fountain as if the solution to the problem might be found there. "I didn't like your father when he arrived in Landover as its new King. You know that, correct?"

She nodded.

"I thought him a play-King, a tool of others, a fool who didn't know any better and would only succeed in getting himself killed because he was too weak to find a way to stay alive. He came to me for help, and I put him off with excuses and a bargain I was certain he could not fulfill."

He looked back at her. "And your mother is one of my least favorite children. She is too much like her own mother, a creature I loved desperately and could never make mine, a creature too wild and fickle ever to settle. Your mother was a constant reminder of her and hence of what I had lost. I wanted her gone, and when she chose to believe in your father, I let her go with my blessing. She would not be back, I told myself. Neither of them would."

"I know the story."

Indeed, she did. Her mother, falling in love with her father in the fairy way, at first sight, had given herself to him. She was his forever, she had told him. He, in turn, had come to love her. Neither had any real idea of what that would mean, and neither had anticipated how hard their road together would turn out to be.

"I did not believe in your father or your mother, and I was wrong about both," her grandfather finished. "That does not happen often to me. I am the River Master, and I am leader of the fairy-born, and I am not allowed to be wrong. But I was wrong here. Your parents were brave and resourceful, and they have become the leaders this land has long needed. Your father is a King in every sense of the word, a ruler who manages to be fair to all and partial to none. I admire him for it greatly."

He gave her a searching look. "Yet you appear to think otherwise. You appear to think that perhaps you know better than he does."

She tightened her lips in determination. "In this one case, yes, I do. My father is not infallible."

"No," her grandfather agreed. "Nor are you. I suggest you ponder that in the days ahead."

"Grandfather . . ."

He held up one hand to silence her, the fringe of black hair a warning flag that shimmered in the half-light. "Enough said about this. I am pleased you have come to me, though I wish it had been under better circumstances. It is a visit that should not have happened. You wish to use me as a lever against your father and mother, and I will not allow it, Mistaya. You must learn to solve your own problems and not to rely on others to solve them for you. I am not about to interfere with your parents' wishes in the matter of Libiris, or to give you sanctuary, as you call it. Hiding out in the lake country will not bring an end to your problems."

She felt the strength drain from her. "But I'm only asking—"

"Only asking me to fight your battles for you," he finished, cutting her short. "I will not do that. I will not be your advocate in this matter. I do not care to challenge the authority of a parent over his child—not even when the child is one I love as much as I love you. I have been a parent with children, and I know how it feels to be interfered with by an outsider. I will not be a party to that here."

He stood up abruptly. "You may spend the night, enjoy a banquet prepared in your honor, and in the morning you will return home. My decision is made. My word is final. You will go to your room now. I will see you at dinner."

She was still trying to change his mind as he turned and walked away.

She was taken to a small cottage close to the amphitheater, one that offered sleeping accommodations not only for her but for the G'home Gnomes, as well. Under other circumstances, she would never have been housed close to them, but she thought that perhaps her grandfather was punishing her for disobeying the code that forbade her from bringing outsiders into the city. Or perhaps he thought she wanted them there, it was hard to tell. He didn't seem to be the man she knew anymore. She was bitterly disappointed in his refusal to let her stay with him. She had never once really believed he wouldn't. She knew he loved her, and she had been certain that this alone would be enough to persuade him to take her in, at least for a few days. Sending her away so abruptly was difficult for her to understand.

Alone in her sleeping chamber, the door tightly closed and the voices of the G'home Gnomes a faint murmur from the other side of the wall, she sat on her bed and tried hard not to cry. She never cried, she reminded herself. She was too old for that. But the tears came anyway, leaking out at the corners of her eyes, and she could not make them stop. She cried silently for a long time. What was she going to do?

She didn't have an answer when she walked down the hall to take her bath. She didn't have one when she was summoned to dinner, either. She ate mechanically of a very lavish feast and was thoroughly miserable the whole time. Her grandfather's family sat all around her, and her cousins had questions about life in her father's world, which she answered as briefly as possible, not caring about any of it. Poggwydd and Shoopdiesel were allowed to eat with the family, but placed at the low end of the table away from everyone except a handful of small children who had asked if they could sit with the strange-looking pair and who spent the entire meal staring up at them in a kind of bemused wonderment.

Mistaya spared them only a glance, somehow convinced that their presence had destroyed any chance she had of convincing her grandfather to let her stay with him. She knew it was a ridiculous conclusion, but she couldn't help thinking it anyway. There had to be some explanation for his refusal to consider her request more carefully. There had to be someone to blame for this.

Dinner went on for a long time, and when it was over there were welcome speeches, music, dancing and a whole lot of other nonsense that left her feeling even more out of sorts. Her grandfather did not even pretend to be interested in the reasons for her foul mood. He spoke with her only once and then just to ask if she needed anything. The rest of the time he spent whispering to the wife he had allowed to sit next to him that evening and to his youngest brother, a dark-visaged youth several years older than she whom Mistaya had never liked and now pointedly ignored.

Back in her rooms, she sat on the bed once more and thought about her situation. It couldn't be any bleaker. She was being sent home, and once arrived she would be dispatched—under guard, in all likelihood—to Libiris. Confined to the moldering old castle in the tradition of fairy-tale princesses in the books her father favored, she would slowly rot away in solitary confinement. The more she envisioned her future, the darker it became and the more trapped she felt.

Then she turned angry, and the angrier she grew the more de-

termined she became to do something about what was being done
to her. She would not permit this sort of treatment, she told herself. She was a princess and she would not suffer it.

Once again, she would have to escape.

Her grandfather, of course, would have already thought of that
possibility and taken steps to prevent it. He knew how resourceful
his granddaughter could be and he probably expected her to try to
slip away during the night and find help elsewhere.

She rose, walked over to the window, and looked outside. There
would be guards keeping watch, she knew. She would not be allowed to leave if they caught sight of her trying to do so. Not that
she could leave Elderew without help in any case, even with the use
of her magic. Magic could only get you so far, and in a land warded
by magic and magic-wielding creatures, even she was at a disadvantage. But she had to try something. She had to get out of there before morning.

Then she saw the cat again.

It was walking just outside her window, for all intents and purposes out on a nighttime stroll, wending its way through the grasses
and flowers of the little gardens. It was the same cat, she was certain. Silver with black markings, slender and aloof in its bearing,
seemingly unconcerned for everything around it.

She watched it a moment, wondering what it was going to do.
Then abruptly it stopped, sat down, and looked over at her. She
blinked. Sure enough, it was watching her. It hadn't done this before, but it was doing it now. *Well, well,* she thought.

Curious, she slipped from her sleeping chamber, went through
the common rooms on tiptoe, and eased out the cottage door and
around the house to the gardens. The cat was still sitting there, looking at her. She stopped at the gardens' edge, perhaps ten feet away,
wondering what to do next.

"Can I help you with something, Princess?" the cat asked suddenly.

And she could have sworn she saw him smile.

EDGEWOOD DIRK

Mistaya stared at the cat, and the cat stared back, its green eyes luminous. Had it really spoken to her or had she just imagined it?

"Cat got your tongue?" the cat asked after a moment's silence between them.

She nodded slowly. "I don't guess you're any ordinary cat, are you? I guess you must be a fairy creature. But you look like an ordinary cat."

"I don't guess you're any ordinary girl, either," the cat replied. "I guess you must be a Princess. But you look like an ordinary girl."

She nodded again. "Ha, ha. What are you doing here?"

"Waiting for you to come out and talk with me. We have a great deal to discuss, you and I. We have plans to make. We have places to go and people to meet. We have a life to live that extends far beyond these woods and your grandfather's rule."

"We do, do we?" She dropped down on her haunches and regarded the beast more closely. She ignored the cool damp of the night air and the silence of the darkness. She didn't even think about the possibility that her grandfather's guards might be watching her talk with this cat and wondering why. Her curiosity pushed all these considerations aside as she studied the cat's inscrutable face. "We have all that to do, you and I?"

The cat lifted one paw and licked it carefully, not looking at her. When it was satisfied with the result, it put the paw back down and blinked at her with an air of contentment. "Allow me to summarize. You have been dismissed from your school and sent home. Your father is unhappy with you and your mother, disappointed. Consequently, they seek to find a way to channel your considerable talents into a project that will further your truncated education. Thus, they choose to send you to Libiris. You view this as punishment, particularly in light of your father's response to Lord Laphroig's marriage proposal, and so you flee to your grandfather in hopes that he will better understand your dismay. But he refuses to let you stay and in the morning intends to send you back to your parents."

It paused. "How does all this sound to you? Have I left anything out, Princess? Would you care to add, subtract, or amend my words in any way?"

She shook her head no. "I think that about covers it, Mr. Cat." She gave it a sharp look. "How do you know all this?"

"It is my job to know things," the cat said. "Cats know lots of things about the world and its creatures, especially people. Cats watch and listen. It is what they do best."

"So you have been watching me?"

"Haven't you noticed me?"

"Once or twice on the way here. Not before then."

"Which points up how unobservant people are when it comes to our place in their lives. We wander about freely, and no one pays much attention to us. It allows us to go almost anywhere and discover almost anything without anyone realizing what we are doing. We know so much about you, but no one ever considers what this means. Cats are highly underrated in this regard."

"Well, I admit to not seeing you before yesterday. But I don't understand why you would want to know anything about me in the first place. What is the point in knowing all this stuff?"

The cat regarded her silently for a long moment and then yawned deeply. "I should think it would be obvious. I am here to help you."

She was aware of a growing stiffness in her legs from her pro-longed crouch, and she stood up carefully, rubbing her muscles. "Could we continue this conversation on the porch so that I can sit properly in a chair?"

"So long as you don't expect me to go into the cottage, we can. I prefer open spaces to cramped ones."

She walked over to the porch and sat down in one of the old rockers that bracketed the front door, wrapping herself in a rough blanket that was draped over one arm. The cat padded its way onto the first step and sat down again. All around them, the night remained deep and silent, and no one appeared to interrupt their conversation.

"How are you going to help me?" she asked after they were both comfortably settled.

"Well, that depends," the cat answered. "For starters, I am prepared to take you away from here. Tonight."

"You can do that?"

"Of course. If you really want to leave and not go home to your parents, I can take you somewhere else and your grandfather's guards will not be able to prevent it. If that is what you really want."

"It is," she said. "Assuming you can do as you say."

The cat said nothing, but instead went back to cleaning another paw—or perhaps it was the same one—licking the fur this way and that, worrying the pads with careful attention to the spaces between, acting as if there were nothing more important in all the world.

"You must possess considerable magic," she said.

"Your father thought so."

"You know my father?"

"And your mother. I have helped them, too, in the past, before you were born. Have they told you nothing of me?"

She shook her head. "I think I would remember you, if they had."

"They should remember me, too. They should remember me well. I did much to help them avoid a rather unpleasant end when the old wizard, the one before Questor Thews, tried to regain control of Landover's throne from your father and very nearly killed him in the bargain. Your father was in flight, too, at the time, wandering the countryside, searching for answers. Very much like you, Princess."

"I didn't know that. They never said anything about it."

"Parents don't tell their children everything, do they? Some things they keep to themselves because they are private and don't need to be shared. Or perhaps people think these things are best forgotten, a part of a past that has gone by and won't—with luck—come around again for a visit. When all this is over, you might not want to talk about what is going to happen to you, either."

"What is going to happen to me?" she asked quickly.

The cat blinked. "We shall have to wait and see, won't we?"

She frowned. "Why should I agree to go away with you?"

"Do you have a choice?"

"Of course I have a choice!" She was suddenly irritated.

"A choice that does not involve going back to your parents?" The cat sounded rather smug. "Besides, you might well ask why *I* should agree to go away with *you,* don't you think?"

"But you just offered!" she snapped.

"Yes, but cats have a habit of changing their minds rather quickly, and I might be in the process of changing mine. You seem to me as if you might be in a lot of trouble, given your rather independent streak and your uncertain temperament. Not to mention all the baggage you carry."

"Baggage?"

"The daughter of the King and Queen of Landover, their only child, on the run in the company of a pair of G'home Gnomes? Yes, I would say you carry more than a little baggage with you. I might not want to burden myself with all that. I might want to rethink my offer to help."

She regarded the cat carefully, studying its inscrutable cat face. "But you won't," she said finally. "You won't because you have a reason for coming to me like this in the first place."

"Perhaps."

"You won't because you are a cat and cats are curious and your curiosity has something to do with you being here and you haven't satisfied it yet."

"Curiosity comes and goes," said the cat.

She nodded. "What's your name?"

The cat looked away for a moment, studying the blackness beyond them as if it had just discovered something of immense interest. "I am like all cats when it comes to names," he said, speaking to the night. "I have as many names as I do lives. I don't even know what they all are yet. The one I prefer now is the one your father knew me by. Edgewood Dirk."

"I like your name," she told him.

"Thank you. Although it doesn't matter one way or the other, you realize."

She took a deep breath. "Does your offer to help me still stand? Will you take me away with you?"

Edgewood Dirk blinked. "All you need to do is gather your belongings, wake your companions, and follow me. No one will see us. No one will stop us. By morning, we will be far away."

"Far away," she repeated, liking the sound of it. Then the rest of what he had said caught up with her. "Wait a minute. Did you say I should wake my companions? Those Gnomes? I don't want them coming with me! I didn't want them coming with me in the first place!"

"Well, we don't always get what we want in life," said Edgewood Dirk.

"Well, they're not coming with me, Dirk, so you can just forget about me not getting what I want in this case!" She glared at him. "Is that all right with you?"

"Perfectly all right," he answered, his cat voice as calm as still waters. "Of course, leaving them behind means that when the River Master finds you gone, he will have to find someone to blame, and those two unfortunate G'home Gnomes might turn out to be his first choice."

She stared at him, speechless.

"Not that this should matter to you, of course," he added.

She knew he was right, and she hated it. She sighed wearily. "All right then, they can come."

"If you are quite certain it is all right, Princess?"

She ignored him, finding him increasingly annoying and suspecting that he would become more so as they traveled. She looked around guardedly. "We just walk right out of here, do we? Right through my grandfather's guards and all the once-fairy who live in the swamps? You know the way out and won't get us lost?"

The cat stared at her, saying nothing.

"Do you mind telling me where we are going?" she pressed.

The cat did not answer.

She put her hands on her hips and bent closer. "Why won't you answer me?" she demanded.

A small noise from behind caused her to straighten up and turn around. Poggwydd was standing there with Shoopdiesel peering over his shoulder, both of them looking bewildered. "Why are you talking to that cat?" the former asked hesitantly. "You know cats can't talk, don't you, Princess?"

He gave the cat an interested look. "But some of them are rather good to eat. Do you suppose this one belongs to anyone?"

Shoopdiesel licked his lips and looked eager.

Her belongings gathered and her mind made up, Mistaya set off through the fairy-born city of Elderew with Edgewood Dirk leading the way and a reluctant Poggwydd and Shoopdiesel bringing up the rear. Neither understood what was happening, and Poggwydd, on behalf of both, had complained loudly about it on being informed. As a result, she had expressly forbidden either G'home Gnome from speaking one single, solitary word until she gave them permission, threatening that if they did not do as she said she would leave them behind to face her grandfather's wrath when he discovered she was missing. Frustrated and out of sorts, they trailed along like restless children, shuffling and snuffling and generally acting as if they had an itch they couldn't scratch. She never looked back at them, and Dirk never looked back at her. In this fashion, single-file and keeping their distance from one another, they passed without notice into the deep woods.

Mistaya couldn't have told anyone why she was doing this. It made almost no sense to trust the cat, even if you got past the part where you accepted that it wasn't all that strange that a cat could talk. This was Landover, after all, and all sorts of things talked that didn't do so in other worlds. The dragon Strabo was a prime example; his vocabulary was both extraordinary and colorful. Not that there were a whole lot of other dragons to compare him with, but that didn't refute her point about creatures that talked. She had grown up in Landover, so a talking animal didn't surprise her, even if it would have shocked the girls of Carrington.

But *trusting* a talking cat—now, that was something else. Cats were not the most reliable of creatures, talking or not. They were independent and self-centered, prissy and devious, and she had no reason to think that this one was any different. Yet here she was, trailing along behind him, ready to believe that he not only knew the way out of Elderew but could actually get clear of the city without being detected. No one else could do this, so why did she think he could?

She guessed it was because she wanted so badly to escape the fate that awaited her if she stayed around until morning. Being sent back to her father would be the ultimate humiliation, and her embarrassment at her grandfather's rejection was quite enough already. Better that she take her chances out on her own than be stymied even in this small gesture of defiance. Better that she trust a talking cat with dubious motives than sit around and do nothing.

She kept silent until they were out of the city and wending their way back through the swamp and quicksand before she tried speaking to him again. She was aware that the Gnomes were listening in, so she kept her voice at a whisper until she grew frustrated and voiced her questions more loudly. But it didn't matter. Dirk ignored her, acting as if he hadn't heard, further convincing Poggwydd and Shoopdiesel that she was suffering from a delusion regarding the abilities of cats.

In the end, she gave it up, and they walked on through the night. By sunrise, they were clear of the woods and had emerged into a broad stretch of grasslands and hill country east, facing into the rising sun.

At this point, Edgewood Dirk came to a stop. Sitting back on his haunches with his tail curled about him, he began to clean himself—an undertaking both meticulous and seemingly endless.

Mistaya couldn't help herself. She had endured enough. "Look here," she said to the cat. "You did well in helping us escape the fairy-born. But now you have to tell us where we are going."

Dirk, predictably, said nothing.

"Stop pretending you can't speak!" she said. "I know you can!"

She glanced over her shoulder at the G'home Gnomes, who were shifting their gazes from her to each other and back again. "Princess, I don't think the cat can—" Poggwydd began.

"Be quiet!" she snapped at him. "I know what I'm doing!"

"But, Princess, cats don't—"

"Did I give you permission to speak?" she demanded, wheeling back on him. "Did I?"

Poggwydd shook his head dejectedly.

"What did I say I would do with you if you did?"

"Leave us behind. But we're safely away now. No one can hear us out here. Besides, you're talking, aren't you?"

She glared at him. "Just don't say anything, all right?"

"But what are we doing out here, following that stupid cat?" he whined miserably. "Cats don't know anything and aren't good for anything except to eat!"

She pointed a finger at him in warning and turned back to Dirk, who had finished cleaning himself and was now staring at her rather accusingly.

"Well, what do you expect me to say?" she demanded.

He continued to stare at her, and she could tell just by the nature of the look what he was thinking. "Oh, all right," she said. She sighed and turned back to the Gnomes. "I'm sorry. I didn't mean to snap at you like that. I'm just frustrated by everything."

And suddenly it occurred to her that perhaps the cat wouldn't speak to her unless they were alone. Hadn't that been the way things had worked last night? "Poggwydd, would you and Shoopdiesel wait for me over there by the trees?" She gestured toward where she wanted them to go. "Just for a few minutes."

The G'home Gnomes trooped off obediently, and she knelt down in front of the cat rather like a humble supplicant. "Now will you speak to me? Please?"

"Since you ask so nicely," said the cat, "I will do so. But not in front of anyone else. You would do well to remember that in the future. That way we won't have to go through this charade again."

"Believe me, I'll remember."

"Excellent. Now then, what is it that you want to talk about?"

She took a deep, steadying breath, submerging her lingering thoughts of strangling him. "Where is it that we're going?"

He cocked his head. "That would be up to you. I promised to take you safely away from Elderew and your grandfather, and I did. I assumed you had a plan. If so, now is the time to implement it."

"Well, I don't have a plan!" she snapped. "I just need to go somewhere my father can't find me while I think this thing through! Mostly, I need to get out of the open!"

She was frustrated and angry by now, suddenly afraid that Edgewood Dirk had taken her from the frying pan into the fire. Dirk, on the other hand, seemed unconcerned.

"Princess," he said quietly. "While you are with me, no one can find you by use of magic. Because I am a fairy creature, I am able to shield those who travel with me. Your father can look for you until next winter, and he will not be able to find you while you are with me unless he comes looking for you himself."

She stared at him. "Are you sure?"

"Cats are always sure. Look at me. I seem an ordinary cat at first glance—though of a particularly lovely sort. But I am much more. I am a Prism Cat, Princess. We possess special magic and are of a unique character."

She frowned, not knowing whether he was serious or not. "I don't think I understand. Can you explain?"

"I can, but I don't choose to. Another time, perhaps. Now, back to the plan you don't have. Where is it that you want to go?"

She sighed. "Somewhere I won't be found, whether you are with me or not. How's that?"

"Poorly conceived and expressed. You will be found quickly, if you are not with me. Which means, you must encourage me to come with you by showing some modicum of intelligence in making your choice of where you might go. Otherwise, I am wasting my time on you."

"What do you mean by that?" she demanded indignantly. "Why do I have to encourage you?"

"Because, Princess, I am not here by chance and I am not bound to stay. I chose to help you in the same way I chose to help your father and your mother. But I need a reason to stay. Cats are curious creatures, you might have heard. But if we lose our curiosity about something, we tend to move on to other, more interesting things. At the moment, I am curious about you. But that could change if you don't find ways to keep me interested."

She sat back on her heels, seething. "I have to keep *you* interested in *me*?"

"You do. How do you plan to do that?"

"The pleasure of my company isn't enough for you?"

"Please be serious."

"I have other friends, you know," she declared. "I have lots of other friends, and they would all be happy to help me."

"You have two G'home Gnomes, and neither has the least idea what to do about your situation. You have no one else. You don't even have your mud puppy anymore, in case you hadn't noticed."

She stared at him in disbelief, and then after looking around quickly began calling for Haltwhistle. But the mud puppy did not appear.

"Where is he?" she demanded, a bit frantic.

"I sent him home to the Earth Mother," said the cat. "It wasn't difficult. You forgot to speak his name, so he would have left anyway."

He was right. She hadn't spoken Haltwhistle's name at all yesterday, and she knew what that meant. If she failed to speak the mud puppy's name at least once each day, he would leave and go back to wherever he had come from. She didn't even know where that was because she had never thought about it. She had always been careful to say his name so that she wouldn't have to worry. But last night, absorbed in her own troubles, she had forgotten.

"Well, I can find him again," she declared bravely.

"Not before your father finds you." Dirk's remonstrance was maddeningly calm. "Now tell me where it is that you are going."

"I don't know," she said miserably.

"Somewhere you won't be found . . . ," he nudged.

"Why won't you just stay with me? Then it wouldn't matter where I went. Why won't you do that?"

Edgewood Dirk licked his chops and closed his eyes. "I know myself too well to make a promise I cannot keep. My nature requires that I be interested in your actions. For that to happen, you have to make interesting choices. Now think. Where could you go that would interest me?"

She shook her head helplessly.

"Put it another way. Where is the last place your father would think to look? Because sooner or later he will give up on talismans and wizards and come looking for you himself." Dirk paused. "Or perhaps he will send someone in his place, someone more effective at finding what is hidden. Perhaps he will send the Paladin looking for you."

Mistaya froze. She knew about the Paladin, of course, even though she had never seen him. Everyone knew about the Paladin. They whispered of it when they thought she couldn't hear, and Questor Thews had talked of it quite openly. They were all proud of its service to the throne, but they were also quite afraid of it: huge and dark of purpose, all armored and armed astride its charger. There had never been anything in memory that had been able to stand against the Paladin.

The last thing she wanted was something as implacable as that searching for her.

"Think, Princess," the cat pressed. "Where will your father look last for you?"

She thought. The Deep Fell was a good choice because magic couldn't penetrate its mists.

"The Deep Fell?"

"He will look there first."

"The Fire Springs!"

"He will look there second. He knows how the dragon feels about you."

"Not Rhyndweir? I won't go there!"

The cat waited. Suddenly Mistaya realized what answer he was looking for. "No!" she said at once. The cat cocked his head. "No! Absolutely not!" she repeated.

"When you wish to hide, the best place is always the one those hunting you are certain you will avoid." Dirk gave her one of those patented looks. "Isn't it?"

"You want me to go to Libiris," she declared.

"I don't necessarily want you to go anywhere. It isn't up to me. The decision is yours. Please make it. I grow bored with this."

She saw the logic to Dirk's reasoning. Her father would never think of looking for her at Libiris. He would look for her almost anywhere else before he looked for her there. But if she went, she was doing exactly what he had asked her to do in the first place. What sort of sense did that make?

"At least you would be going of your own choice and for your own reasons," Edgewood Dirk offered, as if reading her mind.

She toughened her resolve so that she could accept what she now realized she must do. "All right, I will go to Libiris with Poggwydd and Shoopdiesel." She paused. "Are you coming with us or not?"

The cat took a moment to study the countryside, emerald eyes filling with a distant look, as if gone somewhere else entirely. Then he looked back at her. "I believe I will," he answered softly, and then he began to purr.

THE PRINCESS
IS MISSING

Ben Holiday was not particularly worried on that first morning when it was discovered that Mistaya was not in her room. She did not appear for breakfast or lunch, nor was she anywhere in the castle. No one had seen her leave. That might have been cause for alarm in another household, but not in his. Mistaya was famous for her unexpected comings and goings, for choosing to set out on a personal mission or exploration without telling anyone. That she might have done so here was a reasonable assumption, particularly when it was well known that she had been spending her last few days meeting with one of those endlessly troublesome G'home Gnomes that kept cropping up at the castle.

This one, Poggwydd, had already been caught sneaking into the castle for purposes of pilfering whatever he could find—*he* didn't see it that way, of course—and put out again by Bunion right before Mistaya returned from Carrington. She had taken up his cause, thinking that she might help him change his thieving ways. When he had come to the door asking to see her, she'd brought him into the castle for a visit, given him a tour of its many rooms, and spent hours visiting with him somewhere outside Sterling Silver, presumably in an effort to educate him in the error of his ways. She had even made it a point to speak with Bunion about his overly harsh treatment of the little miscreant. All this she had accomplished in the span of little more than the week that she'd been back home.

Ben knew all this because he pretty much knew everything that happened in the castle. His retainers made it a point of telling him, especially when it came to Mistaya. Willow confided in him, too, when she thought it appropriate, and she had done so here because she was proud of the way that Mistaya was handling her ignominious return. Better that she find something useful to do with her time than sit around bemoaning her fate as a suspended student. Ben agreed, and so both of them had left her alone.

By dinnertime, however, he was experiencing the first faint whisperings of the possibility that things were not all right. Mistaya was still missing, and no one had seen her anywhere since the previous night. He decided to voice his concerns to Willow.

"It is possible she is punishing you," she offered, none too helpfully.

"Punishing me?" He frowned. They were sitting together after the dinner had been taken away, talking privately. "What do you mean by that?"

"She's angry with you. You've hurt her feelings, and she doesn't like how that makes her feel. She already told me that much, Ben."

He shook his head. He hated it that the two of them had a private information-sharing arrangement, but it had always been that way, mother to daughter and back again.

"I didn't mean to make her feel bad," he tried to explain. "I was just attempting to——"

"I know." She reached up and touched his lips to silence him. "But she doesn't see it that way. She thinks you should have been more supportive of her situation. Not just about Libiris, but about Laphroig, too. She's unsure of how she stands with you right now. Even when she can think about it rationally, she's still not quite certain what's going to happen."

"So she's gone off somewhere in protest?"

"Just for a little while, I think. Just long enough to make you worry and maybe rethink what you've decided about her future."

He sighed. "That sounds like her, doesn't it?"

Willow nodded. "She's very headstrong, very determined." She smiled and kissed him. "Very like you."

But by the following morning, when his daughter still hadn't reappeared, Ben decided that waiting around was no longer an option. Without saying anything to Willow, he called in Questor Thews and Abernathy for a conference. The three of them gathered clandestinely in Questor's office and put their heads together.

"I don't like it that there's been no word of her from anyone," Ben admitted to the other two. "It's been too long for me to be comfortable with the idea that she's just off sulking somewhere. Is Bunion back yet?"

Bunion wasn't, Questor advised. He sat up straight and prim in his high-backed chair, his colorful robes gathered about his scarecrow frame. "We could ask one of the other kobolds to have a look around, if you wish."

Ben didn't wish. He didn't want anyone but Bunion doing the looking because he could trust Bunion to do so without giving anything away. It was one thing to go looking for Mistaya because he was worried about her; it was another to give her the mistaken impression that he was spying on her.

"No, we'll wait for him to come back," he said. "He should be here by tonight, shouldn't he?"

The wizard and the scribe both agreed that he should. Three days was enough to find out whatever there was to find out about Laphroig, and Bunion would come right back after that.

"Why don't you use the Landsview, High Lord?" Abernathy asked. He cocked his dog ears to emphasize his approval of the idea. "You can find her that way, no matter where she is."

Which was pretty much true, Ben knew, unless she had gone down into the Deep Fell or outside Landover altogether. Neither of those options made a great deal of sense, so there was reason to think that by using the Landsview he might be able to determine where she was and reassure himself that she was all right.

Departing Questor's office, they passed down the castle hallways until they reached the tower that housed the Landsview. From there, they began to climb, winding their way up a spiral staircase to a landing that fronted a massive ironbound oak door. Ben placed the palms of his hands on the graven image of a knight and a castle that had been carved into the aged wood, and the door swung silently inward. They entered the small, circular room that waited beyond. A huge section of the far wall was missing, providing them with an unobstructed view of the countryside beyond. A waist-high silver railing ran along the edge of the opening. At its center stood a silver lectern, its fittings gleaming in the sunlight. Runes had been carved into the surface of the lectern, thousands upon thousands of them, all in a language that no one had been able to decipher in recorded history.

This was the Landsview, Sterling Silver's eye on the world.

While Questor and Abernathy watched, Ben stepped up onto the platform and took hold of the railing in preparation for setting out. He reached down into the leather pouch that hung from one side of the lectern and pulled out a rolled-up piece of parchment. Opening it, he fastened it with clips to the lectern, revealing an ancient map of the kingdom, its rumpled surface thick with names. Various colors of ink denoted forests, mountains, rivers, lakes, plains, deserts, territories, towns, and the like. Everything that could be named was meticulously marked.

Ben stared down at the map a moment, remembering the first time he had used the Landsview. How strange it had been, not knowing what to expect, and then how frightening when the world dropped away so suddenly, as if jerked from beneath his feet. He hesitated despite himself, even knowing that there was no reason for alarm.

Then he focused his concentration on the map, choosing the Greensward to begin his search, calling up the now familiar magic to aid him.

At once the tower and castle and all that surrounded it disappeared and he was whisked out into the blue of the sky. All that remained was the lectern and its railing, and his hands held tight to the latter, even knowing that he had not left the room in which the railing was mounted; the magic only made it seem as if he had, as if he really were flying. He watched the land sweep away beneath him as the Greensward appeared in the distance and the countryside took shape.

The last time he had used the Landsview, it was Mistaya who was missing then, too. Five years earlier, she had been stolen away by the Witch of the Deep Fell, who had hidden her from Ben and Willow with magic. It was Nightshade's intention to subvert her, to turn her away from her parents so she could participate actively in their destruction. Because the Landsview could not penetrate the magic of the Deep Fell, Ben had been unable to find his daughter and had almost lost her forever. But Nightshade was gone and the threat she had once posed was finished, so even though he still could not penetrate the hollows without entering personally, he did not think that this was where his daughter would go.

Still, after almost two hours of scouring his Kingdom—every hidden valley, darkened forest, and mountainous retreat, every town and village, every last possible place in which she might find refuge—he began to wonder. What if he was wrong about Nightshade? Or even about Mistaya's reluctance ever to return to the Deep Fell? Maybe she thought hiding out there was a good idea because she knew he couldn't find her unless he went there himself.

Except that the Deep Fell was a dangerous place, and Mistaya was no fool. She might be angry enough with him to go off on her own for a few days just to spite him, as Willow had suggested, but she wouldn't put herself at risk needlessly.

When he returned to the tower and stepped down off the Landsview, he knew nothing more about Mistaya's whereabouts than when he had set out to find her. "Nothing," he reported to Questor and Abernathy, giving a shrug. He hesitated. "Though I suppose she might be hiding in the Deep Fell."

Both wizard and scribe bristled instantly at the suggestion, insisting that this was not possible, that Mistaya would never go back there after what had happened before. Which, in turn, made Ben feel foolish for making the suggestion, although it also made him feel somewhat better to hear that his friends agreed with his own assessment.

"We have to do something else," he told them as the three tromped back down out of the tower to the lower regions of the castle.

"Maybe Bunion will have a suggestion," Questor ventured finally. "No one knows Landover's secrets better than he does. If there's a hiding place we haven't thought of, he'll remember it."

"Maybe we ought to leave well enough alone," Abernathy growled suddenly. The other two turned to look at him. "Well, I mean that if she doesn't wish to be found, perhaps we ought to respect that. She might have discovered a way to use her magic to hide from us. I don't know that we ought to be so quick to try to undo that."

"What are you talking about?" Questor demanded. "Of course we want to undo it! She's got all of us worried to death!"

"Well, maybe not to death," Ben tried to amend.

"Whatever the extent of our worry, it shouldn't be allowed to continue," Questor declared. His bushy eyebrows knotted fiercely. "She ought to know better than to do something like this! She's a big girl, not a child. We have a right to do whatever we can to find out where she is!"

Abernathy shook his head, ears flopping loosely. "Spoken like a man who jumps without looking."

"Well, I don't see you doing anything to help matters!" Questor snapped in reply. "Should we all just stand around and hope for the best? Is that *your* answer to the problem?"

"*My* answer to the problem is to point out how useless you are when it comes to contributing solutions to problems, Questor Thews!"

The argument continued all the rest of the way down the stairs and well into the beginning stages of Ben's first headache of the day, a headache that only grew worse as the hours lengthened and Bunion did not return.

----◦◦◦----

Berwyn Laphroig, Lord of Rhyndweir—for such was his full name and title—strolled through the weapons room of his castle in an irritated state. He was restless and bored, but the solution to these conditions was not to be found here. There was nothing in this room or even in the whole of his barony that could satisfy his insatiable need to make the young and lovely Mistaya Holiday his wife. There was no other woman who could replace her in his thoughts, none to whom he would give even momentary consideration. Thinking of her only worsened his condition, unfortunately; thinking of her made him even more determined to find a way to have her.

It had seemed easy enough in the beginning, when he had decided he must replace his old wife. Things had not been going well for some time between them, and he could sense that she was looking for a way out of the marriage. Such insolence was intolerable, and he was perfectly within his rights to make certain she could not act on her foolish fantasies. Even her son had become a source of irritation, always clinging to her as if she were a lifeline to a safe place instead of deadweight that would pull him down. He cared nothing for them, really, so it was not difficult for him to decide to dispose of them when he determined they were no longer necessary.

Like his brothers and sisters. Like everyone else who had outlived their usefulness.

His counselors would have been horrified had they realized the extent to which he had gone to fulfill his ambitions. The ambitions alone would have horrified them. Even more certain was the response of his fellow Lords of the Greensward, had he chosen to confide in them. Not that he would ever do such a thing. But if they knew that he had long coveted not only his father's title and lands, but the King of Landover's throne, as well . . .

He smiled despite himself. Not much to guess about there. If they had known, they would have found a way to dispatch him in a heartbeat.

He had confided in no one, however, and given no one reason to suspect the truth. He had disposed of his older brother all on his own. His younger had disappeared shortly after and was never seen again. A poisoner he had enlisted to his cause had taken care of his troublesome wife and son without anyone knowing, and then he had taken care of the poisoner. There was none to bear witness against him, no voices to speak, and no eyes that had seen. It had all been done quickly and quietly, and no trace of his crimes remained to convict him.

Still, Ben Holiday suspected the truth and did not trust him. That might have been worrisome had he thought the High Lord could prove anything.

A door opened at the far end of the room, and his scribe, Cordstick, a wisp of a man with a huge mop of bushy hair, came hurrying across the room. "My Lord," he greeted, bowing low, hair flopping. "We have a problem."

Laphroig didn't like problems and didn't want to hear about them, but he nodded agreeably. "Yes? What is it?"

"We received word from one of our loyal subjects that there was a man—well, not a man, really—but he was asking questions in the town below the castle about you, and he . . ."

He stopped, as if uncertain where to go next with this. "He was asking questions about your family, my Lord, all of them, including your wife and child." He swallowed hard. "About their untimely deaths."

"Get to the point."

Cordstick nodded quickly. "Well, we thought it best to detain him, my Lord. We knew you would want to question him about his interest in your family, not knowing, of course, what his purpose might be. So we sent guards to take him prisoner and hold him for questioning."

He stopped again, looking around the room as if help might be found among the suits of armor and racks of sharp weapons. Laphroig rolled his eyes. "Yes, you took him prisoner. And?"

"After we had done so, we discovered he was not a man at all, but a kobold. Why anyone would confide anything in a kobold, I couldn't say. Perhaps they didn't, but it was enough, it seemed to me, that he was asking these questions. I thought that holding him was the better choice, if it came to a choice about what to do with him, kobold or not, and . . ."

Laphroig held up his hand. "You are trying my patience, Cordstick, and I have very little of it to spare this morning. Who is this kobold? Do we know his name?"

Cordstick looked miserable. "We do. Now, after seizing him. It is Bunion. He is the King's man, a creature of some renown."

Rhyndweir's ruler was angry, but not surprised. Of course the High Lord would try to find out what he could now that he knew Laphroig's intentions regarding his daughter. But that sort of thing couldn't be allowed. Not even by the King. Not in Laphroig's own lands.

"There may be unpleasant repercussions from this business, my Lord," Cordstick ventured. He bit his lip. "Perhaps we should let him go."

"Perhaps not," Laphroig answered at once. "Perhaps we should torture him instead and discover the truth behind this intrusion into the affairs of Rhyndweir. Perhaps we should make an example of him so that Ben Holiday will think twice before he sends another of his spies into our territory."

Then he hesitated, holding up one hand quickly to stay Cordstick's departure.

Torturing one of the High Lord's people, he thought suddenly, would in all likelihood complicate his plans for marriage with the High Lord's daughter. Perhaps discretion was the better part of reprisal in this situation. Yet it galled him that Holiday would feel free to send someone to spy on him in his own barony, no matter what the situation might be. He stewed about it for a moment, thinking that if the kobold simply disappeared—as others who had troubled him had—no blame could attach to him.

"Where is this creature?" he asked his aide.

"Downstairs, in one of the anterooms, safely under guard," the other replied with a confidence that immediately troubled Laphroig.

"Take me to him," he ordered. "I'll decide what to do with him once I've seen him for myself."

Drawing his black robes about him, tilting his head so that his slicked-up black hair cut the air like a shark fin, he swept through the door to the halls beyond, leading the way and forcing Cordstick to hurry to catch up to him. With his scribe barely managing to re-gain the lead, they ascended from the weapons room to the upper receiving chambers, moving from those reserved for invited guests to those well back and better fortified. Always best to take no chances with those who sought to work mischief in your realm, Laphroig was fond of saying.

But apparently chances *had* been taken in this case, Rhyndweir's Lord realized as they approached the holding chamber and saw the door standing ajar. Rushing forward now, the two burst inside and found all four guards hanging by their heels like ornaments from the drapery cords, gagged and bound and weaponless.

Of the kobold, there was no sign.

Laphroig wheeled on a terrified Cordstick. "Call out the guard and find him!" he hissed. "Immediately!"

His scribe vanished as if by magic, and Laphroig stalked from the room in fury, leaving the guards hanging where they were.

It took barely an hour to determine that Bunion was nowhere in the castle, but that before departing he had located and thoroughly searched Laphroig's office and its records. Another might not have been able to determine that anything was amiss, so neat and tidy was the room in question. But Laphroig was immediately suspi-cious, and after tamping down his rage sufficiently to act on his sus-picions had gone directly to his private chambers. There he had discovered that safeguards he had personally installed and were known only to him had been disturbed. His protections had been breached and his personal files and papers examined.

Laphroig sat down for a time to think things through while waiting on the search for the kobold to be completed. He didn't think the creature could have found anything of value, since he made it a point not to keep anything that might give him away. There were no records on his acts, nothing to show that he had dispatched those family members who had stood in his way. There were no notes or revealing pictures or anything of the like. There was nothing that could have helped the kobold in his efforts to discover what role Laphroig had played in the deaths of his family.

He paused, a chill running down his spine.

Unless . . .

He went at once to the bookshelves set in the stone wall to one side of the writing table and looked. Sure enough, the book on poisons was gone—the book that had provided him with the recipes for the nectars necessary to dispatch his wife and son. He took a deep breath and exhaled. He had kept the book only because he thought he might have need of it again sometime. The poisons he favored most were underlined in that book, and the poisoner's notes on the details of their usages were written in the margins. He had forgotten about that, thinking that no one would ever have reason to look at one book shelved among so many.

But the kobold had. How it had found it in the short time provided was a mystery he could not solve. In any case, the damage was done.

He waited until Cordstick appeared with the unsurprising news that Bunion had escaped completely, and then he ordered the four guards still hanging in the library to be cut down and hung from the castle walls instead. Cordstick, grateful that he wasn't the one sentenced to hang, carried out the order swiftly, wondering if perhaps it was time to look into another line of work. If he hadn't served the family for so long that it no longer felt as if he belonged anywhere else, he might have packed his bags then and there.

As it was, he simply made it a point to stay out of his master's way.

It was nearing sunset when he had cause to go in search of Rhyndweir's Lord once more. He felt some small confidence in doing so this time, having news of a different sort to offer up. Although his master kept his counsel close and private, Cordstick knew him much better than he suspected. It was inherent in the nature of his service that he should be able to do so, because knowing the mindset of the master you served had saved more than one servant's neck over the years.

He found Laphroig in his office, slumped in his reading chair with the lights off and the curtains drawn. His black clothes were a rumpled mess, and his black hair was sticking up all over the place. His pale face looked ghostly in the near darkness.

"My Lord," Cordstick ventured tentatively.

"Go away" was the miserable response.

"I have news I think you should hear," Cordstick pressed gently, careful to remain just outside the doorway.

A short silence followed. "About the kobold?"

"No, my Lord. About the Princess Mistaya."

Laphroig was on his feet at once. "The Princess? Close the door! Come over here where we can talk privately. Shhh, shhh, keep it quiet now. Just you and me. Tell me quick—what is the news?"

Cordstick had judged his master rightly. He closed the door to the chamber and hurried over to stand next to him, bending close and speaking in a whisper. "Our spy at the King's court sends news that isn't known as yet by more than a handful of people. The Princess Mistaya has disappeared. The King and his Queen are looking for her everywhere."

"Well, well," Laphroig murmured, his mind racing with possibilities.

"If you were to find her, my Lord . . . ," Cordstick began.

"Yes, that would make the High Lord beholden to me in a way he could not ignore, wouldn't it?" Laphroig finished. He was smiling so broadly that for a moment he assumed a frog-like visage. "Yes, yes."

He put his hand firmly on his scribe's thin shoulder. "You must find her, Cordstick." His grip tightened and his eyes narrowed. "Before anyone else has a chance to."

Cordstick nodded in agreement, shuddering inwardly at the other's rather hideous smile. "As you wish, my Lord," he managed before scurrying from the room.

LIBIRIS

It is not true that things are never as bad as they seem or that the grass is always greener on the other side of the fence or that there is a silver lining inside every cloud. These are things we *wish* were true, but which are more often than not false hopes. So it was with little surprise that as Mistaya and her companions crested the final hill leading up to Libiris, she found all her fears of what awaited her fully realized.

"Oh, no," she murmured, just softly enough that the others could not hear her, and swallowed hard against the sudden lump in her throat.

Libiris was like something out of a particularly nasty nightmare. It rose against the darkening horizon as if seeking to imitate Dracula's castle: stonework all dingy and windswept, mortar cracked and in places crumbling, windows mostly dark and shuttered, and parapets spiked with iron lance heads and lined with razor wire. Towers soared skyward as if seeking to puncture holes in the heavens, and the heavy ironbound wooden doors facing toward her were locked and barred in a way that left no room for doubt about how visitors could expect to be greeted. If this building was intended as a library, she thought, the builders had a peculiar way of showing it. Libiris had the look of something that had been built with the intention of keeping people out, not letting them in.

Things didn't look much better as Mistaya shifted her horrified gaze away from its rugged walls, which oddly enough cast shadows in all directions, a phenomenon she would not have believed possible. Woods surrounded Libiris, dark and deep and unfriendly, the trees leafless and skeletal, the limbs withered, and the forest floor littered with deadwood and bones. She had to look twice and carefully to be certain of this last, but bones there were, some collected in small piles, as if gathered by the wind like leaves. Spiky plants and thorny brush filled in the gaps between cracked and blackened trunks, and the smells were not of fresh greenery but of decay and mold.

It all looked, she thought suddenly, as Sterling Silver had been described to her when under the sway of the tarnish upon her father's arrival years earlier. How odd.

"Let's go home," Poggwydd said at once and backed away.

She was half inclined to take him up on his suggestion. But instead she turned to Edgewood Dirk, who was sitting calmly next to her, washing his paws. "Is this really it?"

"Yes, it is." The emerald eyes gleamed as they found hers. "Might you be thinking of taking the G'home Gnome up on his offer?"

She frowned. They could talk like this comfortably now because her irritating companions would no longer come near the cat. Neither Poggwydd nor Shoopdiesel approached within a dozen yards after the events of last night. Apparently overcome by either greed or hunger, they had attempted to lay hands on Dirk, probably with the intention of parting him from his skin. The effort had failed miserably. She still wasn't sure what had happened, since she had been asleep at the time. A flash of light had awoken her in time to watch both Gnomes run screaming into the night. Today, returned from wherever they had fled to, their fingers burned and their faces blackened, they had made it a point to stay well clear of Edgewood Dirk.

"If I were to leave and go elsewhere, would you come with me?" she asked anxiously.

"No, I would not. I have business here that I must attend to."

"Business? What sort of business?"

"That is for me to know." Dirk's voice tone was insulting. "A cat never discusses his business with humans, not even Princesses. A cat never explains and never apologizes. A cat never alibis. You must accept a cat as it is and for what it is and not expect more than the pleasure of its company. In this case, you must remain at Libiris if you wish to share mine."

She didn't care to remain at Libiris or to share the pleasure of his company, but she didn't really have a choice if she wanted to remain hidden from her parents. If she left Dirk, she left also the concealment that being with him offered. Her father would be quick enough to find her if she acted precipitously.

"What did you do to the Gnomes last night?" she asked, changing the subject. She hesitated. "If you don't mind my asking."

The cat yawned. "I don't mind. I gave them a small sample of what it means to lay hands on a Prism Cat. No one is allowed to do that."

"No, I imagine not."

"Rather like your mud puppy. Magical creatures are not to be handled. We have our defenses, each peculiar to the species or, in some cases, to the individual creature. Touch us at your peril." He glanced at her. "You weren't thinking of trying, were you?"

She shook her head. "No, I was just curious. I don't know anything about Prism Cats. I told you before that my father never spoke of you."

Dirk glanced back at the G'home Gnomes, perhaps to reassure himself that they were still keeping their distance. "I shall speak for myself, then," he said. "You need to know something of the character of the company you keep. My character is obviously impeccable, but a few words of further elucidation couldn't hurt. I am a fairy creature, as you know. I live in the mists except when it suits me. I stay pretty much in one place except when I travel. I keep mostly to myself except when curiosity compels me to engage with others. Such as now, with you."

"Curiosity about me?" she asked. "What do you mean?"

The cat regarded her. "Well, I should think it would be obvious. You are a very curious creature. I want to see what will become of you."

"Become of me?"

"It would help this relationship tremendously if you would stop repeating my words back to me." Edgewood Dirk rose and stretched. "As for what I did to your companions, I simply gave them a small demonstration of what happens when you misbehave around me. Watch."

The Gnomes must have heard this because they began backing away hurriedly. Mistaya held her ground, unwilling to display anything remotely approaching cowardice. The Prism Cat ignored them, closing his eyes and arching his back, his body going so still that it seemed to have turned to stone. All at once, it began to glow, and then it did turn into something *like* stone, changing from fur and flesh to a crystalline form. Emerald eyes glittered out of planes of crystal that shimmered and reflected the forest and the first of Landover's eight moons, which had risen in the east. It ceased to be immobile and began to shift about as if turned to clear liquid glass. He faced her for a long moment, and then the light of his body flooded back into his eyes and he became a cat again.

"There is a small sample," he advised. "If you try to touch me, of course, there is more. Ask your foolish friends for details, when you have a moment. There is more to my magic than this, but I don't think we have to dwell on it just now. It is sufficient to say that not much that walks on two legs or four can stand against a Prism Cat."

Big whoop, Mistaya thought. The cat was so full of himself that there wasn't room for a speck of humility. Irritated, she turned her attention back to the blackened structure in front of them. "So what do you suggest we do now?" she asked him.

The cat followed her gaze and cocked his head. "I suggest that you go up to the door and ask for lodging. Once inside, you can figure things out at your leisure."

She glared at him. "Why don't you go up to the door and ask them to let us in. You're the one with all the magic!"

"Am I?" he asked mildly. He regarded her calmly for a moment, and then stretched anew. "No, I think you had better be the one to ask," he said. "People get nervous when cats speak to them. They are much more accepting of people than animals in these situations, I've found."

"That seems a rather broad generalization, even coming from you. But I guess they can't refuse a Princess of Landover, can they?"

"Probably not. However, I wouldn't tell them who you are, if I were you. Which, thankfully, I am not."

"Why not? I mean, why not tell them who I am?"

The cat blinked. "At the very least, they would let your father and mother know that you've arrived safely."

She grimaced. He was right, of course.

"So I am just supposed to pretend that I'm some peasant girl out wandering the countryside, lost or whatever, and I've found my way here—poor, pitiful me—and I need shelter?"

She glanced into the darkness, where Poggwydd and Shoopdiesel sat huddled together, watching. "What about them?" she demanded, turning back again. "What am I supposed to say about . . . ?"

But Edgewood Dirk had disappeared.

She stared at the empty space he had occupied, not quite believing that he wasn't there. Then she looked all around, searching the darkness. Nothing. Not a sign of him. Anger flooded through her. He had abandoned her! Just like that! He had left her on her own!

"Fine!" she muttered, furious now. "Who needs you?"

She descended the hill in determined silence, not bothering to look behind her to see if the G'home Gnomes were following, knowing that they would be, resigned to the fact that she would probably never be rid of them. The descent took some time, and as she drew nearer to her destination she was able to determine that it did not improve in looks upon closer inspection. Everything seemed to be in disrepair and suffering from obvious neglect. No lights burned in the windows or from the towers, and the darkness suggested a total absence of life. Perhaps that was how things were these days at Libiris, she thought hopefully. Maybe its tenants had abandoned her. Maybe there was no one here anymore, and she wouldn't have to beg for admittance. She would just have to find a way in—and the place would be hers for as long as she wished!

Excited by the idea, she hurried ahead to the ironbound doors, gaining confidence as she neared. Of course there was no one here! Why would there be? Who would live in a place like this? Even the overseer had long since departed, discouraged with the work his charge had required, disappointed in the lack of support he was receiving from the Kingdom. After all, no one had come here for years. Not even Abernathy or Questor Thews had come. They just assumed that someone was still here.

She felt positively buoyant.

She reached the doors, grasped the huge iron knocker, and rapped it hard against the plate, announcing her arrival. The sharp clang of iron on iron echoed through the stillness and slowly died away. Nothing happened. She waited impatiently, already searching for a way to open the door from without. Impulsively, she tried the handles, but the door was securely barred. She might have to chance using magic, just a little, to gain admittance. Or maybe there was another way in, through another door on another wall. Surely there was no reason to keep such a decrepit place as Libiris locked up once it was abandoned.

Then, rather too suddenly, a small door set within the larger doors, close down to the ground, popped open. A head crested with a tuft of white hair poked out, and a pair of gimlet eyes looked up into hers. "What is it?" the owner asked in a dialect she could only barely understand.

"I'm seeking shelter for myself and my friends," she declared, still recovering from her shock at actually finding someone here.

The head tilted upward slightly, and she saw a face that most closely resembled that of a rodent, long and pointed and hairy. The eyes narrowed with suspicion, but she refused to be intimidated and held their gaze with her own. "Can you let us in, please?" she pressed, trying hard to sound both desperate and helpless and not angry.

Teeth flashed behind a wicked smile. "No, I cannot. Go away!"

The head disappeared back inside, and the door slammed shut.

Mistaya stood staring at the tiny portal in a mix of fury and frustration, very tempted to knock down the doors using her magic and march inside, announcing who she was as she did so and demanding that her tormentor be made to answer for his uncivilized behavior. She was cold and tired and hungry, and she did not deserve to be treated like this.

The G'home Gnomes appeared at her elbow, their wizened faces looked up into her own tentatively. "Maybe we ought to just leave," Poggwydd suggested from one side, while Shoopdiesel nodded in hasty agreement from the other.

Maybe that would have been the best thing for it, but Mistaya was already set on doing the exact opposite. She had put up with enough of people pushing her around. She reached up for the knocker and rapped on the plate once more, much harder this time. She had only a few seconds to wait before the smaller door popped open anew. The little man reappeared; he must have been waiting just on the other side. He was angry now and not bothering to hide it.

"I told you to go away!" he snapped.

"Go away to where?" she snapped back. "We are in the middle of nowhere. Don't you know anything of the King's guidelines to hospitality? He wrote them himself when he was made King, years ago. All strangers are to be given food and shelter when they seek it in genuine need; none is to be turned away without good reason. What reason do you have to turn us away? Are you frightened of a girl and two G'home Gnomes? What is your name?"

All this appeared to catch the ferret-faced fellow off guard. He shrank back a bit under the force of her wrath. She watched his mouth tighten and his eyes fix on her belligerently.

"My name is Rufus Pinch!" he snapped. "And I do only what I have been ordered to do and nothing more. I don't know anything about the King's guidelines to hospitality."

"Well, you should!" she shot back, even though she had just made it all up. "I shall be forced to report you to someone who can afford to take the time to come out here and instruct you on their usage! Turning away supplicants in the middle of the night is unacceptable behavior!"

The little man hunched his shoulders and folded his arms across his chest defensively. "Well, I can't let you in," he repeated.

Things seemed to have reached an impasse, but suddenly another section of door—this one apparently the upper half of the smaller—swung open and a second figure stepped into view. It was a boy, not much older than she was, rather tall and angular in build, his black hair worn long, his jaw lightly bearded, and his eyes bright with secret laughter.

"What's happening, Pinch?" he asked the little man, arching an eyebrow at Mistaya. "Is there a problem?"

"This girl wants in, and you know the rules as well as I do. We are not to allow entry to anyone, no matter—"

"Yes, I know the rules. But this is my sister, Ellice. She's here at my invitation." He stepped forward quickly and took hold of an astonished Mistaya's hands. "Hello, Ellice. I gather you got my letter and decided to come help us with the work. I'm very happy to see you."

He bent forward and kissed her lightly on the cheek. *"I'm Thom,"* he whispered in her ear as he pulled away. *"Play along."*

"You never mentioned a sister," Pinch declared accusingly.

"You never asked," the boy answered quickly. "No one ever asks about my family, so I don't talk about them. But I have one, you know. Everyone has a family."

Pinch did not look satisfied. "Well, no one said you could invite her to come here," he pressed. "The rules are the rules. No one is allowed into the building. No one is to be given shelter or fed or encouraged in any way to try to enter or to remain at Libiris. His Eminence has made it quite clear."

"His Eminence has also made it quite clear, on more occasions than I care to think about, that we need someone else to help with the work. You and I and the Throg Monkeys are not enough to accomplish what is needed. You've heard him say that, haven't you?"

"Well, yes, I've heard him, but—"

"Have you done anything to try to satisfy his complaints?" the boy interrupted quickly.

Pinch frowned. "No, I—"

"Then please don't criticize those of us who have. There is a reason I am chief sorter and chronicler and you are an overseer. Now let's go inside and get my sister warm."

Still holding Mistaya's hand, the boy pushed his way past a reluctant Pinch into the doorway. "Wait!" Mistaya exclaimed. "What about my friends? My escort," she corrected quickly. "They must come inside, too."

Pinch stepped quickly to block their way. "I draw the line here!" he declared, glaring at the G'home Gnomes. "These two were not invited to come and are not fit in any case to do the work. They must remain here!"

Thom nodded reluctantly, giving Mistaya a look. "I'm afraid that's so. But there are stables on the south side of the building where they can get out of the weather and sleep the night. I will see that they have something to eat."

"Humpphh," Pinch growled disagreeably. "Very well. But they must leave here tomorrow at first light."

Poggwydd and Shoopdiesel looked very put upon but showed no inclination to argue. Recognizing that Thom had pushed the matter of gaining entry as far as he could, Mistaya nodded. "Good night, my faithful friends," she called over to the Gnomes, not without some small warmth. "Thanks for bringing me. I will see you in the morning to bid you farewell."

She followed Thom through the small door and heard Pinch close and bar it tightly behind her.

—◆◆◆—

Before the unfriendly little man could offer further thoughts on
the matter of Mistaya's arrival and admittance, Thom led her
through a small, tunnel-like entry into a much larger anteroom, its
walls lined with benches and hooks for hanging coats and wraps,
high ceiling intricately carved with figures that in the near darkness
she could not make out. Stray lights burned here and there, but
mostly the room was draped in shadows. The thick smell of must
and stale air filled her nostrils, and a chill had settled with a propri-
etary sense of entitlement.

Thom led and Mistaya followed. The wood floors creaked as they
walked down the length of the room, which was twice as long as it
was wide. A high desk, elevated on a platform to allow whoever
manned it to look down on whoever sought admittance, ran across
the far end of the room, effectively barring entry to whatever lay
beyond a pair of massive wooden doors set in the wall behind. The
desk was old and splintering at its joints, and there were spiders
spinning their webs where space permitted. She assumed there
were spiders elsewhere in the room, as well, in places she couldn't
clearly see. She looked down as they approached the desk and noticed faint clouds of dust rising in small puffs with each footfall.

"Don't mind that," Thom advised cheerfully. "This room doesn't
get much use."

She stepped close to him. "Why did you say that I was your . . ."

His face darkened as he quickly put a finger to his lips and shook
his head. He pointed to his ears and then made a sweeping gesture
toward the walls. *"Later,"* he whispered.

He led her around one end of the desk, but did not try using the
larger portals, choosing instead a small door at one corner of the
room, a door so unobtrusive that she might have missed it completely if he had not taken her right up to it. He grasped a handle
that was all but invisible, pulled the door open, and led her through.
A hallway beyond wound off into a darkness that would have been
complete if not for the handheld lamp he suddenly produced and
fired with his touch, something she recognized immediately as

magic. She arched one eyebrow at him, thinking as she did so that there was more to this place and its inhabitants that she had first thought.

They passed a number of doors, all of them closed, but Thom finally stopped before one and opened it. Inside was a very small, unadorned bedroom, dark and windowless, with a bed, an ancient cedar chest, a small set of shelves, and a table and chairs. There were no decorations hanging from the walls, no rugs on the floors, and no hints of color anywhere. Mistaya looked around in dismay.

"We can talk here," the boy said, giving her a quick, reassuring smile. "They don't listen here. My room, maybe. But not here. These are the servants' quarters, the rooms set aside for the keepers of the stacks and the files, and there haven't been any of those for decades. There's only Pinch and the Throg Monkeys and me. And His Eminence, of course. Sit with me."

He seated himself on the edge of the bed and motioned for her to join him. She did so, feeling braver now, more sure of herself than when she had faced Pinch alone. She didn't know who this boy was, but she didn't think he meant her any harm.

"Why did you help me back there?" she asked him. "Why did you tell that little man—Pinch, you called him—that I was your sister?"

He shrugged. "Oh, I don't know. It just seemed like the right thing to do. I didn't plan it. I saw you, and I just decided to help you out." He shook his head. "I get bored here. There's no one to talk to. I thought anyone traveling with two G'home Gnomes out here in the middle of nowhere would have stories to tell."

"Well, I might not want those stories told just now. Will you make me go if I don't choose to tell them?"

"Not if you tell me some others. I just want someone to talk to. I've been here for almost three years now. I never go anywhere, and no one ever comes to visit. You saw how you were greeted. It's the same with everyone else. Not that there's much reason for anyone to want to come here, anyway." He paused. "Do you know where you are?"

"Of course," she declared at once. "This is Libiris."

"Then why did you come here? Surely, you didn't come by accident?"

She hesitated. "Didn't you just tell me no one ever comes here on purpose?"

He cocked his head. "I did."

"Well, there you are. I got lost. A mistake." She waved one hand dismissively, hoping he believed her. "But what are you doing here?" she followed up quickly. "What keeps you?"

"I'm an apprentice to His Eminence, in service to Libiris."

She pursed her lips. "You keep mentioning that name. His Eminence. Is he some sort of ruler or Lord? How did you become apprenticed to him?"

He frowned. "It's kind of complicated. Can we talk about it in the morning? You look tired."

Again, she hesitated, this time because she sensed he was hiding something. But she really didn't have any right to demand answers to her questions if she wasn't prepared to answer his. Even if it irritated her.

She managed a smile. "I *am* tired and I *do* need to sleep. But can I have something to eat first?"

Thom stood up at once, unfolding his angular frame. "We'll go down to the kitchen. Then I'll take something out to your friends. I still think it's funny that you are traveling with G'home Gnomes."

She couldn't argue with that. But there was much about her life that she found odd of late, so the Gnomes in particular didn't stand out. She stood up with him. "Would you like me to tell you something about those Gnomes?" she asked him.

He nodded eagerly. "I would, indeed."

Together they went off to find the kitchen.

HIS EMINENCE

The trouble with being raised a Princess of Landover is that it makes it very hard to settle for anything less. Sterling Silver, for example, was more than her home; it was her caregiver. A sentient being, it knew instinctively what she needed and provided it for her. A bed that was just right for her size and shape, suitably warmed each night, floors that were heated to order, food prepared and delivered, air that was sweet smelling and always fresh, a channeling of sounds that were pleasing and comforting, clothes to wear, and beautiful things with which to decorate her rooms— these were just a few of the comforts she had been provided, always without her asking. The castle was magical and capable of magical acts, and it had looked after the Kings of Landover and their families since its inception.

Nor was her transition from the castle to the Carrington Women's Preparatory School particularly difficult. She was no longer able to rely on the buildings for special service and care, but if she wanted clean clothes to wear and fresh sheets to sleep on and good food to eat, there were people who could provide them all. And there were a plethora of advantages that even Landover lacked. Her father's world was technologically advanced, so there were movies and televisions and radios and cell phones and computers and vast numbers of retail stores and malls to enjoy. There were airplanes and automobiles and trains and buses for transportation. There were cities that were vast in size and filled with exciting places, some of them actually educational. All in all, it was a fair trade-off for what she was leaving behind in Landover, and she had found it an exhilarating experience (when she allowed herself to do so).

There was nothing at all exhilarating about Libiris. In addition to being dark and dank and cold, it felt like a tomb for the dead. The air was stale and smelled of decay. Her room was a smaller version of the larger structure—close, cold, and dead feeling. Her bed was miserable and her pillow, a rock. She found no clean clothes to wear, no water to drink or bathe in, no toilet facilities of any sort, and no windows to let in fresh air. The silence of her surroundings was like a great weight pressing down on her. Now and then, she would hear a small noise from somewhere far away, but she could never identify it and be reassured that it meant the presence of other living creatures.

She made it through the night, surviving an uneasy sleep, still dressed in the clothes she had worn coming in. She woke to blackness, but when she arose from the bed a tiny light flickered on over the door. More magic, she noted. She found the door unlocked and walked out into the hall. Tiny lights flickered on up and down its length. She wondered where Thom might be sleeping, suddenly anxious for his company. But there was no way of knowing how to find him. She walked the hall from end to end, stopping at each door and listening to the silence beyond as if it might reveal some secret. She did not venture beyond the hall once it turned down other corridors, afraid she would become lost in what appeared to be something of a labyrinth.

Finally, she returned to her room and sat down on her bed to wait. Idly, she began sorting through the few possessions she had brought, laying them out on the bed for study. At the bottom of her duffel, beneath the few items of clothing, she found the compass, the virtual map ring, and the book on wizard spells that Questor had given her. Below all that was the fairy stone she had brought as a present for her grandfather and had failed to give to him. She had carried it all that way and forgotten she had it. She held it in the palm of her hand, feeling immeasurably sad. She found herself thinking about all the things she had taken for granted in her life before this, the way you do when you are feeling sorry for yourself and wondering what has brought you to your present state. But thinking of it didn't make her feel any better, so she shoved such thoughts out of her mind and began concentrating instead on what it was she intended to do with herself now that she was here.

The irony of her situation did not escape her. She had fled from Sterling Silver for the express purpose of not being forced to come to Libiris as her father's envoy, and yet here she was anyway. She could argue all she wanted to that it was a matter of circumstances; that she had come here not because her father wanted her to but because it was her own choice, a choice made out of necessity and one that she could revoke at a moment's notice. She could rationalize that her presence was mostly due to Edgewood Dirk—wherever he was—who had talked her into coming, persuading her it was the only place in which her father would not think to look for her.

But it was all words, and none of them mattered more than the fact of her being here in a place she did not really want to be.

She stewed about it for a while, and then finally there was a knock on the door, and when she called back it opened and Thom stepped inside.

"Good morning," he greeted cheerfully. "Are you all right?"

She brushed back her hair and gave him a short nod, unwilling to admit that she hurt everywhere and hated everything. "Is there somewhere I can wash?" she asked instead.

He took her down the hall to one of the doors she had passed earlier and opened it for her. Inside, there were counters with basins and pitchers of water. On the wall hung towels. None of it looked too clean or too new.

"You can use these," he told her. He looked vaguely embarrassed. "I'll stay outside until you're done. So that no one disturbs you."

When he was gone, she stripped off her clothes and began washing herself as best she could, thinking all the while how much bet-

ter things would be if she were back in Sterling Silver. Halfway
through, it occurred to her that she could make it better simply by
using a little of her magic. A shower with hot water, a soft towel instead of a harsh rag, and a little warmth in the floors would make
things almost bearable. She nearly gave in to the temptation. But
using magic would risk revealing her location to her father and
mother. More than that, it would indicate a certain weakness of
character. If she used magic to lessen her hardship, she was admitting that she wasn't tough enough to deal with things the way they
were. She hated the idea that she wasn't strong enough to endure a
little discomfort. She thought herself better than that, and she
wasn't about to do anything that would prove her thinking wrong.

So she suffered through the cold-water splash and the freezing
air and the rank smells and the rough surface of the towel, and she
was pretty much finishing up when a panel in the wall opened and a
handful of rangy monkeys appeared. At least, that was what they appeared to be as they crowded into the room, all but tumbling over
one another as they pushed clear of the opening. When they caught
sight of her, naked save for the towel she was desperately trying to
wrap about herself, they straightened up as if electrified and hissed
like snakes. She screamed in response—more from embarrassment
than fear—yelling at them to get out.

The door to the room flew open and Thom charged in, caught
sight of Mistaya, made a vague attempt at shielding his eyes, and
then quickly placed himself between the monkeys and her, shouting
loudly at the former until they all piled back through the hole in the
wall and slammed the panel shut behind them.

"Sorry about that," he muttered, keeping his back turned and his
eyes averted. "Those are some of the Throg Monkeys. They aren't
supposed to be in this part of the building, but they seem to go
wherever they want these days. Even His Eminence can't keep them
in line. Guess they've been using this washroom for themselves."

"Can you just keep looking over there until I'm dressed?" Mistaya asked rather pointedly.

"Oh, certainly, of course," he agreed at once. "I wouldn't have come in at all if I hadn't heard you scream, but then I . . . Well, I didn't know what . . . It could have been anything, after all . . . Really, I didn't see anything . . . much."

He trailed off awkwardly, apparently unable to find any good way to end the conversation. She left things hanging there while she quickly finished drying and dressing in her old clothes, promising herself a change as soon as the opportunity presented itself.

"What sort of creatures are those Throg Monkeys?" she asked finally. "Trolls or kobolds or what?"

He shrugged. "I don't know. I don't even know where they came from. His Eminence found them and brought them here to do the heavy work in the Stacks. Which was a waste of effort, it turns out. They don't do very much work at all. They wouldn't do any except that I found a way to make them. They seem to think that work is beneath them. Mostly, they just sit around looking bored."

"Except when they're poking their noses in where they don't belong."

"Except for that." He hesitated. "Did they frighten you?"

"They came through the walls rather suddenly. So, yes, they frightened me. But they won't get a chance to do that again, I can promise you."

She finished tying the stays to her blouse and cinched her belt. "Throg Monkeys, huh. I thought I knew every species of creature in Landover, but I never heard of them."

"I thought the same thing," he agreed. "Can I turn around now?"

"You can." She waited until he was facing her. "There, you see? No damage done. But I am hungry."

He took her back outside and down the hall to the kitchen where he had fed her the night before. The kitchen had been empty then, and it was empty now. She couldn't quite figure out who did the cooking or when they did it, but there was a pot of something bubbling on the stove. Thom ladled them up two bowls of something that might have been thin stew or simply gruel, added hunks of bread, and pumped two cups of water from a sink. They sat at the same table, a small wooden block with benches, and consumed their meal. It did not look appetizing at the outset and did not improve with the tasting. Mistaya ate hers anyway, concentrating on the bread. She needed something in her stomach.

"Now that you're here," he asked her after the meal was nearly consumed, "how long do you intend to stay?"

She thought about it a moment. "How long do you think I will be allowed to stay?"

He shrugged. "Depends. If you want to continue to pretend to be my sister, you can stay as long as you like. Otherwise, I think you better make plans to leave after breakfast."

She stared at him in disbelief. "That's rather abrupt, isn't it?"

"You saw how things are around here last night. If you want to stay, you have to work in the Stacks. That was the excuse I gave for your being here." He gave her a quick smile. "Look, I want you to stay. I told you that last night. I want to have someone to talk to."

He hesitated. "Okay, it's more than that. I don't want to talk to just *someone*. I want to talk to you. I like you."

She almost blushed, but not quite. "Well, I don't mind being your sister if that's what it takes for me to stay. But don't you have to get permission from His Eminence?"

"Oh, sure. But he'll agree. He likes beautiful things, so he'll like you well enough." He faltered, apparently realizing what he had just said. He brushed nervously at his mop of dark hair. "We can go see him after you've finished eating."

"I'm finished," she announced, and she stood up.

He took her back out of the kitchen and down the hallway past all the doorways to the servants' rooms, including her own, until they were back in the front anteroom where the big desk fronted the two huge closed doors. Only now the doors were open, and Thom led her through.

She stopped short when she saw what was there. They had entered a cavernous chamber with ceilings so high she could only just make out massive wooden support beams standing out in stark relief against the shadows. The floor of the room comprised huge stone blocks on which rested hundreds upon hundreds of shelves, row upon row running left to right and back into farther darkness. The shelves were each perhaps twenty feet high and connected by rails on which rolling ladders rested. Books and papers of all sorts were crammed into the shelves and stacked on the floors and dumped in piles in the aisles. Although there were windows high up on the walls on either side, their glass was crusted with grime and dust and cobwebs, and the natural light was reduced to a feeble glow. Usable light emanated from more of the tiny flameless lamps she had seen in the hallways earlier, these attached in pairs at the ends of the shelves, their yellow glow almost, but not quite, reaching to the center of each shelving unit.

"The Stacks," he announced. "It's kind of a mess up here, but better when you go farther in. We've been working back to front and from the middle outward. Don't ask me why; His Eminence ordered it done that way. So those parts are cleaned up and organized." He paused and looked at her. "It's a big job. You can see why we need help."

She could, indeed. As she was thinking that the number of workers necessary to clean up this mess was not a handful, but hundreds, a pair of the Throg Monkeys emerged from the gloom between the stacks, hunched over and conversing in low tones. When they caught sight of Thom and her, they abruptly turned around and disappeared back into the gloom.

"That's the way they are," Thom advised. "They do their level best not to be found so that they don't have to work. They are very good at it, too. Every day, I have to hunt them down and herd them over to the section we're working on. It takes up a lot of valuable time."

She kept staring in the direction of the vanished Throg Monkeys, thinking how creepy they were. "How many of them are there?"

He shook his head. "Don't know. I keep trying to count them, but I can never get them all together in one place. There are a lot, I know." He frowned. "It seems as if there are more all the time, but I don't know how that can be—unless they're breeding, of course, but I've never seen any evidence of that. Fortunately."

He grimaced. "However many there are, there aren't enough since only a small percentage of them ever do any work. The only thing I can trust them to do is lift and haul; they're hopeless at organizing and filing. I keep telling His Eminence that we need better help to finish this job, but he never does anything about it."

He gave her his loopy grin. "But now we have you—my little sister, Ellice. Things are looking up!"

She gave him a grimace of dismay. "How long have you been at this?"

He looked skyward for a moment. "Oh, about three years now."

"Three years? Three whole years?"

The loopy grin returned. "Well, it's slow going, I admit. But His Eminence seems satisfied. Come on. Let me introduce you."

"Wait!" She held up her hand to stay him. "What am I supposed to do when I meet him? What should I say?"

"Oh, that's easy. You really don't have to say much of anything. His Eminence will do all the talking. You just have to play along. Remember your lines. You are my little sister, Ellice. We live in a little village at the south edge of the Greensward called Averly Mills. When I introduce you, bow to him. Always address him as 'Your Eminence' or just 'Eminence.' Can you do that?"

She could if she had to, though she didn't much like the idea. But she held her tongue. "Does he have a name other than 'Eminence'?" she asked instead.

Thom gave her that familiar shrug. "He says his name is Craswell Crabbit, but I think he made it up. It doesn't matter because he won't allow us to use that name anyway. Only 'Your Eminence' will do."

"Is he a noble of the Kingdom? Is that why he insists on being addressed as 'Your Eminence'?"

Thom beckoned with a sweeping gesture of his arm, directing her to follow. "Come with me. You can decide for yourself."

He walked her down the right side of the Stacks and along the far wall until he came to an ornately carved oak door, scrolled with all sorts of symbols and runes and edged in gilt. At the very center and right at eye level was a sign that read:

HIS EMINENCE
Knock Before Entering

The letters, also outlined in gilt, fairly jumped off the polished wood of the door. Directly below was a huge metal knocker resting on a metal plate. It looked to Mistaya as if it would take a fair-sized battering ram to knock the door down if it was secured.

Without hesitating Thom lifted the knocker and let it fall once. A silence followed, and then a rumbling bass voice replied from within, "You may enter, Thom."

How the inhabitant knew who it was who'd come calling was a mystery to Mistaya, but Thom seemed undisturbed and pressed down on the door handle to release the latch.

The room they entered was large but not cavernous, and it in no way resembled the Stacks. Here the wood was polished to a high gloss, the walls decorated with paintings and tapestries, and the floor laid with rich carpet. The ceiling was much lower, but not so low as to make it feel as if it were pressing down, and there were slender stained-glass windows at the rear through which sunshine brightly shone in long, colorful streamers. A massive desk dominated the rear center of the room, its surface piled high with documents and artifacts of some sort. His Eminence sat comfortably behind it in a high-backed stuffed armchair, beaming out at them with a huge smile.

"Thom!" he exclaimed, as if surprised that it was the boy who had entered. Then he stood up and held out his arms in greeting. "Good morning to you!"

Mistaya didn't know what she was expecting, but it wasn't exactly this unbridled display of camaraderie. Nor was Craswell Crabbit quite what she had envisioned. Sitting behind his desk, he looked fairly normal. But when he stood up he was well over seven feet tall, skeletal beyond simply lean or gaunt, a collection of bones held together by skin and ligaments. As if to emphasize how oddly thin he was, his head was at least two sizes too big for his shoulders, an oblong face suggesting that the obvious compression it had undergone hadn't been quite enough to make up for the job done on the body. Because his legs and arms were rather crooked, even given the oddity of the rest of his body, the whole of his appearance was something rather like that of a praying mantis.

"Good morning, Your Eminence," Thom replied promptly. Rather quickly, Mistaya thought, he led her forward to stand before the desk. "This is my sister, Ellice."

"Ah, what a lovely child you are, Ellice!" the spider enthused, reaching out with one bony hand to take her own.

"Your Eminence," she responded quickly, letting the hand he held hang limp as she gave him something between a bow and a curtsy.

"Come for a visit?" he pressed. "All the way from . . . ?"

"Averly Mills, Your Eminence," she answered smoothly.

"Yes, that is the name. I'd forgotten." He smiled. "Missing your brother, are you?"

She noticed now that his head was shaved of hair, but fine black stubble grew over his bald pate and along the smooth line of his angular jaw in a dark shadow that refused to be banished. His sharp eyes locked on her own, and she could feel them probing for information that she might not wish to give.

"Yes, Your Eminence," she answered. "I thought perhaps I might be allowed to remain with him for a time. I am willing to work for my keep."

"Oh, tut, tut, and nonsense!" the other exclaimed in mock horror. "We don't treat our guests that way!" He paused, cocking his head at her. "Then again, we are short of helping hands just now, and our library reorganization clearly lacks the concerted effort it requires. Why, if not for your brother, we might not have made any progress at all!"

"Ellice is a good worker," Thom cut in. "She can read and write and help me with the organizing. She would be an immense help."

"I would be pleased to do whatever I can," Mistaya affirmed quickly, trying out a smile on him.

His Eminence looked charmed in his praying-mantis sort of way. "How very gracious of you, Ellice! I would not ask it of you, but neither will I refuse the offer. You may begin work at once! Please consider yourself a part of our family while you are here. Thom, has she met everyone?"

"Mostly, Your Eminence," the boy answered. "Pinch last night, some of the Throg Monkeys today, although I don't know which ones or whether they even care. Not all of them, I'm sure. They seem to multiply daily. Anyway, thank you for allowing her to stay with me. I miss her every bit as much as she misses me."

"Well, I am certain you do." The oblong face tilted strangely, as if about to fall off its narrow perch. "Though you've never once mentioned her before, have you?"

Mistaya felt a chill go up her spine. But Thom simply gave that familiar shrug. "I never thought it important enough to speak about, Your Eminence. You have so much else with which to grapple that it never seemed appropriate to talk about myself."

The tall man clapped his hands. "How very thoughtful of you, Thom. Indeed, you never disappoint me. Well, then. You've had your breakfast and taken a look around, Ellice?"

"Yes, Your Eminence."

"Then I shall not keep you a moment longer. Your brother goes off to work and you must join him. We shall visit again, later. Goodbye for now."

He gave her another smile and a perfunctory wave that couldn't possibly be mistaken for anything other than a dismissal. Giving deep bows and muttering their profuse thanks, the boy and the girl backed from the room and closed the door.

At once Thom put a finger to his lips. In silence, they retraced their steps back down the aisleway and to the front end of the

Stacks. When they were safely clear of the walls and out in the open, Thom turned to her.

"What do you think now? Is he a noble of the realm?"

She made a rude sound and didn't answer.

⸺⸺◦∞◦⸺⸺

It was only a few minutes later, the boy and the girl gone by then, that a knock sounded in the wall of Craswell Crabbit's office. His Eminence grunted and a hidden panel slid smoothly aside to admit Rufus Pinch. The hirsute little man trundled over to the side of the desk he couldn't see over from the front and peered up accusingly at its occupant.

"Mr. Crabbit," he greeted.

"Mr. Pinch, don't call me that."

Pinch ignored him. "Surely you don't believe their story, do you?"

His Eminence smiled beatifically. "I tend not to believe anything anyone tells me, Mr. Pinch. That way I am never disappointed. Are we speaking of our Thom and his lovely sister, Ellice?"

"I don't know who she is, but she's not who she claims. You can be certain of that."

"That, and much more, I think. But you are absolutely right. She isn't who she claims. But then neither is he, in case it had escaped you."

Pinch looked puzzled. "He isn't?"

Craswell Crabbit steepled his fingers in front of him. "Do yourself a favor, Mr. Pinch. Don't try to do the thinking in this partnership. Leave that to me. Stick with what works best for you. Spying. Keep an eye on those two and find out what they are up to."

He looked deeply thoughtful as he paused. "Because they are almost certainly up to something."

BACK IN THE STACKS

For the remainder of the day, Mistaya worked side by side with Thom in the dark and musty confines of the Stacks, cataloging and shelving the books that were stored there. Each book had to be removed, checked against a master list that His Eminence had supplied to Thom, cleaned and repaired as best as possible, and then returned to its space. The shelves themselves had to be scrubbed, since dust and grime had accumulated in clumps and layers thick enough to provide homes for nests of insects, which had long since gone condo. The work was slow and laborious, and by the end of the day they had barely completed one small section of the acres that required attention.

Of course, the task would have taken a dedicated crew of twenty able-bodied men and women as long as two years to complete, so they were somewhat at a disadvantage having only themselves and the completely unreliable Throg Monkeys as laborers. The annoying little creatures skulked around like evil weasels, appearing out of the gloom and then disappearing back into it once more, coming and going as they pleased. When they bothered to pass by, they regarded Thom with undisguised dislike and Mistaya with malevolent intent. Thom managed to get them to do some work, mostly the heavy lifting of the books from the shelves to the floor for easy reach, using the whistle they hated so to bring them to heel. But mostly they just drifted about, demonstrating no interest in the charge His Eminence, supposedly, had given them.

Still, some work was accomplished, and by the end of the day Mistaya could look with pride on the small area of shelving to which she had successfully lent her efforts. The ancient wood gleamed with waxing and polishing and the books rested upon it proudly, each in its place, giving the space a look of bright promise. She took special pleasure in hearing Thom compliment her on her efforts, pointing out how much easier things were now that she was there to help.

Neither of them made any mention of the fact that Rufus Pinch had been spying on them the entire time, making a poor job of concealing himself as he peeked around corners and through gaps, his eyes narrowed suspiciously. What he was trying to accomplish was anybody's guess, but after their first sighting of him resulted in a quick exchange of wordless looks, they pretty much ignored his pathetic efforts in favor of concentrating on the task at hand. Mistaya did find herself wondering more than once if the little man was intent on making this his life's work, but imagined that eventually he would grow tired of the game.

She also found herself wondering how in the world the job of repairing and restoring Libiris and her books would ever be accomplished if things didn't change dramatically from the status quo. As things stood now, it would not be likely that the work would wrap up in her lifetime. But she wasn't there for that, she kept reminding herself. She was only there to hide until she could figure out a way to bargain with her parents about her future. She was working at Libiris not because she wanted to but because it was the only way she would be allowed to stay. As soon as she was able to do so, she was going to leave this dreadful, dingy place and go somewhere else entirely, somewhere at least marginally reasonable.

All of which reminded her that she was in this mess in the first place because she had listened to Edgewood Dirk, and the cat had not reappeared since.

"Tell me something about yourself," Thom asked her later, as they were eating dinner in the kitchen. As usual, there were only the two of them. Rufus Pinch seemed to have given up spying on them for the day and the Throg Monkeys had gone back into the gloom. "Nothing too revealing; I'm not asking you to give up your secrets. Just something you think I might like to know."

She thought about it a moment, giving him a measured look. "And then you will do the same?"

He grinned. "Of course."

"All right." She thought some more. What could she say that would really amaze him? She wanted to do that, to shock him. But at the same time she had to be careful not to give anything away.

"I know," she said finally. She squared her shoulders. "I have met the dragon Strabo, and talked with him."

He stared at her as if she had lost her mind. It was exactly the reaction she had hoped for. "You have not," he insisted. "You couldn't have."

"But I have. It happened when I was ten years old. I was outside my village, carrying milk to my grandmother's cottage." She was improvising now, making it up as she went. "The dragon landed in a field and ate a cow right in front of me! When he was done, he looked at me and asked me what I was staring at. I couldn't speak, I was so afraid. But the dragon said not to worry, that as a rule he didn't eat little girls. Only now and then, and this wasn't either. Then he flew away."

He exhaled sharply. "Right in front of you? I would have been afraid, too! I've seen the dragon flying, but I can't imagine talking to it." He leaned forward, his face serious. "I think you were very brave."

She blushed despite herself, not so much at the compliment as at the knowledge that she was perpetrating a deliberate deception in order to impress him. She liked Thom, and she wanted him to see her as something more than a runaway with strange traveling companions. Her meeting with Strabo hadn't been anything like what she had described, but she couldn't tell him the truth without giving away her identity.

"I wasn't so brave," she said, making a dismissive gesture. "The dragon wasn't interested in me."

"You would have made a nice snack," he suggested. "Did you believe it when he said he wouldn't eat you?"

She shrugged. "He was scary looking, but not aggressive. He didn't threaten me. He just made that one comment, that's all he did." She was anxious to move on. "All right, now it's your turn. Tell me something about you that I should know."

He gave her his boyish grin and shook his head. "I don't think I have anything to tell you half as interesting as what you just told me." He rested his chin in the cup of his hands. "Let's see. Well, I like books. I read all the time."

"That's not surprising," she challenged. "You work in a library."

"Lots of people work at places they don't have any interest in." He paused. "How about this? I don't like fighting with weapons. I'm not very good at it."

She gave him a look. He didn't seem all that awkward. In fact, she thought he looked pretty capable. "What else?" she pressed. "That's not enough yet. You have to tell me something important, something you wouldn't tell just anyone."

He leaned back, looking much put upon. "You can't expect me to match the dragon story. Well, okay. I saw the dragon once, flying by, high up; I already told you that. Does that count?"

She shook her head. "Something else."

"There isn't anything else!" he exclaimed in mock exasperation. "Wait! Okay, one other thing I can tell you." He leaned forward again, bending close and lowering his voice. "I'm not here because I am an apprentice. I'm here because I'm indentured to His Eminence."

"Indentured? Like a servant or slave? You mean he owns you?"

"Something like that, I guess. My father sold me to him for five years to satisfy a family debt. I have to stay here working for him until my five years are up." He cocked an eyebrow at her. "I'm only in my third year."

She was appalled. "Why would your father do that?"

"Ah," he said, drawing the word out. "That's the question, isn't it?"

She frowned. "Well, you have to tell me!"

He shook his head in rebuke. "Not until you tell me something more about yourself. Then I'll tell you the rest."

She leaped to her feet. "That isn't fair!"

"Who said anything about playing fair?" He stretched lazily. "Anyway, I'm off to bed. We start early around here, and tomorrow is your first full day in the Stacks. You'll need all the sleep you can get."

She stared at him in disbelief, started to say something, then stopped. He was already getting to his feet, picking up his plate, and carrying it to the basin to wash. She was furious, but would not give him the satisfaction of finding that out. Two could play this game. She was already thinking about what she would tell him tomorrow that would shock him even more.

He gave her a cheerful wave as he walked out the door, and she smiled back sweetly.

When she rose the following morning, she was pleased to discover that the washroom was no longer plagued by the threat of uninvited Throg Monkeys. Thom had nailed heavy wooden boards over the panel through which the troublesome little monsters had appeared yesterday, and it looked as if they were shut out for good. Nevertheless, she kept close watch as she washed and dressed herself, a good-sized wooden staff close at hand for head-bashing should the need arise.

Afterward, she did not go directly into the kitchen for her breakfast, but down the hall and through several connected passageways to a small, well-sealed door that opened into a mucky courtyard and stables beyond. She saw Shoopdiesel right away, sitting on a bench next to a woodpile, hunched over and picking pieces of straw and clumps of dirt out of his clothing. He looked as if he might have volunteered for duty as a scarecrow in a windstorm, but she was certain that the explanation was far more complicated.

"Princess!" Poggwydd exclaimed loudly, as he came around the corner of the shed leading a small donkey.

"Not so loud, please!" she hissed, motioning him to quiet down. "And don't call me that! It's Ellice!"

His grubby hands flew to his mouth in horror at the obviousness of his mistake, and he hurriedly nodded his understanding. "Sorry, so sorry," he offered in a hushed voice.

She walked over to him, stopping to take a look at Shoopdiesel, who appeared not just to be coated with straw and dirt but impaled. Moreover, he was the recipient of multiple bruises and cuts. "What happened to him?" she asked Poggwydd.

"Oh." Poggwydd looked embarrassed. "It's a rather long story, Princess . . . I mean, Ellice. Rather long and boring. Perhaps it would be better to tell it another time . . . ?"

"I have time now. What have you two been up to?" She glanced at the animal he was leading. "And what are you doing with that donkey?"

Poggwydd looked all around, as if afraid someone would hear. Shoopdiesel had given up plucking out hunks of straw and earth and was limping as unobtrusively as possible toward the interior of the shed.

"Shoopdiesel, you come back here!" she snapped at him. "Whatever's going on, you're obviously involved!"

"It's really nothing you need to bother yourself with," Poggwydd insisted in something like a whine.

Mistaya shook her head. "Stop wasting my time, Poggwydd. Just tell me what you and your piggy little friend are doing."

Poggwydd seemed to consider the advisability of doing so for a moment and apparently the scales tipped in her favor. "Foraging," he admitted.

She shook her head, despairing that there was any hope for these two. "I thought as much. What did I tell you about that?"

"But, Princess!"

"Don't call me that! Just tell me why you are back to stealing other people's animals!"

"But we're not stealing." Poggwydd managed to look put upon. "Consider our situation. We have been living out here in the stables since we arrived. It's very nice out here, too. Lots of soft earth for burrowing, lots of soft straw for sleeping, and a great many rats for eating. Do you know, Princess, that the stable hands actually *want* us to eat the rats? They encourage it! So we did just exactly as we were told."

He gave a prodigious sigh. "But we have been eating rats constantly since our arrival, and we thought that perhaps we should eat something else. A varied diet is important, you know. A varied diet keeps you healthy of body and mind, Princess."

He saw the look that crossed her face and hurried on. "Well, being of a curious nature, naturally we decided to look around. And what did we find but all sorts of strays that no one has any claim to! We could take our pick! But, admittedly, we got a little carried away. Well, Shoopdiesel did, anyway. He's always been a little too ambitious for his own good. He shouldn't have tried to capture something that big, even if it was just standing out there, waiting for someone to come along and take it away. He should have known better."

"A horse?" she guessed.

"A bull. A rather large, unpleasant bull with big horns and a keen dislike for G'home Gnomes. He threw Shoopdiesel twenty feet in the air and then tried to trample him. Poor Shoop only barely escaped with his life!"

As if on cue, Shoopdiesel began to whimper softly. Mistaya rolled her eyes. "And you, in your wisdom, Poggwydd, have settled on this donkey? Is that right?" she pressed.

He nodded wordlessly, dropping his gaze. "It was just wandering around. No owner was in sight."

"You know, just because you don't see an owner doesn't mean there isn't one," she pointed out. "For instance, if an ear is tagged with a metal clip, like this one?" She reached out and fingered the tag attached to the donkey's ear. "That might suggest that you have overstepped your bounds once again."

"Oh," he said, trying to look abashed. "I didn't see that."

Maybe he hadn't, but maybe he had, too. Who knew? She couldn't be sure with these two. What she did know was that they were becoming increasingly annoying and were going to get into some sort of trouble sooner or later that would call attention to them and therefore to her. She couldn't allow that to happen. Maybe it was time to send them back home.

"You've both been of great help to me," she declared, bestowing on each in turn her most persuasive smile. "I wouldn't have gotten to Libiris without you. But now that I'm here and staying for a while, there's really no need for you to worry further about me. You're probably anxious to get back to your own homes and lives."

The G'home Gnomes exchanged a hurried glance. "Oh, no, Princess," Poggwydd said at once. "We want to stay with you. You still might have need of us. Might'nt she, Shoop?"

Shoopdiesel nodded vigorously.

"If we leave, what will you do for friends if you find yourself in trouble again? That cat can't be trusted. I bet you haven't even seen him since we arrived."

There was no arguing with that. She sighed, resigned to the inevitable. "All right. You can stay a few days longer. But pay attention to me. If you do one more thing that causes trouble, you'll have to leave immediately. I mean it. I'm trying to stay in hiding here, and you don't help matters by doing things that are likely to anger our hosts. So there will be no more foraging. Stick with eating rats, if you must."

The image was nauseating, but then she wasn't a G'home Gnome, either. "Can't you eat grass or something?"

Poggwydd frowned. "G'home Gnomes don't eat grass, Princess."

"That's an example, Poggwydd! I'm just telling you not to eat anything you haven't been given permission to eat. Are we clear?"

Both Gnomes nodded forlornly, their wizened faces crestfallen and their shoulders slumped. They couldn't help being what they were, she knew. They couldn't be something else; they didn't know how. Given all the time in the world, she probably couldn't teach them.

"I have to go eat my own breakfast," she muttered in disgust, turning away.

Beset by images of rats being gnawed on by Gnomes, she discovered that she really wasn't very hungry anymore. Nevertheless, she managed to eat a little bread and cheese and drink some milk before going off to work in the Stacks. By the time she arrived, Thom was already there, sitting cross-legged on the floor as he sorted through the latest batch of books the recalcitrant Throg Monkeys had stacked next to him. He gave her a cheerful greeting, and she was relieved when he didn't say anything about the fact that she was late. Putting thoughts of the G'home Gnomes behind her, she settled down to the job at hand and in no time at all was deeply enmeshed in cataloging and cleaning.

The morning passed quickly, helped along by her concentration on her work. Very little conversation passed between Thom and herself, and when he did speak it was only to ask her if she had slept well, if she had eaten and if she needed anything. She wanted him to say more, was eager to talk with him, but his seeming reluctance left her unwilling to push the matter. She had to content herself with watching the furtive movements of the Throg Monkeys as they slithered through the stacks like wraiths, crouched over and slit-eyed, their purpose and destination unknowable. She might have been frightened of them before, but by now she had grown used to them and found herself mostly irritated that they insisted on lurking rather than helping.

She was aware, too, of Rufus Pinch peering out at her from various hiding places, a spy without spy skills. It didn't seem to bother Thom, who appeared unaware of the wizened face and furtive movements of the little man. Thom just worked along as if nothing unusual was happening, humming to himself, sparing Mistaya an occasional look, but saying nothing. She found herself increasingly irritated with him, too. She wanted him to acknowledge what was going on instead of acting as if he were oblivious. But Thom never once said a word or even gave her one of those conspiratorial looks that he had shared with her yesterday.

Then, just when her patience was nearly exhausted, he leaned forward suddenly and whispered, "Had enough, little sister? Let's go somewhere they can't spy on us."

He took her to the kitchen to gather up bread, meat, cheese, and cups of cold well water for their lunch, then walked her out again and down a hallway to a huge old stone stairway that climbed into gloom and a flutter of bat wings.

"Up there?" she asked doubtfully.

He laughed. "Don't worry. It's safe enough once we're at the top. And we can lock the door when we get there."

She followed him up, ascending the tower steps in steady progression, counting until she lost interest. Slits cut into the walls allowed for just enough light to find the way but not enough to chase the gloom. The bats clung to the walls here and there in shadowy communities, but she couldn't quite decide how they got in since the slits seemed too narrow. It wasn't until she neared the top and the light brightened that she saw barred window openings in the upper reaches of the tower flanking a heavy ironbound door that sat at the apex of the stairs.

Thom reached the door, lifted the latch, and pushed. The door opened with a creaking of metal fastenings, and sunlight poured through in a bright gray wash.

Once through the opening, they were outside the castle, elevated on a battlement that gave a 360-degree view of the countryside beyond. Mistaya could see for miles, even though the day was hazy and the lake country mists snaked through the forests to coil in pools in the vales and deeps. She could see the dark flanks of the mountains south and west, and father north the deep emerald of the Greensward.

She even thought she caught a momentary glimpse of Sterling Silver's bright gleam through the drifting haze.

"What do you think?" Thom asked her, and she gave him a broad grin.

They sat facing each other on a bench at the edge of the battlement, their food and drink settled between them, the sweep of the countryside visible through notches in the ancient stone. It seemed to Mistaya that the battlement had been constructed not so much for defensive as for architectural purposes, and she didn't think it was ever intended for Libiris to be defended against an attacker.

"There really is a throw latch on the door," Thom advised with a wink, "and I threw it. Rufus will have to find something else to do with himself until lunch is over."

"Why is he spying on us, anyway?" she wanted to know.

Thom shrugged. "Hard to say. I'm sure he has his reasons. It's not just you. He watches me, too. Not all the time, but now and then. I think he does it to feel like he's in control of things. Nominally, he's in charge of my work. Practically, he doesn't have any idea at all how I go about it. The Throg Monkeys don't listen to him, either."

"The Throg Monkeys are just plain creepy. I wish we had some other help we could call on."

"I wish that, too. I wish we could do more to put the library back to where it once was. Have you bothered to look at those books you're cataloging? Some of them are wonderful, filled with useful information and strange stories. I love looking at them."

"I would love it better if Pinch wasn't watching all the time." She gave him a look. "I guess I haven't paid much attention to what's in the books. If they're so useful, why isn't anyone reading them?"

He shrugged anew. "People haven't come here in decades. Not since before you and I were born. Most don't even know about the library. As a matter of fact, most don't even read. They've forgotten how or don't take the time. They have all they can do to keep food

on the table. Life isn't easy for most living here in Landover. They
have to work very hard."

She frowned, aware that she hadn't given the matter much
thought. "I suppose that's true."

He didn't say anything more for a moment, munching solemnly
on his food as he looked out across the countryside. "When I come
up here, I like to pretend that all the lands, for as far as I can see, belong to me, and I can do whatever I want with them."

She laughed. "What would you do, if you had the chance?"

"Oh, that's easy. I'd give them away."

"Give them away? To whom?"

"To all those people we've been talking about. Most Landoveri-
ans living in the Greensward have to work for the Lords because the
Lords hold title to all the land. Half of what they farm or earn or
forage belongs to their masters. They owe allegiance in case of war.
They owe fealty oaths of all sorts. They really don't have anything
that they can call their own. I'd give them the land."

She nodded, thinking. "Hasn't the King thought of this? I heard
he made a lot of changes in the old feudal system."

"He did. More than any King before him. He's done a lot of
good. But he can only do so much. If he tried to take the land away
from the Lords of the Greensward, there would be a war. Only the
Lords can give away their own land."

"But doesn't the King own this land?" she pressed, gesturing at
their immediate surroundings. "Isn't Libiris his?"

"Libiris is his, but the land isn't. As a matter of fact, title to this
particular piece of land is held jointly by the Lords and the River
Master. It took years for them to agree on using even this small
piece to build Libiris. I don't think they've ever agreed on anything
since."

"Maybe they could be persuaded to do more," she said.

He laughed. "Why don't you be the one to persuade them, then?
A girl who talked with the dragon Strabo and lived to tell about it
should be able to deal with mere mortals!"

"Maybe the King could do something," she suggested impulsively.

He gave her a look. "You know, I was once inside the castle and saw the King."

She felt her throat tighten. "How did that happen?"

"I was with a group of boys carrying baggage for one of the Lords. So I was allowed inside for a bit, and I saw the King and his Queen. I even saw their little girl."

She nodded slowly, measuring his look. "How long ago was this?"

"Quite a while. I don't remember a lot about it. I was just a boy. The little girl was just a child. She would be older now. Your age, maybe." He grinned. "But she wouldn't be nearly so interesting or pretty as you are, I bet."

She was suddenly anxious to change the topic of conversation. "Tell me the rest of how you ended up being sent here as an indentured servant."

He finished the last of his bread and meat and washed it down with several swallows of water. "As I recall, the bargain was that you were supposed to tell me something interesting about yourself first. Something other than that story about you and the dragon."

"That wasn't a bargain I made. That was your condition for finishing the story—a very unfair condition, I might add."

He thought about it. "All right, maybe it was. If I finish the story, will you tell me something else about yourself afterward?"

She stuck out her hands. "Let's shake on it."

They shook, his hands strong and firm as they grasped hers. She liked the feel of them—not too rough, but they had seen hard work.

"Well, then?" she asked, withdrawing her hands from his.

"There's not much more to tell," he said. "My father sold me into indenture to His Eminence because he felt I might find a better future here than if I stayed with him. There wasn't much work in the village and no one to teach me a useful trade. Or at least not a trade that interested me. He thought that coming here, working with books I could read and studying on my own when I wasn't working, might better serve me."

"Well, couldn't he have sent you to study with His Eminence instead of indenturing you for five years? It would have been the same thing!"

Thom shook his head. "His Eminence wouldn't allow it. No one gets to come to Libiris and stay without a reason. His bargain with my father was that if I came, it was as an indentured servant. That was the condition to my apprenticeship. When I am done working, I owe His Eminence half of my first five years' earnings in my chosen trade, as well."

"That's unfair!" Mistaya was indignant. "He can't do that!"

Thom laughed. "Tell you what. When you talk to the King about persuading the Lords to give up their lands to the poor people, put in a good word for me, too."

"Maybe I will," she declared boldly.

He leaned over and brushed her hair back from her face in a curiously tender gesture. "You have a good heart, little sister. Whoever you are and wherever you came from, you have a good heart."

She didn't know what to say. "I think you have a good heart, too," she managed.

There was a moment when their eyes locked and time seemed to freeze. She waited, her anticipation of what might happen next so sharp it made her ache.

Then abruptly he stood up. "Come along. Back to work. Rufus will grow bored if we're not there to be spied upon."

She certainly wouldn't want that, she thought. She felt a pang of disappointment that their time alone together was over. She wanted more. She determined that she would have it.

Picking up their plates and cups, she followed him back through the tower door and down the stairs to work.

It was late in the afternoon, the time nearly run out on their day's efforts, when Mistaya heard someone calling. The voice was so faint and so distant that at first she thought she was mistaken. She stopped what she was doing and listened for a long few moments without hearing anything more. Her imagination, she supposed. A place this cavernous could play tricks on you, deceive you into hearing and seeing things that weren't there.

She had risen to begin sorting through a new stack of books when she heard it again. She stood listening anew, staring off into space and trying to pinpoint the location. She thought it had come from somewhere back in the Stacks, where the darkness was so thick and deep that it was virtually impenetrable. But there was only silence.

"Did you hear something?" she asked Thom finally.

He glanced up and shook his head. "No. Did you?"

"I thought so."

He shrugged and went back to his sorting. She watched him for a few moments, absorbed in his work, and then she quietly rose and started walking toward the interior of the Stacks, searching the gloom. The shelves ran on endlessly into the darkness, finally disappearing altogether. How far back did they go? How big was this room, anyway? She kept walking, glancing over her shoulder once to where Thom knelt on the floor, absorbed in his work. The silence was deep and pervasive, broken only by the soft sounds of her footfalls and Thom's rustling of pages.

Then she heard the voice again, and this time she was certain that it came from somewhere in the direction she was going.

"Ellice!" Thom called out suddenly. "Wait!"

She stopped and turned. She was surprised to find that she had gone far enough down the aisle that he was almost out of sight. "What?"

He was approaching her at a run. "Don't go any farther!"

She stared at him. "What are you talking about? I was just . . ."

"I know what you were doing," he interrupted. His face was flushed as he came to a stop in front of her, and she was shocked to catch a glimpse of fear on his angular features. "I don't want you going into the Stacks by yourself. Not ever. Not without me. Understood?"

She nodded, not understanding at all. "What's back there?"

"Nothing," he said quickly. Then he shook his head in denial. "Maybe nothing. But maybe something, too. I don't know. I just know it might be dangerous." He saw the look on her face and grimaced. "I know how that sounds. But I know what can happen because it happened to me."

She gave him a look. "Are you going to tell me what it was?"

He nodded. "But not here. Not now. Tonight. Just promise me you'll do as I say."

She was touched by his concern. He was genuinely worried for her. "All right, I promise. But I still think I heard something."

She followed him back to where they had been working, quietly dissatisfied. She had told him she would not to go back into the Stacks alone, but she had already decided she was doing exactly that the first chance she got. It wasn't lying exactly; it was more like . . .

Well, she didn't know what it was more like. But it was not his decision to make; it was hers.

She had heard the voice clearly the last time it called, and she didn't think there was any way she could ignore its plea.

Help me, it had begged.

THEY SEEK HER HERE,
THEY SEEK HER THERE

High Lord Ben Holiday, beleaguered King of Landover and increasingly troubled father of Mistaya, was up early the next morning. He had been unable to sleep for yet another night and had slipped out of the bedroom and come down to his desk in the library to do some work. Even though he was consumed by thoughts of his absent daughter, there were pressing issues in the governing of his Kingdom that required resolution. And even though much of what he did in those still-dark morning hours consisted of rumination and paper rearranging he still felt as if he was doing something.

He looked up in surprise as Bunion appeared in the doorway and announced the arrival of a messenger from the River Master. Ben was still in his robe and pajamas, not accustomed to receiving visitors either at this hour or in this state of dress. Still, he would make an exception here. He told Bunion he would see the messenger, and the kobold disappeared without a word. Within minutes the kobold was back, their visitor in tow. The messenger entered with a slight bow, an oddly misshapen creature with twigs and leaves growing out of his body and patches of moss attached to the top of his head.

"High Lord," he growled softly, a strange guttural sound that caught Ben by surprise. "The River Master awaits you on the far side of the causeway. He wishes to speak to you of his granddaughter."

Ben was on his feet at once, asking Bunion and the messenger to wait where they were. He headed down the hallway and up the stairs to wake Willow. They were washed and dressed in minutes and on their way downstairs to meet Mistaya's grandfather. The River Master refused to go inside man-made structures, which were anathema to him. All meetings had to be conducted out in the open. Ben was used to this and didn't let it bother him. The River Master almost never left his home in Elderew. The fact that he had come to Sterling Silver said much about the importance of his visit. In any case, Ben would have gone anywhere to meet him if he had news of Mistaya.

He glanced at Willow as they descended the stairways of the castle in the company of Bunion and the woodsy-clad messenger. She looked calm and alert despite the circumstances, her beautiful face serene. The fact that she had been awoken from a sound sleep seemed not to have affected her at all. Nor did she seem bothered by the unexpected visit from her father, who was indifferent to her in the best of times. Ben knew she had grown used to his coldness, the result of his inability to accept her mother's refusal to become his wife, a betrayal of which Willow's birth reminded him every day of his life. His grudging acceptance of her marriage to an outsider and her status as Queen of Landover was the best she could hope for. If not for Mistaya, he would undoubtedly have less to do with either of them than he did, so she was probably grateful just for that, though she never spoke of it.

Ben studied her a moment—the slender curve of her body, the smooth and graceful walk, and the strange mix of emerald-green hair and moss-green skin. He had loved her from the moment he had encountered her so unexpectedly, twenty years ago, standing in the waters of the Irrylyn, naked in the moonlight. She had told him he was for her, and that in the fairy way they were bound by fate. He could not imagine now, though he had been doubtful then, that it could have turned out any other way.

She glanced over at him suddenly and smiled, as if she knew what he was thinking. She was almost prescient, at times. He smiled back, reaching over and taking her hand in his. Whatever else happened in their lives, he knew they would never be apart again.

They left the castle through the main gates and crossed the drawbridge and causeway to the far shore of the mainland from their island home. The River Master was waiting just inside a screen of trees not two hundred yards from the moat. He stood with a single retainer, his tall, spare form as still and hard as if it were carved from stone. He wore a look of obvious distaste, which might have had something to do with the people he was meeting or the purpose of his coming or even the weather—there was no way of telling. His nearly featureless face, smooth and hard, turned toward them as they approached, but gave no sign of interest one way or the other.

Ben nodded as he reached Willow's father. The leader of the once-fairy nodded back, but spared not even a momentary glance for Willow.

"I've come about my granddaughter," he announced tonelessly.

How typical of him to refer to Mistaya as *his* granddaughter, Ben thought. As if she belonged to him. As if that were what mattered.

"She came to Elderew to ask for 'sanctuary,' as she referred to it," he continued, hurrying his sentences as if to get through quickly. "She complained that she was being misused and generally misunderstood by her parents. I don't pretend to understand all of it or even to care. I told her that her visit was welcome, but that sanctuary was not a reasonable solution to her problems. I told her she must go home and face you directly rather than trying to use me as a go-between."

He paused. "In short, I did what I would have expected you to do should one of my children come crying about their treatment."

Something about the way he said it suggested that he was referring in oblique fashion to Willow. Ben didn't get the connection, but thought it best not to comment. "But she didn't take your advice, I gather?"

The River Master folded his arms. "She disappeared sometime during the night and was not seen again. The once-fairy, on my orders, attempted to track her and failed. That should not have happened, and I worried over the reason. Only a true fairy creature could hide its tracks from us. Was she in the company of one? I waited for her to return, as I thought she might. When she didn't, I decided to come here to tell you what had happened."

Ben nodded. "I appreciate that you did."

"I should have done more. She is my granddaughter, and I would not forgive myself if something happened to her."

"Do you have reason to think that something has?" Willow asked suddenly, speaking for the first time.

The River Master glanced at her, as if just realizing she was there, and then looked off into the distance. "She came to Elderew with a pair of G'home Gnomes. She claimed they were friends who had helped her. I thought them untrustworthy traveling companions for a Princess, but she is never predictable. Her mud puppy was with her as well, however, even though we did not see him, so I thought her safe enough from harm."

"How can you know he was with her if you didn't see him?" Ben demanded, no longer feeling quite so calm about things.

"Fairy creatures, such as Mistaya's mud puppy, leave a small but unmistakable trace of magic with their passing. Even if they are not visible to the eye, they can be detected by the once-fairy. So we knew he was there with her when she arrived. But when she left, there was no longer even a tiny trace of him."

"Perhaps it was the mud puppy's doing." Ben was trying to put a good face on things, even though he wasn't feeling good about this piece of information. Haltwhistle, a gift from the Earth Mother, was his daughter's constant companion and protector in Landover. He was as close to her as her shadow. "Couldn't he have covered their tracks?"

The River Master shook his head. "A mud puppy can transport a charge to another place. It cannot hide its own or another's passing. Mistaya's trail was hidden from us. Another magic was required for that. Only the most powerful of fairy creatures would possess such magic."

Ben thought immediately of Nightshade, but quickly dismissed the idea. The Witch of the Deep Fell was gone. There was no indication that she had returned. He was letting his imagination run away with him.

"I shall continue to search for Mistaya, Ben Holiday," the River Master added. "I shall do everything in my power to find out where she has gone."

Ben nodded. "I know you will."

"There is one thing more I need to say. I know what you and my daughter think of me. I know I have brought some of this on myself. But I would do nothing to undermine you with Mistaya. When she asked to stay with me and I told her she could not, I told her as well that when I had doubted your ability you had proven me wrong, that you were the King that Landover needed. I told her, as well, that you and my daughter were good parents to her and that she should listen to you and trust you."

He shifted his gaze to Willow. "I have been hard on you, I know. I wish it could be otherwise, but I am not sure it ever can. Although I have tried, I find I cannot put aside entirely the pain even your presence causes me. You are your mother reborn, and your mother is a ghost that haunts me daily. I cannot escape her memory or forgive her betrayal. When I see you, I see her. I am sorry for this, but there it is."

Willow nodded. "It is enough that you do what you can for Mistaya, Father," she said quietly. "She looks up to you. She respects you."

The River Master nodded but said nothing. There was a momentary silence as they stood facing one another.

"Will you take something to eat?" Willow tried.

The River Master shook his head. The bladed features showed nothing as they faced her squarely for the first time. He looked as if he might say something more, but then abruptly he turned away, and with his retainers in tow he disappeared back into the trees and was gone.

Ben stood close to Willow, staring after them. He said softly, "He does the best he can, I think."

There were tears in her eyes as she nodded.

"We have to do something more about finding Mistaya," he added, anxious to leave the subject of her father. "I'm starting to worry about her. Perhaps the Landsview will help this time, if I . . ."

"No," she said at once, her voice firm and steady. "We'll go to the Earth Mother, instead. She will know where our daughter is."

Ben nodded and put his arm around her shoulders, hugging her close. She always made the right choice.

They went back inside the castle, ate their breakfast, packed for an overnight journey, had Bunion saddle their horses, and by mid-morning had set out with the kobold as their escort to find the Earth Mother. It wasn't a given that they would. You didn't find the Earth Mother just by looking for her. What was needed was a visit to the northern borders of the River Master's country, close by the swampy areas where the Earth Mother dwelled. If she wished to see you, she would send a mud puppy to guide you to her. If she had better things to do, you would wait a long time and had better have other plans for the interim.

Ben was happy to have Bunion back in one piece. The kobold hadn't spoken to him directly of his misadventures at Rhyndweir, but Questor had uncovered the truth of things and passed it along. He had also given Ben the book on poisons that Bunion had stolen from Laphroig's library. The notes and markings pretty much revealed the fate of Laphroig's unfortunate wife and child and reaffirmed Ben's suspicions. By itself, it wasn't enough to convict Rhyndweir's Lord of murder, but it was enough to underline the importance of keeping him well away from Mistaya until such time as he overstepped himself in a way that would allow him to be stripped of his title and punished in a court of law.

The day was hazy and cool, unusual for this time of year, and the grayness lent a faint despondency to their travel. Without wishing it so, Ben found himself growing steadily more pessimistic about his missing daughter. Where he had come from, there was a reasonable amount of danger for teenagers. But Landover was dangerous on a whole other level, and even Mistaya, for all her talent and experience, need only make one misstep to invite fatal consequences. He should have gone out and found her and brought her back the moment he knew she was missing. He should never have waited for her to come back on her own.

But after a while his pessimism gave way to reason, and he accepted that what he had done was the right thing and he should just have a little faith in his recalcitrant daughter. Didn't Willow have faith, after all? Had she once expressed serious concern for Mistaya?

On the other hand, Willow was a sylph whose father was a wood sprite and whose mother was a creature so wild that no one could hold her fast. Willow was a woman who periodically turned into a tree and sent roots down into the earth for nourishment so that she could survive. How could he equate his own sensibilities with hers? She could function emotionally on a whole separate plane of existence than he could.

So the morning passed away and then the early part of the afternoon. They stopped once to rest and feed the horses and to eat lunch themselves. Ben was feeling much better about things by then, although he couldn't have said why. Perhaps it was the fact that he was doing something besides sitting around waiting. He had used the Landsview every day since Mistaya's disappearance without success. Now, at least, he had reason to think they might find her.

They camped that night by the shores of the Irrylyn. Before eating their dinner, while the twilight shadows settled in about them in purple hues, they went down to the lake to bathe together. Bunion remained behind to set camp for them, and they were alone as they stripped off their clothes in a secluded cove and walked down to the shore. As they sank into the waters—he was always surprised that lake waters could feel so warm and comforting—he was reminded anew of their first meeting. He had been new to the role of King and not yet accepted by anyone beyond Questor and Abernathy. He had come in search of allies, thinking to start with the River Master, and

Willow had appeared to him as if by magic. Or perhaps it *was* magic, he thought. He had never questioned the how and the why of it. But it had changed his life, and every day he was reminded of it anew.

They washed and they held each other and stayed in their quiet, solitary place for a long time before coming back to the camp. Ben thought it was over too soon, thought they could have stayed there forever, and wished with lingering wistfulness that they had.

He slept well that night for the first time, free of dreams and wakefulness, his sleep deep and untroubled.

When he woke again, it was nearing dawn, and a mud puppy was sitting right in front of him, watching. The Earth Mother was summoning them to a meeting as they had hoped.

"Willow," he said softly, shaking her gently awake.

She opened her eyes, saw the mud puppy, and was on her feet at once. "That's Haltwhistle, Ben," she whispered to him, an unmistakable urgency echoing off the words.

They dressed hurriedly, and leaving Bunion to watch over things they let the mud puppy show them the way. Haltwhistle gave no indication that he knew who they were, and to tell the truth Ben wasn't sure he could have identified the creature without Willow to help him. Mud puppies all looked the same to him. But if it really was his daughter's, then Mistaya was out there somewhere on her own without her assigned protector, and that was not good.

He took a moment to recall all the times that the Earth Mother had helped them in the past, both together and individually. An ancient fairy creature come out of the mists eons ago when Landover was first formed, she was the kingdom's caretaker and gardener. Wedded to the earth and its growing things, an integral part of the organic world, she nevertheless maintained a physical presence, as well. She was wise and farsighted and ageless, and she loved Mistaya.

They walked for a long time, leaving behind the Irrylyn and the surrounding forests and descending into mist-shrouded lowlands in which the ground quickly grew soggy and uncertain. Patches of standing water turned to acres of swamp, and stands of reeds and grasses clogged the passage in all directions. But the mud puppy maneuvered through it all without pausing, leading them along a narrow strip of solid ground until at last they had reached a vast stretch of muddied water amid a thick forest of cedars.

Haltwhistle stopped at the edge of this water and sat. Ben and Willow stopped next to him and stood waiting.

The wait was short. Almost immediately the waters began to churn and then to heave and the Earth Mother appeared from within, rising to the surface like a spirit creature, her woman's form slowly taking shape as she grew in size until she was much larger than they were. Coated in mud—perhaps formed of it—and her body slick with swamp waters, she stood upon the surface of the mire and opened her eyes to look down on them.

"Welcome, King and Queen of Landover," she greeted. "Ben Holiday of Earth and Willow of the lake country, I have been expecting you."

"Is that Haltwhistle who brought us here?" Ben asked at once, wasting no time getting to the point.

"It is," the Earth Mother confirmed.

"But shouldn't he be with Mistaya?"

"He should. But he has been sent home to me. He will remain here until Mistaya summons him anew."

"Why would Mistaya send him home?" Willow asked.

The Earth Mother shifted positions atop the water, causing her sleek body to shimmer and glisten in the misty, graying light. "It was not your daughter who sent Haltwhistle home to me. It was another who travels with her."

"The G'home Gnomes?" Ben demanded in disbelief.

The Earth Mother laughed softly. "A mud puppy will not leave its master or mistress and cannot be kept by humans. A mud puppy is a fairy creature and not subject to human laws. But powerful magic wielded by another fairy creature is a different matter. Such magic was used here."

Ben and Willow exchanged a quick glance, both thinking the same thing. "By Nightshade?" Ben asked quickly. "By the Witch of the Deep Fell?"

"By a Prism Cat," the Earth Mother answered.

Ben closed his eyes. He knew of only one Prism Cat, and he had crossed paths with it more than once since coming to Landover, almost always to his lasting regret. "Edgewood Dirk," he said in dismay.

"The Prism Cat found your daughter in the lake country and took her away with him. But first the cat sent Haltwhistle back to me. The message was clear."

Clear enough, Ben thought in dismay. But what did Dirk want with Mistaya? The cat always wanted something; he knew that much from experience. It would be no different here. The trouble was in determining what he was after, which was never apparent and always difficult to uncover. The Prism Cat would talk in riddles and lead you in circles and never get to the point or answer a question directly. Like cats everywhere, he was enigmatic and obtuse.

But Edgewood Dirk was dangerous, too. The Prism Cat possessed a very powerful magic, just as the Earth Mother had said. Yet the extent of that magic went far beyond his ability to manipulate a mud puppy. Ben felt a new urgency at the thought of Dirk's proximity to Mistaya.

"Where is Mistaya now?" he asked the Earth Mother.

"Gone with the Prism Cat," she answered once more. "But the Prism Cat covers their tracks and the way of their passing, and even I cannot determine where they are."

Ben felt a slow sinking in the pit of his stomach. If the Earth Mother didn't know where Mistaya was and couldn't find her, how could he expect to?

"Can you reverse the magic used to send Haltwhistle home to you?" Willow asked suddenly. "Can you send him back out again to find our daughter?"

The elemental shifted again, scattering droplets of water that sparkled like diamonds shed. "Haltwhistle can only go to her if she calls him now. She has not done so, child. So he must remain with me."

All the air went out of Ben on hearing this. His one chance at finding his daughter had evaporated right before his eyes. If the Earth Mother couldn't help him find her, he didn't know if there was anyone who could.

"Can you tell us anything to do?" Willow asked suddenly, her voice calm and collected, free of any hint of desperation or worry. "Is there a way to communicate with her?"

"Go home and wait," the Earth Mother said to her. "Be patient. She will communicate with you."

Ben tried to say something more, but the elemental was already sinking back into the swamp, slowly losing shape, returning to the earth in which she was nurtured. In seconds she was gone. The surface of the water rippled softly and went still. Silence settled in like a heavy blanket, and the mist drew across the water.

Haltwhistle looked up at them, waiting.

"Take us back, mud puppy," Willow said softly.

They walked back the way they had come, weaving through the swamp grasses and reeds, winding about the deep pools of water and thick mud, carefully keeping to the designated path. Neither Ben nor Willow spoke. There was nothing either of them wanted to say.

On reaching their camp and Bunion, Haltwhistle turned back at once and vanished into the mist. Ben shook his head. He had the vague feeling he should have done something more, but he couldn't say what. He walked over to where their camping gear was already packed and ready to be loaded and sat down heavily.

He looked at Willow expectantly as she sat next to him. "What do we do now?"

She smiled, surprising him. "We do what the Earth Mother suggested, Ben. We go home and wait for Mistaya to communicate with us."

This was not what he was hoping to hear, and he failed to hide his disappointment. "I don't know if I can leave it at that."

"I know. You want to do something, even if you don't quite know what that something is." She thought about it a moment. "We can ask Questor if he has a magic that can track a Prism Cat. He might know something that would help."

Sure, and cows might fly. But Ben just nodded, knowing that he didn't have a better suggestion. Not at the moment, anyway. Not until he thought about it some more.

So they loaded their gear on their horses and set out for home, and all the way back Ben kept thinking that he was missing something obvious, that there was something he was overlooking.

THEY SEEK THAT
PRINCESS EVERYWHERE!

The sun was just cresting the horizon when Questor Thews slipped from his bed, drew on his favorite bathrobe (the royal blue one with the golden moons and stars), and his dragon slippers (the ones that looked as if his toes were breathing fire), and padded down to the kitchen for his morning coffee. He had discovered coffee some years back during one of his unfortunate visits to Ben's world and had secured several sacks in the process, which he now hoarded like gold. Mistaya had been good enough to add to his supply now and again during her time at Carrington, but since she had been dismissed, he wasn't sure how long it would be before he could replenish his stock.

He finished brewing a pot and was in the process of enjoying his first cup of the day when Abernathy wandered in and sat down across from him. "May I?" he asked, motioning toward the coffee.

Questor nodded, wondering for what must have been the hundredth time how a soft-coated wheaten terrier could possibly enjoy drinking coffee. It must be a part of him that was still human and not dog, of course. But it just looked odd, a dog drinking coffee.

"Any new thoughts as to where our missing girl might be?" Abernathy inquired of him, licking his chops as he took the first swallow of his coffee.

Questor shook his head. "Not a one. The High Lord is right, though. I think we are missing something important about all this."

Ben Holiday had voiced his opinion on this late last night on his return from the lake country, more than a hint of discouragement coloring his voice and draping his tired visage. He had thought that he and Willow would find her there, but instead they had found only clues that seemed to lead nowhere. If neither the River Master nor the Earth Mother could help, it didn't look good for the rest of them.

"What could Edgewood Dirk want with her?" Abernathy asked suddenly, as if reading his thoughts.

Questor grunted and shook his head. "Nothing good, I'm sure."

"He wouldn't be going to the trouble of hiding her tracks if his intentions were of the right sort," his friend agreed. "Remember how much trouble he caused the last time he showed up?"

Questor remembered, all right. But on thinking back, it didn't seem that Dirk had been the cause of the trouble so much as the indicator. Something like a compass. The Prism Cat had appeared at the behest of the fairies in the mists, a sort of emissary sent to nudge the High Lord and his friends in the direction required for setting aright things that had gone askew—all without really telling them what it was exactly that needed righting. If that were true here, then Mistaya might be headed for a good deal more trouble than she realized.

Questor sighed. He was at his wit's end. He could continue to do what Ben Holiday and he had done every day, which was to go up to the Landsview and scour the countryside. But that had yielded exactly nothing to date, and it felt pointless to try yet again. He had thought about approaching the dragon, always a daunting experience, in an effort to see if it might be willing to help. But what sort of help might it offer? Strabo could cross borders that the rest of them couldn't—he could go in and out of Landover at will, for example—but that would prove useful only if Mistaya were somewhere other than Landover, and there were no indications at this point that she was.

"I remember when the High Lord was tricked into believing he had lost the medallion and Dirk trailed around after him until he figured it out," Questor mused, turning his coffee cup this way and that. "He was there when the High Lord was trapped with Night-shade and Strabo in that infernal device that Horris Kew uncovered, too. Dispensing his wisdom and talking in riddles, prodding the High Lord into recognizing the truth, if I remember right from what we were told afterward. Perhaps that is what's happening here."

"You make the cat sound almost benevolent," Abernathy huffed, his terrier face taking on an angry look, his words coming out a growl. "I think you are deluding yourself, wizard."

"Perhaps," Questor agreed mildly. He didn't feel like fighting.

Abernathy didn't say anything for a moment, tapping his fingers against his cup annoyingly. "Do you think that perhaps Mistaya might be trapped somewhere, like the High Lord was?"

Possible, Questor thought. But she had been wandering around freely not more than a few days ago in the company of those both-ersome G'home Gnomes and the cat. Something had to have changed, but he wasn't sure it had anything to do with being trapped.

"We need to think like she would," he said suddenly, sitting up straight and facing Abernathy squarely. "We need to put ourselves inside her head."

The scribe barked out a sharp laugh. "No, thank you. Put myself inside the head of a fifteen-year-old girl? What sort of nonsense is that, wizard? We can't begin to think like she does. We haven't the experience or the temperament. Or the genetics, I might add. We might as well try thinking like the cat!"

"Nevertheless," Questor insisted.

They went silent once more. Abernathy began tapping his fingers on his cup again. "Well?"

"Well, what?"

"Well, what are your thoughts, now that you've taken on the character of a fifteen-year-old girl?"

"Fuzzy, I admit."

"The whole *idea* of trying to think like a fifteen-year-old girl is fuzzy."

"But suppose, just suppose for a moment, that you are Mistaya. You've been sentenced to serve out a term at Libiris, but you rebel and flee into the night with two unlikely allies. You go to the one place you think you might find a modicum of understanding. But it is not to be. Your grandfather takes the side of your parents and declares you must return to them and work things out. You won't do this. Where do you go?"

Abernathy showed his teeth. "Your scenario sounds unnecessarily melodramatic to me."

"Remember. I'm a fifteen-year-old-girl."

"You might be fifteen, but you are also Mistaya Holiday. That makes you somewhat different from other girls."

"Perhaps. But answer my question. Where do I go?"

"I haven't a clue. Where do I go? Where Edgewood Dirk tells me to go perhaps?"

"If he tells you anything. But he might not. He might speak in his usual unrevealing way. He might leave it up to you. That sounds more like the Prism Cat to me."

Abernathy thought about it. "Well, let me see. I suppose I go somewhere no one will think to look for me." He paused, a look of horror in his eyes. "Surely not to the Deep Fell?"

Questor shook his head and pulled on his long white beard. "I don't think so. Mistaya hates that place. She hates everything connected with Nightshade."

"So she goes somewhere else." Abernathy thought some more. He looked up suddenly. "Perhaps she goes to see Strabo. The dragon is enamored of her, after all."

"The dragon is enamored of all beautiful women. Even more

so of Willow." Questor pulled on one ear and plucked at one eye-brow. "But I've already considered that possibility and dismissed it. Strabo won't be of much use to her in this situation and she knows it. Unless she wants someone eaten."

"A visit to the dragon *doesn't* seem likely, does it?" Abernathy sounded cross. "Nothing seems likely, when you come right down to it."

Questor nodded, frowning. "That's the trouble with young people. They never do what you would expect them to do. Frequently, they do the exact opposite. They are quite perverse that way."

"Perverse, indeed!" Abernathy declared, banging his coffee cup down on the table, his ears flopping for emphasis. "That is just the word! It describes them perfectly!"

"You never know what to expect!"

"You can't begin to guess what they might do!"

"They don't listen to reason!"

"The word doesn't exist for them!"

"You expect them to do something, they do something else entirely!"

"They very last thing you'd imagine!"

They were both revved up now, practically shouting at each other.

"Tell them what you want them to do, they ignore you!"

"Tell them what you don't want them to do, they do it anyway!"

"Go here, you say, and they go there!"

"No, no!" Questor was practically beside himself. "Go here, and they tell you they won't, but then they do anyway!"

The air seemed to go out of them all at once, that final revelatory sentence left hanging in the wind like the last leaf of autumn. They stared at each other, a similar realization dawning on both at the same moment.

"No," Abernathy said softly. "She wouldn't."

"Why not?" Questor Thews replied just as softly.

"Just to spite us?"

"No, not to spite us. To deceive us. To go to the last place we would think to look for her."

"But her tracks . . ."

"Covered up by Edgewood Dirk for reasons best known to him."

"And maybe to her. An alliance between them, you think?"

"I don't know. But isn't Libiris the very last place we would think to look for her?"

Abernathy had to admit that it was.

Much farther east, on the far end of the Greensward, another was contemplating Mistaya's disappearance, though with much less insight. Berwyn Laphroig, Lord of Rhyndweir, was growing increasingly vexed at the inability of his retainers to track down the missing Princess, a chore he felt they should have been able to accomplish within the first thirty-six hours of learning that she was missing. She was a young girl in a country where young girls did not go unescorted in safety. Thus she had chosen to accept the company of a pair of G'home Gnomes—this much he had managed to learn through his spies. This, and not much more. Since the discovery that she had turned up at her grandfather's in the company of the Gnomes, not another word had been heard of her.

In something approaching a rage, he had dispatched Cordstick to personally undertake the search, no longer content to rely on those underlings who barely knew left from right. Not that Cordstick knew much more, but he was ambitious, and ambition always served those who knew how to harness it. Cordstick would like very much to advance his position in the court, abandoning the title of "Scribe" in favor of something showier, something like "Minister of State." There was no such position at this juncture; Laphroig had never seen the need for it. But the title could be bestowed quickly enough should the right candidate appear. Cordstick fancied himself that candidate, and Laphroig, eager to advance his own stock in Landover by way of marrying Mistaya Holiday, was willing to give the man his chance.

If Cordstick failed him, of course, the position would remain open. Along with that of "Scribe."

A page appeared at the open door of the study where Laphroig sat contemplating his fate and crawled across the floor on hands and knees, nose scraping the ground. "My Lord," the man begged.

"Yes, what is it?"

"Scrivener Cordstick has returned, my Lord. He begs permission to give you his report."

Laphroig leaped to his feet. "Bring him to me at once."

He walked to one of the tower windows and looked out over the countryside, enjoying the sound of the page scraping his way back across the stones. He admired the sweep of his lands in the wash of midday sunlight, though he had to admit that his castle was rather stark by comparison. He must find a way to brighten it up a bit. A few more banners or some heads on pikes, perhaps.

He heard movement behind him.

"Well?" he demanded, wheeling about. "What have you—" He broke off midsentence, his eyes widening in shock. "Dragon's breath and troll's teeth, what's happened to you?"

Cordstick stood to one side, leaning rather uncertainly against a stone pillar. He was standing because it was apparently too painful for him to sit, although it might have been a toss-up had there been a way to measure such things. He was splinted and bandaged from head to foot. The parts of his skin that were not under wrap were various shades of purple and blue with slashes of vivid red. His right eye was swollen shut and enlarged to the size of an egg. His hair was sticking straight up and here and there were quills sticking out of his body.

"What happened?" Cordstick repeated his master's words as if he was not quite able to fathom them. "Besides the porcupine, the bog wump, the fire ants, the fall from the cliff, the beating at the hands of angry farmers, the dragging through the fields by the horse that threw me, and the encounter with the feral pigs? Besides being driven out of a dozen taverns and thrown out of a dozen more? Not a lot, really."

"Well," Laphroig said, an abrupt utterance that he apparently intended to say everything. "Well, we'll see that you get double pay for your efforts. Now what did you find out?"

Cordstick shook his head. "I found out that I should never have left the castle and may never do so again. Certainly not without an armed escort. The world is a vicious place, my Lord."

"Yes, yes, I know all that. But what about the Princess? What have you found out about her?"

"Found out about her? Besides the fact that she's still missing? Besides the fact that looking for her was perhaps the single most painful undertaking of my life?"

His voice was rising steadily, taking on a dangerously manic tone, and Laphroig took a step back despite himself. There was a wild glint in his scribe's eyes, one he had never seen before.

"Stop this whining, Cordstick!" he ordered, trying to bring things under control. "Others have suffered in my cause, and you don't hear them complaining."

"That's because they are all dead, my Lord! Which, by all rights, I should be, too!"

"Nonsense! You've just suffered a few superficial injuries. Now get on with it! You try my patience with your complaints. Leave all that for later. Tell me about the Princess!"

"Might I have a glass of wine, my Lord? From the flask that is not poisoned?"

Laphroig could hardly miss the irony in the wording of the request, but he chose to ignore it. At least until he got his report out of the man. It was beginning to look as if Cordstick might have outlived his usefulness and should be dispensed with before he did something ill advised. Like trying to strangle his master, for example, which his eyes suggested he was already thinking of doing.

He poured Cordstick a glass of the good wine and handed it to him. "Drink that down, and we'll talk."

His scribe took the glass with a shaking hand, guided it to his lips, and drained it in a single gulp. Then he held it out for a refill.

Laphroig obliged, silently cursing his generosity. Cordstick drank that one down, too.

"My Lord," he said, wiping his lips with his shirtsleeve, "I understand better now why those who do your bidding do so as spies and not openly. That is another mistake I will not make again."

If you get the chance to make another mistake, an enraged Laphroig thought. *Where does this dolt get the idea that he can criticize his Lord and master in this fashion? Where did this newfound audacity come from?*

"Just tell me what you found out, please," he urged in his gentlest, most reassuring voice, hiding every other emotion.

Cordstick straightened. Or at least, he made a failed attempt at it. "My Lord, there is nothing new on where the Princess has gone or what she is doing." He held up one bandaged hand as Laphroig started to vent. "However, that is not to say that our efforts have been totally unsuccessful."

Laphroig stared. "Exactly what does that mean?"

"It means that we know one more thing that we didn't know before I set out to find the Princess, although I'm not sure it's worth the price I had to pay to discover it. The Princess Mistaya has not disappeared for the reasons we thought. Nothing bad has happened to her. No abduction, no spiriting away, nothing like that. Apparently, she had a falling-out with her parents and left of her own volition. Because of the nature of the falling-out, it is thought she has no immediate intention of returning."

Laphroig shrugged. "Forgive me, Cordstick, but I don't see how that helps us."

"It helps, my Lord, because she is seeking sanctuary with an understanding third party. Her grandfather, the River Master, turned her down. She must be looking elsewhere." He paused. "Do you happen to know anyone who might be willing to grant her sanctuary, should I eventually find her and have a chance to speak with her?"

"Ah," said Laphroig, the light beginning to dawn. "So you think she might come here to live?"

"Beggars can't be choosers." Cordstick rubbed his bandaged hands and then winced. "If she agrees to let you act as her guardian, she becomes your ward and you gain legal status in determining her future. As her guardian, you will have ample opportunities to . . ." He trailed off, cleared his throat, and smiled. "To persuade her to your cause."

"Indeed, indeed!" Laphroig sounded positively enthusiastic at the prospect. He began to pace, as if by doing so he were actually getting somewhere. "Well, then, we must find her right away before she has a change of heart!" He wheeled on Cordstick. "*You* must find her!"

"I must?" His scribe did not sound in the least convinced.

"Yes, of course! Who else can I depend upon?" He dropped his voice to a near whisper. "Who else, but my future Minister of State?"

Cordstick gave him a calculating look. "I was just about to hand in my resignation and retire to the countryside, my Lord."

"No, no, we can't have that sort of talk." Laphroig was at his side instantly, patting him on his good shoulder. Gently, he walked him over to the window, where they could look out over the countryside together. "That sort of talk is for weaklings and quitters, not for future Ministers of State!"

His scribe frowned. "Would you care to put that in writing?"

Laphroig gritted his teeth. "I would be happy to do so." He could always deny he'd written it.

"Witnessed by two nobles of the realm?"

The teeth gritting turned to teeth grinding. "Of course." He could always have the nobles put to death.

"With copies to be sent to a personal designate for delivery to the King should anything unfortunate happen to me?"

"You are starting to irritate me, Cordstick!" Laphroig hissed. But he saw the look on the other's face and quickly held up his hands. "All right, all right, whatever you say. Is there anything else you require?"

Cordstick was edging toward the doorway. "I will find the Princess, my Lord. You have my word. But this time I will require a personal guard so as to avoid all the unpleasantness of this past out-ing. I think perhaps fifty or sixty armed men would . . ."

He ducked through the doorway just as the brass candlestick Laphroig had flung flew past his head and crashed into the wall be-yond. The padding of his limping feet could be heard receding into the distance.

Laphroig closed his eyes in an effort to calm himself, and he un-clenched his teeth long enough to whisper, "Just find her, you idiot!"

THE VOICE
IN THE SHADOWS

Mistaya returned to work in the Stacks the following morning and did not speak to Thom even once of the voice. She listened for it carefully, but the hours passed, and no one called out to her. The longer she waited, the more uncertain she became about what she had heard. Perhaps she had only imagined it after all. Perhaps the shadows and the overall creepiness of the Stacks had combined to make her think she was hearing a voice that wasn't there.

By midday, she was feeling so disillusioned about it that when Thom declared almost an hour early that it was lunchtime, she didn't even bother to argue.

Seated across from each other at the wooden table in the otherwise empty kitchen, they ate their soup and bread and drank their milk in silence.

Finally, Thom said, "You're not still mad at me for yesterday, are you?"

She stared at him, uncomprehending. Yesterday? Had he done something?

"When I told you I didn't want you going back into the Stacks by yourself?" he added helpfully.

"Oh, that!" she declared, remembering now. "No, I'm not mad about that. I wasn't mad then, either. I just wanted to have a look at what was back there because I thought I heard something." She shook her head in disgust. "But I think I must have imagined it."

He was quiet a moment. Then he said, "What do you think you heard, Ellice?"

His face was so serious, his eyes fixed on her as if she might reveal mysteries about which he could only wonder, that she grinned despite herself. "Actually, I thought I heard someone calling."

He didn't laugh at her, didn't crack a smile, didn't change expression at all. "Did the voice say, 'Help me'?"

Her eyes widened, and she reached impulsively for his hand. "You heard it, too?"

He nodded slowly, his shock of dark hair falling down over his eyes. He brushed it away in that familiar gesture. A lot about him was getting familiar to her by now. "I heard it. But not yesterday when you did. I heard it a few weeks ago, before you came."

She leaned forward eagerly, lowering her voice. "Did you go back into the Stacks to see if someone was there?"

"I did. That was when I found myself in the trouble I warned you about yesterday. We were supposed to talk about it last night, but you forgot. I think you were still wondering about the voice when you left me. Am I right?"

She nodded quickly. "I thought about it all night. And I did forget to ask you what happened. Will you tell me now?"

He leaned close as well, taking a careful look about the kitchen. "Two weeks ago, around midday, I heard the voice. Not for the first time, you understand. I'd heard it before, very faint, very far away. I was always alone, working on cataloging the books. I'd made myself believe I was hearing things. But this time, I couldn't ignore it. I went back into the darkest corners of the Stacks when everyone else was eating lunch or off doing something." He had dropped his own voice to a whisper to match hers. "I have good eyesight, so I didn't take any kind of light that might give me away to Pinch. You know how he's always lurking around. Anyway, I had heard the voice very clearly this time. It was saying the same thing, over and over. 'Help me! Help me!' You can imagine how I felt, hearing it pleading like that. I decided to try to track it down."

He paused, glancing left and right once more. "There were Throg Monkeys back there, dozens of them. But they weren't paying any attention to me. They were carrying books, but they didn't seem to be going anywhere. Some of them glanced my way before disappearing back into the shelving. One or two hissed at me. But they do that all the time, and I keep them under control with the whistle. So they let me pass without trying to stop me. It got darker and more shadowy as I went, and everything seemed to lose shape. Like it was all underwater, except it wasn't, of course. But the Stacks seemed to ripple and shimmer as if they were."

"Did you hear the voice while you were back there?" she interrupted.

He shook his head. "Not once. I listened for it, but didn't hear anything. The farther back I went, the deeper the Stacks seemed to go. I couldn't find the end. I don't mind telling you that it gave me the shivers. But I kept going anyway. I thought I was being silly feeling scared like that. After all, I hadn't been attacked or anything. Nothing had threatened me."

He took a deep breath. "But then something happened. Something grabbed at me. Not like a hand or anything. More like a suction of some kind, pulling at me with tremendous force. It happened all at once, and I lost my footing and fell down. I was being dragged along the floor toward this darkness that looked like a huge tunnel. I started screaming, but it didn't help. I managed to catch hold of one of the legs of the shelving and pull myself up against it. I clung to it with everything I had. Finally, I was able to pull myself back along the shelves until I was out of its grip. It took a long time, and no one came to help me. Which was probably a good thing, because if I'd been caught snooping I don't think I would still be here and I wouldn't have met you."

Mistaya rested her chin in her hands. "So you never did find out about the voice? Or any of the rest of it?"

He shook his head. "I didn't. And I didn't hear it again, either. I kept thinking I would, but I didn't. So I ended up doing what you did. I convinced myself I was mistaken. I knew I wasn't supposed to go back into the Stacks in the first place——His Eminence and Pinch had made that pretty clear. I just chalked the whole thing up to not doing what I had been told and almost paying the penalty for my disobedience. Not that I didn't wonder; I just didn't know what I should do."

"So what do you think we should do now?" she asked him. "Now that I've heard the voice, too. Now that we know something is back there." She watched his face as she said it, curious to measure his response. "Shouldn't we do something?"

He gave her a momentary look of disbelief, and then he grinned. "Of course we should do something. But we have to do it together, and we have to be very careful."

"We should have a better chance if there are two of us," she declared excitedly. "We can protect each other."

"We'd better go in at night, when everyone is asleep. Maybe whatever is back there will be sleeping, too."

She nodded eagerly. "When do we go?"

"Soon as possible, I guess. Tonight?"

She grabbed his hand impulsively and squeezed it. "I like you, Thom of Libiris! I like you a lot!"

To his credit, he blushed bright red and looked immensely pleased.

They spent the afternoon planning their nighttime excursion, talking about it in low voices as they worked on the cataloging of the books, aware that Rufus Pinch was never far away and always listening. They decided they would go in around midnight, when everyone should be sleeping and no one would be working in the Stacks. They would take glow sticks to give them light, since the shelf torches were always extinguished at night, and they would make their way back into the shadowy recesses of the cavernous room until they found its end. If they were lucky, they would hear the voice while they were doing so. If not, they might at least find the back wall and see what was there.

Several times, as their conversation drifted on to other subjects, Thom remarked again that some of the books from the library seemed to be missing. It was impossible to tell which ones because all he had been given to work with by His Eminence was a list of catalog numbers. The only way he could even tell that books were missing was because he couldn't find a match for some of the numbers on the list, and occasionally he noticed gaps in the books on the shelves.

"Why don't they give you the titles instead of just the numbers?" Mistaya asked him.

He shrugged. "I don't know. His Eminence said I didn't need the titles, only the numbers. Maybe he was trying to save on ink."

"Did you tell him that there were books missing?"

"I told him. He said that maybe they weren't really missing, that they were just misplaced. But finding any of them would have meant searching the whole of the Stacks, and I don't have that sort of time. I try to keep an eye out for them, but I haven't found any yet."

She thought about it a moment. "Do the catalog numbers have any relationship to one another? If they did, maybe we could figure out what section the missing books came from."

"The numbers are all different. They don't share any common points that I can determine. Hey, would you hand me that book right there? The one with the red lettering on the cover?"

The subject was dropped again, and they continued with their work in silence. Mistaya soon found herself thinking about how long ago and far away her time at Carrington seemed. It wasn't really either one, but it seemed that way thinking on it. From studying the literature, sciences, and history of a world that wasn't even her own to cataloging ancient books in a library no one ever used in a world no one outside her own even knew existed struck her as bizarre. Neither endeavor seemed particularly important to her, nor compelling in a way that made her feel she was using her time well. She had felt trapped at Carrington and she felt trapped all over again here at Libiris. Why couldn't she find a way to make herself feel useful? Why did she feel so adrift no matter what she was doing?

For a moment, a single moment, she thought about leaving and going home. How bad could it be, if she did? She would have to face up to her father's disappointment and possibly his anger. She would have to prepare herself for a heated discussion about what would happen next. But what was the worst that could come out of that discussion? Maybe she would be sent back to Libiris, but maybe not. If she could manage to keep her temper in check and argue logically and forcefully, perhaps she could manage to talk him into having her do something else. Wouldn't that be better than what she was doing now?

Still, that would mean leaving Thom, perhaps for good, and she wasn't quite ready to do that. She liked being with him; even though most of what they did was work, she was having fun.

"Have you ever asked His Eminence for a copy of his master list of the books shelved at Libiris?" she asked after a while, frustrated by finding yet another set of gaps in the shelves.

Thom shook his head. "I don't think he would give it to me."

She stood up abruptly. "Maybe not. But I think it's worth asking. Let me try."

"Ellice, wait," he objected.

"I'll just be a minute," she called back to him, already on her way. "Don't worry, I won't cause trouble."

Without waiting for his response, she crossed the room to the far wall and followed the aisles through the shelving back to the door leading to Craswell Crabbit's office. The Stacks felt huge and empty, and even her soft footfalls echoed in the cavernous expanse. She could not quite shed her distaste for the feelings the library engendered in her.

As she drew closer to her destination, she heard voices from inside. To her surprise, the door was cracked open.

She crept closer, curious now, taking slow, measured steps so as not to give herself away. She could hear Crabbit and Rufus Pinch, their conversation low and guarded. As if they didn't want anyone to hear, she thought. She slowed further. If she was caught sneaking around like this, she would no doubt be tossed through the front door of Libiris instantly.

" . . . easier if we had them on this side of the wall," Pinch was saying. "Then we wouldn't have to worry about hauling them all back again."

"Easier, yes," His Eminence agreed, "but ineffective for our needs. To work their magic, they need to be right where they are."

"I don't trust our so-called allies," Pinch pressed, his voice a low growl that bordered on a whine. "What if they go back on their bargain?"

"Stop fretting, Mr. Pinch. What possible reason could they have for doing that? They want out, don't they? And not just into Landover. They need me to accomplish that. They don't have the skills and the experience to read the necessary passages."

"They might know more than you think."

"They might . . ." His Eminence paused. "Mr. Pinch, did you leave that door open when you entered? That wasn't very wise of you. Close it now, please."

Mistaya tiptoed backward as swiftly as she could to where the shelving unit ended and flattened herself against the wall. She held her breath until she heard the door close, then stayed where she was for another few minutes before moving silently away.

When she got back to Thom, he asked, "Any luck?"

"I didn't ask," she told him. She gave him a shrug and what she hoped was a disarming grin. "He was busy with something else."

--―∞―--

She thought about the conversation between His Eminence and Pinch for the rest of the afternoon. She was still thinking about it at dinner that night, sitting with Thom, and later when she went to bed.

But when Thom woke her at midnight, leaning close and gently shaking her shoulder until she came awake, it was all forgotten.

"Shhh!" he whispered, putting a finger to his lips. "No talking, no noise at all!"

She was already dressed as she rolled out of her bed and slipped on her boots. The room was dark except for a sliver of moonlight that slanted down through the single high, narrow window on the east wall. She straightened her clothing, retightened her belt, and gave him a nod. He handed her one of the two glow sticks he was carrying, but she didn't light it. By previous agreement, they would work their way into the Stacks in the dark and light the glow sticks when they could no longer see at all.

They slipped from her bedroom with Thom leading the way, their footfalls virtually noiseless in the deep silence. The hallway beyond was empty and dark, and they passed down it without seeing or hearing anything or anyone. When they reached the Stacks, Thom held up his hand for a moment while he studied the larger room carefully. She listened as well, but heard nothing. When both were satisfied that it was safe, they slipped from the shadows of the hallway into the cavernous silence of the Stacks.

In the dark upper reaches of the room, something scurried along the beams and was gone. Mistaya exchanged a hurried glance with Thom, but he shook his head. Whatever was up there wasn't interested in them.

They crossed the open space to the beginning of the shelving aisles and started for the back of the room.

Somewhere behind them, a door opened and closed on squeaky hinges, the sound echoing in the deep silence.

They froze as one, halfway down the aisle at the first set of shelves, eyes peering back over their shoulders, waiting. Mistaya quit breathing for long moments, certain that someone was about to appear. But no one did, and the sound of the squeaking hinges did not come again. They continued to wait, not wanting to make a mistake, to take an unnecessary or foolish risk. If either one decided to call it off, they had agreed, the other would not argue. They would simply wait and try another time.

Finally, long moments later, they looked at each other and nodded wordlessly. The hunt would go on.

Back into the darkness they crept, moving carefully between
shelving units that had the feel of confining walls. The small amount
of moonlight let in by the high windows at the front of the room
slowly faded behind them, leaving the darkness thicker and more
impenetrable. At last they could see almost nothing, and they had to
feel their way ahead by using the shelves as guide rails.

When the last of the light dimmed to nothing more than a distant glimmer, Thom brought them to a stop. They still hadn't
reached the back wall, and there was no indication that they would
anytime soon.

"We have to use the glow sticks," he whispered in her ear. "Remember. They only last for two hours, so we have to get back before
time runs out."

She nodded that she understood. Together they broke off the
tips, and a soft, golden glow spread away in a pool of light that extended about six feet from each bearer. The way forward made
clear, they started ahead once more.

By now, Mistaya thought, they must have covered several hundred yards. But that was impossible. The Stacks couldn't be that
deep. There had to be magic at work, and she wondered who had set
it in place and why. She reached out for its source, but couldn't find
it. She also wondered at the blackness of the space. She seemed to
remember from her work in the daytime that windows on both
walls extended back for as far as she could see. Why weren't those
windows permitting any moonlight to enter the room? She knew
the moon was full and the sky clear that night. Was the magic that
made the room seem so much larger also blocking the light and
cloaking the room in shadows?

Time slipped away, and still they didn't find the back wall. Mistaya began to grow impatient—and more than a little uneasy.

Finally, Thom brought them to a halt once more. "We need to
start back," he whispered in her ear. His face was so close she could
feel the heat of his body. "The glow sticks are half gone."

"Why is it taking so long?" she hissed.

"I don't know. It didn't take this long before. It took much less time. Something is wrong."

"I think it's magic that's making us think the room is much larger and the way much longer!" She hesitated. "I know a little about how it works."

To his credit, he didn't ask for an explanation. "You want to go on?"

"For a little longer. I think we can find our way back."

They pushed on, their sense of urgency growing exponentially. Mistaya wasn't certain how much longer they could search, but she didn't want to give up until she absolutely had to. Thom, she sensed, wouldn't quit before she did, no matter what. His pride wouldn't let him. He was the older and stronger of the two; he would tough it out for as long as she did.

Then, all of a sudden, she heard the voice.

Help me! Help me!

From the way Thom drew up short, his body going rigid, she knew that he had heard it, too.

"Just ahead!" she whispered encouragingly, even though she wasn't at all sure that this was so.

But then she felt the pressure from whatever it was that had gripped Thom two weeks earlier, a sucking at the air about her that gripped her and held her fast, pulling her forward. She saw Thom lurch and stumble, his arms flailing. They collapsed in a tangle of limbs, grasping first at each other and then at the shelving units, trying unsuccessfully to get hold of something as they skidded along the floor and down the aisle. Whatever was pulling them forward was more powerful than she had expected, an irresistible force she could not fight against. She tried to get into a kneeling position, yet the force not only pulled her relentlessly ahead but held her down. The glow stick flew from her hand and was lost. She almost lost her grip on Thom, but just barely managed to hang on to one of his strong legs.

Ahead, a huge blackness hove into view, a tunnel of such impenetrable darkness that it looked as if it would swallow them whole. In that moment, she thought they were lost. So much so that she began to summon her magic in a last-ditch attempt to save them.

But Thom, resourceful as always, finally managed to grab hold of a leg of one of the shelving units and pull them both over to huddle against the heavy structure, anchoring them in place against the sucking force. She heard a sound like breathing, deep and powerful, and the force increased. But Thom held them fast, refusing to give in to it. She pressed herself against him, tucking her head against his leg, her face flattened to the worn wooden floor of the room.

Which was when she felt the sudden flush of warmth against her face. She jerked away in surprise, but then pressed down again with her cheek to make sure. The floor was pulsing softly, a sensation that was unmistakable. There was a life force embedded in the wooden boards. She felt the beating of its heart, and the entire experience was suddenly so familiar that she could hardly believe it. She knew what this was! She had known since she was a child!

It was Sterling Silver, the castle that cared for and nurtured the Kings and Queens of Landover and their families. It sheltered and protected them against the elements and enemies alike. It warmed them when they were cold and cooled them when they were hot. It provided them with food and clothing. It could determine their physical needs and to a very large extent satisfy them.

It was her home!

But how could that be? Sterling Silver was a sentient being formed of magic-infused materials, and it was the only one of its kind. Was it really the castle's life force she was feeling? If so, how had it found its way here when it was rooted in the bedrock of the island on which it had been built?

The glow stick that Thom held went out, and they were left in blackness. The sucking force continued to pull at them for a long time after that, but finally it eased into a soft breathing and then ceased altogether. Mistaya and Thom lay together, listening to the silence, waiting for something more. Mistaya kept her face pressed to the floor, but the warmth she had felt earlier was fading away.

Don't go, she thought. *Don't leave me.*

But there was nothing she could do to make it stay, and seconds later it was gone.

She sat up again cautiously, placing her back against the shelving unit that had served as an anchor, the darkness deep and unbroken all around. The warmth she had felt in the floor and the pulsing of the life that had created it had both disappeared.

Mistaya could not understand. What had just happened?

"I think we should quit for tonight," Thom said softly, a disembodied voice in the black.

"I suppose so," she agreed. She was silent a moment, and then she said, "Thom, did you feel anything in the floor?"

She could hear him sitting up next to her. "Like what?"

"A pulsing, a warmth?"

"I don't know," he admitted. "I was busy trying to hold on to the shelving so we wouldn't be sucked down into that tunnel. Did you feel all that? The pulsing and the warmth?"

She wasn't sure what to say now. "I might have been mistaken," she answered. "I was pretty scared."

He laughed quietly. "So was I. It wasn't any easier this time, even knowing what to expect. But I won't give up if you won't."

She reached out and squeezed his arm. "You know I won't give up. Thanks for sticking with me."

They rose and began groping their way back down the aisle, using the edges of the shelves to guide them, careful to keep together in the deep gloom. They didn't speak of what had happened, knowing it was better to wait until later. Mistaya wondered how much time had passed. If magic had obscured distance and light, it could have obscured time, as well. It could have obscured everything they had experienced. Nothing might have been what they thought it was.

Yet she couldn't dismiss the strong feeling of recognition that had flooded through her. She wasn't mistaken about that, but she didn't know what it meant. Was she sensing the presence of her home? Had Sterling Silver reached out to her somehow? Was it a warning that something was wrong at home? Or perhaps it wasn't the castle at all. Perhaps it was Libiris she was feeling. But if so, why did it feel like it was alive?

Those questions, in turn, made her wonder anew about the voice. Exactly who was it that was calling?

They had almost reached the front of the Stacks and Mistaya was thinking of how good it was going to feel to sleep when a hunched figure appeared abruptly in their path, and a familiar wizened face lifted into the pale wash of the moonlight.

"Out for a little nighttime walk, are we?" asked Rufus Pinch with a visible sneer.

"We were just . . . ," Mistaya began.

"Just looking for . . . ," Thom picked up.

Pinch held up both hands. "Doing what you were expressly forbidden to do. That's what you were doing! Well, now you're going to have to pay the price for your disobedience, aren't you? His Eminence will know how to deal with you!"

Mistaya felt her heart sink. She had ruined everything.

"Off to your rooms!" Pinch ordered, making shooing motions with his hands. "Don't even think of trying to do anything else. Lock yourselves in and remain there until sunrise. Then report to His Eminence first thing. Now go! Get!"

Obediently, Mistaya and Thom headed out of the Stacks. Mistaya was miserable. She would be sent home for certain. In all likelihood, Thom would be punished in some equally unpleasant way. And it was all because of her.

"Don't worry," Thom declared cheerfully as they parted for the night.

"I won't," she promised. But of course, she already was.

She reached her bedroom sunk in a miasma of gloom and dark thoughts, opened the door, and nearly jumped with fright when a tall, gangly figure seated on the edge of her bed abruptly stood.

"Hello, Mistaya," said Questor Thews, and held out his hands in greeting.

REVELATIONS

Mistaya gave a small cry of mingled relief and joy and rushed over to her old friend, wrapping her arms about him with such ferocity that she could hear his shocked gasp. She crushed his body against hers, the feel of his bony frame, all the angles and knobs so wonderfully familiar and welcome. Her reaction surprised her, but it didn't lessen the intensity of her enthusiasm. She had never been so glad to see anyone in her life.

"Mistaya, goodness!" he managed, his voice a bit strangled, but obviously pleased. "Did you miss me so much?"

"I *did* miss you," she whispered into his shoulder. "Oh, I'm so glad you're here!"

The long, thin hands patted her hair comfortingly. "Well, I would have come sooner had I known you were in such distress. Of course, it would have helped if you had told me just where you were."

"I know, I know. I'm sorry. But I just couldn't . . ."

She gave a deep, long sigh, and then she backed away from him far enough that they were eye-to-eye. "How *did* you find me?"

"It was a guess," he advised, rather sheepishly. "When we couldn't find you any other way, Abernathy and I tried to think where the last place was that we would expect you to go. A kind of reverse psychology, I suppose. We put ourselves in your shoes—

which isn't all that easy to do, I might add—and we came up with Libiris. It didn't make a whole lot of sense, but we were running out of options. So we decided to come here and see if we might possibly be right."

"Abernathy is here, too?"

"Outside with the G'home Gnomes." The blue eyes twinkled. "They gave you up, I am afraid. They couldn't help themselves. They denied everything, but when G'home Gnomes deny everything, it is usually true. I left them in Abernathy's care and came inside for a look."

"But how did you manage that? This place is guarded like a fortress!"

"Oh, I know a few tricks about how to get in and out of places." He took her hands in his own and squeezed them. "Come. Sit down on the bed while we talk. My bones do not allow for prolonged periods of standing in place anymore."

They sat on the bed, the scarecrow wizard and the young girl to whom he had always been mentor and friend. She kept one arm around him, as if afraid she might lose him. It was uncharacteristic of her to be so clingy; she saw herself as independent and strong, not as a child in need of an adult's protective presence. But just now, in this time and place, all that seemed unimportant.

"It wasn't their fault, you know," she told him. "Poggwydd went with me to grandfather because I made him. I threatened him. I told him that if he didn't come with me, he'd be blamed for my disappearing because he was the last one to be seen with me." She felt embarrassed by her admission, but didn't back away from it. "The truth is, I was afraid to go alone. Shoopdiesel just happened along and stayed because he's Poggwydd's friend."

Questor Thews nodded. "I thought it might be something like that. Their attempts at an explanation suggested as much. They kept insisting that they only did what was necessary to look after you. I guess that included bringing you here, too."

"No, they didn't have anything to do with that. That was all because of the cat."

"Edgewood Dirk?"

She sighed, somehow unsurprised that the wizard knew. "He showed up at Elderew after Grandfather said I would have to go home. He was the one who suggested that nobody would think to look for me at Libiris. He said he'd come with me and hide me with his magic from any other magic that might uncover my presence." She shrugged. "I don't know what I was thinking, coming to the one place I said I wouldn't go. But I came, anyway. It just seemed to be the only thing to do. He was pretty persuasive."

"Edgewood Dirk can be like that. But you have to be careful of him."

"I guess so. Once we got here, he disappeared, and I haven't seen him since. I don't know where he went."

Questor grimaced. "If I know Dirk—and I do—he will not have gone very far away. You have to understand. A Prism Cat is a fairy creature, and his motives are his own. But he always does things for a reason, and bringing you here was not accidental. He brought you here for a purpose. You just don't know what it is yet."

He gave her a reassuring smile. "Now tell me everything else that happened."

Well, she wasn't about to do that, of course. And she didn't. But she did tell him some of it: her arrival at Libiris and Rufus Pinch's refusal to admit her; Thom's intervention; His Eminence's decision to let her remain and work with her "brother" in the Stacks; the terrible impossibility of the task to which she and Thom had been set; the ways in which they were spied upon and mistrusted by both His Eminence and Pinch. Finally, she worked her way around to the two questions that weighed most heavily on her mind and to which she was hoping he might provide the answers.

"A couple of very strange things happened during the last few days, Questor," she began. "Yesterday, I heard a voice calling out to me. Or to someone, at any rate. I heard it clearly. Thom heard it too, both tonight and several weeks earlier, before I got here. We talked about it. We don't think we were mistaken."

She chose her words carefully. She had no intention of revealing too many details. If Questor thought she was in any real danger, he would take her away at once, and she wasn't yet ready to go. For starters, things with Thom were just getting interesting. Besides, she didn't think that she was in any real danger.

Questor nodded as if he understood. "You probably did hear something."

"All right," she continued, wanting to get the rest of it out before she heard what he had to say on the matter. "The other thing is that while I was lying on the floor, just resting for a moment"—she was making it up as she went—"I put my cheek against the wooden boards and felt a pulse and a warmth that reminded me instantly of Sterling Silver. But I don't understand how that could be."

She waited for his response, which wasn't given immediately. Instead, the wizard pursed his lips, cocked first one and then the other eyebrow, narrowed his eyes, and then drew in and let out a long, sustained breath.

"Well," he said, as if that pretty much covered it.

"Well, what?"

"If you had not gone off on your own, so determined that none of what has already happened *would* happen, if instead you had taken the time to learn about Libiris first, you might have avoided a good deal of the confusion in which you now find yourself mired."

He held up one finger in warning as she was about to object. "I just think you need to hear how difficult you have made things for people who love you before I tell you what you want to know. You caused us all a great deal of worry, Mistaya. It isn't as if you didn't know we would wonder whether something had happened to you. We have all been thinking of little else since you disappeared. If your grandfather had not sent word that you came to see him, we might not even have known that much."

"I know," she said. She had left them dangling, running off like that. But what choice did she have? Still, an apology couldn't hurt. "I'm sorry," she added, only half meaning it.

He gave an emphatic nod. "Then we shall put this behind us. Let me tell you a few things about Libiris that you do not know. Things, I would point out again, that I would have told you much earlier had you agreed to come here voluntarily with me as your companion. But it is not too late to rectify that now."

He paused. "I suppose I should start by telling you that you are not mistaken in believing that Libiris feels like Sterling Silver. It does, and there is a good reason for it. The buildings share a commonality that you know nothing about. Sterling Silver was constructed of materials and magic in equal parts in a time long since forgotten. She was created to be a sentient being, a caregiver for Landover's Kings and Queens, a protector for their families. You know all this from your studies. Libiris shares something of those same characteristics, though to a lesser extent. When the old King had her built, back in the years before your father became ruler, he did so using materials taken from Sterling Silver. He did so in hopes that Libiris, like Sterling Silver, would take on a life of its own and become a living organism that would care for its books just as the King's castle cared for its royal family."

He gave her a knowing look. "Why could this be so? Because the Kings of Landover had discovered over the years that left to her own devices and occupied by a true king, Sterling Silver would take care of herself without human or fairy assistance. She could repair damage, brighten tarnish, clean off dirt and grime, and generally revitalize herself all on her own. It only became a problem for her to perform when no King sat upon the throne and the central purpose of her existence was undermined.

"The old King, then, instructed the court wizard to remove shelving throughout the castle to form the foundation for the Stacks and to take some stone from the battlements and ramparts to cap the walls of the library buildings. Just enough magically infused material to give Libiris a life of her own. Just enough so that she, too, would be able to function as an independent entity. Of course, this process was not an exact science, and the old King's belief that you could graft pieces of one building onto another and get the same results was flawed. Nor did it help that his court wizard was my brother, who was already planning to take control when the old King was dead."

He sighed. "So the effort failed, although not altogether. Libiris did become a sentient being, but on a much lower level of intelligence than Sterling Silver. There simply were not enough magically enhanced materials employed to achieve the desired result. The old King ended up with a building that was little more than a child. It could perform basic tasks, but it lacked the capacity for critical thought and problem solving. Its ability to care for itself and the books it housed was severely limited."

"But was it Libiris that I heard calling out to me?" she pressed.

"Of course. The feeling of life in the flooring of the stacks and of a pulse that signaled a living presence was not something you imagined. Libiris is alive, and she obviously *chose* to call out to you and to make herself known. Perhaps she senses a kinship born of your connection with Sterling Silver. I don't know. I can only guess."

Mistaya thought about it a moment. Questor's story explained most of what she had encountered, but not all. There was nothing that explained the black hole in the back of the Stacks or the fact that the Stacks themselves seemed to go on endlessly or that there was magic being employed to disguise time and place and to mute light. She didn't think this could be the work of Libiris, given her limitations. This was someone or something else. Then there was the matter of the conversation she had overheard between His Eminence and Pinch. Clearly, it had something to do with what was happening at Libiris.

But she couldn't tell him any of this or even talk about it in general terms without giving him too many reasons to spirit her back home.

"What do you think I should do about the meeting tomorrow morning with His Eminence?" she asked instead. "How do I explain what Thom and I did so that he won't banish us?"

Questor Thews frowned reprovingly. "You are a Princess of Landover, Mistaya Holiday, and you do not answer to people like Craswell Crabbit or Rufus Pinch for anything. Once you have revealed yourself to them, we can dismiss this matter and return home."

"What?" She jumped to her feet, her worst fear realized. "What are you saying? Go home? I can't go home!"

Questor was suddenly flustered. "But why not? I can't just leave you here, Mistaya! What do you expect me to do—go back and let your parents continue to wonder what has happened to you?"

Well, in point of fact, she did. But she also knew from the way he said it that she had better change her thinking. Besides, he was right. She couldn't just leave her parents hanging with the possibility that she might be injured or in trouble. Still, she didn't want them to interfere with what she was doing.

She took a deep, steadying breath. "I won't give up on what I'm doing as if it didn't matter," she said to the wizard, emphasizing her words. "I have to see this through, and I don't want to do it as a Princess of Landover. I want to do it as Thom's sister, Ellice. I don't expect you to understand this. But it's something I've started that I intend to finish. I want to know more about that voice trying to communicate with me. I think there was a reason for it, Questor, and I have to stay long enough to find out what it is."

The old man shook his head. "I don't like it. I don't trust Crabbit or Pinch. Especially Crabbit. You don't know him as I do, Mistaya. For starters, he is a wizard and a very dangerous one at that. He was exiled to Libiris by the old King, well before your father's time in Landover, for that very reason. It was necessary to put him somewhere that he wouldn't cause trouble."

"What sort of trouble had he caused earlier?" she asked, curious now.

Questor sighed. "This and that. He was an ambitious sort and lacked anything remotely connected to scruples. He was intent on advancing his position at court, and he didn't care what it took to achieve that end. The position he coveted most was my own. Unfortunately for him, it was occupied at the time by my brother, the man who recruited your father to Landover and very nearly added him to a long list of failed rulers. But my brother was a more formidable adversary than Craswell Crabbit anticipated, and he was quick to recognize the other's ambitions and was responsible for his exile. Crabbit's magic made him a dangerous man, but my brother was more dangerous still."

"But he didn't try to come back to Sterling Silver when you became court wizard and my father King?"

Questor shook his head. "No, and that was something of a surprise. I had thought that after my brother was disposed of and your father made King, he would be one of the first to make his appearance and offer his services. That would be very like him. But he failed to do so, and after a while I simply stopped thinking about it."

She frowned. "Yet you were prepared to send me here?"

"Not alone, I wasn't. Only if I was in your company, your supervisor for this job of reopening the library and your protector against any threats. I wasn't worried about Crabbit specifically. Frankly, it had been so long that I wasn't even sure he was still here. I thought he might have moved on. I regret that I was wrong and regret even more that you had to encounter him on your own."

"It hasn't been such a problem," she declared quickly, shrugging the matter off. She paused. "Let me make a suggestion," she said impulsively. "A compromise. You leave me here and go back to my parents and tell them where I am. Let them know I'm fine, and I'm doing what Father sent me to do in the first place. Sort of, anyway. Ask him to give me a chance to work on this a little while longer before he hauls me home. Tell him all I want is a chance to prove myself. Besides, Thom risked a lot for me, and it wouldn't be right if I just walked out on him."

"I am not comfortable with the idea of leaving you here alone," the old man declared, pulling at his whiskers. "If Craswell Crabbit were gone, as I had hoped he would be by now, I would feel better about your staying. As it is . . ."

"I'll be careful," she promised. "I have my magic to protect me, don't I? Didn't you train me yourself? Besides, I don't think I'm in any real danger. His Eminence hasn't threatened me or anything."

"He won't bother with threatening you if you get in his way. I know him. He is a snake. He never should have been appointed director of the library, but the old King was failing and didn't see." Questor shook his head. "Are you sure he doesn't know who you are?"

"He hasn't said or done anything that would suggest he thinks I'm anyone other than Thom's sister, Ellice."

But she wondered suddenly if she had missed something. Was it possible that His Eminence had recognized her and was keeping her here for reasons of his own? The possibility sent a sudden chill up her spine.

"This business with the voice bothers me, too. I just don't like any of it, Mistaya. I think you should come with me."

She shook her head stubbornly. "It was your idea for me to come here in the first place," she pointed out, brushing aside her concerns about His Eminence. "Yours and Abernathy's. Well, I did what you wanted. What my mother and father wanted, too. And now you want me to just walk away, to give up. Like I did at Carrington?"

She reached out and took the old man's hands in her own. "Please, Questor. Let me stay. Let me see this through. This is as much for me as it is for Thom; I know that now. I need to do this. Please!"

Questor Thews cleared his throat. "If I agree to this—and I am not saying yet I will—I want your word that you will not do anything to place yourself in danger. I do not know what hearing that voice means, whether it is Libiris speaking or someone else, but before you go off investigating the source—no, no, Mistaya, let me finish—before you do anything that puts you at risk, you will call on one of us to help you. And I do not mean this boy, whoever he is. I mean myself or your father or someone else who can protect you. Otherwise, you can pack your clothes and prepare to leave right now. I want your word."

"You have it," Mistaya declared, prepared to say or do whatever it took to get him to agree to let her stay.

"Then I have something for you." Questor reached into his pocket and withdrew a round stone not much bigger than a pebble.

It was infused with striations of various colors that swam through its surface like the currents in a river. "Take this," he ordered.

He handed it to her, and she held it in the palm of her hand, looking down at it. "This is a rainbow crush," the wizard advised. "Should you need to call for help, this stone will allow you to do so. You give it a message and tell it who you want the message to reach—you say the words in your mind—then drop the stone to the ground and stamp on it. Whoever you summoned will hear your voice speaking the message and respond accordingly. If you feel you are in any danger at all, you are to use it at once. Understood?"

She nodded. "Understood."

"You are not to rely on your own magic to protect you except as a last resort. You are well schooled in its use, but you are not well practiced. Too many things can go wrong. Use the crush instead and summon one of us."

She was tempted to remind him that her magic had helped save his life five years earlier, but decided that was pushing things. "I've never heard of a rainbow crush," she said instead.

"That is because there are only a few in existence. They are very precious and difficult to come by. So take care of yours and use it wisely." He stood up. "Time for me to be going. Morning is almost here, and I do not want to be found inside these walls when it arrives."

She put the rainbow crush in her pocket and hugged him to her. "Thank you, Questor, for trusting me. You won't regret it."

"I'd better not," he declared. "Do not forget that when I leave here, I go back to the castle and your parents. I cannot speak for what they will choose to do; they may come here whether you like it or not. So whatever you need to do, do it quickly."

"All right." She stepped back from him. "But you can tell them you've seen me and I'm fine. Assuming His Eminence doesn't throw me out after our meeting. After hearing from Rufus Pinch, he might do exactly that. Thom and me both. I might be home before you are."

He gave a disapproving grunt. "That would not be the worst thing in the world. Think of the satisfaction you will feel if he does throw you out and you return as Princess of Landover and his new employer. Then you can throw him out!"

She grinned. "That does have a certain appeal."

"Just remember one thing." He was serious again, his frown back in place. "Craswell Crabbit is no one to fool with. He has skills and trickery of his own to call on if he needs them and an appalling lack of morals to back them up. If there is something to be gained, he will not hesitate to sacrifice anyone or anything that stands in his way. You keep on being the poor little peasant girl who doesn't know anything and let him toss you through the door if that is what he wants. No heroics."

"I promise to be careful." She kissed him on the cheek. "Now you'd better go."

"One thing more," he added, turning back as he reached the door. "I am taking those G'home Gnomes with me. Keeping them here is just asking for trouble. All they are doing out there is plotting ways to steal the livestock. That does nothing to help you. *They* do nothing to help you, come to that. So back they go!"

She felt a momentary pang of regret for Poggwydd and Shoopdiesel, who had tried so hard to help her. But she also felt a huge relief. "Say good-bye for me."

He smiled anew, nodded his approval of something or other, and disappeared through the door into the darkness of the hallway. She stared after him, smiling back. When he was gone, all that remained was the whisper of his robes and the warmth she felt on thinking how lucky she was to have him as her friend.

"It seems you have a problem understanding the difference between obedience and disobedience," His Eminence declared, his overlarge head cocking to one side as if somehow dislodged from his neck. He rocked back in his chair with his fingers steepled and gave them a stern look. His tall, angular, skeletal form seemed to fold over on itself as he leaned forward suddenly. "A rather serious problem, it appears."

It was first light, and Mistaya stood beside Thom on the other side of the desk facing their judge and jury. Rufus Pinch lurked off to one side, hunched over and frowning, which was pretty much what he did the rest of the time, so there was nothing troubling there. His Eminence, on the other hand, was scowling in a way suggesting that the outcome of this trial was unlikely to be favorable to them no matter what their defense.

"The rules are quite clear about use of the Stacks," he continued, looking thoughtful. "You are to be there only during working hours. You are to stay in your assigned area of work. You are to concentrate on the task you have been given and no other. You are not to go outside your area of work and never are you to go back into the Stacks unaccompanied and without permission. I believe I made that quite clear to you, Thom, on your arrival, did I not?"

"Yes, Your Eminence, but—"

One bony hand lifted quickly to cut him off. "Your time to speak will come later. Just answer my questions." He turned to Mistaya. "Did Thom explain the rules to you, Ellice?"

"Yes, Your Eminence."

"So when you went into the Stacks at midnight or whatever hour it was, you knew you were there in violation of the rules, didn't you?"

"Yes, Your Eminence."

Craswell Crabbit glanced over at Rufus Pinch, who managed a sour smile and a curt nod. "Mr. Pinch?"

"They were where they weren't supposed to be and they were obviously doing something they weren't supposed to do. The evidence is quite clear. Our course of action should be just as clear. This is a flagrant violation of the rules."

"So it seems." His Eminence gave a huge sigh, turning back to the accused. "Have you anything to say for yourselves?" he asked, looking from one to the other.

"Yes, Your Eminence, I do," Mistaya said suddenly, stepping forward. She lifted her chin and met his judgmental gaze bravely. She deliberately did not look at Thom. "If you please."

He nodded. "Say whatever it is you want to say, Ellice."

"None of this is Thom's fault. It is entirely mine, and whatever punishment you care to deliver I will accept it without complaint. But Thom was only trying to help me, the way big brothers do their little sisters when they discover that their hearts have been broken."

"Is that so?" His Eminence sounded only marginally interested. "Please explain yourself."

Mistaya never hesitated. "While working in the Stacks the other day, I lost a pendant, a family heirloom. A gift, actually, from my mother. I wear it everywhere, but somehow the chain broke and the pendant was lost. I didn't realize it right away, and when I did, I looked for it and couldn't find it. I was devastated. I searched for it two days straight, looking all around the areas in which we worked. I looked for it in the kitchen and all the common rooms and even my bedroom. But it was gone."

She paused, taking time to look as if she were composing herself. "Then it occurred to me that one of the Throg Monkeys might have taken it. Maybe just to look at, but maybe to keep. So I begged Thom to go with me back into the Stacks while everyone was sleeping to see if it might have been carried back there somewhere. It was a foolish thing to do, but that pendant meant everything to me."

She cried a little, real tears. "It was all I had left to remind me of my mother," she whispered, sobbing softly. "We lost her not long ago . . ."

"It was my fault as much as hers, Your Eminence," Thom cut in suddenly. "I knew how much she valued that pendant. I didn't want her to lose it. So I said I would take her into the Stacks to look for it."

"Knowing you were breaking the rules?" His Eminence pressed.

"Knowing I was," Thom agreed. "I admit it. I hoped no one would find out, but Rufus was on watch, as usual."

"Of course I was on watch!" the little man snapped. "I am always on watch against the likes of you and your sister!"

"Rufus, Rufus," Craswell Crabbit soothed.

"Well, it's true!" the other hissed.

"But we didn't get very far," Thom added quickly. "We were afraid to do something that bold. We only looked a little way before coming back. The Stacks are too huge for a search of the sort that was needed, and if the Throg Monkeys took the pendant—which they might have done, since they take things all the time—then I needed to confront them and find out what they had done with it."

"Yes, yes, I'm sure that all this is true." His Eminence looked and sounded bored. "But rules are rules."

"Your Eminence," Thom replied, straightening. "I will save you the trouble of making a decision on our punishment. A mistake has been made and a rule violated. There is no excuse. Ellice and I will pack our bags and leave immediately. After seeing my sister safely home, I will return and complete the remainder of my service working in the stables."

Rufus Pinch looked pleased. But His Eminence held up both hands and shook his head slowly. "No, no, that won't do at all. Your service here is not for mucking out stables, it is for cataloging and organizing books. You will stay and work as you have committed yourself to doing."

He turned to Mistaya. "As for you, Ellice, I have a different plan in mind. Because I am by nature a generous and forgiving person, I am going to make an exception this one time and give you another chance. You may stay to help your brother. But as punishment for your disobedience, you will do service in the stables every third day for an entire month cleaning up after the animals. Mind you, young lady, should you violate the rules again—any rules—you will be dismissed immediately. There will be no discussion, no excuses, and no further leniencies. One misstep, and you are gone. Do we understand each other?"

Mistaya hung her head meekly. "Yes, Your Eminence."

He ignored Rufus Pinch, who was looking at him with a mix of astonishment and rage, his face twisted, his fists balled, and his entire body arched like an angry cat's.

"You will begin your month of stable service tomorrow morning," he said to Mistaya.

"Yes, Your Eminence," she repeated.

"Very well, the matter is closed. Now get back to work, both of you."

Once the door had closed behind the so-called brother and sister, Rufus Pinch wheeled on His Eminence, so enraged that he was hopping up and down. "What are you doing? They were lying, Craswell! Lying from first word to last! Couldn't you tell that, you idiot?"

"Watch your tongue, Mr. Pinch," the other cautioned, holding up one finger and touching his long nose. "Or I shall have to remove it."

But Rufus Pinch was too furious to take notice of what he perceived to be idle threats. "They were lying!" he screamed.

His Eminence smiled and nodded. "Yes, I know that."

The other man stared at him. "You know that? Then why aren't you doing something about it? Why don't you throw them out?"

"Because I wish to keep them working in the Stacks, Mr. Pinch. I am keeping them here for a purpose, though I am quite sure you don't have the faintest idea what it is. Besides, I want to see what they are up to. You don't happen to know, do you?"

"Of course I don't know!"

"Well, there you are then. You have your marching orders. Shadow them when they are together and find out what they are up to. They have gone to great pains to keep it from us, so it must be something important. We should know what it is before we decide what is to be done with them."

Pinch shook his head in dismay. "You take too many chances! We would be better off getting rid of both of them right now!"

His Eminence shook his head and shifted his long body to a more comfortable position. "Oh, no, Mr. Pinch. We would be much worse off if we got rid of them. Trust me on this. They are valuable, those two. Not for who they seem, but for who and what they are."

He winked at his companion. "You do know, don't you?"

"No, I don't know!" Pinch spit at him. "Why don't you just tell me?"

His Eminence laughed. "And what fun would that be, Mr. Pinch? Tell me that. Why, no fun at all!"

His laughter increased until he was practically rolling on the floor. Rufus Pinch looked at him as if he had lost his mind, decided that perhaps he had, and stalked from the room.

CAT'S PAW

Mistaya spent the remainder of the day working side by side with Thom in the Stacks, and although they talked about it at length—keeping their voices at a barely audible murmur to avoid any chance of being overheard—neither one attempted to go outside the assigned area. Rufus Pinch was lurking close by, sometimes visible and sometimes not, but always a discernible presence. He would be looking for them to do something like that, something that would allow him to insist that they be banished from Libiris for good. Or at least that *she* would, since it appeared that Thom was doomed to serve out his indenture no matter what crimes he committed. Whatever the case, she did not want to be the cause of either happening, and so for the moment she knew she must be content mulling over ideas for another nighttime foray.

The situation reminded her a little of her adventures at Carrington, where she was always in the forefront of one underground revolution or another. Except that here, she knew, the consequences of being caught out might be a bit more extreme than at a women's prep school.

By now, she had told Thom of the conversation she had overheard between His Eminence and Pinch, and together they had puzzled over the identity of the unknown allies and the origins of the books taken from the Stacks and the nature of whatever magic was being used, but had been unable to come up with a reasonable explanation for what it was all about. Someone was using magic, someone was trying to get out, and somehow Crabbit and Pinch were involved. That was about all they could agree upon.

She had said nothing to him of the visit from Questor Thews. Nor could she think of a way to speak to him of what the wizard had confided about the origins of Libiris. Doing so would require an explanation of how she had come into possession of such knowledge, and she couldn't think of one that didn't necessitate her telling him who she really was.

She considered doing that, but quickly dismissed the idea. If he found out she was a Princess of Landover, it would change everything between them, and she didn't want that.

"We have to give it a few days, at least, before we try to go back there again," Thom was saying as time wound down toward the close of the day. By then the discussion had been ongoing for hours.

"I don't think waiting is going to help," she replied, sorting through the stack of books closest at hand. Another one was missing, she noticed. Another in an ever-increasing number. "Pinch won't give up watching us no matter how long we wait."

"He's like that," Thom agreed. He brushed his dark hair out of his eyes. "Maybe he'll get sick."

"Maybe we could make him sick." She gave him a look.

"Maybe," he agreed. "But he never eats anything he doesn't prepare himself."

"We could get around that."

"We could."

They were quiet for a moment, thinking through various scenarios that would allow them to poison Pinch's food enough to render him temporarily unable to function. But poisoning was an uncertain science, and neither wanted to do anything worse than make him sick.

"This would all be much easier if we had a way to make ourselves invisible," Thom said finally. "If they couldn't see us, they wouldn't know what we were doing."

Mistaya nodded absently, thinking that her magic would allow her to make them invisible, at least for a short time. But using her magic might give her away. Then again, maybe that didn't matter anymore. Her father and mother would know where she was by tomorrow at the latest, and they were the ones she had been worried about before. Still, she also found herself thinking suddenly of Craswell Crabbit, of whom Questor had told her to be especially careful. If he had the use of magic, he might be able to detect hers and determine its source. Not a pleasant prospect when you considered the consequences of being caught out.

She sighed. Questor had told her not to use her magic except in an emergency, and their hunt for the source of the voice probably didn't qualify. At least, not yet.

They didn't talk after that, concentrating on the sorting and cataloging of the books, their thoughts kept private until it was time to quit and they were walking toward the kitchen.

"We're not going to give up on this, are we?" Thom asked her quietly, giving a quick glance over his shoulder for what might be lurking in the shadows.

"I'm not," she declared firmly.

"Then I'm not, either. But we have to find a different way."

"What if we don't find a different way?"

Thom shook his head. "Sooner or later, we'll have our chance. We just need to be patient." He frowned. "You didn't hear the voice again, did you? It didn't call out to you or anything?"

She sighed. "Not since the last time. But I think it will. Soon."

"I do, too." Thom's mouth tightened into a thin line. "There has to be a way."

As it happened, he was right, but when opportunity knocks, it doesn't always appear the way we expect. Thus, as Mistaya was walking back to her bedroom after finishing her dinner, already dreading tomorrow's workday in the stables, she was surprised to find herself suddenly in the company of Edgewood Dirk. As usual, the Prism Cat appeared out of nowhere and with no warning. One moment he wasn't there, the next he was. For a moment, Mistaya just stared, not quite believing what she was seeing.

"Where have you been?" she demanded, recovering herself sufficiently to demand an explanation.

The cat's face was inscrutable as he glanced over at her. "Here and there," he said, showing no inclination to offer anything further by way of explanation.

"Well, you certainly were quick enough to disappear once you'd brought me here!" She was steaming and not the least bit interested in keeping it to herself. "What about all those promises you made about keeping me safe and hiding me from discovery?"

The cat didn't even glance at her. "If I remember correctly, I never said anything at all about keeping you safe. What I promised is that you wouldn't be discovered through use of another magic. I didn't promise that Questor Thews wouldn't figure out on his own that you might be here and come looking for you." He paused, reflecting. "Although such initiative is quite unlike him, I admit."

"At least he offered to try to help me!" she snapped back. "He listened to what I had to say and then he tried to do something about it. At least he *talked* to me. What have you done lately? Disappeared and stayed disappeared, is what!"

"I wasn't aware that I was under any obligation to do anything other than what I had promised." The smooth, silky voice was infuriating. "I didn't promise to help you or talk to you or do anything else. I'm a cat, in case you hadn't noticed, and cats don't do anything for people unless they choose to. I didn't so choose. Or at least I didn't before this and may not still if you don't keep a civil tongue in your head."

She forced down the retort she wanted to make and kept quiet a moment, considering her options. They were almost to her bedroom door now, and she glanced up and down the hallway to see if anyone was watching. Rufus Pinch came to mind.

"No one but you can see me," Dirk advised, obviously reading her mind. "Spying is poor form, even for humans. I don't allow that sort of thing."

She sighed. "Of course you don't."

They reached the door, and she opened it. The cat walked inside, jumped up on her bed, and assumed a Sphinx-like pose, forelegs extended, head raised, rear haunches tucked against his lean body. His fur glistened in the dim candlelight, as if encrusted with diamond chips or dappled with morning dew.

"Shall we start over again?" the cat asked.

She nodded. "Please. Do you know what's happened to me since I arrived? Do you know about the voice and the darkness in the back of the Stacks?"

Edgewood Dirk closed his eyes in contentment. "I am a cat. I know everything that happens. Did you think that because you couldn't see me, I couldn't see you?"

"I just didn't know if you would bother."

"Oh, Princess, you cut me to the quick! I bother with anything that engages my curious nature. You do know about cats being curious creatures, don't you?"

"I believe we already established that in an earlier conversation." She gave him a look. "What about the old saying that curiosity killed the cat?"

"Lesser cats, perhaps. Not Prism Cats. We are not the kind to let curiosity kill us. Which is not true of young girls like you, I might point out. Especially in situations like this one."

"Are you saying I'm in danger?" she asked quickly. "What aren't you telling me?"

"Lots and lots," he replied. "But most of it does not pertain to your present circumstances, so we can skip all that. Let's start with something pertinent. For example, your efforts at exploring the darker regions of the Stacks have not met with much success to date, although they have placed you in a tenuous situation with the library's present administration. Perhaps you would like to see that change?"

She brightened instantly. "Of course I would. Can you do something to help?"

"Perhaps. If you are serious about this." Dirk rose, stretched, and yawned. "I'll be back at midnight to see if you are awake."

He hopped down off the bed and walked over to the door. "Be alone when I come. The boy may not go with you. Do you understand?"

She understood well enough, although she didn't much like it. But what choice did she have if she wanted to learn something more about the voice? She could always tell Thom later what she had discovered.

"I understand," she replied. "He's not to know anything about you."

The cat nodded, and the door opened of its own accord and then closed behind him as he strolled out. Mistaya sighed and decided she might consider coming back as a Prism Cat in her next life.

----⟨∞⟩----

At exactly midnight, the bedroom door opened anew and there was Edgewood Dirk. She was sitting on the bed waiting for him, dressed in dark clothing and wearing soft boots to muffle her passage. The cat gave her a quick glance, then turned away without a word. Eyes forward, he started down the hallway toward the Stacks, not waiting to see if she would follow.

She caught up to him quickly but didn't say anything, preferring the quiet. She kept glancing around for Pinch but didn't see any sign of him. Even when they reached the Stacks, entering the cavernous room and crossing to the beginnings of the shelving, the odious little man had not appeared.

"Nor will he," said Dirk, apparently reading her mind. "He fell asleep in his room a while back. I believe he wore himself out earlier in the day, keeping watch over things. Now he needs to sleep. Come with me."

They worked their way down the aisles and deeper into the Stacks. While there were no lights lit on the shelving units and they carried no glow sticks, they had no trouble finding their way because Dirk's fur radiated a pale silvery light that let them see where they were going. Mistaya kept glancing around, unable to shake the feeling that someone must be watching. The shadows surrounding them were impenetrable beyond their small light, and her imagination was working overtime as she tried to detect a presence that wasn't there. Not only was Pinch absent, there was no sign of the Throg Monkeys, either. Apparently Dirk was as good as his word.

"What are we doing?" she whispered finally.

"Exploring," he whispered back.

"Exploring for what?"

"Whatever we find that looks interesting. Keep your eyes open. That is what cats do; humans should learn to do it, too."

That wasn't much of an answer, but she decided to let it go for the moment. She concentrated instead on wending her way through the shadows, keeping close to the Stacks on her left as she progressed, wary of the sucking wind that sooner or later would try to draw her into the deepest part of the blackness waiting ahead. Although the Throg Monkeys were not in evidence, she kept looking for them, thinking they must be there, hiding and watching. She glanced repeatedly at Dirk for some sign that she should start worrying. But the cat seemed unconcerned, ambling down the center of the aisle, tail twitching and eyes shining like bright, tiny lamps.

After they had gone a long way back, although not as far as she had gone with Thom, and there was still no sign of the black tunnel or the sucking wind, her patience gave out.

"Why aren't we encountering the tunnel or the wind that was here before?" she asked the cat. "What's happened to them?"

"Nothing," he said. "They are still here. But we don't see or feel either because they are dormant."

"How can that be?"

"The magic that sustains them is unaware of us."

"Unaware of us?"

"I am shielding us. I told you I could hide us from other magic when I chose to do so."

"Well, why didn't you shield Thom and me when we came down here before? Wouldn't that have saved us both a lot of trouble?"

The cat arched his back, and all his fur stood up on end. Mistaya backed away, afraid suddenly that she had stepped over an invisible line.

"That," Dirk declared in a voice that brooked no argument, "would have put you in a good deal more trouble than you've gotten into so far. If you don't know what you are doing—and you don't—then it is best that you leave it to those of us who do. Shielding with magic is tricky business, and doing it for one is difficult enough without trying to crowd in two. Besides, if left on your own, you and that boy wouldn't have found your way to what's waiting."

She compressed her lips into a tight line. "What *is* waiting, if you don't mind my asking?"

"I don't mind your asking, but I think I'll leave it to you to find that out for yourself."

Stupid cat, she thought, furious all over again. "Some kind of monster, I suppose?"

"That would be monsters, plural," said Edgewood Dirk.

She sighed. "Can I ask you something else? Are these monsters the ones causing the blackness and the wind?"

She didn't really expect an answer, but he surprised her by providing one. "No, the monsters have nothing to do with either one."

"Well, who does, then? Someone must!"

The cat stopped where he was, turned toward her, and sat. "It appears your impatience cannot be contained a moment longer, so perhaps it is best if we satisfy it here and now. This is just one more example of why cats are vastly superior to humans. Cats understand patience. You never see a cat unable to wait. Humans, on the other hand, cannot stand to be put off even for a moment. If the delay goes beyond their limited ability to cope, they implode. I will never understand."

Nor would she ever understand cats, she supposed, especially this one. "We are fragile vessels in many ways," she conceded wearily. "But you were about to say?"

The cat gave her a long, steady look. "You are quite bold,

Princess. Even for a child of Ben Holiday." Its strange eyes glittered. "Very well. Listen carefully."

It lifted one paw and licked it, then set it down carefully again. "Libiris is a living creature, though of limited ability and intelligence. You already know this. But all creatures share a commonality, no matter their origins or talents. If they are injured, they will be in pain. And if they lose purpose, they lose heart. The former is self-explanatory, the latter less so. Purpose is individual to each creature. Purpose gives meaning to life. Take away that purpose, and the creature starts to wither inside."

He gave her a moment to digest this, now licking the other forepaw. "Let me give you an example. Sterling Silver was created to serve the royal family. When there was no King, as when Ben Holiday came into Landover, the castle ceased to function as she should. She was both injured and bereft of purpose. Holiday found her tarnished and emotionally damaged. Yet when he entered her and became her new King, she came alive again and began to heal. So it is with Libiris. Do you understand?"

"So the wind and the blackness are symptoms of injury and loss of purpose? Symptoms generated by Libiris?"

"Just so. They are a reaction to both conditions. But can you guess what injury she has suffered and what purpose has been stolen from her?"

Mistaya had no clue. She shook her head. "I don't know."

The cat stood up and started walking. "Then we'd better hurry on so you can find out."

They moved ahead once more, penetrating deeper into the Stacks, and for a long time Mistaya was convinced that they were simply going to slog ahead forever without finding anything. Nothing around them changed; nothing suggested it ever would. There was no wind and no tunnel of blackness into which it could suck you, but there was nothing else, either. There was a gloomy sameness to things that filled her with an unexpected sense of despair.

"Why is this taking so long!" she hissed at Dirk in exasperation.

"It isn't all that long; it just seems that way." The cat barely glanced at her. "The distance is an illusion; Libiris seeks to protect herself."

"Protect herself from what?"

But the cat had apparently lost interest in the conversation and did not answer. Letting the matter drop, she trudged on.

Finally, she caught a glimmer of light from somewhere ahead. She felt an urge to run toward it, to escape the darkness. But Edgewood Dirk kept moving at the same maddeningly unchanging pace, as if it made no difference whether they reached the light in the next few seconds or the next few days.

Then, as the light grew nearer and brightened sufficiently, it took on a crimson hue. She could see that it marked an opening in the library's rear wall that was ragged and cracked all around its edges. The light seemed to emanate from the breach itself rather than from whatever lay beyond; the air was thick and misty and concealing. More disturbing to her, the light's crimson hue suggested a wound.

Edgewood Dirk stopped abruptly and sat down. "This is as far as I go. You have to go on alone from here."

She looked at him doubtfully. "Why is that?"

"I cannot pass through that opening. It would be much too dangerous for me. I will wait here for you to return."

"I can go somewhere you can't?"

"Because I am a fairy creature, I am at much greater risk than you. Once you pass through, you will understand." He gave her another expressionless cat look. "You need not worry. I shall still be shielding you. Just be careful. Don't go too far in. Touch nothing. Just take note of everything you see. It will be interesting to discover how much you understand."

Thanks ever so much, she wanted to tell him. But she didn't. She just nodded. "Go straight ahead, through that opening?"

"I believe I have already made that clear. Is there a problem? Are you too afraid to go through? Was I wrong when I said you were a bold girl?"

She felt like spitting at him, but instead she simply looked ahead again, studying the ragged, red-tinged rent in the wall and the deep gloom beyond. Well, she was either going to do this thing or turn back. Turning back was not an option.

She took a deep breath to steady herself and started forward.

---◈---

She entered the hole in the wall without incident, paused only momentarily for a quick look about to reassure herself that she wasn't missing anything, and then continued through to the other side. She moved more cautiously after she did, taking slower, more careful steps, listening for sounds, searching for movement.

She found both much more quickly than she anticipated. The hazy gloom cleared and she found herself in what appeared to be a tunnel that quickly turned into a winding stairway descending into the earth. She kept going only because she hadn't found anything yet and had made up her mind she wasn't going back until she did. She went down the stairs, hugging the wall to one side, her steps more cautious still. Strange glowing rocks embedded in the walls at regular intervals illuminated the darkness enough that she could see to make her way. The mist followed her down, a clinging presence that felt damp and cold against her skin. She ignored it as best she could, concentrating on the task at hand, putting one foot in front of the other, reminding herself that she wasn't completely helpless here, that she had magic of her own to protect herself even if Dirk should abandon her. Not that she had any reason to think he would, of course. Although he had abandoned her before for all intents and purposes after she was inside Libiris, so maybe she shouldn't be so sure about what might happen here.

Stop being so paranoid, she scolded herself. *There's nothing to be frightened of!*

But several hundred feet farther down the stairway, she changed her mind.

The stairs leveled out onto a sort of shelf before continuing on down, and the wall opened up at this point in a kind of window to reveal a cavernous chamber below. She crouched down, peered over the wall's edge, and was instantly reminded of the Stacks in Libiris. Perhaps this was because she was suddenly looking at row upon row of shelving, most of it filled with books. For a moment, she had the sensation that somehow she had returned to Libiris, although a different Libiris than she had left, a rather surreal one. Throg Monkeys were everywhere, carrying books to and fro, arranging and stacking and organizing.

Amid the little monsters were black-cloaked figures carrying tablets on which they were writing, presumably making lists of those books. In one shadowy corner, tightly clustered and hunched over a massive red, leather-bound book, a trio of the black-cloaked figures chanted the same words over and over again. Even from as far away as she was, she could tell that neither the list makers nor the chanters were human. Their hands and wrists were blackened and withered and clawed and gnarled, and once or twice she caught a quick glimpse of their faces, which were of the same terrible aspect, with eyes that glittered like embers.

At the periphery of all this activity were creatures that resembled monstrous wolves, huge muscular beasts that prowled back and forth along the edges of the workers like guard dogs. Their muzzles were drawn back to reveal rows of sharpened teeth.

Overhead, circling through the misty gloom above the shelving and the workers, things that resembled huge raptors flew in great sweeps, an endless and unchanging patrol.

What in the world was going on?

She watched it all for long minutes, crouched down on the rock shelf, pressed close against one edge of the opening so that she would not be seen. Perhaps with Dirk warding her, she *couldn't* be seen, but she wasn't about to take that chance.

The intricacies of the scene below slowly began to take shape. Books were being cataloged and placed on shelves in some sort of order by the Throg Monkeys and the list makers. Here and there, some of the list makers were actually reading some of the books and writing things down. All the while, the wolves and the flying creatures—whatever they were—kept watch against intrusions.

Intrusions from whom?

While she was puzzling it through, she sensed movement behind her. She turned, but before she could find a place to conceal herself a Throg Monkey was coming down the stairs, descending from Libiris and the Stacks. Its arms were loaded with books, but even as burdened as it was there was no way it could miss seeing her. She pressed against the wall, prepared to fight, already planning her attack and flight back up the way she had come. But the creature passed right by her, not once glancing in her direction. She held her breath until it was out of sight, and then exhaled sharply. Dirk's shielding magic was working!

She stayed where she was, waiting for another of the Throg Monkeys to pass. Eventually, one did. But this time instead of trying to conceal herself, she kept her attention focused on the books that the creature was carrying. There were three of them, and two of the titles were clearly legible on the spines.

Principles of Ancient Magic: A Court Wizard's Critical Overview, read the first, and *Fables and Fairy Tales Revisited,* read the second.

Books of magic! They were stealing books of magic! That was what Crabbit and Pinch had been talking about when they had argued over hauling something back and forth!

She turned back to the opening in the rock wall to study with fresh eyes the scene unfolding below. Who was doing the stealing? Why bother when all you needed to do was to go into Libiris and read them?

She decided she needed to take a closer look at what lay below her. She eased her way across the open shelf, praying that no one could see her, gained the stairs on the far side, and started down. She crept forward around a bend until she could see that the stairs continued on down past the room below in a long winding spiral that eventually disappeared entirely into a mix of mist and blackness.

Her mind spun. *What could be down there? What sort of creatures could live underground in such conditions?*

It came to her all at once—not just the answer to that question, but the answers to all of the others, the whole convoluted truth, everything she had come to find out and everything that Edgewood Dirk had wanted her to realize.

She turned away and climbed back up the stairs as fast as she could manage. She needed to find Dirk and let him know. And then she needed to find Thom and figure out how to stop it!

MISDIRECTION

Mistaya made her way back up the stairs to the opening in the library wall, twice encountering Throg Monkeys on their way down with more books. Each time she pressed herself against the rough stone of the passage wall, terrified of discovery, and each time they passed by without slowing. She kept thinking that sooner or later someone had to see her, as clearly visible as she appeared to herself. But Edgewood Dirk's fairy magic was protecting her, and she remained undiscovered.

She found the Prism Cat sitting pretty much right where she had left him, not too far inside the Stacks. He was washing himself as she came up to him, and when she tried to tell him what she had discovered he quickly held up one paw to silence her while he finished his bath.

"Now then," he said, once he was satisfied that he was clean. "What have you learned?"

She knelt down next to him, keeping her voice at a whisper, just in case. "Well, this is what I *think* is happening. The Throg Monkeys are stealing books of magic out of Libiris and taking them down through a tunnel to a cavern chamber. The chamber is a part of Abaddon, and the thieves are Abaddon's demons. Some of the demons are counting and cataloging the stolen books, and some are reading from them and chanting, working some sort of spell to keep

the wall leading into Libiris open. There are flying things and wolves
keeping watch while the demons work so that no one interferes. I
don't know what their arrangement is with His Eminence and
Pinch, but it has something to do with letting the demons out of the
underground. I heard Craswell and Pinch talking about it earlier, although I didn't know then what it meant."

She took a deep breath. "I understand now what you were saying
earlier. Taking those books from Libiris is just like leaving Sterling
Silver without a King. Like you said—stealing her heart. She can't
function when the thing she has been given to do is taken away.
She's supposed to care for her books, but now many of them are
being stolen and she can't stop it, so she's in pain and calling for
help. Isn't that right?"

Edgewood Dirk cocked an ear. "Be sensible. I'm a cat; what
would I know?"

She frowned, ignoring him. "But why are they doing all this? Not
the demons, but His Eminence and Pinch. What do they want?"

The cat yawned, bored. "Reason it through."

"All right." She glared at him. "Father locked the demons away
years ago when he first came to Landover. The demons had united
under the leadership of the Iron Mark and broken out of Abaddon.
They were able to escape because the restraints that imprisoned
them had weakened. Landover had been too long without a King for
the wards to hold, and so the demons got out and were challenging
Father for the throne."

She hesitated. "So they're trying to do the same thing now. Only
this time they're using the books of magic they're stealing out of Libiris. The books are providing them with spells they can use to
break free, and the chanters are calling up some of those spells so
that . . ."

She stopped herself. "But why would His Eminence and Pinch
help them? I don't see what they have to gain by letting the demons
get loose."

The cat blinked. "I'm sure I don't, either. But you can be certain
there is something in it for them and it's not anything Ben Holiday

would be happy about. In any case, that isn't your problem to solve. Your problem is staring you in the face. What are you going to do about the theft of the books?"

"What am *I* going to do? What about you? You're the one who brought me here and showed me all this. You have to help!"

"I have been helping, in case you haven't noticed." Dirk's reply bordered on insolence. "What else have I been doing but helping. Given the fact that fairy creatures like myself are not able to go down into Abaddon, I have done a great deal. I brought you here, and I showed you the problem. I shielded you from discovery. Now that you know the situation, it is up to you to correct it."

She stared in dismay. "How am I supposed to do that?"

"You might start by asking yourself what needs doing."

"All right. That's easy. The books *need* to be taken back so that the spells can't be chanted and the damage to the library walls can be healed and the demons shut away again. Libiris is organic, like Sterling Silver. She can heal herself if her purpose is restored. You said so."

"Then you had better get busy and return those books, hadn't you?" The cat regarded her with luminous eyes. "How are you going to do that, by the way?"

It was a good question. She couldn't very well carry all those books back again, even if she could find a way to do so without being discovered. It would take days, maybe weeks. She could ask Thom to help, but even the two of them wouldn't be enough.

"I can use magic," she announced after a moment.

"Can you?" asked the cat.

She ignored him. "Maybe I can shrink the books to the size of pebbles, put them in a sack, and carry them out all at once. Then I can enlarge them when they're back in the Stacks and put them back where they belong."

"An excellent idea," Dirk announced. "Except for one small problem. You can't use magic on those books because they are protected by magic of their own and will resist your efforts if you try to change them in any way."

She gave him a look. "How do you know this?"

He didn't exactly shrug, but almost. "Cats know these things because cats pay attention. Also, fairy creatures know that certain rules apply in all situations. That books of magic are unalterable is one of those rules. You'll have to find another way."

Of course, I will, she thought irritably. She thought about it some more. Maybe she needed to talk this over with Thom. But if she did that, she would have to tell him how she'd found all this out, and that would require telling him who and what she was. She couldn't explain why, but this seemed like a bad idea. It would almost certainly change the nature of their relationship, and she didn't want that to happen. Besides, what could Thom do that would make a difference in things?

Nevertheless.

"If I brought Thom down here to help me, could you . . . ?"

"Haven't we had this discussion?" Dirk barely gave her a glance. "Shielding you is hard enough. I am not without my limits."

She wasn't sure that she believed that, but she didn't care to challenge him on it. Anyway, the possibility of bringing Thom into the mix was gone. She would have to do this by herself. She thought about it anew. She couldn't use magic to change the books. Could she use it in some way to move them?

"What if I made the books lighter?" she asked Dirk. "You know, took away all that weight so that I could . . ."

"You are not paying attention," he interrupted rather irritably, enunciating each word carefully. "You cannot use magic. Not any kind of magic in any way. Not on these books. Am I being clear enough?"

She wanted to smack him. She forced herself to think of something else. Okay, she couldn't use magic on the books—she got it. She paused suddenly in her thinking. But even if she couldn't use magic on *those* books, maybe she could use it on some of the others.

And on the book thieves.

"Are the Throg Monkeys demons?" she asked Edgewood Dirk.

"They are not. They are a species of troll, brought down out of the Melchor Mountains. Why do you ask?"

She ignored him. "His Eminence brought them here?"

"He did."

"Are there a lot of them?"

"Dozens."

"And they answer strictly to him?"

"They do. What is it that you are thinking of doing?"

"Patience. Can I use magic on other books in the Stacks—ones that aren't books of magic?"

"Yes, yes. What are you up to?"

"How long can you keep me from being seen while I'm down here? Can you do it all the rest of tonight?"

The cat was watching her closely now. "I can shield you for as long as you like, if it doesn't involve you trying to carry out books for endless days. You're not going to suggest that, are you?"

"I'm not," she agreed. "I'm going to suggest something else."

And she told him what that something was.

She positioned herself just back from the hole in the library wall in the shadow of the Stacks where she could work her magic without risking a direct encounter with the Throg Monkeys. They came by regularly, sometimes in twos and threes, but mostly alone, carrying one or two books toward the hole to take down into Abaddon. They seemed absorbed in their work, eyes fixed on the way forward and wicked little faces set in a permanent grimace. They all looked pretty much the same, so she couldn't be sure at first which ones she had spoken to already and which ones she hadn't. In the end, she just kept speaking to them all, not trying to make a distinction, but just trying to make sure she didn't miss anyone.

They didn't know she was there. All they saw was the looming figure of His Eminence deep in the shadows, his voice a dark, booming whisper in the silence.

"Stop where you are! What are you doing? You are going in the wrong direction! The books are supposed to *come out of* Abaddon and *back into* the Stacks! Turn around and take that book back where you found it. Then go down the steps and bring out the rest! Replace each one you remove with a book from the shelving section directly across the aisle from me—there, behind you. Look for the ones with the words *magic* and *conjuring* and *sorcery* in the titles. Spread the books you carry out of the tunnel all over the shelving units of the Stacks so that they aren't all in one place. Hide them, if you can. Work day and night until the task is finished. Do not speak of this to anyone, especially the demons! Do not let the demons find out what you are doing! Distract them so that they do not see. Do what I say! Do it now!"

This pronouncement was accompanied by a small spell that induced a feeling of confusion and a desire to make up for it by doing exactly what was being asked. She allowed each recipient of her spell a glimpse of His Eminence's face, wreathed in displeasure and impatience, a further inducement to act swiftly. Each Throg Monkey left hurriedly to carry out her instructions.

It was child's play, really—one of the easiest spells she had learned in her time studying with Questor, a spell that was effective in part because those affected were almost always on the verge of confusion and uncertainty to start with and were quite prepared to believe that they were doing something wrong. She didn't know anything about Throg Monkeys, but she had a feeling that His Eminence would value obedience over independent thought in a situation like this. Or, to put it another way, matter over mind.

The books she was sending down into the tunnel as replacements for the real books of magic were farming volumes with the titles altered. Unless a close inspection was conducted, no one would know they weren't what they appeared to be. By the time the truth was discovered, she hoped to have all the real books of magic back on the shelves of Libiris. It was the old sleight-of-hand trick, and there was no reason to think it wouldn't work here.

She stayed at it for most of the night. She quit finally when she no longer saw any of the Throg Monkeys emerging from Abaddon without carrying books. She had reversed the flow of traffic, which was the best she could do for now. It would all work out as long as the demons didn't catch on. She would come again tomorrow night to see how matters were progressing.

Leaving Edgewood Dirk at her bedroom doorway, having extracted his rather indifferent promise to meet her again at midnight next, she tumbled into bed.

She woke late and unrested, having barely managed two hours of sleep. She stumbled down to breakfast, skipping her morning bath entirely since this was her first day of work in the stables anyway and she didn't see the point. Rumpled and disgruntled, she sat down heavily across from Thom.

"I hope you won't be offended," he said after a few moments of complete silence, "but you look terrible. Are you all right?"

She nodded. "Fine. I just didn't sleep much."

He studied her doubtfully. "It looks to me like it might be something more than that." He pushed back his stool and got to his feet. "I'm going to ask His Eminence to have you assigned back into the Stacks for today, at least. You can begin your punishment in the stables tomorrow."

He was out of the room and down the hallway before she could object.

To his credit, Thom got the job done. His Eminence seemed unconcerned that the punishment was to be postponed, agreeing without argument to let Ellice work with her brother in the Stacks so that Thom could make certain she was all right. Mistaya was grateful for the reprieve and told him so. She even went so far as to give him a hug. Thom was a better friend than she deserved, she decided. After all, he wasn't hiding things from her the way she was hiding them from him.

"Have you been thinking about the voice?" he asked her at one point as they toiled over the cataloging.

She was thinking of nothing else, of course, but not in the way he was. Mostly, she was wondering if her plan was working and the

Throg Monkeys were still carrying the missing books of magic back out of Abaddon as she had ordered them to. There was no way she could check on this now; she would have to wait for tonight, when Dirk could go with her. But that didn't stop her from worrying over the possibility that her efforts had failed.

"I've thought about it," she admitted.

"Good. So have I. When do we do something? When do we go back into the Stacks?"

She shook her head. This was not a conversation she wanted to have just yet. "I don't know. When I'm feeling better, I guess."

"Pinch was sick all yesterday and again today. He can't seem to get out of his bed. Maybe that's what you've got." Thom paused, glancing around. "If you feel well enough, we should try again tonight."

That was the last thing she wanted, but she couldn't tell him so. "Let's talk about it later," she suggested finally, and went back to work feeling inexplicably guilty.

When it was finally time to quit, Mistaya was so exhausted that she could only just manage to eat a little of her dinner before announcing to Thom that she was off to bed. Because of her obvious exhaustion he was quick to tell her that they would talk about their plans for returning to the forbidden regions of the Stacks later on. He offered to help her to her room, but she insisted she could get there on her own, a task that turned out to be just manageable.

She slept without waking or dreaming until something soft touched her face, and she woke with a start. Her bedside candle was still burning, if barely, or she wouldn't have been able to make out Edgewood Dirk seated next to her, whiskers brushing her cheeks as he washed himself. She blinked and tried to sit up, but failed.

Dirk jumped down from the bed and walked to the door. "Coming, Princess? It is already after midnight."

She didn't know what time it was and she didn't care. All she wanted to do at this point was go back to sleep. But at the same time she realized the importance of finding out what was happening in the Stacks and in the cavern down in Abaddon. She needed to know whether her magic was working on the Throg Monkeys.

So she climbed from the bed, still wearing the clothing she had fallen asleep in, pulled on her boots, and followed the Prism Cat out the door. They didn't say a word to each other as they walked down the hallway to the library and entered the Stacks. Mistaya was too tired for conversation. Dirk, taciturn as usual, sauntered on with no apparent concern for whether she was keeping up or even following. She found herself thinking how bizarre it was that she was trailing after a talking cat in a library filled with something called Throg Monkeys in search of stolen books of magic, and she wondered how Rhonda Masterson, were she there, would feel about doing something like that. Some things, she guessed, were best left to the imagination.

She was suddenly, inexplicably homesick. She missed Sterling Silver and her mother and father and Questor Thews and Abernathy and all the other creatures that were so much a part of her life. If she could have made a wish that would have taken her home at that very moment, she would have seized it with both hands.

But she was stuck with things as they were, so she pushed the feeling aside and tried to concentrate on the task at hand. She couldn't help thinking as she did so that all this was much tougher than she had imagined. She wished she could do more using her magic, but it was too dangerous. It was risky enough using magic to deceive the Throg Monkeys. Attempting anything more would almost certainly give her away.

Once they had gotten deeper into the Stacks, she began seeing her unsuspecting accomplices. They crept down the aisles and through the shadows like gnarled wraiths, their arms loaded with books. To her delight, they were carrying the books away from Abaddon. Apparently her plan was still working.

"I need to go back down to that cavern to see how far they've gotten," she told Dirk.

The cat nodded wordlessly, and she left him at the entrance and

passed through the breach in the wall. Was she imagining things or
was the hole getting smaller? She stared at the rough edges, trying
to remember how they had looked the day before. Larger and more
jagged, she thought. She hadn't heard the building's voice for a
while, either, an indication that it wasn't as desperate for help as it
had been. Perhaps because that help had been given? By her? She
smiled to herself, liking the idea and feeling good about the possibility that she had helped it come to pass.

The passageway leading down to the cavern where the books
were stored was empty as she descended. She was only yards from
the opening in the wall before she passed the first of the Throg Monkeys she had seen since starting down, a group of three, all with
arms laden. She caught a glimpse of titles on the spines, some con-
taining the word *magic* in bold print, so she had her proof that things
were going as intended. She was surprised at how easy this had
been, how simple the solution to the problem.

At the opening in the wall, she crawled out onto the rock shelf,
taking care to crouch as she did so, still not entirely convinced that
she couldn't be seen. Edgewood Dirk could promise to shield her,
but there were counterspells that could undo his efforts. She knew
that much from her time studying with Questor.

When she peered down, she was excited to discover that the
shelves that had held all the stolen books were virtually unchanged.
Wolves continued to patrol the perimeter and winged sentries still
flew overhead while some of the black-cloaked figures walked
among the books and others chanted spells from the book with the
red leather cover. No one seemed to notice that anything was
wrong. Perhaps they didn't know the difference between magic and
farming, she thought, muffling the urge to laugh. She could see the
Throg Monkeys watching these wraiths, avoiding them whenever
possible. Now and then, one of the little monsters would snatch a
book furtively from the shelves, replace it with one it was carrying,
and edge away from the tally takers until it was able to slip up the
stairway unnoticed.

Her plan was working! She wanted to shout it aloud, but managed to restrain herself.

How much longer would it be until all of the books were replaced? How many more books were there? She couldn't think of any way to find out that didn't involve her going down into the cavern and having a closer look. That seemed too risky, even if she was supposed to be invisible. She could ask the Throg Monkeys, perhaps. Or she could wait until they were no longer bringing books back out of Abaddon. That way she would know they were all safely spirited away.

Would that be enough to close the hole in the library wall, or was something more needed?

She stayed where she was for a little longer, reading what she could into what she was seeing. Finally, unable to determine anything more, she turned away and crept up the steps to the hole and back into the Stacks.

Edgewood Dirk was waiting, sitting on his haunches and studying her. "Is your plan working?" he asked.

"I think so. But what should we do about the hole in the wall? Can we close it over?"

Dirk blinked. "Libiris is organic, like Sterling Silver. She will heal herself if the wound is not enlarged by further thefts and by the continued chanting of spells."

"Then we need to make sure that it all stops, don't we? We need to do something about His Eminence and Pinch."

The cat hesitated. He arched his back in a long stretch, his fur shimmering with a strange, silvery glow. "Perhaps you should leave that to Ben Holiday and his companions. They seem more suited to that sort of work."

"But I started this and I want to finish it!" she insisted. "I know how to be careful."

The Prism Cat gave her a long, steady look that suggested he might be weighing the merits of this assertion. Then, his interest in the subject exhausted, he turned away and started back down the aisle toward the front of the room. "Time to go back to sleep," he called over his shoulder. "We can discuss this further tomorrow."

She thought it a reasonable suggestion, even though she was already certain that she wasn't going to change her mind no matter what sort of arguments he mounted. This was her chance to make up for Carrington, her opportunity to prove herself to her parents. Once she had restored Libiris and exposed His Eminence and Pinch, they could no longer deny her request to remain in Landover and to take charge of her future. She would be allowed to continue her studies with Questor and Abernathy. She would be accepted as an equal and no longer treated as a child.

The trek back through the stacks was endless. Mistaya was bone-weary and muddle-headed from lack of sleep, and she could barely manage to put one foot ahead of the other. If Edgewood Dirk noticed or cared, he was not giving evidence of it. He minced along ahead of her, a cat on its way to someplace of its own choosing. She might have been wallpaper for all the difference she made to him.

Somewhere along the way, he simply disappeared. She barely noticed, her thoughts only on getting to bed and going to sleep. Shouldn't be any problem tonight, she thought with a smile. Nothing would keep her awake after this.

Taking a quick look up and down the hallway before she did so, she opened the door to her room and stepped inside.

She knew immediately that something was wrong.

"Taking a nighttime stroll, Princess?" she heard His Eminence ask her from the darkness.

Then she caught a whiff of something bitter and raw, and she tumbled away into blackness.

SADLY MISTAKEN

When Mistaya came awake again, she was lying on a straw pallet in a dark, windowless room with only a single candle sitting on the floor beside her for light. She had a splitting headache, but otherwise she felt all right. She lay without moving for long moments while her eyes adjusted, trying to remember exactly what had happened to her. When she did remember, she wished she hadn't.

A figure moved out of the darkness, coming over from another part of the room to sit on the bed beside her. She flinched involuntarily and hunched her shoulders, frightened that it was His Eminence or Rufus Pinch. But when she saw Thom's worried face, she exhaled sharply in relief.

"Are you all right?" he asked her, leaning close, his voice a whisper.

She nodded. "Are we alone?"

He nodded back. "But they might be listening."

"They brought you here, too?"

"Actually, they brought me here first, then you."

She tried to lift one arm to rub her pounding head, but her hands were surprisingly heavy. When she glanced down to find out why, she saw that they were encased in what looked like clouds of swirling mist that completely hid them from view.

"What's happened to me?" she gasped, shaking them wildly, struggling to free them. "Who did this?"

"His Eminence." Thom put his hands on her arms to quiet her. "No, don't. Not yet. Stay still. Your hands are bound with magic so that you can't work spells. If you try to free them, you will only hurt yourself."

She stopped thrashing and stared at him. "He knows everything, doesn't he? He knows who I am. I heard him call me by name before I passed out. What did he use on me?"

Thom shook his head. "A spell. He had me frozen in place with another one so that I couldn't do anything to help. He's a much more accomplished wizard than we gave him credit for. And, yes, he knows who you are."

She gave a long sigh and lay back. "So now you know, too."

He smiled. "Oh, I knew who you were all along. Right from the moment I saw you standing in the doorway." He laughed softly when he saw the look on her face. "I told you I saw you when I was at court all those years ago, when you were just a child. You looked different then, but you had the same eyes. No one could ever mistake those eyes."

To her horror, she found herself blushing. Her face turned hot, and it was only the darkness that hid her reaction. "You must have gotten closer to me than I would have thought possible for a servant."

He shrugged. "Other things gave you away, as well. Your hands are too soft for a village girl's. Also, you are too well spoken, and you've had training in how to carry yourself."

"You seem awfully well informed about Princesses."

"Not really. I just pay attention to things."

"Why didn't you tell me you knew?"

He seemed to consider. "I'm not sure. Once I had you here, I didn't want you to leave. I wasn't making that up, you know. I was afraid that if I told you I knew you were Mistaya Holiday, it would change the nature of our relationship and you might decide you had to go. It just seemed easier to go on pretending I believed you to be who you said you were." He paused. "I actually do have a sister named Ellice, but she's much older than you."

She grimaced. "I don't know whether to be angry with you or not. I guess I'm not. It just feels funny, knowing I was pretending with you for nothing."

"We were both pretending. It was a game. But there wasn't any harm done. Except now that it's out in the open that you're a Princess, I'm afraid you might not want to have anything more to do with me."

She laughed despite herself. "It doesn't much matter what I want at this point, does it? I'm a prisoner of His Eminence, and so are you. We can't pretend much of anything now. What do you think he plans to do with us?"

Thom shook his head. "I don't know. He didn't say. He brought me here and left me, and a little later he brought you here, too."

"If he knows who I am, and he's keeping me prisoner anyway, then we are in a lot of trouble. He can't be planning anything good for either of us if he's willing to risk all that."

"No, I don't suppose so."

"This is all my fault," she declared, sitting up next to him, resting her mist-encased hands in her lap. She was already trying to think of a spell that would free her from the bindings, running through the lessons she had studied under Questor's tutelage. "If I'd stayed in my room instead of going back into the Stacks, none of this would have happened. I was so stupid it makes me want to scream."

"So that's where you were. I came looking for you earlier, but you weren't in your room."

"I didn't want to tell you," she admitted, giving him a rueful smile. "I'm sorry about that. I wish that I had."

"It isn't too late for you to do so now, is it?" he asked.

She smiled and proceeded to tell him everything she had been keeping from him. She even told him about Edgewood Dirk, despite her promise to the cat. It was necessary, she reasoned, given her present situation.

She had kept so much from him, she told Thom, because she was worried about involving him further.

"Also, I was worried about the same things you were," she added. "I thought it would change how you felt about me, and I didn't want you not to be my friend."

He cocked an eyebrow at her. "Funny that we were both so worried when there was no reason for it."

"Funny peculiar," she agreed, just managing to meet his gaze. Then she looked quickly away. "Anyway, I messed up."

He looked away. "Maybe I was the one who messed up. Your getting caught might not have been your fault. It might have been mine. If I hadn't come to your room looking for you and then gone prowling around out in the Stacks, His Eminence might not have caught me and found out about you."

"Well, it doesn't much matter now. It's over and done with, and we can both take some share of the blame." She swung her legs around to rest her feet on the floor. "Where are we, anyway?"

"One of the storerooms, down by the kitchen. There's no way out; I've already searched. Even if there were somebody who might try to help us, the walls are two feet thick. We can yell all we want, but no one will hear." He paused. "Any chance the Prism Cat might help us?"

She shrugged. "There's always a chance. But Dirk thinks mostly of himself. I don't think his attention span is all that long, either. If he knows we're here and feels so inclined, he might choose to help us. But he might just as easily not."

"Some friend."

"I wouldn't call Edgewood Dirk a friend. More on the order of a particularly nettlesome aunt or a nagging teacher." She was thinking now of Harriet Appleton. But that wasn't fair, she knew. She tossed the comparison aside. "Dirk is unpredictable," she finished.

He shifted himself on the pallet so that he was sitting closer. "You told me how you happened to come to Libiris, but not why. You said you were escaping from your grandfather and hiding from your family so you wouldn't have to come here. But why was your family making you come here in the first place?"

She told him. She started all the way back with her time at Carrington and her troubles with the school administration, culminating in her suspension and disgraced return to Landover. She related the events surrounding her flight from Sterling Silver, although it was unexpectedly hard to explain why she hadn't wanted to come to Libiris but had ended up coming anyway and then staying. He listened without comment to all of it, and not once did she see even the flicker of a grimace or a look of disbelief cross his face.

"I guess I still don't understand what happened," she finished. "I mean, I still don't know exactly how I ended up here."

"Well, I think you just wanted it to be your idea," he said, giving a shrug to emphasize that it wasn't all that complicated for him. "I think you wanted to come here on your own terms, and that's what you did. I also think you did the right thing."

"You do?"

"Yes. Both for you and for Libiris. Maybe for your father and the Kingdom, too. After all, you've stopped the book theft and done something to heal the library so that the demons no longer have a way to escape Abaddon."

"But His Eminence will already have found out what I've done! He'll put everything back the way it was!" She felt suddenly disheartened. "A week ago, it wouldn't have mattered. I didn't even want to be here. Libiris was just an ugly building. But now I know the truth about her. She's so much more—and she's in such pain, Thom! I wanted to help her get better, and I thought that by tricking the Throg Monkeys into returning her books I had. But it will all have been for nothing."

Thom shook his head quickly. "Don't be too sure of that. He didn't say much of anything when he caught up with me. He doesn't necessarily know what you've done."

"Maybe. But he'll figure it out quickly enough, don't you think?"

"I don't know. Just don't give anything away. He'll try to get you to do that. Make him find it out for himself."

"Don't worry, I won't do anything to help him."

"Tell him he has to let you go. You are a Princess of Landover, and if your father finds out what's happened, His Eminence won't be able to run fast enough or far enough. That ought to make him sit up and take notice." He paused. "Wait a minute! I've got a better idea. Tell him your father already knows you're here!"

"Of course!" she exclaimed, remembering suddenly. "Questor told him! And Father's on his way here to bring me home!"

"That's right! He might even get here before sunset today!"

Mistaya looped her bound arms over his head and shoulders and hugged him as hard as she could. "Yes, yes, he might!"

Thom hugged her back instantly, and then as if realizing what they had done, they released each other at the same moment and looked in different directions, eyes lowered.

"Well, that deserved a hug," she declared finally, looking him in the eye again.

"I thought so," he agreed, and gave her one of his quirky grins.

They sat together in the small glow of the candle until the tiny flame went out, leaving them in darkness save for a faint wash of sunlight creeping with a thief's hesitancy under their locked door from the hallway beyond. Time passed with agonizing slowness, and no one came. Mistaya was hungry and tired, but there was no food to eat and sleep was impossible. Instead, she talked with Thom about ways they might escape and things they might do to make His Eminence sorry for what he had done. The conversation helped keep her growing fears at bay—fears that seemed increasingly well founded. The more she thought about it, the more convinced she became that His Eminence was not going to be intimidated by anything she said. If he was willing to lock them up in the first place, he couldn't be all that worried about what her father might do.

She spent a goodly amount of time during the silences between exchanges thinking about how she could summon spells that would help them. The problem was that virtually everything she knew how to do required a combination of voice and hands. You had to speak the words and make the signs if the spells were to work. It was a safeguard against accidental summoning and unfortunate consequences. If all that was needed to conjure a spell was a word or two, you might act inadvertently. But if you also needed to gesture, it was less likely that you would make a mistake. Questor had taught her this, explaining that using magic always required measured consideration beforehand.

She wished suddenly that she hadn't left all her possessions tucked away in her sleeping chamber. She might find something useful in Questor's book of magic if she could get her hands on it. There were all kinds of spells, incantations, and conjuring in there—maybe even something that didn't require the use of her hands.

Nor, she realized with a shock, did she have the rainbow crush on her. That, too, was back in her sleeping chamber. She had been so sure she wouldn't need it, so sure of herself.

Well, maybe Edgewood Dirk would come to rescue her.

Sure, and maybe cows would fly.

She had no idea how long she had sat in the darkness with Thom when she finally heard footsteps outside the storeroom door and the sharp snick of the lock releasing. She sat up straight at once, readying herself for whatever was to come. Beside her, Thom whispered, "Remember. Don't tell him anything. Don't let him trick you."

The door opened and a flood of light spilled through, momentarily blinding her. His Eminence appeared, tall and vaguely spectral, his strange head canted over to one side, as if it were too heavy for his neck. Rufus Pinch followed close on his heels, sour-faced and pale from his illness, apparently determined not to miss out on whatever punishment was to be dispensed to the prisoners.

"Good day, Princess," His Eminence greeted, beaming down at her. "Good morning, Thom," he added, nodding to the boy.

"You had better let us go, and right now," Mistaya snapped, glaring at him as she came to her feet and stood facing him, ignoring the weight of the restraints on her hands.

"Had I?" asked the other, an astonished look crossing his face. "Oh, dear. What will happen if I don't?"

"My father will find out, that's what!"

"Well, I certainly hope so."

"He already knows I'm here, you realize. Questor Thews visited me secretly two days ago, and when he left he . . ." She caught herself, realizing suddenly what he had said. "You hope so?" She repeated his words back to him, not quite believing she had heard right.

His Eminence held up his hands and patted at the air, glancing at Pinch to share a secret smile before turning back to her. "Let me save you the trouble of puzzling it through. I already know Questor Thews was here. You both thought he got into the building without my knowing, but that is quite impossible. You talked, and he departed. I don't doubt that in doing so he made you aware of the fact that he would have to report your whereabouts to your father. Am I right?"

She nodded dumbly, not at all liking where this was headed. "He said Father would be coming to get me." This was not so, but she thought she needed to suggest that there was an urgency to things. "He's probably already on his way."

His Eminence looked even happier. "Excellent! Exactly what I was counting on!"

Mistaya stared. "What are you talking about? You hold me prisoner, and you're telling me you want my father to come here to do something about it?"

"That is not exactly right. I do want him to come, but I do not want him to think you are a prisoner." He held up one finger, as if lecturing. "In point of fact, if you hadn't gone into the Stacks against my express orders, there wouldn't be a reason for you to *be* a prisoner. But you just couldn't help yourself, could you? Whatever was it that you were doing back there, little Princess?"

She ignored the question. "Why do you want my father to come visit me at all?"

He sighed heavily. "Well, the answer to that question is complicated. Boiled down to its simplest form, it has to do with his position in Landover versus my own. I think his is slightly more elevated than necessary and mine is very much in need of improvement. If he comes to see you, he will of necessity have to see me, and I might be able to persuade him of the need for reassessment."

"Reassessment?"

"Of our respective positions."

She shook her head. "I don't understand."

"Princess, you had a falling-out with your parents and you ran away from home. Of that much, I am certain. Why you came here, I haven't a clue. But I view it as a type of divine intervention. Higher powers than those to which I have access have sent you my way. I knew you at once for who you were; surely you realize that now, even if you didn't before. You are too well known to pretend to be a village working girl. Nor was there any hope that Thom could pass you off as his sister. No, you were Princess Mistaya Holiday, and you were here to help me in my efforts to improve my fortunes and reinvent my future."

Behind him, Rufus Pinch cleared his throat meaningfully. "Yes, yes, Mr. Pinch, and yours, as well," Crabbit added wearily.

"I don't see myself doing much to help you achieve that end," she snapped at him. "You have made me a prisoner against my will. You have kept Thom in indentured servitude for years, an act that my father would never—"

"I did what?" His Eminence demanded, interrupting her. "Indentured servitude?" He looked sharply at Thom. "Is that what you told her? That I was holding you against your will?"

Mistaya was confused. She looked quickly at Thom, who was clearly uncomfortable with the attention. "I did," the boy said simply.

"Goodness, no wonder the two of you got caught out! Co-conspirators, and you don't even trust each other enough to reveal your true identities! Oh, this is really too much! Did she tell you who she is, Thom? She didn't, did she? And you didn't tell her who you are, either, did you? I will never understand young people. So,

I ask you again, Princess. What was it you were doing back in the Stacks? And please don't tell me you were looking for a lost piece of family jewelry."

Mistaya tightened her lips. "I heard someone moaning. I was trying to find out who it was."

His Eminence and Pinch exchanged another glance. "Someone moaning," the former repeated. "Did you discover who that someone was?"

She shook her head. "It was too dark to see anything. And there was a wind of some sort that kept pulling at us. We were frightened and turned back." She hesitated. "But then I went back into the Stacks again last night for another look. I thought I could find a way to get through the wind and the darkness. But I couldn't."

His Eminence smiled rather unpleasantly. "After standing toe-to-toe with the Witch of the Deep Fell five years ago and somehow besting her to the extent that she has not been seen since, you failed to find a way to get past some wind and darkness? Really, Princess?"

He came forward until he was standing right in front of her, looming over her like a big tree. "I don't believe a word of it. I think you know exactly what we are doing here, and I think you have been trying to interfere with our efforts. I don't know that you have succeeded, but I suspect you have worked some sort of mischief and I intend to find out what it is. Meanwhile, you will stay locked in this storeroom until your father comes to take you home. You and *Andjen Thomlinson* both. You are not going to be allowed to disrupt my plans further."

He was grinning so hard that all his teeth were showing, and Mistaya stepped back despite herself.

"Now, I know something of magic, little girl," the other continued softly. "In fact, I know a great deal more than you do. I have bound up your hands with a spell that you cannot undo without my help. That way, you won't try something foolish. You and Thom will stay here as my *guests* for as long as I wish it. Thom owes me continued service under the terms of our bargain and you owe me some days in the stables. I intend to collect from both of you, on that and maybe more. I have a special use for you, Princess, one that requires you remain here awhile longer. Think on that and make of it what you will."

He wheeled about. "Come along, Mr. Pinch. We are done here. Leave them fresh candles so that they can see each other's faces while they confess the truths they keep trying to hide."

Pinch grinned wolfishly at Mistaya and Thom. "You were warned, weren't you? See what your disobedience has gotten you!"

He dumped a handful of candles on the pallet and followed His Eminence out of the room. The door slammed shut behind them with a bang, and its locks slid into place. The girl and the boy, standing next to each other, were left in blackness once more.

As soon as they were alone, Thom found and lit one of the candles. "What do you think he meant when he said he had a special use for you?"

Mistaya didn't know, and right at the moment she didn't particularly care. "Andjen Thomlinson?" she asked, giving him a stony look.

"My given names," he admitted.

"You knew who I was all along, but after listening to His Eminence, I get the impression that maybe I don't know everything about you. That doesn't make me feel very good. It makes me feel a little foolish and a whole lot angry."

"You have a right to be angry, but I was just protecting myself out of habit." He sat down on the pallet, looking up at her. "I've been hiding my identity now for the entire three years I have been at Libiris. I don't even think about it anymore. I'm always just Thom, the boy from the village. I'm Thom to everyone."

She sat down next to him. "But it appears that you are actually someone else."

Thom nodded. "I am. Thom was the name I took when I came to stay here. I was looking for a place to hide, and His Eminence offered me one. He said no one would ever think to look for me here.

We agreed that I would be Thom, a boy from a distant village, come to work off an indenture. I wasn't making something up on the spur of the moment when I told you that; I was just repeating what I told everyone. Actually, it's not so far from the truth. I committed myself to serve His Eminence for five years for the privilege of hiding out here. He needed someone to take over the cataloging of the books, and I had the necessary skills."

He paused. "At least, that's what I thought when we made our bargain. Now I don't know why he let me stay. It obviously doesn't have anything to do with cleaning up the library."

"You should have told me the truth," she said quietly. "You should have trusted me."

He shook his head slowly. "I think so, too, now. But when you first came, I was afraid that telling you the truth would be a very bad mistake. I was afraid it would make you hate me."

"Why would you think that?" she demanded, suddenly angry all over again. "What did I do or say to make you think I wouldn't like you if I knew who you were?"

"Nothing. It isn't you. It's me. It's the truth about who I am. I'm not some village boy. I came to Libiris to hide after my father died and one of my brothers murdered the other and banished my sisters to various places around the Greensward."

He paused. "I came here to hide because Berwyn Laphroig is my brother."

FROGS, DOGS, AND THROGS

"I know you've explained it, but I still have a very hard time thinking of The Frog as your brother," Mistaya said.

She was back to sitting next to him on the pallet, the clouded balls that bound her hands resting in her lap. Food had arrived, finally, and since she couldn't feed herself, he was helping her by spooning into her mouth small portions of something that was just a notch above gruel on the nutritional meter. She was eating without tasting, her concentration elsewhere ever since His Eminence had departed, leaving behind his latest pronouncement on her fate.

"Well, it does take some getting used to," he agreed.

"At least he isn't your real brother. That would be even more difficult to accept."

"We had different mothers. Really, we're nothing alike. We share a common father and that's the extent of it."

"I wouldn't ever think you were like him," she said after a moment of chewing and swallowing. "No one would."

Thom smiled. "He's not like anyone, really. He was never interested in being friends with other people. He only wanted one thing from the time he could walk—to be Lord of Rhyndweir." He paused. "Actually, I think he wants a great deal more than that. That might have something to do with his interest in you."

She thought about it for a moment. It made sense. If he married her, he would be her spouse when she took the throne. *Took the throne.* That sounded so weird. She almost never thought about it. She couldn't quite make herself believe it would ever be necessary. The idea of her father not being King of Landover was inconceivable. Laphroig wouldn't think that way though; he would already be anticipating her father's demise.

"He wouldn't be satisfied with being married to me unless he could be King, would he?"

"He would want you to bear him a son he could raise as future King while he acted as regent during the child's minority. That's how he thinks. You would be a means to an end and not much more."

"Then he would get rid of me," she agreed. Thom didn't say anything. He didn't have to. She accepted another spoonful of whatever it was he was feeding her. "Well, I hate to disappoint him, but none of this is going to happen. I'm not ever marrying The Frog or bearing his child—ugh—or having anything to do with him. Once we get out of here and tell my father what he's done, we won't either of us have to worry about him ever again!"

Thom had related the details of his story earlier, laying it all out for her once she had calmed down enough to listen. After his father's death, he had lasted through the brief reign of his oldest brother, thinking that things at Rhyndweir might actually improve, since his brother was a decided improvement over his intractable and impetuous father. But when his brother had died under circumstances that were decidedly suspicious and his sisters had been shunted off to the farthest corners of the Greensward, he had recognized the writing on the wall. His other brother, who was now the new Lord of Rhyndweir and almost certainly responsible for everything, would soon get around to disposing of him. Telling no one, he departed his home in the dead of night. Once safely away, he resolved to wait things out until he knew which way the wind was blowing. When Berwyn's wives began dying one after the other, he abandoned any thoughts of returning and resolved to stay away as long as necessary. Shortly after, he reached Libiris, a refuge he had been considering from the first, and convinced His Eminence to let him stay.

Thom finished feeding her and put her bowl and spoon aside to take up his own. He ate with studied disinterest, eyes downcast and his usually cheerful demeanor subdued.

"What's wrong?" she asked him after a few minutes of silence.

"I was just thinking. After I fled Rhyndweir, my brother announced that I was dead. He did it in part, I think, to see if I would reappear to dispute it and in part to make everyone stop thinking about me. The first didn't work, but the second did. All this time, ever since I left, everyone has believed it. My mother, my sisters, my friends—everyone. I don't have a place in their lives anymore. I'm just a memory to them."

She looked down at her bound hands. "Don't be sad. All that will change once we're out of this mess." She gave him a tentative smile. "Think how happy they'll be to have you back."

He shrugged. "I just wish I knew how to make that happen. His Eminence isn't going to let us go; he can't afford to do that now that he's made a prisoner of you. Not to mention that he clearly has something bad planned for your father."

"I know," she agreed. "It has something to do with using me as bait to lure him to Libiris. He made that clear enough. My so-called special use. I wonder what it is."

"Whatever it is, he plans to improve his situation at our expense. Or maybe at your father's. I don't even trust him to keep his agreement to hide me, though he's done so up until now. If he thinks it will gain him anything, he will give me up in a heartbeat. Laphroig has never stopped hunting for me. If he finds me, I know what will happen."

Mistaya knew, too. Laphroig was ruthless and ambitious, and he had demonstrated on more than one occasion that he would eliminate anyone who got in his way.

"We're going to get out of here, Thom," she said suddenly, standing up as if ready to do so right that moment. "He can't keep us locked up forever. Sooner or later, we will find a way to get out."

He arched one eyebrow at her. "It had better be sooner. I don't think we have all that much time. Whatever he's got planned, it's going to come about pretty quickly now."

She was about to reassure him that it didn't matter what His Eminence had planned for them, that they would find a way to escape, when the cell door opened and in strolled Edgewood Dirk. The Prism Cat looked sleek and relaxed, his brilliant fur shining in the near darkness, his eyes agleam and his tail aloft and twitching left to right, right to left. He glanced at Thom, but mostly he kept his eyes on Mistaya as he came up to her, sat down so that they were facing each other, and began cleaning himself.

She watched him with ill-concealed frustration, but kept silent while he performed his ablutions.

"Good day," he greeted when finished, sounding as if he believed it actually was.

"I see that you've abandoned your insistence on never talking in front of anyone but me," she responded with as much irony as she could muster.

"I've abandoned it because you've compromised me by telling your friend everything you know about me," the cat replied. "There's not much point in pretending to be ordinary when you've already let the cat out of the bag, so to speak."

She sighed heavily. "Of course, I should have realized. But about that cheerful greeting you just offered?" She purposefully placed her hands where he could not miss seeing them as anything but balls of swirling, misty smoke. "It might be a good day for some, but not necessarily for me."

The cat cocked his head. "I see what you mean."

She waited a beat. "Well, then, perhaps you can do something about it? I would like to have the use of my hands back."

Edgewood Dirk seemed to consider. "I am afraid I cannot help you."

"You can't help me," she repeated flatly, exasperation flooding through her like a riptide beneath the water's surface.

"I'm a cat, you see."

"I do see. But you are so much more than an ordinary cat. You are a Prism Cat, in case you have forgotten. A fairy creature, possessed of special magic, if I am not mistaken."

"You are not mistaken. I am possessed of special magic, although I might choose a different word than *possessed* to describe my gifts. But while I have the use of special magic, I do not have the use of either fingers or opposable thumbs." He held up one paw to reinforce his point. "In case *you* have forgotten."

She shook her head. "What has that got to do with anything? All I want you to do is employ enough magic to rid me of my shackles!"

The cat cocked his head the other way. "I understand that. But it isn't easy for me to undo other spells. True, I have formidable skills with which to protect myself and sometimes others. I also have the ability to shield those I think might need it, such as you. But there are many things I cannot do because I lack the ability to weave spells in conjunction with speaking words. I believe that is your current problem, in point of fact, isn't it?"

"You have to use your hands to get rid of this spell?" she demanded in disbelief. She gave a quick glance over at Thom, who was eyeing the cat with some suspicion but clearly not interested in getting involved in this argument. "You can't set me free?"

"Lacking fingers and thumbs, I cannot make the necessary signs, even though I can speak the words. So, no, I cannot set you free."

Mistaya wanted to scream aloud her frustration. What was she supposed to do now? Dirk was her last real hope for getting out of there.

"Can you open the door and let us out?" Thom asked cautiously.

The cat lifted one paw and licked it, and then set it down again. "I can open the door for you. I can even shield you from discovery. I can do this, Andjen Thomlinson, and I will, even though the Princess broke her word and told you about me. But I can only help you, not her. So long as she wears her shackles, she can be tracked easily. For her, escape is impossible. She wouldn't get a dozen feet from the doorway before her captors were after her."

He paused. "So, then. Do you want me to help you escape? You alone?"

Thom shook his head reluctantly. "No, I won't leave Mistaya."

"So here we sit, awaiting our fate, helpless victims of your lack of thumbs and fingers," Mistaya declared with a flourish that was somewhere between theatrical, disgusted, and clumsy.

"Well, not entirely helpless," the cat advised. "You do have family and friends who might try to help you. And you do have your own considerable intelligence on which you might rely, just as you did with the problem of returning the books to the Stacks."

She stared at him. Had he just paid her a compliment? "His Eminence is already seeking to undo what I have done, so it may all have been for nothing. My family and friends have been told to let me be, so I don't look for them to come to my rescue." She paused. "And my considerable intelligence is drained of ideas."

"Perhaps you need to have a little more faith both in yourself and in others. You like being mistress of your own fate, but when you've needed help, hasn't it always been there?"

She thought back to her adventures with Nightshade. She considered her term of imprisonment at the Carrington Women's Preparatory School. "I suppose so. But that might not be the case this time."

"Faith, Princess," the Prism Cat repeated. "It is a highly underrated weapon against the dark things in this world."

He stood up, stretched and yawned, and turned for the door. "I have to be going now. I have other things to do and other places to be. But we will see each other again. Be patient with yourself. Cats are enormously patient, and as a result we almost always get what we want. I advise you to try it out for yourself."

"Wait!" she exclaimed, leaping up. "You can't just leave us!"

The cat was at the door. He stopped and turned. "Cats can do whatever they want, whenever they want, without regard to what anyone says or does. Rather like Princesses."

The door opened of its own accord. He sauntered out, and the door closed behind him, the locks refastening.

Mistaya looked at Thom. "That cat has a rotten attitude," she said.

In the somewhat subdued and somber chambers of Sterling Silver, a different attitude was in evidence. Ever since Questor Thews had returned from Libiris with news of Mistaya's whereabouts, the members of the inner circle of Landover's high court had been mulling over the King's decision to honor his daughter's choice to remain where she was. There were mixed feelings about this, and no one was resting easy. Knowing that Mistaya was with someone as notoriously unpredictable as Craswell Crabbit took a good deal of getting used to. No one was comfortable with the idea that the Princess was alone with such a man, yet no one was willing to press the point with her parents. After all, no one was more aware of the risks than they were, and they did not need reminding.

This did not mean, however, that their friends and retainers were able to stop worrying about it.

Abernathy in particular was distressed. He had been thinking it through from a somewhat different perspective than the others, being both man and dog and, thus, subject to the genetic breeding and emotional makeup of both, and he was beginning to see things that they might have missed.

First, he didn't much care for the idea of a fifteen-year-old being mistress of her own fate. A child unlike others, but a child still, Mistaya should be held accountable for her actions, and he did not think she should be telling her parents what to do. There was no reason for her to remain at Libiris and in such close proximity to Craswell Crabbit, a man Abernathy had been worried about from the beginning. She should come home and face Ben and Willow and then, after having aired her grievances, she might petition them to go back in the company of either Questor or himself. But she shouldn't be there alone.

Second, he was beginning to have a strong suspicion about

Thom. At first, he had dismissed the boy as someone of no importance. But the more he thought about it, the more he wondered
why Crabbit, who never did anything unless there was a strong
chance for personal gain, had allowed the boy to stay on. Because he
was court scribe, he knew Landover's history and everyone connected with it intimately, and he had come to suspect that the mysterious Thom might be Andjen Thomlinson, the younger brother of
Laphroig, who supposedly had been dead for three years. Abernathy
had always been suspicious of that story; there had never been any
proof that Kallendbor's youngest had indeed died. They would be
about the same age now, the Princess and the boy, and what Mistaya
had related of Thom to Questor suggested he might be less a village
boy and more an equal. Which made Abernathy wonder if Crabbit,
who was no fool, might have recognized this, too.

Because, third, he was almost certain that Crabbit knew who
Mistaya was. How could he not? Everyone who had even the small-
est link to the royal court knew of the King's only daughter. Her
physical features were striking and hard to mistake. Her history was
common knowledge. They knew what she looked like and they
knew her history. Crabbit should have figured it out by now. If so,
then why was he keeping it a secret from everyone, especially from
Mistaya? This bothered Abernathy because he knew it meant that
Crabbit was up to something.

Finally, he was troubled that Questor had managed to sneak in
and out of Libiris without being caught. This was a terrible thing to
admit, but he knew that the odds against the frequently inept wizard successfully bypassing the wardings and locks that the overlord
of the library would have set in place were huge. Crabbit was too
smart. Abernathy suspected that he had deliberately allowed
Questor to come and go, and that meant, once again, that he was up
to something.

So went the soft-coated wheaten terrier's thinking.

He mulled matters over for an entire day before he finally came
to the conclusion that he had to say something to someone.

The question was, To whom should he speak?

He did not want to alarm Ben and Willow; he needed his listener to have a clear head about what he was going to say. The depth of his concern for Mistaya's safety suggested he should bypass the King and Queen. The kobolds, Bunion and Parsnip, were good choices, but their judgment in these matters was suspect. Bunion, in particular, would favor a full-fledged frontal assault on Libiris and her caregiver.

That left Questor Thews, but speaking to him openly might prove awkward—especially if Abernathy questioned his wizarding abilities.

But he decided to take his chances, and following breakfast on the second day after coming to his decision to speak up, he sought the other out. He found him in his workshop, cataloging chemicals and compounds in his logbook and humming absently to himself. Abernathy stood in the open doorway for several long minutes, waiting to be noticed. When it became obvious he might stand there the rest of the day, he knocked loudly to announce his presence and stepped through.

Questor looked up, clearly annoyed. "I am quite busy at present, so if you don't mind . . ."

"But I do mind," Abernathy interrupted quickly, "and unless you are on the verge of making a breakthrough in your efforts to find a way to turn me back into a man, perhaps you ought to listen to what I have to say. It concerns Mistaya."

He sat himself down on a stool next to the wizard and proceeded to tell him everything. Well, almost everything. He chose to leave out the part about the suspicious ease of Questor's entry and exit from Libiris and focus on the rest. Irritating the wizard probably wouldn't do much to help his cause, whether what he had to say was valid or not.

"What are you suggesting we do?" the wizard asked when the other was finished. He pulled on his ragged white beard as if to free up an answer on his own. "Are we to try to persuade the High Lord that he should change his mind and go fetch Mistaya back?"

Abernathy shook his head, vaguely annoyed that the action

caused his ears to flop about. "You promised the Princess that you would do the exact opposite. I think you should keep that promise. Sending the High Lord would only cause trouble for everyone. I think we should go instead, just you and me."

"To have a closer look at things?"

"Without attempting to bring the Princess back home unless we encounter problems with Craswell Crabbit. Which I am almost certain we will. Call it intuition, but there's something going on there that we don't know about. Once we determine what it is, then we can decide whether or not to tell her she has to come home."

Questor sighed. "I don't fancy a trip back to that dreary place, but I see the wisdom in your thinking. Sometimes you quite amaze me, Abernathy. You really do."

"For a dog, you mean."

"For a court scribe, I mean." Questor Thews stood up. "Let's make something up to explain our absence and pack our things. We can leave right away."

At about the same time that Abernathy and Questor Thews were deciding on a course of action, two ragged figures were trudging north along the western edges of the Greensward, bound for a home they didn't particularly care to reach. Poggwydd and Shoopdiesel had been walking since early the previous day, when High Lord Ben Holiday had satisfied himself that they had told him everything they knew about the Princess and had released them with a stern warning to go home and not come back again anytime soon. The G'home Gnomes, used to much worse punishments, had considered themselves lucky to be let off so lightly. Shouldering the food and the extra clothing they had been given for the journey, they had set out with an air of mingled happiness and relief.

But the good feelings didn't last out the day. By nightfall, they were already pondering the dubious nature of their future. Poggwydd had left home under something of a cloud, and Shoopdiesel had chosen to throw in with him, so neither could expect to be welcomed back with open arms. In truth, neither cared anyway, since neither liked his home or wanted to return to it, even had things been different. What they really wanted was to stay at Sterling Silver, close to the Princess, whom they both adored. Add into the mix their ongoing concerns for her safety, which they did not feel certain about at all, and you had a pair of decidedly unhappy travelers.

Unfortunately, things were about to get worse.

The Gnomes were engaged in a heated argument about which form of gopher made the best eating or they might have caught sight of the rider before he was right on top of them. He seemed to appear out of nowhere, although in fact he had been tracking them for some distance, watching and waiting for his chance. He reined to a stop right in front of them and gingerly climbed down from his mount, looking decidedly grateful to be doing so. He was an innocuous-looking fellow, nothing of an apparent threat about him, rather smallish and thin with a huge shock of bushy hair, so the Gnomes didn't bolt at once, although they remained poised to do so.

"Gentlemen," the man greeted, giving them a deep bow. "It is an honor. I have been searching for you ever since you left the Princess behind at Libiris. Is she safe?"

Poggwydd, who was the smarter of the two friends, was immediately suspicious and held his tongue. But poor Shoopdiesel was already nodding eagerly, and the damage was done in an instant.

"Good, good!" exclaimed the stranger, who was now suddenly looking decidedly less innocuous and more predatory. "We must act swiftly, then. You do wish her safety assured, I assume? You would go back with me to help her, wouldn't you?"

Again, Shoopdiesel was nodding before Poggwydd could stop him. He glared at the other G'home Gnome and gave him a punch in the arm to make him aware that he was doing something wrong. Shoop stopped nodding instantly and looked at him in wide-eyed bafflement.

"What my friend means—" Poggwydd began, intending to undo as much of the damage as possible.

"Tut, tut," the stranger interrupted, holding up his hands to silence him. "No explanations are necessary. We all have the same goal in mind—to keep the Princess from harm. Now then. I need you both to come with me."

Poggwydd frowned. "Come with you to where? We are on our way home."

"Well, going home will have to wait a little longer," the stranger advised. He brushed at his mop of red hair in a futile endeavor to straighten it. "A little detour is required before your journey can continue."

"Who are you?" Poggwydd demanded, his query ending in a high-pitched squeak as other, more formidable horsemen rode out from behind trees and boulders, armed knights aboard chargers.

Cordstick smiled. The information supplied him through his network of spies had been accurate. These fools had been at Libiris and now they had revealed that the Princess was there, too. He could already envision his rapid advancement at court, the newly created position of Minister of State eagerly bestowed on him by a grateful Laphroig.

"Come with me, gentlemen, and I will take you to someone who will explain everything."

THE LESSER
OF TWO EVILS

His Eminence, Craswell Crabbit, sat at his oversized desk in his overblown office contemplating a list of the secret books he never let anyone see, not even Rufus Pinch. Some time back, when his grand scheme was first taking shape, he had decided there was no reason to share such information with someone who might one day outlive his usefulness. The Throg Monkeys had seen the books, but they were dull and incurious creatures and no threat to his plans. They knew to find the books, to bring them to him for cataloging, and then to take them down into Abaddon. They had no real idea of their purpose or their worth.

Only he understood that.

Only he knew that these were books of old magic and ancient conjuring with power enough to alter entire worlds.

The list in his hands contained the names of those books, but not their locations. Over the years, the books had been scattered throughout the Stacks by those who had owned them previously and brought them here to store. Some had been placed haphazardly, some given false titles, and some deliberately hidden in more creative ways. Finding them anew and collecting them was the trick. It was, although young Thom didn't realize it, the task to which Crabbit had set himself when he had put the boy to work cataloging inventory. While seemingly organizing the library, he was secretly searching out the missing books of magic and transporting them down into Abaddon.

At first blush, that might have seemed self-defeating. What was the point of finding all these books only to turn them over to the demons? Wouldn't he have been better off keeping them for himself? The answers were not immediately obvious. Keeping the books in his personal possession would have been the ideal choice. But he needed the demons to achieve the goal he had set himself, which meant letting them have access to the books and their spells. It was a clear quid pro quo. The demons wanted a way out of Abaddon, and there were spells in the books of magic that could give them that. He wanted Landover's throne, and the demons could give it to him.

Well, to a large degree. They could give him the army he needed to take control of the Kingdom once Ben Holiday was out of the way. They could give him power over the Lords of the Greensward and the River Master and his once-fairy and all the rest.

And then he would rid himself of the demons by sending them outside of Landover into the myriad worlds to which she was linked.

This last was the tricky part, of course, but he believed he had worked it out. Demons, by nature, were never satisfied, and if they could be freed from Abaddon's prison they would migrate willingly to other places.

He allowed himself a satisfied smile. A fair-minded man would have blanched at what he was planning, but he was not a fair-minded man by any stretch of the imagination. Such men littered the pages of history books under the category heading "Losers, Failures, and Weaklings." He had no intention of being remembered as one of these. He would be remembered as a great and powerful man, a leader, a ruler, and a conqueror.

He was contemplating his place in history, visualizing lesser men reading of his prowess as they pined over their own inescapable shortcomings, when Rufus Pinch appeared in the doorway, wild-eyed.

"Craswell, we have a serious problem!" he exclaimed breathlessly and collapsed into an overstuffed chair to one side, mopping a bright sheen of perspiration from his wrinkled brow. "A very serious problem," he added.

His Eminence, who did not like serious problems unless they belonged to someone else, looked stern and unforgiving. "Get to it, Mr. Pinch. And what did I tell you about the proper form by which to address me?"

Rufus Pinch glared at him. "You have much bigger problems than what I choose to call you, Mr. Craswell Crabbit, Your Esteemed Eminence!" He spit out the names with such vitriol that Crabbit was taken aback. "Now do you want to hear what I have to say or not?"

His Eminence exhaled wearily and gave an assenting gesture. "Proceed."

"Berwyn Laphroig, Lord of Rhyndweir, is standing at the front door and demanding to be admitted. He wants you to come out to speak with him."

"Did you tell him that no one . . . ?"

". . . is to be admitted, yes, of course, I told him! But he didn't care for that answer, and he has threatened to gain entry by force if denied it by acquiescence. He has fifty armed knights and a battering ram to back up his threat, I might add."

His Eminence stared. "Did he say what he wants?"

"Yes, Your Eminence. He wants you. Downstairs. Speaking with him. Right away. If you refuse, he will break down the doors, seek you out, and do things to you that I don't care to repeat!"

The other man frowned anew, not at all pleased with this bit of information. He thought momentarily of summoning magic enough to melt the entire attack force into lead dumplings, but discarded the idea as too radical. Better to talk to Laphroig first and see what it was he wanted. He could always fry him up for dinner later.

"Come with me," he said, getting to his feet and coming around the desk. He got as far as the door before he changed his mind. "No, wait. Stay here. Keep an eye on our little friends in the storage room, just in case. Whatever happens, we don't want them getting out and stirring up additional trouble. Not that I think they will, but it doesn't hurt to be cautious, Mr. Pinch."

Grumbling about everything in general and nothing in particular, his associate trundled away in a huff. His Eminence watched him go, thinking anew that perhaps the value of their friendship was diminished sufficiently that it was time to sever it. Relationships gone sour should be ended swiftly and completely. It was a harsh, but necessary, rule of life for great men.

It occurred to Craswell Crabbit, as he crossed from his office to the entryway of the building, that the reason for Berwyn Laphroig's visit could have to do with the fact that he had discovered his younger brother was alive and hiding at Libiris. How he had found that out was anyone's guess, but it would certainly explain his insistence on being allowed entry. If that were the case, His Eminence reasoned, he might well be forced to give up young Thom just to avoid the unpleasantness that would almost certainly follow otherwise. He had hoped that Thom might one day prove valuable as a bargaining chip, a way to gain leverage over Rhyndweir's Lord should that prove necessary. But the boy's presence couldn't be allowed to interfere with his current plans, so if push came to shove young Thom would have to go under the ax. Literally.

He reached the entry, passed through, and, taking a moment to compose himself, opened the doors to Libiris.

Bright sunshine spilled out of a nearly cloudless blue sky, momentarily blinding him. He squinted through the glare at the dozens of armored knights sitting their horses in tight formation not two dozen yards from where he stood. At their forefront, rather incongruously, two hapless-looking G'home Gnomes sat trussed and bound atop a single charger. Craning his neck in order to make himself even taller, His Eminence searched for Laphroig. Instead, he found a stick-thin fellow standing just off to one side of him looking exceedingly distressed, rather as if he needed help with loosening pants that were too tight. His frantic movements, constrained and half formed, were puzzling.

"Crabbit!" barked a voice directly in front of him.

He jumped back, startled, and discovered that Berwyn Laphroig, a man barely taller than Crabbit's belt buckle, was staring up at him. "Good day to you, Lord Laphroig," he offered, recovering his equanimity. "I understand you wish to speak with me?"

"You took your time getting here!" the other snapped. "We must talk, just the two of us, alone. It concerns your guest."

So there it is, His Eminence concluded. *He's found out about his brother and come to take him away.* Shrugging his reluctant agreement, he led Rhyndweir's diminutive lord inside the entryway, closing the door behind him. He stopped him there, blocking his way forward.

"So, then?" he asked, testing the waters. "Of whom do you speak?"

Laphroig was incensed. His face colored and his neck tendons strained. "You know perfectly well who, Craswell Crabbit! Mistaya Holiday, Princess of Landover! You are hiding her here, presumably so that her father cannot find her. But I have found her, and I intend to take her back to Rhyndweir with me."

His Eminence stared at him in surprise. This put a different twist on things. Apparently, Berwyn Laphroig still knew nothing of young Thom, only of the Princess. "You wish to return her to the High Lord?" he pressed, trying to navigate murky waters.

"What I wish is my business and none of yours!" the other snapped.

"Well, she is here for safekeeping and under my protection," His Eminence advised. "I don't intend to turn her over to you or anyone without a very good reason for doing so."

The Frog glared. "This isn't a request, Crabbit. It is a demand. From a Lord of the Greensward with fifty armed knights looking for an excuse to break down your front door. You will give me the girl or I will simply take her."

"By force of arms? From me, a trained wizard?"

"I don't care what it takes or what you are, the girl will be mine. I am determined on it. She is to be my wife."

Ah, thought His Eminence, *the light begins to dawn. He wants the Princess of Landover for his bride.*

"You are already married, are you not?" he asked, using his most solicitous tone of voice.

"News travels slowly in this part of Landover, I see," the other snapped. "My wife and son are dead, more than several weeks now, and thus I am left with neither spouse nor heir to my throne. Mistaya Holiday will provide me with both."

And so much more, His Eminence added silently. "But why would she choose to marry you, if you don't mind my asking? Not that any girl in her right mind would pass on such an opportunity, but I have discovered that this particular girl can be most obstreperous."

Laphroig squared his shoulders, sweeping his black cloak behind him dramatically. "I will tame her. She will come to see that I am the right husband for her. It is an excellent match, Crabbit. I will give her freedom from her parents, which she obviously desires, and she will give me sons to rule!"

She will give you a foot in your backside, His Eminence thought but did not say. "Time is an issue here, is it not?" he said instead. "Her father will learn of her presence at Rhyndweir and come to take her home. Likely, she will agree. What to you plan to do about that?"

Laphroig looked momentarily nonplussed. "He won't find out about her right away. I will have my chances to win her over."

"But winning over a girl of fifteen might take some doing, especially if she is a Princess of Landover. If you force her in any way, she will go straight to her father and your head will be on the block." His Eminence saw his chance now and determined to take it. "Suppose I was able to persuade her to accept you as her husband and to enter into marriage with you immediately? You cannot force a girl of fifteen to marry you, but if she signs a valid consent the marriage is binding. What if I were able to produce such a consent? Even a King would be bound by such a document."

The Frog frowned and shook his head. "How could you manage this, Crabbit? What sort of hold do you have over her?"

His Eminence shrugged. "She came to me for shelter and I provided it. She has come to trust me. I am persuasive when I need to be."

"You are a purveyor of horse pucky, is what you are. Come to trust you, has she? Persuasive when you need to be, are you? Nonsense! You must know a spell that will bind her to your command. You must have a way to trick her using magic."

His Eminence glared. "Do you want my help or not? Because if you don't, then let's put an end to this. You risk everything by insisting on taking her by force, but that is certainly your choice."

The Frog considered. "What do you get out of all this? You wouldn't expect me to believe that you are helping me out of the kindness of your heart, would you?"

His Eminence smiled. "Let us be perfectly open with each other, Lord Laphroig. Your intentions go well beyond the obvious. You hunger for Landover's throne, and by marrying Mistaya Holiday you put yourself in a position to claim it. If the royal line should diminish sufficiently, rule of Landover could fall to you."

He held up his hands in warning as the other started to object. "Wait, wait, I am not being in any way critical of your ambitions. I, too, would like to see Ben Holiday removed as King. Having his daughter here furthers that goal. But I think it might be in our best interests to work together on this. Essentially, we both want the same thing. You want access to Landover's throne, and I want Ben Holiday off it. What if there was a quick and easy way to make that happen?"

Berwyn Laphroig pulled his black cloak closer about him and glanced around uneasily. "You are speaking treason, Crabbit."

His Eminence had endured being called "Crabbit" just about as long as he could, but he forced himself to stay focused on the matter at hand. "Yes or no? Where do you stand?"

"How would you make this happen?" the other whispered, leaning close enough that His Eminence was forced to take a step back to avoid his rather noxious breath.

"Mistaya Holiday will acquiesce to your marriage and sign a consent in the bargain. I will perform the ceremony myself; I am authorized to do so. You shall remain with her at Libiris when the nuptials are concluded; your conjugal rights shall be concluded and an heir assured. Her father will come to rescue her, but when he does he will find a rather unpleasant surprise awaiting him—a rather long drop down a deep hole. It will be over before he realizes what is happening. A trap has been set and remains in place. His demise will be swift, and your path of ascension to the throne of Landover will be cleared."

He paused, doing his best to look humble. "All I ask is that I be given free rein to continue my work here as royal librarian."

"I become King and you become royal librarian?" Laphroig did not look convinced.

His Eminence shrugged. "With certain guarantees. I would also be granted immunity from prosecution for my continued experimentation with magic. There are certain . . . ah, conjurings I would like to attempt that could have rather unpleasant side effects for the people involved. Of course, I would only use peasants and the like, creatures of no value." He paused. "You would be welcome to attend at your convenience. You might enjoy it."

He could see that Laphroig was already envisioning himself as King of Landover and that none of the rest of it mattered. He would wed Mistaya Holiday, engender an heir, and then rid himself of the girl. Ben Holiday and his Queen would be dead and gone by then, the royal family wiped out save for his newborn son. As husband of the Princess and father of the only surviving heir to the throne, he would have an indisputable claim. No one would be able to challenge his right of rule once the boy died, too.

What he didn't know, however—what he would *never* know until it was too late—was that he would be dead, as well. Craswell Crabbit did not much care for partnerships, especially with creatures like Laphroig.

Moreover, he would do much better as King of Landover than Rhyndweir's unstable and unpopular Lord.

"Do we have an agreement?" he asked brightly, beaming down at the smaller man.

Berwyn Laphroig nodded slowly. "We do. If, Crabbit, you can persuade the Princess to marry me right now and without argument."

"Please wait right here," His Eminence said, thinking as he turned away that this was the last time Berwyn Laphroig would get what he wanted in this life.

Neither caught sight of the black-and-silver cat sitting quietly and unobtrusively in the shadows, licking its paws.

━━━◦≫◦━━━

Mistaya and Thom were sitting side by side on the pallet in the candlelit storeroom, lost in silent contemplation of their predicament and puzzling through methods of escape, when they heard the rasp of the lock bar being drawn back. They rose as the heavy wooden door opened and His Eminence stepped into view. He glanced from one to the other and back again, smiling.

"Well, you both seem to be holding up well enough. How would you like to get out of here?"

The girl and the boy exchanged a suspicious glance. "You know the answer to that question already," Mistaya replied. "What do you want from us now?"

His Eminence rubbed his hands eagerly. "To begin with, I would like to have a private conversation with you. Thom, would you mind stepping outside and waiting in the storeroom next door? All I ask is that you make no attempt to escape while you are there. It would be a huge mistake for you to try. Mr. Pinch will be there to reinforce the point."

Thom looked at Mistaya questioningly. "I'll be all right," she told him. "Won't I, Your Eminence?" she added, giving Crabbit a meaningful glance.

"Perfectly all right. This won't take but a few minutes."

A reluctant Thom went out the door, closing it behind him. His Eminence waited a few moments more, cocking his elongated head to one side, giving it a Humpty-Dumpty-sat-on-the-wall look. Then he moved closer to Mistaya and stood staring at her. She could tell from the look alone that whatever was coming was going to be bad.

"I will make this brief and to the point," His Eminence declared. "You deserve that much, at least. Berwyn Laphroig has discovered you are here and has come to take you to Rhyndweir. He intends to make you his wife and the mother of his children. Of his sons, if all goes well. I have argued with him, but to no avail. The matter is complicated by the fact that he also knows about Thom. The one concession I have been able to wring from him is that if you marry him voluntarily, executing a viable written consent to the match, he will leave Thom in my safekeeping. Otherwise, he intends to dispatch Thom immediately. Am I being perfectly clear on all this?"

Mistaya nodded wordlessly. If she didn't marry The Frog, Thom would be killed. If she did marry The Frog, she would have to kill herself. Figuratively, anyway.

She gave him a chilly smile. "No one has the right to tell a Princess of Landover whom she may wed. Not even my parents. Certainly not you. I will wed when I am good and ready and not before, and I will wed a man of my own choosing. I refuse to be married to The Frog. What's more, if any harm comes to Thom, I will see to it that your head is posted on your own gate until there is nothing left of it but bone. Am *I* being perfectly clear on all *this*?"

His Eminence stared at her silently, shaking his head. "You do live in a fairy-tale world, don't you, Princess? All you see is what you want to see. If you don't want to think about something or face up to something, it simply doesn't exist for you. Goodness. But this is the real world, not some make-believe story in which you are the heroine. So perhaps you ought to rethink your situation before you start making threats."

He snatched the front of her tunic and pulled her close enough that she could feel his breath on her face. He towered over her, and she could see the anger in his eyes.

"You are my possession, Princess!" he hissed softly. "You belong to me. I can do with you what I want. Do you understand me?"

She nodded without speaking, her eyes riveted on his. For the first time since she had come to Libiris, she was genuinely scared. She was terrified.

"Well, then," he continued, his voice still a whisper, "it ought to be simple for you. I don't choose to make you do anything you don't want to do, even though I can. But this is the reality—you hold a boy's life in your hands. So you need to consider your choices carefully and spare me your idle threats. You need to consider the consequences of those choices. Listen now—here they are again. If you fail to walk out of here and tell Berwyn Laphroig that you will marry him and bear his children, I shall be forced to turn young Thom over to him and you will have the unfortunate experience of watching him die right in front of your eyes, knowing it was all your fault! Is any of this not clear?"

When she failed to answer, he sighed wearily. "I shall take it from your silence that you understand. Now let's try it again. Think carefully before you speak. Will you agree to this arrangement or not? Will you marry Berwyn Laphroig or shall I send young Thomlinson out for a short reunion? Give me your answer."

She compressed her lips into a tight line. "My father will never countenance this! He will not let me be used in this way! You had better release me right now!"

His Eminence pulled a face, released her tunic front, and stepped back. "Very well. I shall deliver your answer—and the boy—to his brother. Good luck to you, Princess."

Without waiting for any further response, he turned for the door. He had reached it and was pulling it open when she called to him. "Wait, no. Don't do that. Don't tell him that. Tell him I accept his proposal. But I want something in writing signed by him, something in the marriage contract that says he will not harm Thom now or ever."

His Eminence turned back and gave her a long, searching look. "Done," he said finally, and went out the door.

Alone again, she collapsed onto the pallet and stared into space. Tears she was unable to hold back trickled down her cheeks. She wanted to bury her face in her hands and shut out everything, but she couldn't do so while the magic held them bound. The room was dark and empty, and Thom did not return. She wished she were back in school or home or anywhere but here. She wished she had listened to a whole lot of advice that she had chosen to ignore.

What was she going to do?

She knew she couldn't let anything happen to Thom, no matter what. If she were responsible for his death, she could never live with herself. The trade-off was horrendous, but she kept thinking that even if she went through with this, her father would find a way to undo it. But what if he couldn't? What if no one could? She kept thinking that something would happen to stop all this, but she couldn't think what that something would be.

She stopped crying finally and tried to think clearly about how things stood. She didn't have the use of her magic and wouldn't have while her hands were bound. She had to find a way to free them, if only for a minute. She didn't have the rainbow crush, so she couldn't summon help. But even if she had it, whom would she summon? Not her father—that was what His Eminence wanted. Questor? No, he had been duped once already, and Crabbit was probably the superior wizard. Her grandfather? No, no! She brushed it all aside as wishful thinking. There wasn't much chance that she would be allowed back into her room unaccompanied, and that was the only way she could get her hands on the crush anyway. Thom could retrieve it if he knew it was there and was free to go get it. But he didn't and he wasn't, so that was that.

She got to her feet and crossed to the door and stopped, placing her hands against the rough wood, her mind racing. How could she stop this from happening? There had to be a way!

From beyond the locked door, she heard footsteps in the hallway.

She thought suddenly of Haltwhistle, whom she might still have been able to count on if she had remembered to speak his name and hadn't gotten so caught up in her own concerns that she had forgotten him. Edgewood Dirk might have sent the mud puppy away, but she was the one who had made that possible. Was it too late to call him back? Was he gone from her forever?

"Haltwhistle," she whispered, and it was almost a prayer. "Halt-whistle," she said again, louder this time.

She jumped in shock as the latch on the door released. She wiped her tear-streaked face on her shoulder. She shouldn't be crying, she told herself. She was tougher than this. She was better than what she was showing.

"Haltwhistle!" she said a final time, bold and determined.

But as the door opened it wasn't the mud puppy who appeared but His Eminence, Craswell Crabbit. "Time to go, Princess," he announced. "Your future husband awaits."

And with a dramatic sweep of his arm he beckoned her through the open doorway.

BRAVEHEART

As she trudged from her storeroom prison into the hallway, dutifully trailing a clearly elated Craswell Crabbit, a strange thing happened to Mistaya Holiday. One moment she was subdued and submissive, riddled with self-doubt and fear, her future a bleak certainty from which she could find no escape, and the next she was so angry that the rest of what she had been feeling was swept away in a tidal wave of rage. It happened all at once and for no discernible reason that she could identify, a shift of such monumental proportions that it shook her to the core.

It also focused her in a way that nothing else had.

Her posture changed, her mind cleared, and her confidence hardened. She was not going to let this happen. It might seem to those who sought to use her so badly that it would, but they were in for a big surprise. Whatever it took, whatever she had to do, she was going to put a stop to all of it.

And to them.

In that instant, she was once more the child of three worlds and three distinct cultures, the little girl born of Landover, fairy, and Earth all grown up and ready and willing to fight. She had stood against Nightshade, the Witch of the Deep Fell, and defeated her when it seemed impossible. She would do the same with His Eminence and The Frog and all their minions. She would not stand by and let them ruin her life and betray her country and her parents for their own personal gain. She would not let them disfigure Libiris or subvert and misuse her books. She would find a way to prevail.

As they passed Rufus Pinch, standing watch before the door of the storeroom in which Thom was held prisoner, the little man called out, "Have a good life, Princess!"

She stopped at once and turned on him. The look on her face sent Pinch stumbling back against the door, hands raised defensively, face terror-stricken. "What I meant, Your Majesty . . . ," he tried to say as the words dried to dust in his mouth.

"Thank you for your good wishes," she replied sweetly. Then, turning to Crabbit, who was waiting for her, she said, "I want Thom to witness this."

His Eminence frowned. "That is a terrible idea. He might do something foolish to try to stop it. Worse, he might further antagonize his brother. He is better off where he is."

"He won't interfere. Let me speak with him, and I will make certain of it. If he disobeys, the fault will be mine and the penalty will be his to bear. But I want him there. I have to be certain he accepts that this marriage is real."

His Eminence looked as if he might deny this out of hand, but then abruptly he shrugged. "You may speak with him. If he promises to behave, he can come out. But Mr. Pinch will be watching him closely."

Pinch appeared to be on the verge of a heart attack. "Crabbit, you fool, you can't trust . . . !"

"Mr. Pinch!" the other snapped, his voice as hard and cold as ice. "You forget yourself! Remember your place! You serve me at my pleasure and not the other way around. You are here at my sufferance. Remember that, as well. And do not ever again call me by name!"

Pinch had shrunk to the approximate size of a walnut, which given his general appearance wasn't as difficult to do as it might seem. Reluctantly, he unlocked the door to the storeroom and stepped aside. Mistaya, giving him her sweetest smile, walked in.

"The door will remain open, Princess," His Eminence called after her.

Thom stood up from the bench on which he had been sitting and came to her immediately, the relief in his face obvious. "I thought something bad had happened to you!" he whispered excitedly.

"Something bad *has* happened to me," she said, feeling his strong hands on her arms. "Now back up, away from the door."

He did as she asked, guiding her into the deeper shadows, never taking his hands from her. "What is it?" he demanded.

"I'm to marry your brother," she told him. "No, don't say anything!" she continued as he started to object. "Just listen to me! I don't intend for the marriage to happen, but it has to look as if I do. His Eminence has agreed to let you watch, but you have to agree in turn not to do anything to disrupt the ceremony or cause trouble. Will you do that?"

He looked horrified. "No, I won't do that! I can't just sit by while my brother . . ." He broke off, unable to finish. "Why would you agree to this in the first place? You're a Princess of Landover; you don't have to marry someone like him!"

"If I don't agree to it, they will give you over to be killed."

"Then let them do so!"

She took a deep, steadying breath. "No, Thom, I won't. But I won't let them marry me off, either. You have to trust me on this."

"But what can you do to stop it?"

In truth, she didn't know. She just knew she would do something. "I'll find a way," she assured him. "Just wait for a sign to break free of Pinch. He'll be watching you closely."

Thom shook his head. "I should just stay with you—"

"You should just keep quiet," she said, cutting him short.

He stopped talking and stood there, looking at her.

"Kiss me," she told him impulsively. "Right now. Like you mean it. Like you might not get another chance."

He did so, on the mouth, a long kiss that caused Pinch, standing in the doorway, to gasp and mutter in dismay. She closed her eyes and leaned into the kiss. So sweet, so exciting.

"Enough, children," His Eminence called over the other's shoulder. "Do we have a bargain or not?"

"We do," Mistaya said, breaking off the kiss reluctantly but not looking away from Thom. "Don't we?" she asked him softly.

"We do," he whispered reluctantly.

His Eminence beckoned Mistaya from the room and shoved Pinch in to replace her. "Take young Thom aside and wrap him up in a cloak. Bring him out only after the ceremony has started. Do you understand me, Mr. Pinch?"

Pinch glared at him and hustled Thom away. His Eminence watched them go, shaking his head. "So hard to find good help," he mused. "Come, Princess."

She followed silently, eyes downcast as if she'd become entirely submissive, while her mind worked furiously. If she was to do anything to help herself, she had to free her hands. Everything depended on being able to invoke her magic, and her magic was needed if she was to free herself from the spell that bound them. But how could she persuade His Eminence to release her long enough for her to invoke a spell that would help? And what sort of spell would it take for her to gain freedom? Not just for herself, but for Thom, as well. It would do no good for her to escape without him. She thought of the many forms of magic she had learned from Nightshade. She thought of all the spells that Questor had taught her to cast. Which among them would work to help her here? A battle fought with killing magic would be risky for everyone involved, but what sort of magic could she call upon that would effectively put a stop to the plans of His Eminence and Laphroig?

Then suddenly she knew exactly what she must do. It was so simple, she was surprised she hadn't thought of it earlier. She almost smiled, but managed to keep from doing so by remembering that her plan might still fall flat.

Just at that moment she caught sight of something moving along the wall far ahead, nearly lost in the shadows. It was there and gone in the blink of an eye, and she had not seen enough to be certain, but she thought it might be Edgewood Dirk.

Or not. She grimaced.

They reached the door to His Eminence's office. Crabbit glanced back at her as if to reassure himself that she was prepared for what waited on the other side, his oblong head cocked as he fixed his gaze on her young face. "It is surely a pity you have to be given to him," he commiserated. "You would have been better served with another husband, but such matters are not for either of us to decide. We only do what we must, don't we, Princess?"

She wanted to wring his neck and promised herself that when she got the chance, she would. "Yes, Your Eminence," she agreed docilely.

He opened the door, and there stood Berwyn Laphroig. All in black, his pale frog face radiating expectation and a few other unmentionable things, he charged forward to greet her. "Princess Mistaya!" he purred. "How lovely to see you again. I trust our last encounter hasn't left any bitter feelings? There mustn't be any of those. But you are here! Dare I hope that you have reconsidered my proposal to wed?"

He certainly didn't waste time with small talk, she thought in dismay. "I have reconsidered," she agreed. "His Eminence has been very persuasive."

"A well-considered decision, Princess!" He was practically jumping up and down, his froggy eyes bulging, his tongue licking out. "And Crabbit! Excellent work, Crabbit!" He gave His Eminence a short bow of acknowledgment. "We must proceed immediately with the wedding, then!"

His Eminence ushered her all the way into the office and closed the door behind them. "Yes, well, there are a few legal matters to be settled first. Paperwork to be filled out, agreements to be signed, that sort of thing. A consent to the marriage agreed upon and signed by both parties is requisite."

Laphroig flushed. "Well, get about preparing it then! Don't keep the Princess waiting!"

His Eminence sat down to work while Laphroig crowded close to Mistaya, looking her up and down in the way a buyer might a new horse, smiling as if all were right with the world. Or maybe just as if all were right with him. She tried not to shrink from him, did her best not to show her loathing, and held herself firmly in check.

"Would it be possible for you to free my hands?" she asked suddenly, looking not at His Eminence, but at Laphroig. "A bride on her wedding day shouldn't appear in shackles."

Laphroig glanced down and seemed to see for the first time the swirling ball of darkness that bound her hands. "What's this, Crabbit?" he snapped. "What have you done to her?"

His Eminence glanced up, sighing. "It is for her own good. And yours."

"Well, I don't like it. How can it appear that consent is given voluntarily if she weds me looking as if she is shackled in some mysterious way? Even the appearance of coercion is unacceptable. Signing the consent is sufficient, I should think. Set her free!"

Craswell Crabbit shook his head firmly. "That would be immensely foolish, my Lord."

"I promise not to try to escape," Mistaya said quickly. "I won't run from you. You have my word as a Princess of Landover. I have made my decision, and I will see the wedding through to its conclusion. But don't make me marry you like this."

She tried to sound pathetic and put upon instead of desperate, casting a pleading glance at The Frog.

"Crabbit seems rather convinced that it would better if you did." Laphroig was experiencing doubts, as well. "The word of a Princess of Landover ought to count for something, I realize, but you are known for your troublesome nature, Princess."

"But I promise! What more can I do?"

Laphroig smiled. "I am sure I could think of something." He leered. Then he shrugged, refocusing on the matter at hand. "I can't see that it would do any harm. Not if you give us your promise."

His Eminence looked at him as if he had lost his mind. "You are seriously contemplating setting free a young woman with magic enough at her command to burn us all to ash? Have you lost your mind, Laphroig?"

"Watch your tongue, Crabbit! Unlike you, I am not afraid of a fifteen-year-old girl. I have fifty knights waiting just outside the door, and should she prove too troublesome, I might give her over to them for a bit of sport." He gave Mistaya a look. "So I don't think we need be concerned."

"Your Eminence," Mistaya said quickly, ignoring the threat. "My word is good. I will not break it. I have more than one reason not to do so, as you well know." She flicked her eyes toward the office door, reaffirming her commitment to Thom. "Besides," she added, "won't I need my hands free to sign the documents of marriage? Won't I need them in order to don my wedding dress? You do have a wedding dress for me, don't you?"

His Eminence stared at her for a long moment. "Naturally, I shall provide you with a wedding dress, Princess. And since Lord Laphroig seems set on this, I shall set you free. But I warn you, disobedience at this juncture would be a big mistake. The matter is in your hands. Be careful."

He made a few quick gestures, spoke a few short words, and the swirling ball that held her hands imprisoned faded away. She rubbed her wrists experimentally as His Eminence watched her like a hawk and then allowed them to drop harmlessly to her sides. "There, you see?" she said.

His Eminence went back to preparing the documents of marriage while Laphroig launched into a long, rhapsodic dissertation on the joys that awaited her once she was married to him. She nodded along agreeably, thinking through her plan as she did so. It was a risky gamble, but it was all she could do. If it failed, she was in deep trouble.

She found herself wishing momentarily that she could use her newfound freedom to break from the room, race to her bedroom, produce the rainbow crush, and stamp on it while calling for her father. But her father might be as much at risk as she was—perhaps more so, if what she had heard His Eminence say earlier was to be believed—so she would die before she summoned help from that quarter.

In any case, there was no time left for second-guessing and nothing to be gained by wishing for what might have been. She had made her choice, and she was going to have to live with it. If she were given half a chance, things would work out.

His Eminence straightened at his desk. "All done. Please sign on the lines here and here," he advised Mistaya and Laphroig, indicating the required spaces.

Laphroig signed without reading, impatient to get on with things. Mistaya took her time, skimming quickly but thoroughly, and found the promise not to harm Thom embedded deep in the document in language that was clear and concise. Whatever happened to her, she would have protected Thom to the extent that she was able to do so. She took a deep breath and signed, knowing that if the marriage went through now, it would be binding on her and on her parents under Landover's laws.

She sat back, thinking that if all else failed, perhaps she could leave Landover behind and go back to school at Carrington for the rest of her life. *As if.*

"Now, about my dress?" she queried His Eminence.

Crabbit moved her back a few steps, worked a quick conjuring with words and gestures, and she was suddenly clothed in a stunningly beautiful white gown that left Laphroig with his eyes wide, his mouth open, and his tongue hanging out.

"Princess, I have never seen anything—"

"Thank you, my Lord." She cut him short with a perfunctory wave of her hand. "Shall we go outside into the open for the ceremony?"

Again, His Eminence didn't look pleased with this suggestion, but Laphroig leaped on it like a starving dog on a bone and proclaimed that, indeed, the wedding must take place outdoors before his assembled knights, who would act as witnesses.

So out the office door they went, then down the hall to the front of the building and out into the sunlight. The knights still sat their horses, and the G'home Gnomes were still bound and gagged atop their mule. Cordstick had gone from looking distressed to looking euphoric. Mistaya ignored them all, resisted the urge to look back for Thom, and kept her eyes fixed straight ahead as His Eminence marched her out to a small grove of rather wintry trees and placed her side by side with the Lord of Rhyndweir.

Craswell Crabbit cleared his throat. "Be it known, one and all, from the nearest to the farthest corners of the realm, that this man and this woman have consented . . ."

He droned on, but Mistaya wasn't paying attention. She was thinking through her plan, knowing that she must put it into play quickly. If the wedding got too far along, there might not be enough time for things to come together as she needed them to.

Mistaya gazed out at the assembled knights, who had removed their helmets out of respect for the ceremony, whatever it was, and the girl, whoever she was, most of them obviously having no clear idea of what they were all doing there. The G'home Gnomes were moaning softly through their gags, and every so often the two guards bracketing them would lean over and cuff one or the other or both.

"Mistaya Holiday, Princess of Landover, do you take this man, Berwyn Laphroig, Lord of Rhyndweir to be—"

"What?" she asked, snapped back into the moment by the question. She looked blankly at His Eminence and then at Laphroig.

"Of course she does!" The Frog snapped. "Get on with it, Crabbit!"

Craswell Crabbit looked flummoxed. "Well, we need rings, then. One from each of you."

Laphroig began pulling at the rings on his fingers, of which there were plenty, trying to loosen one to give to her. Mistaya glanced at her own fingers. She wore only two rings, both given to her by her parents as presents when she left home for Carrington. She grimaced at the thought of giving either up.

She made a show of trying to remove the rings, but in effect began the process of casting her spell, weaving her fingers and whispering the words of power. His Eminence was preoccupied with watching Laphroig, who was thrashing wildly now in his efforts to loosen one of the rings he wore.

As he finally succeeded, turning back to Mistaya, reaching for her hand to slip the ring in place, she said abruptly, "My Lord, I lack a ring to seal our bargain, but I give you this gift instead!"

She wove her hands rapidly, completing the spell. His Eminence tried to stop her, but he was too slow and too late.

Crimson fire blossomed across the sky above them, an explosion of flames that dropped the wedding party to its knees and caused the mounts of the knights to rear and buck and finally bolt in terror.

"I warned you, Princess!" His Eminence shouted at her, covering his head with his hands as he did so. "I warned you!"

Laphroig had dropped flat against the ground, his eyes darting every which way at once, trying to discover what was going to happen to him. "You promised!" he screamed at Mistaya. "You gave your word!"

Overhead, the flames parted like the curtains on a stage, and the dragon Strabo appeared.

TILL DEATH
DO US PART

Strabo was the perfect incarnation of anyone's worst nightmare, a huge black monster with spikes running up and down his back in a double row, a fearsome horn-encrusted head, claws and teeth the size of gate spikes, and armor plating that could withstand attacks from even the most powerful spear or longbow. He was impervious to heat and cold, no matter how extreme; he was able to fly high enough and far enough to transverse entire worlds whenever he chose. He was contemptuous of humans and fairy creatures alike, and he regarded their presence as an affront that he did not suffer gladly.

The dragon burst through the flames and swooped down toward the wedding party. Rhyndweir's knights and their mounts scattered for a second time, taking the unfortunate G'home Gnomes with them. Cordstick dove for cover under the trees. Mistaya stood her ground, watching the dragon approach. Laphroig had flattened himself against the earth at her feet, screaming in a mix of fear and rage, and His Eminence was crouched to defend himself, apparently the only one prepared to do so.

For just an instant, Strabo loomed over Libiris and the surrounding woods like a huge dark cloud that threatened to engulf them all. Then he turned to smoke, vaporized in an instant without warning, and was gone.

There was a stunned silence as everyone but Mistaya waited for his return. Then, quite slowly and deliberately, Laphroig climbed back to his feet, brushed himself off, turned to Mistaya with a smile, and struck her as hard as he could across the face. She managed to partially deflect the blow, but went down anyway, her head ringing.

"You witch!" he hissed at her.

His Eminence stepped in front of Rhyndweir's Lord, blocking his way. "Enough of that, Lord Laphroig. Remember our purpose here. Time enough for retribution later, after the wedding."

Mistaya heard him and took his meaning, but pretended not to. She hung her head for a moment, waiting for the ringing to stop and her vision to clear, her eyes filled with tears.

Then she climbed back to her feet. "It was only pretend," she said to Laphroig, brushing at her eyes. "It wasn't meant to hurt anyone. I kept my word; I did not try to escape. I thought that a demonstration of what my magic can do might make your knights respect you even more. If you have a wife who can—"

"Spare us your bogus explanations," Craswell Crabbit interrupted. "Your intention was to distract us and escape. The only reason you are still here is that your magic was insufficient to allow for it."

He made a quick series of gestures, spoke a few brief words, and Mistaya's hands were again bound, encased in the swirling mist. She stared at them in dismay, even though she had known that this would happen, that her momentary freedom would be taken away. But escape would have put Thom at risk, and she wasn't about to do anything that would allow for that. Her plan was to see them both freed, and anything less was unacceptable.

Laphroig moved over to stand so close to her she could smell his mix of fear and rage. "When this is over, Princess," he whispered, "I shall take whatever time it requires to teach you the manners you so badly need. And I shall enjoy doing it, although I doubt that you will."

He stalked away, calling back his knights, some of whom still remained close enough to hear his voice. Those who responded he dispatched to gather up the others. The wedding would proceed with all present, including those who had fled. Even Cordstick had managed to put himself back in the picture, standing by uneasily, trying to look as if nothing much had happened.

It took awhile—quite a while, in fact—but eventually all were gathered together once more, and His Eminence rearranged the bride and groom and began to speak anew.

"Be it known, one and all, from the nearest to the farthest corners of the land, that this man and woman have consented to be joined . . ."

"You've already said that!" Laphroig roared. "Get to the part where you left off and start from there, and be quick about it!"

His Eminence looked at Laphroig as he might have looked at a bothersome insect, but he held his tongue. Mistaya had hoped that he would say he had to start over in order for the ceremony to be valid, but apparently that wasn't the case. She shifted her feet worriedly, gazing down anew at her shackled hands. She could feel time slipping away and her chances with it.

His Eminence took a deep breath and began anew. "Having spoken their vows and pledged their love, having exchanged rings—ah, rings and other gifts—to demonstrate their commitment, I find no reason that they should not be man and wife. Therefore, by the power invested in me, as a certified and fully authorized delegate of the crown, I . . ."

"Run!" someone screamed from behind him, someone who seconds later went tearing away from the wedding party and across the hills, waving and shouting and pointing.

"Isn't that your man Cordstick?" His Eminence asked.

"Yes, *Cordstick*." Laphroig spit out the name distastefully. "Whatever is the matter with him?"

As the words left his mouth, a huge shadow fell over the assemblage, sweeping out of the skies like a thundercloud falling from the heavens, thick with dark rain. It was winged and horned and spike-encrusted and black as the mud pits of the lower Melchor, and when Mistaya saw who it was, she felt her heart leap with impossible gratitude.

"Strabo!" she exclaimed.

His Eminence and Laphroig were caught between emotions, not knowing whether to run or to stand their ground, looking from the dragon to Mistaya and back again as they tried to figure out how she had made this latest apparition appear. What sort of magic was she using now that her hands were shackled anew? But there were no answers to be found, and by the time they had determined that this dragon was not an apparition, but the real thing, and that headlong flight might be a good idea, it was too late. Cordstick was gone, the knights had scattered once more, taking the G'home Gnomes with them, and the wedding party of three found itself abandoned to its fate.

Strabo settled earthward with a flapping of wings that knocked Mistaya and her captors to their knees and then landed with such force that the earth shook in protest. The dragon glared as it folded its massive wings against its sides and showed all of its considerable teeth in row after blackened row.

"I thought I made myself perfectly clear, Princess!" he snarled. "Was my warning too vague for you to understand?"

"It was perfectly clear," she replied. "You said if I used magic to create an image of you again, especially if it was to frighten someone, you would pay me a visit much quicker than I would like."

"Yet you did so anyway?" The dragon swung his triangular head from side to side in dismay. "What do I have to do to convince you that I am serious? Eat you?"

She held up her hands, encased in the swirling ball of mist. "I took a chance that you were as good as your word. I needed someone to help me, and I couldn't think of anyone more capable. So I deliberately made an image of you so that you *would* come, and here you are!"

She said it with great satisfaction. She couldn't help herself. Her plan had worked exactly as she had hoped, and now she had a chance to get free from His Eminence and Laphroig for good.

The dragon looked at her magically shackled hands and hissed. "What is this?" he demanded, looking now at her captors, his great brow darkening. "Have you done this?"

Well, there was no good answer to that particular question, and neither His Eminence nor Laphroig tried to offer one. They just stood there, staring in horror at all those teeth.

"They are holding me prisoner and trying to marry me off against my will," she declared. "To Berwyn Laphroig!"

The dragon hissed at the accused. "You are forcing her to marry you, Lord of Rhyndweir?"

"No! Not at all! She's doing so voluntarily!" Laphroig was grasping at straws. "She loves me!"

Strabo breathed on him, and the combination of stench and heat knocked him from a guarded crouch to his hands and knees, gasping for fresh air. "It doesn't sound like it to me. Set her free at once."

"I can't!" sobbed Laphroig. "He did it!" His trembling hand pointed toward His Eminence. "It's his magic that binds her!"

The dragon shifted his gaze to Crabbit, who held up his hands defensively. "All right, all right, I'll release her. She's more trouble than she's worth, in any case."

He made a few gestures, spoke a few words, and the swirling mist dissipated. Mistaya was free once more.

Strabo bent close to Laphroig and His Eminence. "I've a good mind to eat you both. A snack would do me good after flying all this way to straighten you out. What do you think of that?"

"I think I would be most grateful if you only ate him," His Eminence replied, gesturing at Laphroig. "This was all his idea."

"Liar!" screamed Laphroig. "You were the one who—"

"You both agreed to this marriage idea," Mistaya pointed out. "I don't think either of you should try to blame the other."

"It isn't a good idea to force young girls to marry," Strabo lectured, looking from one man to the other. "Marriage, in general, isn't a particularly desirable institution. It causes all sorts of trouble, from what I have observed over the centuries. In any case, a Princess shouldn't marry this young, the issue of the advisability of marriage aside. She should be free to grow up and spend time with more interesting creatures than prospective husbands. Dragons, for instance. We're much more interesting than you, Laphroig. Or you,

Craswell. So be warned. If I hear of any further attempts at forcing this girl to marry either one of you or anyone you know or even anyone I think you know, I will not be so lenient."

His Eminence and Rhyndweir's Lord nodded eagerly, babbling their understanding in a jumble of hurried promises.

Strabo backed away a few yards, still watching them. "I don't know. I'm awfully hungry. Eating you now would solve a great number of potential problems later."

Mistaya didn't want that to happen quite yet, so she stepped forward quickly. "I wonder if I could ask one further favor. An associate of His Eminence is holding my friend Thom prisoner, too. Can he be released, as well?"

Strabo licked his chops as he nodded. "Have her friend brought to me right away, Crabbit."

His Eminence looked as if he might implode, but he turned to the building and shouted for Rufus Pinch to produce Thom. Laphroig still didn't know who they were talking about, but as soon as Thom appeared, sliding past him quickly to stand next to Mistaya, he turned purple with rage and screamed a long string of bad words that don't bear repeating.

"You knew about this, Crabbit! You knew, and you kept it from me! You will pay for this, I promise you." He wheeled on Thom. "As for you, I won't make the same mistake twice. I'll hunt you down once this is finished, no matter how long it takes, and when I find you—"

"You won't do anything, if you're inside Strabo's belly," Mistaya pointed out smugly.

But all of a sudden Strabo reared up and wheeled away, his attention diverted. "What's that I smell?" he growled.

They all looked and saw a handful of mounted knights racing away across the hills, trying unsuccessfully to escape notice. Apparently, they had recovered from their earlier fright and finding themselves on the wrong side of escape had decided to circle back north and try to slip past the dragon.

"Oh, my favorites!" Strabo enthused. "Crunchy on the outside

and chewy on the inside. And all that iron is fuel for my inner child."
He glanced at Mistaya. "I have to go now, Princess. I need a snack
after all that flying. Good luck to you."

He wheeled away, spread his wings, and soared off into the sky,
Mistaya and her captors forgotten in an instant. Already they could
hear the rumble of his internal furnace as the bellows heated the
flames to cooking temperature.

Mistaya was so shocked by the dragon's abrupt and unexpected
departure that for a moment she just stood there. How could he
leave like that, right in the middle of rescuing her?

Then Laphroig looked over at her and His Eminence did the
same, and she realized how much danger she was in.

She brought up her hands in a warding motion. "Don't even
think about it. This wedding is over. Just stay right where you are.
I'm not your prisoner now, and if you try to make me one, I'll fry
you where you stand."

"I think that it is dragons who fry people, Princess," His Eminence purred, his fingers flexing. "In any case, you are no match for
me, free or not. You are young and inexperienced, and you are
alone. Thom can't help you, either. His brother will see to him
while I see to you."

The oblong head bobbed and a smile played across the odd face.
"I would let you go if I didn't think you already knew too much for
your own good. Best if you come back inside and remain as my
guest until your father gets here."

Mistaya kept one eye on his hands, the other on Laphroig. "My
father isn't coming. Didn't you know?"

"Oh, I think maybe he is. I sent him a message."

She didn't know if he was lying or not, but it wasn't something
she wanted to chance. "It doesn't matter. I'm not helping you trap
my father by staying. We're leaving."

Laphroig stepped forward quickly. "You'll leave when I say you
can leave, you little snot-nosed whelp! You're mine, wedding or
not, and I will do with you as I wish. By the time the dragon finds
out what's been done, it will be too late. Crabbit, I will deal with

you and your lying ways later. For now, bind her hands and my brother's, too, and get out of my way."

To emphasize the point, he produced a wicked-looking dagger from beneath his robes and held it in a way to suggest that he was ready to use it on any one of them should they give him reason.

His Eminence looked taken aback. "Who do you think you are, issuing orders to me, Laphroig? I am not one of your lackeys."

He shifted away slightly, putting himself at the same distance from Laphroig as he was from Mistaya. "I've had enough of you, Lord of Rhyndweir. I think perhaps it is time for you to take your leave. You can do so voluntarily or I will help you on your way. Mr. Pinch? Do you have the crossbow pointed at his back?"

"I do, Mr. Crabbit," the other replied from just behind Laphroig. "As you instructed me to do earlier when I warned you that he was a snake in the grass and not to be trusted."

Laphroig smiled. "A crossbow won't do the job, Crabbit. I am armored against such weapons. And before you can work a spell, I will have this dagger through your throat. Now do as I say and stop playing games."

Mistaya was at a loss as to how to proceed. The standoff had pitted them against one another. If one attacked, the others would retaliate. She took two steps back and bumped into Thom.

"Get behind me, Mistaya," he whispered in her ear.

She shook her head. "Stay out of this."

"I won't. I can help."

"Not with this." She didn't dare take her eyes off His Eminence and Laphroig to look at him. "Please, Thom."

"Princess," His Eminence called out suddenly, "what of your promise not to try to escape? Does that mean nothing to you? Have you abandoned your word and your honor, as well?"

"I kept my word," she replied. "I said I wouldn't do anything during the wedding. The wedding is off, so I am released from my promise."

"Some of us might argue with you."

"I think we are beyond arguing, Your Eminence."

Although she was pretty sure by now that talking was the only thing keeping her would-be captors at bay. She had to find a way to break this off without provoking an attack, and then she had to find a way for both Thom and herself to leave.

She wondered suddenly what had happened to Edgewood Dirk. She had thought the Prism Cat would be there to help her at this point. But it appeared he had abandoned her in the same way as Strabo. She regretted anew that she hadn't done a better job of keeping loyal Haltwhistle at her side. He would never have left her.

"Haltwhistle," she whispered to herself in a voice so low that even Thom, standing right next to her, couldn't hear.

"Lord Laphroig," His Eminence called. "Let's put our differences aside long enough to deal with the Princess. She remains our common enemy and the lure by which we might still trap her father. You and I can settle up later, once she is incapacitated."

Laphroig seemed to be thinking it over, and now Rufus Pinch was turned toward her, too, crossbow pointed. Mistaya saw her window of opportunity slipping away. She had to do something, and she had to do it right now.

Suddenly she saw Haltwhistle standing just at the edge of the trees behind His Eminence and Laphroig, hackles raised. She took a long moment to register his presence, to make certain she wasn't mistaken. But there he was, good old Haltwhistle, not an apparition but the real thing.

She took a deep breath. "Haltwhistle," she whispered a second time, and the sound of his name almost made her cry.

"Mr. Pinch?" His Eminence called softly.

In the next instant, everyone moved at once. Pinch released the trigger on the crossbow, Laphroig flung the dagger, and His Eminence leveled a dark charge of magic with lightning quickness. Mistaya retaliated with her own magic, already waiting at her fingertips, to protect both Thom and herself, and as she did so she felt Thom slam into her, knocking her aside. As all of this was happening, she saw Haltwhistle's hackles turn to frost and his magic lance out in a sudden rush.

Dagger, crossbow bolt, and magic seemed to arrive at the same moment, exploding in front of her in a cloud of smoke. The force of the explosion sent her sprawling, so she didn't see clearly what happened next, except that the confluence of magic and dagger and crossbow bolt seemed to rebound from her own defenses and carom away, sharp flashes indicating results she could not make out. She found herself sprawled on the ground, the stench of His Eminence's powerful magic raw and pungent in her nostrils, the heat of it layered against her skin. She lay stunned for a moment, entangled with Thom, who had also been upended by the attack. Struggling to disengage, she tried to peer through the clouds of smoke and the mix of random flashes to see what had happened, but everything was obscured.

As she scrambled to her feet, she took a deep breath of air that was suddenly sharp and bitter and assailed her mouth and nostrils with suffocating power. She tried to fight it off, failed, and lost consciousness.

She came awake with a blinding headache. Everything seemed hazy and a bit vague, as if she were viewing it through gauzy curtains.

"Mistaya!" Thom whispered from somewhere far away. She felt his hand squeeze her arm. "Are you all right?"

She wasn't entirely sure, but at least she could breathe again. She opened her eyes and looked into his. "Are you?"

"The dagger missed me," he replied.

She wasn't so sure how that could be. Right at the last, he had tried to save her and put himself in the path of the blade. It hadn't looked to her, in the split second she'd had to witness the attack by his brother, that it could have missed him. But maybe her magic had deflected it.

Haltwhistle nudged into view through the haze, his hackles lowered again, his coat smooth. Things must be all right after all, she thought. She sat up slowly and smiled. "Good old Haltwhistle. I'm so sorry for not taking better care of you. I won't do that ever again."

The mud puppy's beaver tail wagged eagerly as he sat down close by, but safely out of reach. If he didn't think there was any danger, there probably wasn't. With Thom helping, Mistaya climbed back to her feet, searching for her adversaries, the last wisps of smoke wafting away on the breeze.

Then she saw Laphroig. He was standing approximately where she had last seen him, one arm raised in the follow-through of a throwing motion, his face twisted with anger. He wasn't moving.

Chances are he wouldn't ever move again.

He had been turned to stone.

She looked farther around the clearing. But there was no sign of Craswell Crabbit and Rufus Pinch.

"What happened here?" Thom asked quietly.

Mistaya didn't know. It was entirely possible, she decided, that she never would.

DEMONS
AT THE GATES

Mistaya and Thom conducted a hurried search of the grounds but failed to find any trace of Crabbit and Pinch. Their complete disappearance suggested that the pair might have been vaporized or spirited away to some other corner of the Kingdom. After all, a collision of magic as powerful as those commanded by herself, His Eminence, and Haltwhistle could result in almost anything.

Nor was there much she could do about The Frog. She was not particularly adept at reversing magic spells, and the one that had turned him to stone was no exception. She decided it was best to leave him as he was and see if Questor could do anything to help.

She was about to suggest to Thom that they search within Libiris itself just to make certain Crabbit and Pinch hadn't somehow gotten past them when a huge squalling sound from inside the building signaled that whatever the fate of those two villains, something else was clearly amiss. With Thom at her side, she charged back through the front doors toward the entry into the Stacks, tracing the cacophonous noise to its source.

They had not yet reached their destination when dozens of frantic Throg Monkeys came pouring out, flinging their arms wildly and howling as if they had lost their minds. Some few made it all the way out of the building and disappeared into the woods, but most

seemed to lose their sense of direction before they reached the outside. As Mistaya and Thom entered the Stacks, they could see
dozens more of the little monsters charging about, racing up and
down the aisles, climbing shelving units, clinging to the ceiling
rafters, and generally milling around to no recognizable purpose.

Then Mistaya saw it. From the rear of the chamber, back in the
deep gloom where the wall had been broken through, a wicked
crimson light was pulsing to the steady rhythm of a coarse and omi-
nous chanting.

The demons of Abaddon were trying to break out on their own.

"Thom, stay here!" she shouted and raced down the closest aisle
for the darkness ahead.

Thom apparently had no thought of obeying. He caught up with
her in nothing flat. "*You* wait!" he called over to her as he sped past,
flashing his familiar grin.

She was furious with him and at the same time scared. He had no
business going back there like this! He had risked an encounter with
magic once and it had almost killed him. Now he was risking another. The demons of Abaddon would brush him aside like a fly.
What was wrong with him?

Well, she knew the answer to that one before she finished the
thought. He was doing it for her, because he cared for her and was
trying once again to protect her. It made her chest ache with pride;
it made her want to do the same for him. She increased her pace,
flying through the near darkness, darting from one pool of shadows
to the next, dodging errant Throg Monkeys and books that lay scattered about. All the while the air throbbed with the sound of the
chanting and the invisible pulse of demon magic. She had no idea
what she was going to do, only that she had better do something or
all of her efforts would have been for nothing.

Her worst fears were realized as the rear wall of the Stacks came
into view. The hole opened in the building wall by the theft of the
books of magic and the release of their power was clearly outlined
by the crimson light. The hole was enlarged anew, a torn, aching
wound filled with the dark shapes of the demons and their minions,

all grouped around the black-cloaked form that held the red leather book. This demon, the largest of them all, led the chanting, holding up the book to the glow of torch flames so that the others could see, crimson light leaping off the pages as the reading stole the magic of the words and turned it back against the hapless building. Throg Monkeys too scared to flee were crouched in the shadows just on the other side of the opening, eyes wide. The scene was a bizarre tableau, all the characters frozen in place against the ebb and flow of the crimson light.

Now Thom slowed, uncertain what to do. He glanced over at Mistaya, searching for direction, but she had none to give. There was a screen of clear light across the opening; she could see a distension where the demons pressed up against it. It was all that held them back, and it was being stretched more thinly as the magic eroded the library walls and widened the opening. Mistaya's gamble in tricking the Throg Monkeys into returning the stolen books had worked for a time, but something had gone wrong. Either the demons had discovered her ruse or her battle with His Eminence had triggered this new response. Whatever the case, the demons weren't waiting any longer to break free.

They were coming out now.

Mistaya stood a dozen yards away, squarely in their path, and summoned a conjuring of storm-strength repulsion that she had learned from Questor Thews. She brought it to her fingers and threw it at the demons, a white-hot explosion that knocked them backward into the tunnel, turning them into a sprawling dark mass of arms, legs, teeth, and claws.

But in the process of stopping their advance, she had destroyed the thin membrane that held them at bay.

She stared. She couldn't believe how foolish she had been. She had acted impulsively, out of haste and fear; she had responded to the danger without thinking things through.

Already the demons were back on their feet, a knot of twisted dark faces and feral eyes searching her out. She summoned an iron-infused blocking spell, throwing it up across the opening, and they were stopped short. But only for a few precious moments, she knew; the spell would not last.

They plunged ahead again in seconds, the big demon with the red leather book leading the way. He held the book clutched close against his chest, claws gripping it tightly. Following in his wake, the foremost invaders cleared the tunnel opening and were suddenly inside the library before her third casting—this one a combination of tornado-force wind and hurricane rain—threw back the entire pack once more.

She dropped to one knee, nearly exhausted by her efforts. She had used the best of the conjurings she had learned from Questor. She had nothing left to try.

She caught herself. She *did* have another weapon: one of the deadly incantations she had learned from the witch Nightshade, one that would burn the demons to ash, that would steal the life from them with a certainty that was frightening even to think about.

It *would* stop them—if she could use it. If she could react as Nightshade had taught her and not think of what it meant.

But, no, she wouldn't do that. Not even against creatures like these. Not even to save Libiris.

Then she saw the book. The leather cover glistened, shards of wicked red light seeping from between the pages even though its covers were closed. The book was lying on the floor just inside the library where the big demon must have dropped it when her spell struck.

Thom had seen it, too, and he was already racing toward it.

"Thom, no!" she screamed.

Too late. He was already there, just ahead of the demons that had regrouped inside the tunnel and were charging for the opening once more. Thom snatched up the book and stood frozen in place. The demons were almost on top of him, tearing at the space that separated them, claws eager for something more substantive. Mistaya waited for him to run, to drop the book, to save himself. But he just stood there, holding his ground against the onrush.

"Thom!" she screamed in desperation. "Throw me the book!"

He glanced back at her, his face bloodless.

"Throw me the book, Thom!" she repeated, gesturing wildly.

For a moment, he didn't move. Then, abruptly, he turned from her and flung the book over the heads of the demons, a whirling, spinning missile.

Mistaya understood at once what he was trying to do: turn the demons around, using the book as a lure to send them back into the tunnel. He was trying to save her.

Mistaya reacted instinctively, doing something entirely unexpected, even to herself, something she had sworn she would never do.

She summoned one of Nightshade's spells.

Her hands a blur, her voice a hiss, she dispatched a chaser bolt of killing green fire, one that could have incinerated the demons but here was meant for something else. It caught the red leather book in midflight over the heads of the demons and broke through its protective magic. The leather covers flew open, the pages tore free, and the book disintegrated into hundreds of pieces that scattered everywhere. The demons tried to snatch them out of the air, but some burst into flames and others eluded their grasp and flew away like tiny birds. The demons howled and gave chase, but their efforts were futile.

Mistaya didn't wait. As soon as she saw that the book had lost its power, she put her magic to work creating a healing spell that would close the breach in the library wall. Weaving her fingers, she spoke words of power and brought the spell to life, spinning it out toward the opening. It wasn't as strong or complete as she would have liked, but it was enough. Libiris, freed from the book's wounding magic, was already healing on her own, able once more to begin repairing the breach. Mistaya could see the results—the rent smoothing and tightening, the hole narrowing, the wall strengthening anew.

A handful of the demons trapped inside turned from their efforts to salvage the book and rushed to stop what was happening. Thom grabbed a huge iron stanchion, knocked aside the candles it bore, and prepared to use it as a club, placing himself in their path. Mistaya could do nothing to help; trying to stop the demons now meant abandoning her spell, and she could not afford to do that. But luck was with them. The demons that reached the opening were unable to pass through. They tried a second time and then a third with no better results. Without the magic of the red leather book to aid them in their efforts, they could not break free.

In moments, they had fallen back to join their fellows. The largest demon looked back at Mistaya, rage bright in its yellow eyes. But the gash was healing, the opening slowly shrinking. Soon the space had emptied of everything but shadows and the lingering wisps of ash and smoke.

The way out of Abaddon was closed.

NO PLACE LIKE HOME

Even supposing that the danger was over, she decided to stay where she was, braced before the opening with her arms extended, until her strength left her. Exhausted by her efforts, she sat cross-legged on the floor with Thom and waited longer still to be sure that nothing else was going to happen. Then she and Thom went back into the Stacks and took stock of her efforts to return the missing books of magic. It was impossible to know how successful her plan had been. The Throg Monkeys had all fled, even the ones that had cringed about the opening at the end of things. She had no idea where they had put the books she had ordered returned from Abaddon, and no idea where those never taken might be. It would take a thorough search of the library to discover their whereabouts, and she wasn't up to it just now.

She was disappointed in losing the red leather book, but then she could hardly blame Thom for its destruction. When it came right down to it, he had probably saved their lives.

It was enough that he had done so.

Satisfied, she turned her efforts anew to finding out what had become of Crabbit and Pinch.

She received only marginal assistance from Questor Thews when he arrived late in the day with Abernathy in tow and not before she got a stern lecture that had something to do with not lis-

tening to the warnings of her elders. Which warnings those were
and how listening to them would have helped she wasn't sure, but
she endured it all and at the end kissed and hugged them both and
told them she loved them dearly. This seemed to placate them,
and not another word was uttered about what she should have
done.

Unfortunately, her patience did not yield much in the way of re-
wards. Questor was not able to shed much light on the disappearance of Crabbit and Pinch or do anything about The Frog's
unfortunate condition. He was pretty certain that the spell that had
turned The Frog to stone had come from His Eminence, intended
for Mistaya but redirected by Haltwhistle. It was typical of what
happened when you attacked someone under the protection of a
mud puppy. The strange little animal couldn't actually harm you,
but it could turn your efforts against you or deflect them. Something of the sort had happened all those years ago when Nightshade
had attempted to retaliate against Mistaya.

"So I would guess that was what occurred here," he finished, giving a shrug of dismissal. "Wherever they are, Craswell Crabbit and
Rufus Pinch will have to find someone else to manipulate."

"And good riddance!" Abernathy added with an audible growl.

On a more positive note, when Questor went back inside with
her to inspect the damage to the back wall, he was enthusiastic.
After taking measurements of the magic still in use by the building,
he pronounced her well on the way to a full recovery, adding that
Mistaya and Thom had done extraordinarily well and he couldn't
have done better himself.

"Damned by faint praise," Abernathy whispered in her ear and
gave a small bark that approximated a dog laugh.

They decided they would spend the night at Libiris. Thom took
them all into the little kitchen and fixed them dinner, more cheerful than at any time since Mistaya had known him. He laughed and
joked with her and even managed to charm Abernathy out of his
usual pessimistic attitude.

"Andjen Thomlinson," the royal scribe declared at one point, ebullient and expansive, "you will make a fine new Lord of Rhynd-weir."

Thom instantly went still. "It wasn't ever my intention to become Lord of Rhyndweir," he answered at once.

"Perhaps not your intention, but quite possibly your destiny," Questor chimed in. "Rhyndweir needs a master, and you are next in line and the logical choice. More to the point, I think Abernathy is right. You are most suited to the task."

"But there is still so much work to be done here," Thom objected.

"Thom, you can still supervise that work," Mistaya cut in quickly. "Why not? Father will give you authorization; I will ask him myself. You can bring all the help you need from the Greensward and send those dreadful Throg Monkeys back to wherever they came from."

Everyone but Thom thought this a grand idea, and in the end he promised to sleep on it.

"And you, Mistaya," Questor said. "Will you continue to work here with Thom?"

She knew what Thom wanted her to say, but she wasn't yet sure of her own wishes, so she shook her head and shrugged. "Like Thom, I have to sleep on it. I also have to go back to Sterling Silver and straighten things out with my parents. They may not want me coming back."

So they talked on through the meal, agreeing that the best thing for The Frog was to have him transported back to Rhyndweir and placed somewhere in a park where those who chose to do so could visit him at their leisure. Perhaps to comment on how much better behaved he was now than before, Abernathy observed. Perhaps to provide recalcitrant children with an object lesson on what could happen if you were not a good person, Questor added.

After dinner was over, Questor took Mistaya aside, putting his hands on her shoulders as he faced her. "I want you to know how proud I am of you. Well, how proud we both are, Abernathy and I. You have conducted yourself with courage and demonstrated both wisdom and determination. You stayed when you could have left—

when I told you to leave, in fact—and you were right to do so. Had you followed my advice and not discovered what Crabbit and Pinch were up to, we all might have found ourselves in a much more dangerous situation down the road. And your father would have been in considerable peril as a result. The trap set for him on his arrival was cunningly conceived and well hidden. He might not have been able to avoid it, even with the help of the Paladin."

"What sort of trap was it?" she pressed him quickly.

"The sort I don't care to talk about."

"But shouldn't I know?"

Questor shook his head. "What you need to know is that the disappearance of the man who contrived it effectively put an end to its usage. Your father is safe now, and he can thank you for that."

She frowned. "You won't tell me?"

"I won't tell him, either. But I will tell him that you helped save him from his enemies and that no blame should attach to your behavior during these last few weeks. I will tell him you are every inch a true Princess of Landover."

Then he kissed her on the forehead. "Mistaya Holiday, I do believe you are growing up."

Several days later, she was back home. The walls of Libiris were continuing to heal, the books were safely back in place, and the library would soon be under new management that Questor had promised he would personally arrange. The demons of Abaddon were shut away again, perhaps without fully understanding what had happened to derail their plan, but that was their problem. Laphroig's spy at Sterling Silver had been rooted out, a cook's assistant with ambitions for advancement whose reach exceeded his grasp. An irate Parsnip, in ways that the kobold would not discuss and summarily dismissed when questioned, had disciplined him. All was right with the world, and there had been no reason to stay longer at a place she still didn't much care for, so off Mistaya had gone.

Now she was sitting with her father on the south lawn at the edge of the castle walls, enjoying the sunlight and the sweet smell of lilies wafting on the summer breeze. She had told him everything by then—well, almost everything; there were one or two things she was keeping to herself—and to her surprise he had not scolded or criticized her for anything she had done. Not even for running away. Not even for trying to hide from him. Not even for worrying her mother and himself to the point of distraction.

"I'm mostly just glad you're back," he said when she asked if he was mad at her. "I'm glad you're safe."

She was both relieved and pleased. She had no desire to engage in another confrontation with him. While she had been in hiding, she had thought a lot about her attitude toward her parents and decided that it could use some improvement. So one of the first things she did on her return, once they were reassured that she was unharmed, was to tell them how sorry she was for not trying to understand better that they had only her best interests at heart. Her father responded at once by telling her he was sorry he had treated her as a child.

"I still think of you that way," he told her. "Maybe I always will. Parents do that. We can't help ourselves. We can't help thinking that you need us to look after you. We can't get used to the idea that you are growing up and need space to find your own way. We don't like it that you might one day discover you will be just fine without us."

"I would never be fine without you and Mother," she had replied and hugged him so hard he thought she might break something.

Thom had come back with her, deciding that he would return to Rhyndweir as successor to his brother. This decision had more to do with his determination to change the way things were done in the Greensward than anything to do with Questor's repeated references to destiny and fate. Ben had received him warmly and told him that he could count on the throne to support him. He had suggested that he send Questor to the Greensward to make certain the transition went smoothly. Not that he believed there would be any problem, he was quick to assure the boy. Berwyn Laphroig had not been well liked, and the people of Rhyndweir would be happy to have a new Lord. They would be especially accepting of one who seemed so willing to put the welfare of his subjects ahead of his own.

"He wants to give the land to the people," Mistaya had told her father later. "He wants the people to feel they have a vested interest in it, something they can call their own and pass on to their children. All he wants in return is for them to agree to pay a reasonable tax to the crown. He has a plan to accomplish all this, and it is a good one. Listen."

Her father did so, and after asking a number of questions he was inclined to agree. Perhaps Thom's openness would provide a working model for the other Lords of the Greensward, one that would revolutionize the old practices and herald the beginning of an era of fresh cooperation between the Lords of the Greensward and their subjects.

Perhaps.

"I think Thom will become a valuable ally, Father," Mistaya finished. "I think you'll come to like him very much."

She had not missed the way the boy looked at her, of course, and she knew how he felt about her. What she didn't know was exactly how she felt about him. The two had shared a very dangerous and exhausting ordeal at Libiris, and that sort of experience had a way of bonding people. She liked Thom, but she wasn't sure she liked him in that way—even though she couldn't stop thinking about the way he had kissed her in that storeroom at Libiris when she was to be married to Laphroig. It still sent chills up and down her spine when she thought about it. It still made her want to try kissing him again. Someday.

She sat with her father for a long time after that without speaking, comfortable just to be together. She couldn't remember when they had last done this, and she was almost afraid to say or do anything that might break the spell. One or the other of them was always rushing away, and time spent doing nothing, father and daughter sharing space and nothing more, was a rarity. Thinking on it, she felt a pang of regret that it might be another broad stretch of time before they would do it again.

She caught him looking at her and said, "What?"

He shook his head. "I was just thinking about how much I enjoy being with you like this. Just sitting and not saying anything or doing anything. Just . . ."

He trailed off, unable to finish. "I know," she said. "You don't have to say it. We don't do this like we did when I was a little girl."

"You remember, do you? I thought that maybe all that was so far in the past that you had forgotten."

"I haven't forgotten any of it. We would go on picnics, and I would sit next to you and watch everything you did. Mother would set things out, but I would sit with you. Sometimes you would carry me on your shoulders into the trees and pretend you were my charger."

He grinned. "I did do that, didn't I?"

"You did a lot for me—you and Mother both. Since coming home, I've been thinking about it. I've been doing a sort of self-assessment. There might be some areas of improvement needed. What do you think?"

He arched one eyebrow at her. "You've got to be kidding. You don't really expect me to answer that one, do you?"

"Not really."

"Then don't ask me things like that. I'm trying to walk a fine line here between parenting and friendship."

"They're supposed to be the same thing, aren't they?"

"When the stars align properly, yes. But you might have noticed over the past few weeks that sometimes you have to work at it."

She looked at him thoughtfully. "Well, I guess I did notice something of the sort."

They were quiet again for a time, and then her father said, "What do you think you will do now, Mistaya? Now that you've come back home."

She had thought of little else. "I don't know."

"You have a lot of options open to you. You've probably thought of a few that I haven't. I'm not asking this to try to persuade you to do anything in particular. The choice is yours, and whatever you decide is fine with your mother and me. I think."

"Thank you."

"So do you have any ideas?"

"Some."

"Care to talk about them with me?"

He sounded so eager, she could hardly make herself give the reply she had already decided on. "Maybe later. Can we just sit here like this for now?"

He said they could, but she thought that he would have preferred the discussion he had suggested. Trouble was, she just wasn't ready. She didn't know what she was going to do. She thought it might take some time to figure it out.

--------◦◦◦◦◦◦◦◦◦◦--------

As it turned out, she was wrong. She went for a walk outside the castle grounds late in the afternoon, needing to stretch her legs and find space to think. She was in a meditative mood, and movement always seemed to help spur her thinking. In addition, she wanted to see if there was any sign of the G'home Gnomes, Poggwydd and Shoopdiesel. After the horse to which they were tied had galloped in terror away from a hungry Strabo, they had thought themselves doomed. The dragon had caught up to them almost immediately, but then it had refused to eat them after finding out they were G'home Gnomes. Even dragons had limits when it came to food choices, Strabo had observed archly before abandoning them to fly after tastier morsels. Eventually, Questor Thews and Abernathy had come across them on their way to Libiris, still bound and gagged astride their grazing horse. Showing considerably more compassion than others, they had released the pair and, after hearing how they had revealed Mistaya's hiding place to Laphroig, had sent them packing, and no one had seen them since. Mistaya wouldn't have blamed either one for refusing to have anything to do with her from that day forward and wouldn't have lost a great deal of sleep over it, either. But she felt certain she hadn't seen the end of them.

So she went looking for them that afternoon, out to the woods where she had first encountered a dangling Poggwydd some weeks earlier on her return from Carrington. Maybe they had come back and made a new home, a fresh burrow in the soft earth. Maybe it wasn't that they didn't want anything to do with her. Maybe they were waiting to see if *she* wanted anything to do with *them,* given that they had betrayed her whereabouts to The Frog.

But a thorough search of the area revealed nothing, and she was just about to turn around and start home again when she saw Edgewood Dirk.

The Prism Cat was sitting at the base of an ancient broadleaf, his emerald eyes fixed on her, his silver-and-black coat glistening in a wash of hazy sunlight. She stopped and stared, making sure she wasn't seeing things, and then she walked over to stand in front of him.

"Good afternoon, Princess," the Prism Cat greeted.

"Good afternoon, Edgewood Dirk," she replied. "I wondered what had become of you."

"Nothing has become of me. I've been here all along, watching."

"Watching? Me?"

"Not simply you. Everything. Cats like to watch. We are curious creatures."

She smiled despite herself. "So you know what happened back at Libiris?"

The cat blinked. "I know what I care to know, thank you. All's well that ends well, it seems."

"Do you know what became of His Eminence and Pinch?" She arched one eyebrow at him. "You do, don't you?"

"Perhaps."

"Will you tell me?"

"Someday, if the mood strikes me. But the mood doesn't strike me just now. Now is the wrong time. Why don't you tell me something instead?"

She sighed. She could have guessed that it wouldn't be that easy. Dirk revealed what he knew of things only now and then. "What would you like to know that you don't already know?"

"What do you intend to do now that you are back home again?"

"You sound like my father. He wants to know that, too. But I guess I haven't decided, so I don't have an answer to your question."

"Perhaps you do. Perhaps you just need to consider the possibilities."

She glared. "Why don't you save us both a lot of time and list them for me. In fact, why don't you just tell me what you think I should do and save me the trouble of having to decide anything at all?"

The cat blinked and then began washing himself. He took a long time in doing so, a rather deliberately slow process that she was certain was intended to aggravate her. But she held her tongue and waited.

Finally Dirk looked at her. "It isn't my place to tell you what to do with your life. But I do think putting things off is not a good idea. Or leaving things undone. Cats never do that. They always finish what they start before going on to anything else. Cats understand the importance of completing what they start. They are easily distracted, as you know, so it is necessary for them to establish good life habits early so that they learn to focus."

He paused. "It might be true of young girls, as well. Although I do not pretend to understand young girls in the same way I understand cats."

She studied him a moment, and then she nodded. "I think you probably understand young girls pretty well. For a cat."

Edgewood Dirk closed his eyes and then slowly opened them. "Just the ones who merit understanding. And only once in a very great while."

Suddenly she heard her father calling her, although later she could never be certain that she had heard anything at all, and she turned toward the castle to look for him.

When she turned back again, Edgewood Dirk was gone.

She stood staring at the spot he had occupied for a very long time, as if by doing so she could make him reappear. She could hear him speaking in her mind; she could hear his words quite clearly. They jumbled together at first and then they sorted themselves out, and suddenly she discovered she knew exactly what she was going to do. Maybe she had known all along, but just hadn't realized it. In any case, it hadn't taken any time at all to figure it out. It had just taken a few words of wisdom from a very unusual cat.

She started back to the castle. She would tell her parents at dinner. She would tell them that it was important to finish what you start and to make a habit of doing so. She would tell them that she had learned this from a rather unexpected source, and now she must act on it.

DÉJÀ VU

Vince stopped when he reached the aviary and stood looking for what he already knew wasn't there. He couldn't seem to help himself. Every day he came and every day he looked and every day it was the same thing. The bird was gone. The crow or whatever it was with the red eyes. After all these years, it had disappeared. Vanished. Just like that.

No one knew for sure what had happened. Most hadn't paid much attention to the bird for months—years, really, if you didn't count the ornithologists. Some still didn't realize it was gone. There were more important matters to occupy their working lives and dominate their conversations. But Vince was of a different mind. He didn't think there was anything more important than the disappearance of the bird. Even if he wasn't sure why, he sensed it.

That bird shouldn't have gotten free. Security should have taken greater care than they did when they opened the door and took those two madmen into custody. But they weren't paying attention to anything but the two men, and the crow would have been watching.

Just like it was always watching.

Vince knew, even if the others didn't. It gave him a creepy, uncomfortable feeling, thinking about it. But he knew.

Five weeks gone now, and things were pretty much back to normal. No one had forgotten that day, a day that had started out pretty much like every other. He wasn't the first one to notice the two men in the aviary, but he heard Roy shouting and rushed over to see what was happening, and there they were—these two guys, trapped in the aviary, kicking and hammering on the bars and shaking the cage in their efforts to get free. Odd pair of ducks—that was Vince's first thought when he saw them. They were wearing clothes of the sort you sometimes saw on those people who spent their weekends playing at being knights and fighting with swords. They didn't have any armor on, but they wore robes and tunics and scarves and boots and big belts with silver buckles. One was tall and skinny with a head that looked too big for the rest of his body, and the other was short like a dwarf and all wrinkled and whiskery. They did not look happy, their faces contorted and flushed with anger and frustration. They wanted out, but neither Vince nor Roy was about to help them. How they had gotten into the cage in the first place was hard to guess, considering that the cage door was still locked. But they had no business being there, whatever their excuse. At best, they were trespassing on city property, and it was likely that by interacting with the animals without authority they had broken a few more laws, as well.

Roy had already called security, so Vince and he stood side by side watching the two men rant and rave. Neither could understand anything the pair was saying. Roy thought they were speaking an Eastern European dialect, although how he would know that, being of Scottish descent, was a mystery to Vince. Vince thought it more likely that they were speaking Arabic. He thought the emphasis on the hard vowels suggested one of the Middle Eastern languages, and even if the big one was as pale as a ghost, it wasn't impossible that he might be an Arabic albino or something. He might have been raised in Egypt or Morocco, Vince thought—even though he had never been anywhere outside the state and didn't know the first thing about either of those countries.

Nevertheless, the two speculated on the matter until security got there and hauled the interlopers out of the cage in handcuffs and tossed them into one of those holding pens on wheels they used when the animals needed to be moved to a new enclosure. Shut the doors and took them away, and that was the last anyone had heard of either one. Vince guessed the authorities would try to find out where they came from and send them back. But he heard later that they didn't have any identification on them, and no one could figure out what language they were speaking. That last was especially puzzling. In this day and age, with people all over the world moving here and there at the drop of a hat, you would think they could find *someone* close by who could speak any language in existence.

But not in this case, apparently. So the pair had ended up in the hands of the Homeland Security people to determine if they might be terrorists. But if no one could understand them or figure out where they came from, what could Homeland Security do?

It was odd that the two men had appeared just like the crow with the red eyes. Exactly the same way: not there one day, there the next, and no explanation for how they got there. It was as if animal shelters and aviaries were some sort of transport devices, like in that TV show *Star Trek*. Beam me up, Scotty. Maybe the madmen and the bird had been beamed up from another planet.

Staring at the aviary now, in the aftermath of all the excitement, Vince shrugged his disinterest. What did it matter? If there were answers to be had, they weren't going to be given to him. They were gone, all three of them, and they likely weren't coming back. The crow with the red eyes especially. It wasn't coming back for sure. Any fool who had watched it as he had could tell you that. Now that it was free, it was long gone. It wouldn't be caught again, either. Not that bird.

He wondered where it would go. Somewhere far away, he hoped. He didn't like that bird. He didn't want to see it again. Better if it were someone else's problem.

That bird was trouble waiting to happen.

ABOUT THE AUTHOR

TERRY BROOKS is the *New York Times* bestselling author of more than twenty-five books, including the Genesis of Shannara novels *Armageddon's Children, The Elves of Cintra,* and *The Gypsy Morph; The Sword of Shannara;* the Voyage of the *Jerle Shannara* trilogy: *Ilse Witch, Antrax,* and *Morgawr;* the High Druid of Shannara trilogy: *Jarka Ruus, Tanequil,* and *Straken;* the nonfiction book *Sometimes the Magic Works: Lessons from a Writing Life;* and the novel based upon the screenplay and story by George Lucas, *Star Wars®: Episode I The Phantom Menace.*™ His novels *Running with the Demon* and *A Knight of the Word* were selected by the *Rocky Mountain News* as two of the best science fiction/fantasy novels of the twentieth century. The author was a practicing attorney for many years but now writes full-time. He lives with his wife, Judine, in the Pacific Northwest.

www.shannara.com
Terrybrooks.net

ABOUT THE TYPE

This book was set in Perpetua, a typeface designed by the English artist Eric Gill, and cut by The Monotype Corporation between 1928 and 1930. Perpetua is a contemporary face of original design, without any direct historical antecedents. The shapes of the roman letters are derived from the techniques of stonecutting. The larger display sizes are extremely elegant and form a most distinguished series of inscriptional letters.